A Literary Playground

Short Stories

by

James Ball Naylor

Dr. James Ball Naylor
Photo courtesy of the Morgan County Historical Society

A Literary Playground

Short Stories

by

James Ball Naylor

Edited and Annotated

by

Theresa Marie Flaherty

www.TurasPublishing.com

Photo Credits:
Front Cover Photo: Courtesy of Rick Shriver (The boy is Walter Willis)
Back Cover Photo: Courtesy of Lucile Naylor
Naylor Portrait: Courtesy of the Morgan County Historical Society
Map of Locale by Melanie McBride

A Literary Playground

Short Stories

by

James Ball Naylor

Edited and annotated

by

Theresa Marie Flaherty

ISBN-13: 978-0-9832342-2-7

Cover Design: Michael Flaherty

www.TurasPublishing.com

Tribute Series

A Literary Playground
Short Stories
is the third book in a Tribute Series
to James Ball Naylor

Table of Contents

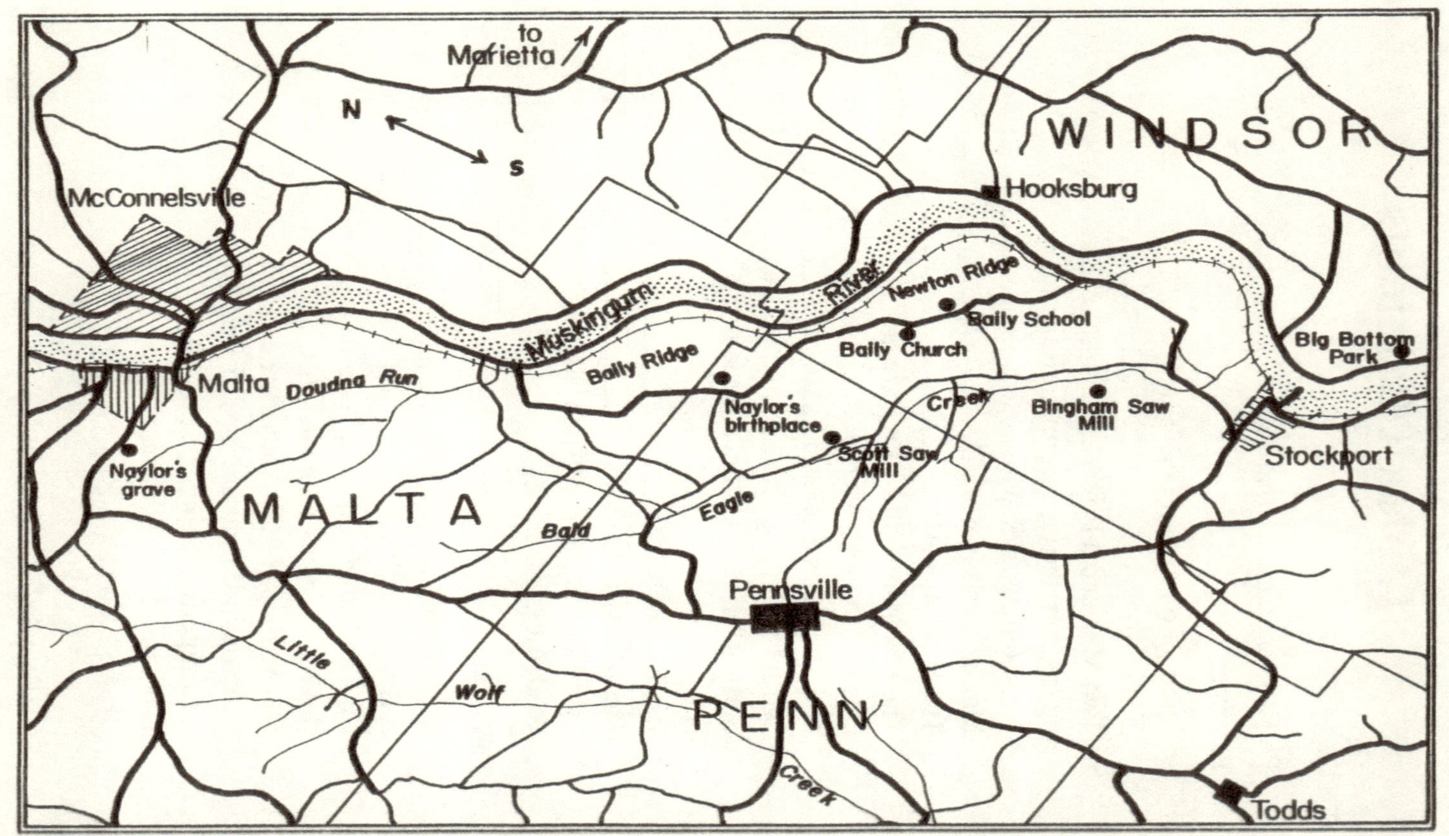

to Marietta
N
S
WINDSOR
McConnelsville
Hooksburg
Muskingum River
Newton Ridge
Bally School
Big Bottom Park
Malta
Doudna Run
Bally Ridge
Bally Church
Naylor's birthplace
Creek
Bingham Saw Mill
Scott Saw Mill
Stockport
Naylor's grave
MALTA
Bald
Eagle
Pennsville
Little
Wolf
Creek
PENN
Todds

PREFACE

A Literary Playground - Short Stories by James Ball Naylor is the third book in my Tribute Series to Dr. Naylor. By bringing Naylor's works back to life, I hope that his legacy will be fully appreciated. He was one of the most well known authors in the country at the turn of the twentieth century; however, after his death in 1945, he faded into obscurity. His rise from an impoverished childhood, his fight to get an education, his struggle through hardships in becoming a country doctor in rural Ohio, and his passion for writing is an inspirational story that I told in *The Final Test – A Biography of James Ball Naylor.* Naylor's lifetime of literary work includes eight novels, three children's books, numerous short stories, six volumes of collected verse, political sketches, fifteen years of mostly daily newspaper columns, and a myriad of ephemera, such as pamphlets, broadsides, and greeting cards, etc.

The first book in the Tribute Series, *Vintage Verse,* includes poetry by Naylor that for the most part did not appear in any of his published volumes. The second book in the series is a reformatted reprint of *Ralph Marlowe,* his 1901 best seller, and it includes additional material—notes and analyses, many contemporary reviews, and numerous period photographs—much of this material was not publicly accessible. Like the previous two books in the Tribute Series, most of Naylor's works in this book were not publicly available.

Naylor began to write short stories and longer serialized stories for newspapers and magazines, the "social media" of the day, sometime around 1896. Perhaps he began experimenting with this genre because poetry was not the profitable endeavor that he had hoped; more likely, he recognized an opportunity that had evolved earlier around 1836 when Charles Dickens published the first serialized story. Newspapers discovered that by publishing several serialized stories staggered over the course of several weeks they could attract and retain more readers. Before one serialized story finished, another began, thus ensuring that readers would keep coming back.

At a time when less than six percent of all Americans had graduated from high school, when two out of every ten adults could not read or write, when the average life expectancy in the U.S. was only 47 years, newspapers played an important role by providing not just news, but entertainment as well.

Naylor's family maintained a scrapbook of most of his stories that appeared in print; however, the date or the name of the newspaper or magazine that published it was often missing. Jean Naylor Finley, Naylor's youngest daughter, graciously allowed my mentor, D.W. Garber, an Ohio historian, and me to copy these stories in 1974. Since that time, in the course of my ongoing research, I have discovered only a few of the stories elsewhere.

A majority of Naylor's short stories appeared before 1900, written using his pseudonym, S. Q. Lapius, a play on the name of the Roman god of healing, Esculapius (Naylor was also a physician). These early stories comprise Part One of this book. Part Two contains the stories written after 1900 when he dropped the use of S.Q. Lapius and began identifying all of his writings with his full name, James Ball Naylor. Exactly when the stories were written or their order of appearance can no longer be determined.

The division of Naylor's short stories into two distinct sections has less to do with the arbitrary date that separates them and more to do with the nature of their content. Writing short stories was for him like playing on a literary playground, discovering what worked and what did not, finding his "voice," and learning to follow, and to bend, the rules. Ever the student, he was also his own teacher. In Part one Naylor experiments with a variety of characters, settings, and styles, but it is in the stories in Part Two that this effort coalesces in a way that grabs and holds the reader's attention.

Because these stories were written more than one hundred years ago, sometimes obscure words occur that are difficult to decipher or an otherwise familiar word may refer to an alternate or no longer relevant meaning. Footnotes identifying such words and their intended meanings are included for the reader's benefit.

Theresa Marie Flaherty

Part One

Short Stories

by

S. Q. Lapius

Introduction

Part One

Naylor wrote about what he knew. He drew on memories of his childhood growing up in southeastern Ohio, and his recall of those years and of his feelings and awe of nature come across clearly in these short stories that comprise Part One. His deep love for his family shines through in the little details that define relationships between characters. The magnitude that his medical practice played in his life is especially noteworthy since most of these stories are peppered with that knowledge. The Civil War colored his life for most of his early years and clearly influced his writing. He lost his father in the war, as did many of his friends, and neighbors lost fathers, sons, and brothers.

Naylor appears to have used short stories as a playground, exploring different topics and ways to bring his own experiences to life on the written page. The stories in Part One reflect experimentation with childhood, family, his medical practice, and the Civil War. He explores boyhood emotions and ways of building drama, and he experiments with dialect to embellish his characters—all aid in creating vivid pictures in the reader's mind. In some cases, Naylor took ideas from one of his short stories and reworked them for use in other stories or novels. If questioned about this he might well have replied as he did on one occasion, "For may I not do which I like with mine own production?"

Some of his most charming stories are written about children, and it is clear that he often relied on his own childhood memories to bring his stories to life. For example, "Ben's Adventure," the first story in Part One reflects his warmest childhood memories when he spent days running wild and free, wandering barefoot through the woods intent upon discovery. Newton Ridge, where he grew up, was a constant attraction with its many forested areas along the Muskingum River.

The "Diversions of Dicky Dare," about a boy with a penchant for poetry, could well have been an actual episode in his life. "Two Men and a Boy," eloquently illustrates two episodes that affected Naylor deeply. Written from the heart, a young boy's tender emotions are skillfully revealed.

Naylor's earliest known serial, "Beggars Awheel," appeared in *The Ohio Farmer* in eight chapters in a section for "Young Folks" from December 3, 1896, through January 21, 1897. In characterizing the boys, Naylor again drew on experiences from his own boyhood, vividly presenting childhood emotions that held the reader's attention. The adventure story about two teenage boys on a 250-mile bicycle trip, was written at a time when bicycles were considered strange contraptions. The rustic characters met along the way add much to the drama, and Naylor's use of dialect enhanced the characterization. The boys are fascinated with threshing operations on a farm and with water-powered mills, the sweet memories of Naylor's own childhood. It is an entertaining story that for today's readers provides an interesting contrast to the present.

"Wild Tom," the last story in Part One, is one of the author's most delightful stories, a heartwarming tale of a friendship between a crusty railroad engineer and a youngster who brings meaning into his life.

By the end of 1895, Naylor, a loving father, was blessed with "four little queens." A son followed in 1897 and his last child, Jean, was born in 1903. Inspired by their presence, he wrote many touching poems about them. He drew on his own family life for the short story, "Mamie's Prisoner," about a young girl and her little brother.

Naylor's exercises in characterizing young boys found fruition in main characters in three of his novels, *The Cabin in the Big Woods, The Kentuckian,* and *The Scalawags.* The main character in last novel, *The Misadventures of Marjory,* was based on his oldest daughter, Olive Nance. Like her real-life counterpart, Marjory proved to be a delightful and controversial young woman.

Despite all the endeavors that occupied his time, Naylor was first and foremost a physician, and this comes through clearly in these short stories. Again, Naylor uses his personal experience to enrich his stories, with medical situations sometimes the central theme of the story, and other times medical knowledge is peripheral, as when he experiments with writing a mystery or bringing light to a social issue.

"The Story of a Skeleton" is a macabre tale of a skeleton given to a young American doctor by a French colleague. Many doctors as medical students pondered the stories behind the skeletons they handled, but Naylor took it a step further and created at least one story for a skeleton.

During the early years of his medical practice, Naylor faced stiff competition from older physicians. Younger doctors seeking to establish practices provided another problem. "Two Consultations at Mam Starling's" illustrates different approaches to the treatment of one patient, ninety-year-old Mam Starling who is on her deathbed.

"Stuff of Which Doctors are Made" contains recognizable minor incidents from Naylor's past. Drawing on his own background, Naylor portrays young Tom with a poverty-stricken background much like his had been, and the local doctor, who takes an interest in the boy's future, as caring as Naylor hoped himself to be.

More than a hundred years before "CSI" became a staple of prime time television, Naylor recognized the fascination of the uninitiated in matters of medicine. Medical details play a large part in "The Coming of Sawlus," one of his longer stories. Naylor's attitude toward religion is also explored. Considered a bit unorthodox, he was sometimes mistakenly thought of as an atheist or agnostic. He was neither. He called himself "a fixed scientist and a rationalist." But Naylor was definitely suspicious of the smooth-talking evangelists who came to town for weeks at a time putting on revivals. These ideas were later explored in greater detail in his autobiographical novel, *Ralph Marlowe*. This was one of his longer stories, and it allowed him to expand on his characterizations and to add more plot devices. The idea of a letter, intercepted and misinterpreted, was used again in a later story and in more than one of his novels.

"The Blackmer Affair," also a longer story, is a more complicated murder mystery, and the main characters' medical knowledge is also used to find a killer.

Although the main character in "Did It Pay?" is a doctor, the focus of the story is on a major social issue that is still of concern today, an employer's responsibility to pay a "living wage." The main character in "Mills of the Gods" is a doctor as well, but the story itself is about betrayal and retribution.

Naylor lived through the Civil War as a young child, so his feelings about it ran deep. He wrote several stories related to it. "A Spike from the Underground Railroad," based on a true incident, was also one of his first ventures into historical fiction. Written barely more than thirty years after the end of the war, the story is set in a village easily recognized as Pennsville, Ohio. Naylor lived there for a time in what had been a strongly abolitionist village that figured prominently in the "underground railroad."

"One of Morgan's Men," is based on a true historical episode associated with the Civil War in Morgan County. It is an interesting story about a man under the command of the Confederate guerilla commander, General John Hunt Morgan, on his 1863 raid through Ohio.

"Jud Trainor's Ghost" is also set during the Civil War. Naylor's character descriptions in this story test the limits of believability because the main character is so extremely flawed and self destructive.

Again, Naylor used elements and ideas from these stories about the Civil War in a novel, *The Kentuckian,* said by some to be the best of his novels. In one instance, a situation similar to one in "One of Morgan's Men" is introduced when a character discovers that another's view of slavery is very different from her own.

Theresa Marie Flaherty

Ben's Adventure

"Nancy, I'm goin' down to the lower end o' the corn patch to see if I can find where them shoats[1] gits into the corn."

"Well, Dan, don't you go traipsin' off huntin'. Dinner 'll be ready in an hour 'r so, an' when you have a gun on your shoulder you don't know when to come back," replied his wife.

"All right," was the non-committal answer; and Dan closed the cabin door and strode away in the direction of the corn patch. As he reached the wood pile in front of the rude domicile that he called home a bright faced lad of 10 years dropped the load of wood he had in his arms.

"Are you going?" His father asked.

"Yes, in just a minute. I got to take this wood to mam." He carried the armload of sticks into the cabin, and throwing them upon the floor in a sprawling heap, ran out to rejoin his father. Together they climbed the low rail fence that surrounded the house, and chatting merrily they proceeded on their way to the corn patch down by the edge of the forest.

Mr. Daniel Hartzell—for such was the settlers name—carefully inspected the fence all along the border of the woods, but could discover no break in it through which an enterprising porker might force its way; and he was about to abandon his search and return to the cabin, when the rattling of the corn blades and a startled grunt admonished him that the marauder was in the corn patch at that very moment.

"Ben," he said, addressing his son, "you run up there in the corn an' start that shoat down this way. We'll chase him out, an' thereby find out where he got in; fer I'm sure there ain't more'n one place he gits through." Ben did as directed, and soon the shoat dashed past Mr. Hartzell and made its egress at a point that the latter had just carefully examined.

---

1 **shoat** - a young pig that has just been weaned

"Don't that beat all creation!" muttered the settler; "talk about sense—that shoat's got more mother wit than half the people in the valley."

Ben examined the place and burst out laughing. A hollow log ran through the bottom of the brush pile, communicating with the corn patch on the one hand and the forest on the other; and through this log—as through a tunnel—the cunning pig was in the habit of passing into the enclosure and out again.

"I'll soon stop that cunnin' bugger's tricks by closing up his gate," remarked Ben's father, tugging at the log.

He dragged it from its position and rolled it out of the corn patch into the woods; then he took his axe and cut a quantity of green limbs, with which to repair the gap that had been made by removing the log.

"Now, Ben" he said, sitting down to rest, "call up the shoats and let's see if they're all here."

"Peeg—peeg! Pooy—pooy!" bawled Ben, lustily, making a funnel of his fat hands.

A serious of grunts and squeals, resounding from points far and near in the woodland, was the immediate result of Ben's strange bellowing.

One—two—three—four—" counted Mr. Hartzell, until he reached ten. "W'y there's only ten shoats here, an' there ought to be 'leven. That tarnal[2] she bear over on Turkey Run's got another one of 'em. Ben, you run up to the cabin an' say to yo' mam that I've gone over that way to git a shot at the bear. I'd give a horn o' powder to draw a bead on 'er jest once. She wouldn't eat no more shoats."

"Can I go, too, pap?" pleaded the boy, sniffing the battle a-far off. "I can ketch up with you after telling mam."

"I don't care—ask y'r mam. Be off now."

And Mr. Hartzell shouldered his long gun and strode away as Ben sped in the direction of the cabin. The latter, on reaching the house, informed his mother of his father's intentions; and then, without wasting time to gain her permission, he sprang away in pursuit of his male parent.

———————————

2 **tarnal** - damned

He had passed the corn patch, and was flying over the ground as fast as his sturdy young legs could carry him, when his attention was attracted to a clump of bushes a few yards to his right. A strange commotion seemed to be going on in that clump of bushes, and Ben paused momentarily to investigate. As he did so he was surprised to see a cub bear tumble into the open and waddle toward him.

It was a fat little thing, not much larger than a full-grown raccoon, and as playful as a puppy. Ben immediately relinquished all idea of following his father. He would capture the bear cub and take it home in triumph.

He started toward the cabin, proudly bearing his burden, and had just reached the edge of the corn patch, what a bloodcurdling sound—half growl, half roar—caused his hair to stand on end and his youthful knees to knock together. It was the mother bear, and she came lumbering out of the forest in pursuit of the kidnapper of her offspring.

Ben hugged the cub to his breast and ran as fast as he could scamper. He was so badly scared that he never thought of dropping the source of all his trouble and danger. The mother rapidly gained upon him, and, glancing over his shoulder, he was horrified to see her but a few feet distant, standing on her hind legs, her paws outstretched, and her open jaws dripping foam and ready to catch him.

He screamed at the top of his voice, but hugged the cub the tighter, and ran on. An obstacle appeared in his way—it was the hollow log that had served as a secret tunnel for the enterprising porker. It lay directly in the boy's path, and he attempted to spring over it, with the result that he stumbled and fell, dropping the cub and bruising his own shins. The baby bear set up a pitiful whining, and the mother gnashed her teeth and reached for the unfortunate youngster.

Ben scrambled to his feet, but the bear was almost upon him, and he gave himself up for lost. He staggered to the end of the log, over which he had fallen, and in a fit of sheer desperation, dropped quickly to his hands and knees and nimbly crawled into it.

The log was about fifteen feet in length, and much smaller at one end then the other. Ben had entered the larger end, and had crawled nearly to the middle of the cavity. Here his further progress had been stopped by the lessened caliber of the hole; so, drawing his legs well under him, he waited and trembled.

The bear sniffed at the log, peered into it, and then tried to gain entrance; but her bulky body refused to be squeezed into so small a space, and she was compelled to abandon the project. She uttered a growl of exasperation and disappointment, and thrust first one paw and then the other into the log, in a vain endeavor to reach the crouching and cowering lad.

Finding that her former efforts and devices had failed, she commenced to claw and gnaw at the log in the most cruel and bloodthirsty manner. The hollow cylinder rested upon a sloping bit of ground, and the mother bear, in her earnest endeavors to tear it to pieces, dislodged it and sent it rolling over and over, into a little hollow fifty feet from its former resting place.

Ben could not imagine what had occurred. He was whirled over and tossed about until he hardly knew where he was. When the log came to a sudden halt from striking against the stump of a tree, he was thrown into a promiscuous heap, and realized that he had received a number of abrasions and contusions, as a result of his revolving ride.

Ben lay quite still for a long time, his cramped limbs aching and throbbing painfully. Not hearing or seeing anything of his enemy, he at last determined to take the risk and crawled from his uncomfortable position. This was a resolve easier made than executed, for a large and strong splinter on the inside of the log had penetrated the back of the boys coat and with each backward movement on his part it prodded deeply into his flesh and prevented his exit.

He squirmed and twisted, but all to no purpose. He could not dislodge the splinter and he could not bear the excruciating torture, so he crawled still further into the log and gave himself up to thought. He was a self-reliant little man, schooled in all the hard lessons of poverty and adversity, and to the life of a back woodsman's family, and he had no idea of tamely submitting to the situation.

How hungry he was! He must get out in some way, there was no gainsaying[3] that—but how? He succeeded at last in grasping the perverse splinter, and by bending and twisting it in various

---

3 **gainsay** - deny or contradict (a fact or statement)

directions separated its tough fibers. Then he breathed easier and gave a great sigh of relief.

"Well, I think it won't be long till I have a taste o' pone[4] an' milk," he murmured, as he worked his way backward.

He was doomed to bitter disappointment; however, for as his feet reached the rim of the cavity they came in contact with the solid substance that completely blocked the opening. The log had stopped with its larger end pressed squarely against a stump!

Little Ben had an inkling of the true state of affairs, and knew instinctively that he could not get out by his own unaided efforts. His father—as his mother had said—never knew when to return when he started out with his gun; and probably would not come back to the cabin till nightfall. He would not be uneasy about his son for he would suppose that the mother had refused to let the lad follow him. Ben's mother, on the other hand, would suppose that the boy was with his father, and would give the subject no further thought. Ben reasoned this all out as he lay full length in the hollow log. He occupied an easier position and was not wholly uncomfortable except that he was very hungry.

The autumn afternoon waned, and the shades of night grew apace, and still no one came to release the little fellow from his prison house. He called and called, but received no answer, and at last his native stoicism gave way and he broke down and cried; then he fell asleep.

When he awoke it was quite dark. The first sound that greeted his ears was the sniff of some animal at the smaller end of the log. His first thought was that the bear had returned, and was again seeking a chance to devour him; so he again crawled toward the center of the cavity and drew his legs under him as before. He was relieved, however, for the lusty bay of a large dog resounded upon the bright air.

"Hyur, bingo—good dog—good dog!" Ben called. And the dog capered about frantically and barked louder than ever.

"What you doin' there, Bingo? Hunt 'em up—hunt 'em up!"

The boy recognized his father's voice and hellooed as loudly has as he could.

---

4 **pone** - a type of cornbread

"Here I am, pap—here I am!"

"By the ghost o' Dan'l Boone!" shouted Mr. Hartzell, explosively; that's Ben's voice. Where are you, young'n?"

"Right here in this holler log, pap."

"What the nation you doin' in there, boy? Me 'n y'r mam's been 'most scared to death 'bout you, an' been huntin' you everywhere."

"Let me out an' I'll tell you," answered Ben.

Mr. Hartzell rolled the log from its position and dragged forth his son. Ben's mother hugged him to her breast and rained kisses upon his sunburned little face. After he had given his parents a full account of what had happened to him his father caught him up and said:

"I s'pect you're purty hungry, lad, seein' that you hain't had no dinner n'r no supper; but you can have all the bear steak you want— you can help to eat the old beer that wanted to eat you. I killed 'er jest about sundown; an' the cub's at the cabin, jest a-spillin' fer a play with you. Me an' y'r mam jest 'bout give you up fer lost."

And Ben's chubby hand, fondlin' his father's bearded face, felt something warm drip upon it.

◆–◆–◆

Two Men and a Boy

He was just a barefoot country boy, carrying a heavy bag upon his bony shoulder. He had trudged into the village, from two miles out among the hills—where the log cabin he called home bashfully hid itself in a hollow so deep the sun found the hut only at midday. The boy's clothing was neither gorgeous nor superfluous. His trousers, precariously supported by one knit suspender, were patched in front and rear; and one leg of this nether[1] garment was turned up rakishly and the other hung dejectedly over a stone-bruised heel. A ragged check shirt and a battered bit of a straw hat completed the youngster's gay attire.

Diffidently he made his way into the village hardware store; and, screwing up all the boyish courage he possessed, he said to the prim and punctillious[2] proprietor: "Do-do you buy old iron?"

The skinny little hardware dealer nervously stroked his stiff chin whiskers, glared at the boy as if the diminutive urchin was guilty of a piece of unpardonable impertinence, and replied icily: "Yes; bring the stuff back this way."

The two went to the back of the store. There the proprietor weighed the scrap iron, and paid the boy the few cents it brought. Not a word was spoken during the whole transaction. The boy, awed by the little man's arctic demeanor, was too scared to speak; the man apparently considered the lad beneath notice—and was too reserved to speak. The deal over, the youth started out, the empty bag over his arm.

But, near the front of the store, he paused and fixed his gaze upon the contents of a showcase containing cutlery. Longingly he looked, shifting his weight from one bare foot to the other. The proprietor was at his elbow.

---

1 **nether** - located beneath or below; lower or under
2 **punctilious** - precise; scrupulous

"How—how much is that big knife in there?" The lad asked—his whole soul in his words and manner.

"Oh, get out—get on out!" the frigid little man with the frostbitten ego cried irritability. "You haven't got money enough to buy that knife. Get on out, now."

The boy didn't wait for further orders. He hurried out the door, and set off up the street. Not a word did he say—not even to himself; his thoughts were too tumultuous and conflicting to be formed into words—just at that time. But his lips were tremulous, his eyes were moist with tears of anger and mortification. When he reached the far end of the dusty and deserted village street, he paused momentarily, knuckled a grimy fist into his smarting eyes and cast a hasty glance back over the course he had come. Then he silently and carefully counted his pennies; and proceeded on his way—his heart filled with bitterness and his head filled with rash resolves.

A year later, the family to which this twelve-year-old boy belonged moved into the village. The boys of the town, with whom he soon became acquainted and struck up a comradeship, all had bats and balls. The country lad had none. But he traded a pack of walnuts for a bat; and was at the end of his available commercial assets. However, he must have a ball. He appealed to his mother; he had faith in her resourcefulness. His confidence was not misplaced. The mother had learned lessons in the school of hard-luck; she knew what to do. She raveled out some cast-off woolen socks for the yarn; tore up an old rubber shoe to obtain the elastic material necessary; and fashioned and formed the ball. It was a good piece of handiwork, too—of requisite size; elastic and fairly spherical; and well-sewed with twine. But it had no leather cover; and the son couldn't conceal his disappointment. His discerning mother saw that he was dissatisfied, and said: "Doesn't it suit you?"

"Oh, why y-e-s," he replied hesitatingly; "but I'd like—like to have it covered—with leather."

The good mother confessed that she was dubious about her ability to design and sew on the desired cover. However, she remarked consolingly:

"You find some leather; and I'll try the thing. I can't do worse than fail."

The boy hunted for an old boot or piece of carriage cover; but failed to find anything suited to the purpose he had in mind. Then he thought of the village saddler's shop; he had seen a pile of leather cutting in front of the door of that small and weather-worn edifice—where the sadler had swept them. The lad had little expectation of finding a piece of leather large enough for his ball-cover; but he didn't know where else to search. So down to the saddler shop he hastened—fast as his strong and nimble legs could carry him.

The door of the shop was open. The saddler was busy at work, just inside, seated upon his sewing-horse—one leg tucked under him. He was a stooped and sallow man; lame in one foot, and with a wealth of iron-gray hair and whiskers; but he had two of the brightest black eyes—and out of these clear windows his ego looked, and laughed at the world and all its cares.

The boy entered upon his vain search, industriously stirring the pile of leather cutting and softly whistling to himself. The saddler heard him; and leaned far back on his sewing-horse, that he might look out the door, and watched him for several seconds. Presently the boy looked up. His eyes met those of the saddler fixed upon it. The timid lad was disconcerted; he instantly recalled his experience of the year before, with the hardware man—and the recollection frightened him.

"What're you doing out there?" the saddler demanded brusquely; but the kindly expression of his homely features belied his tone and words. So the boy instantly forgot his fear; and truthfully replied: "I'm trying to find a piece of leather big enough to cover up a ball."

"Got the ball with you?" the saddler inquired in the same gruff voice and manner.

"Yes, sir"

"Come in here."

The boy silently obeyed.

"Let me have that ball," the saddler ordered, extending his yellow, claw-like digits.

The lad obeyed.

The saddler slowly descended from his perch; hobbled across the floor, to his cutting-table; and, humming a tune, pulled a flank of leather toward him. The youngster dropped upon a stool, and silently looked on—his mind in a state of wonder and doubt, mingled. What was the man going to do—keep the ball, or—or what?

The saddler continued to hum his long-meter tune and turn the flank of leather this way and that. Presently he picked up a pair of calipers and measured the ball. Next he took a pair of compasses and scratched a circle upon the leather. Then he caught up a knife, whet it a little upon a convenient stone, and began to cut out a cover for the ball.

The boy, for the first time, realized what the saddler meant to do; and the youngster was scared stiff. Under his breath he muttered:

"He thinks I told him to cover the ball; and he's going to do it—and I haven't got a cent to pay him."

But the urchin's mouth was so dry he couldn't say a word aloud; he could only sit and suffer expectantly—picturing to himself the dilemma he would be in when the job was finished, and the punishment that might be his. Maybe the old saddler would whip him, or throw him out, or even send him to jail. He devoutly wished he was anywhere else than where he was; almost wished the earth might gape and engulf him. Oh, how had he got himself into such a predicament—and how was he to get out of it!

The saddler deliberately cut out the cover—all the while humming his hymn tune; and wet and stretched it. Next he reseated himself upon his sewing-horse; tacked the cover to the ball; clamped the ball firmly in the jaws of his horse; and sewed the cover in place. Then he again descended to the floor and returned to his cutting-table. There he took a wooden mallet and hammered down the seams; and, finally, he oiled and polished the cover—till the beautiful ball shown with the rich brown luster of a ripe chestnut. And all the time the old fellow kept humming that long-meter tune.

The boy was in a mental state bordering on panic or collapse. The saddler suddenly cried out:

"Are you a good catcher?"

And, with the words, he tossed the ball to the boy. The lad gasped and swallowed spasmodically; but at last succeeded in saying:

"I'm aw—awful glad to have the ball covered; but I haven't got—got any money to pay you."

"Well, who in the world asked you for money—or expected money, hey?" laughed the saddler. "Run along and play, now."

The boy shouted—"Thank you," and bounded out the door—his heart filled with gratitude and gladness.

Why have I detailed these two truthful anecdotes? Well, listen: a boy is a young savage—with all the primitive merits and defects, all the primitive trends and tendencies of an aborigine. He's virile in his loves and hates; he long remembers kindness or injury, courtesy or insult—real or fancied.

This particular boy grew to manhood. The congealed and methodical hardware man ran for the office of township treasurer. The boy had become a voter; and he deliberately went into the booth and intentionally voted against the hardware dealer—although the latter's name was on the ticket the former usually voted.

On the contrary, this same boy—after he became a middle-aged man—traveled a dozen miles to a county fair, for no other reason than that he had heard the old saddler was to be there. And he hunted the grounds over, till he found his benefactor; and, with tears in his eyes, he shook the hand of the tottering old saddler—and recalled to the old fellow's mind the latter's kind deed of other days.

The moral? Oh! well, do as I do—draw it to suit yourself.

A Spike from the Underground Railroad

Kirkertown is not the real name of the place, but it serves as well as another to conceal the identity of the little town of which I wish to write; and as it is a modest, unassuming hamlet and would never recover its equanimity if once brought into notice, I wish to shield it.

Kirkertown is a collection of white cottages, green shutters, and neat doorways; a quiet, rural place, knowing little of the great outside world—and caring less. It occupies the crest of a high ridge, with Bald Eagle creek on the one hand and Wolf creek on the other and is hedged in by a fruit and grazing country.

Its inhabitants are sober and industrious, for the most part, as it is the center of a large Quaker settlement. Those peace-loving people came from Pennsylvania years ago, and their descendents occupy the farms that their ancestors cleared, and still cling tenaciously to the religion, dress and manners of their forefathers.

Situated among the grass-clad hills of southeastern Ohio, a few miles from the picturesque Muskingum river, Kirkertown is a quaint and delightful pastoral Eden.

At the time of which I wish to speak it was of much greater importance to the general public than it is today. It had several "general" stores, a tannery, a tobacco warehouse and two or three cooper and blacksmith shops, besides the two-story brick tavern that stood at the junction of the two principal streets.

It was one of the regular stopping places on the old stage road from Zanesville to Marietta, and was, also, one of the main stations on the great "Underground Railway" from Kentucky to Canada. An incident connected with the same underground system furnishes material for the following sketch:

The Quakers of Kirkertown were an intensely liberty-loving people, and uncompromising abolitionist. They made it a part of their religion, as it were. The black man had no better friends anywhere. They gave lavishly of their time and money to aid him, and many were the responsibilities they assumed and the risks they ran to keep him on his way to Canada—and freedom.

This much by way of explanation; and now to my story.

One raw and rainy Saturday evening in the autumn of 1842, three black fugitives found temporary refuge in Kirkertown, at the house of a good Friend named Jason Halpin; and a few hours later their pursuers—also three in number—arrived in the village and put up for the night at the brick tavern.

It was not customary to carry passengers over the underground in daylight, except in cases of emergency; but in this case it had been absolutely necessary to do so. The three blacks had been secreted at the farm of Richard Barkhurst, six miles south of Kirkertown, but the slave hunters had been so close upon them, that it had been thought best to move them at once to the next station—Kirkertown.

The fugitives had been brought in a covered express wagon to Halpin's, and were concealed in his haymow near the edge of the village. The express wagon had arrived and departed so quietly— just before dusk—that not a half dozen villagers knew of its arrival at all; and the few that did know of it were loyal and could be depended upon to keep the secret.

Halpin carried supper to the cowering black wretches at the barn, and made arrangements to spirit them away sometime during the night; but the arrival of the slave catchers complicated matters greatly.

These latter worthies dismounted from their jaded horses at the tavern door, ordered their beasts fed and watered, and went in to their suppers. After they had eaten heartily of the primitive fare that the tavern afforded, they wended[1] their way to the tavern bar-room, and entered into conversation with the congregated village idlers.

The spokesman of the trio was a tall, raw-boned Kentuckian who bore the very appropriate name of Jack Bassett. He was "hail fellow well met" with everybody, treated indiscriminately, and did not attempt to conceal his mission. On the contrary, he said boldly:

---

1 **wend** - go in a specific direction

"Yes, we're slave catchers, an' we know that we're close onto the three black rascals that we followed clear from Kentucky. They're in the village somewhere, an' we mean to have 'em. I'll give any man a gallon o' whiskey that'll tell me right where they are."

No one answered.

"They can't escape us," Bassett went on, "an' if anybody knows right where they are an' wants to earn a gallon o' good whiskey let him speak out."

Still no one offered to accept his munificent[2] offer. The crowd was a motley one of villagers, countrymen and teamsters, but with the exception of a possible two or three they were all rank abolitionists. Besides, not a man of them knew where the slaves were hidden; in fact, the first intimation they had that slaves were near came from Bassett himself.

"Does anyone want a gallon o' red liquor?" insisted the Kentucky giant in his most wheedling tone.

"S-s-say!" it was stuttering Ike who spoke, crossing his long legs and refilling his black pipe at the same time. "S-s-say, do you mean w'at you s-say, m-m-mister?"

"Of course I do," replied Bassett, eagerly.

"W-w-well, fill up the jug an' I'll t-t-tell you."

"Will you tell me right where they are?"

"Y-y-yes, of course."

Bassett ordered the florid faced host to fill a gallon jug with his best liquor; while the crowd sat in amazement at Ike Taylor's perfidy[3], for he had always been considered a trusty abolitionist. "There," Bassett said, handing the heavy vessel to Ike; "there's your whiskey, now where's my cattle?"

Ike took the jug, removed the cork and sampled the contents freely, smacking his lips and winking at his comrades between gulps.

"Y-y-you want to know r-r-right where they are?"

"Certainly!" cried Bassett impatiently.

Taylor edged toward the door, jug in hand. As he reached it he turned—himself and the doorknob at the same time—and stuttered:

---

2 **munificent** - showing great generosity
3 **perfidy** - deceitfulness; untrustworthiness

"M-m-mister, as near as I can t-tell you, they're in their skins!"

He darted out just in time to escape the vicious kick that Bassett aimed at his retreating coat tails.

The assembled loafers burst into a roar of mingled shouts and laughter, in which Bassett's two companions heartily joined.

The Kentuckian was furious, but perceiving that his anger but enhanced the enjoyment of the others, he bawled out: "That was a purty slick Yankee trick, wasn't it? Come up an' have a drink, everyone o' you!"

While these events were transpiring at the tavern, the friends of the black men were by no means idle.

In the darkened kitchen at Jason Halpin's sat a number of stern, resolute men planning how Bassett might be outwitted.

"What does thee propose to do under the circumstances, Jason?" came from the corner occupied by Barclay Penstock. Halpin in his slow earnest way told him his plans.

Does thee think James Milburn can be depended upon to carry out thee plans?" William Worthington inquired. "He is inclined to be somewhat rash and boastful, thee knows, Jason."

"Thee has no cause for worry, William," answered Halpin; "James Milburn will do as I bid him."

"What thee does, thee must do quickly," remarked Barclay Penstock in a musing tone. "These ungodly slave dealers will not long remain idle. They will be scouring the premises in an hour from now."

"Again I say that thee need not worry, brethren; my plans are completed and the black men will escape—depend upon it. I will ensure the success of the undertaking, if the Lord vouchsafe[4] his willingness," answered Halpin somewhat nettled.

The meeting dissolved, the members slipping out one by one, silently as shadows. Halpin went directly to the barn to complete arrangements. A few minutes afterward a large farm wagon, drawn by two strong horses and covered by a tarpaulin, moved out of the barnyard and rattled at a brisk rate of speed along the village street.

Just as it came opposite the brick tavern, James Milburn, the

---

4 **vouchsafe** - bestow, confer, accord

driver, put whip to the horses. The surprised animals broke into a gallop, and amid a shower of mud the swaying wagon disappeared up the dark and sloppy street. Barclay Penstock and William Worthington were standing on the street corner as the unwieldy vehicle rolled by.

"It is just as I feared and just as I told thee," groaned Worthington. "James Milburn is far too rash—he will betray all!"

"I very much fear that thee is right," sighed Penstock in return. "If those men of violence hear him, they will be in hot pursuit."

The two Quakers turned and walked away together, and a third slouching figure, that had been crouching in a neighboring doorway, arose and hurried in the direction of the tavern.

It was Corson Furrier, the dissipated[5] son of Dr. Furrier, and there was little that was mean and disreputable that he would not do for the price of a night's dissipation.

Sliding into the tavern ballroom, he drew Bassett aside and said: "Do you want to ketch them slaves o' yours? If you do, you'd better be after 'em."

"What do you mean?" asked Bassett, excitedly.

"If I tell you all about it an' you capture the niggers will you give me a gallon o' whiskey?"

Bassett nodded hastily and eagerly, and Furrier went on: "There ain't no sell about this; I don't want the whiskey till you get your niggers."

"Yes, I'll do better than that. I'll give you the whiskey an' five dollars. Now out with it," and Bassett bent forward to hear.

Furrier told the Kentuckian what he had seen and heard. Bassett quickly and quietly informed his companions, and procuring horses the three slave hunters, accompanied by their informant, started in pursuit of the flying vehicle.

They left the tavern, watched by the excited habitues[6] of the ballroom, and following the course taken by James Milburn, traveled the ridge road for about a mile. At this point the road forked; so Furrier dismounting, struck a match and examined the ground.

---

5 **dissipate** - intemperate in the pursuit of pleasure; dissolute
6 **habitués** - a regular patron

"The wagon's gone down onto the creek road," he announced as he remounted. "He's breakin' fer ol' man Wendell's place with 'em, about a mile from here on Bald Eagle. He expects to hide 'em there until the hunt's over."

The four pursuers hastened forward as rapidly as the nature of the road and the night would permit, Bassett cursing and raving incessantly.

When within a quarter of a mile of Wendell's farm they heard the clatter of an approaching wagon and paused and listened. It was coming from the direction of Wendell's, and Bassett and his companions could hear the driver talking and chirruping to his team as the heavy vehicle bounded and rumbled along the rocky bed of the creek road.

"That's him—that's Jim Milburn," said Furrier triumphantly. "He's unloaded his pets at ol' Wendell's. We'll get 'em now, never fear."

The wagon drew nearer and nearer.

"Hullo!" called Bassett in his leonine[7] voice.

The driver quickly pulled up his team and replied: "Hullo theeself."

"That's him," again whispered Furrier.

"Is your name Jim Milburn?" inquired Bassett, riding forward and peering into the intense darkness.

"I was christened James Milburn. May I ask by what right thee stops me at night, on the public highway, and asks thee question?"

"My name's Jack Bassett, an' I want to know what you've done with my niggers—an' you better be quick about telling it," returned Bassett menacingly.

"I know nothing of thee chattels[8], friend. Will thee be kind enough to let me pass?"

"Listen how a Quaker can lie!" muttered Furrier to himself. Then aloud to Bassett: "Ther' aint no use to fool with him. He aint got half sense nohow. We'll find 'em at Wendell's. Let's go on."

Bassett acted on Furrier's suggestion; first, however, searching the wagon and finding it empty.

---

7 **leonine** - characteristic of a lion
8 **chattel** – a personal possession; an it of property other than real estate

When the slave hunters were beyond hearing, Jim Milburn indulged in a bit of laughter that almost precipitated him from the high wagon seat; then he drove on in the direction of Kirkertown.

It was a little after ten o'clock when Bassett and his followers reached the residence of Thomas Wendell. Riding up to the house, that stood on a knoll a short distance from the creek road, the party stopped and had a whispered consultation.

It was agreed that Bassett should go to the door, while the others stationed themselves at various points around the house, to prevent the escape of the slaves.

Fortifying his courage by means of a drink from his pocket flask, Bassett thundered with his clenched hand upon the oaken panels. After a short interval a smooth, resonant voice called out from within: "Who is there and what is wanted?"

Bassett told his name and business. The door opened, and the tall, spare form of Thomas Wendell stepped out upon the porch. He was without coat or hat, and the night breeze blew his thin white locks about his shaven, leathery face, as he said: "Friend, I have no knowledge of thee slaves. Why has thee come to me?"

"They're in your house, an' I want 'em," returned Bassett curtly and decisively.

"Have I not told thee that I know nothing of thee slaves? Does thee doubt my word?"

"Ther's no use denyin' it—they're in there," almost shouted the Kentuckian. "The house is surrounded, an' I mean to have 'em. If you don't want to git yourself into trouble, stand out o' the road an' let me in."

Wendell drew his gaunt figure to its fullest height, and his pale blue eyes glistened dangerously as the lamplight from the open door fell full upon his face.

"I am a law-abiding citizen, friend," he said quietly. "I suppose thee has a search warrant that thee demands to search my premises?"

Bassett admitted that he had not.

"Then," resumed the old Quaker in the same quiet way, "thee cannot come in. I will bid thee good night!"

And stepping quickly inside, he shut and locked the door in the surprised and enraged slave dealer's face.

Another consultation was held, and as a result Bassett dispatched one of his men to Kirkertown for a search warrant, while he and the others remained to guard the house.

In an hour and a half the man returned and reported that the justice—Barclay Penstock—had said: "I will issue no warrant to search the premises of Thomas Wendell. I do not believe that the chattels are there."

When the man told the result of his mission, Furrier swore a mighty oath and hissed: "Oh! Barclay Penstock's a cussed abolitionist—he's trying to fool us. Send down to Marlow fer a warrant."

Again acting on Furrier's suggestion, Bassett, himself, started for Marlow, five miles away.

Kirkertown and vicinity was thoroughly aroused by this time; and the men came flocking in from all directions—abolitionists and slavery sympathizers alike bent on seeing "fair play," and enjoying the gossip and excitement.

The slavery sympathizers gave as their opinion that "Thomas Wendell had got his foot in it, this time;" and many of the abolitionists, also, were alarmed at the situation and exercised[9] in regard to the outcome of the affair.

Wendell stubbornly kept his doors locked, alike to friend and foe. Bonfires were kindled about the premises, and the place with its neighing steeds and tramping men resembled a miniature army encampment. The fact that many of the men on both sides were armed with guns and pistols added to the impression.

It was almost daylight when Bassett returned from Marlow, accompanied by a constable with a search warrant. Following in their wake came a number of citizens from the latter place, to swell the constantly increasing throng.

A surprise was in store for all. Without protest Wendell threw open his doors to the officer of the law, requesting only that the crowd be kept out.

---

9 **exercised** – occupied with the attentions of, especially so as to be worried or vexed

From cellar to garrett[10] the search was prosecuted diligently and thoroughly, but all in vain—not a slave was to be found!

At the distance of a few yards from the residence stood a small log cabin. After the former had been rummaged completely the Constable and Bassett attempted to enter the latter. But Thomas Wendell, rifle in hand, planted himself in front of the door and said:

"Thee has a warrant to search the house of Thomas Wendell. This house is my mother's—the warrant does not cover it, and thee cannot enter!"

Here was a dilemma! Bassett swore and the Constable argued and pleaded, but the stern old man remained inflexible.

Just when the Kentuckian was about to start again for Marlow, to procure a second warrant, Jason Halpin arrived on the scene. He whispered a few words to Wendell, who immediately changed his mind and invited the officer to complete his search.

The slaves were not there, however, and Bassett retired discomfited.

It is almost needless to say that the negroes were never caught; and it is equally needless to say that they had never been at Wendell's. The whole thing was a ruse to throw the slave catchers off the scent—James Milburn's hurried trip, the conversation of Worthington and Penstock within hearing of Furrier, and all! As soon as the hue and cry had been started toward Wendell's, the fugitives had been taken from Halpin's to another station a dozen miles away. They finally reached Canada in safety.

Barclay Penstock was wont[11] to remark in a lugubrious way, "Thee knows that James Milburn is but half witted and inclined to be rash and boastful. Thee cannot depend upon him!"

---

10 **garrett** - a room or unfinished part of a house just under the roof
11 **wont** - customary behavior in a particular situation

The Coming of Sawlus

Part I

"The glad earth throbs with joy that he
   Is come. Hot, pulsing, passionate June!
   Of whom the poets love to tell,
   For whom the merry wild birds tune

Their throats. A reign of love is his
   With licensed freedom to the smart
   And active God of Love to send
   An arrow through each youthful heart."

So quoted the brown haired, brown eyed maiden of eighteen summers, as she leaned listlessly from the second floor window of a large barn-like structure that rose to the height of three barren stories from the dock at the edge of the sparkling river. Her fair oval face was clouded with the discontented, far away look, and her red lips were pursed into a pretty pout of vexation. The shapely hand that supported her dimpled, baby-like chin was white and soft; and the loose leaves of gauzy stuff that fluttered in the lazy breeze, revealed glimpses of an arm of ivory purity.

A fascinating, intelligent girl was Amy Stanwood, daughter of the wealthy Captain Stanwood of Dartmore. She numbered her friends and admirers by the score, for she was the acknowledged belle of the village and surrounding country.

Her father, Captain Charles Stanwood, was a moving and directing spirit of Dartmore. He owned a large store, had a controlling interest in a half dozen other industries, and possessed several fine farms in the immediate vicinity of the village. He was a hard-headed, far-seeing business man of fifty years, and a widower with two children—Amy and her brother James, a young man of twenty five.

James Stanwood, as everyone in the village called him, was a revised edition of his father in appearance, general intelligence and business sagacity; but here the resemblance suddenly ceased. The father was industrious and economical; Jim was easy-going and prodigal. The father had little education and cared nothing for music, painting or literature; Jim was scholarly, with a passion for the fine arts. He would rather thrum a guitar and sing a song to a crowd of kindred spirits in Tarbell's barroom than keep accounts in his father's dusty office; and he immeasurably preferred a lolling on the sofa in the darkened parlor at home—with pipe and book to console him—to superintending any one of his father's numerous enterprises.

James Stanwood was a source of vexation and bitter disappointment to his father; and Lish Finley, the old ferryman, voiced the opinion of those who knew the facts in the case, when he said:

"Jim Stanwood's a disappointment to the ol' Cap'n. He's been sent to college an' eddycated, but all he'll do is plink-plunk on an ol' banjo, 'r somepin o' that kind, 'r lay aroun' an' read books and study out pictur's. He's a good-hearted feller, Jim is, but he's awful shif'less, I tell you. An' his loafin' roun' Tarbell's ain't doin' him no good, neither. His drinkin' an' gamblin's a growin' on 'im. Anybody kin see that. He gits pretty well rossumed sometimes, an' it's jest a worryin' the ol' Cap'n to death. Jim ought to be ashamed o' hisself, as good a chance as he has. He could make money if he would. Lord knows he's smart enough! But he's jest like his mother an' her folks—rather spend ten dollars than 'arn one. His mother was a good woman, but land sakes! she'd ruther write po'try an' paint pictur's than eat when she's hungry. Jim looks like his daddy, but lawzee! he ain't. The ol' Cap'n he's stood it bout as long's he will. There'll be the allfiredest rumpus there one o' these days—they're both mighty high-strung, Jim an' the ol' Cap'n both.

"Now ther's Amy—she's more like the ol' man. Looks like 'er mammy, though. She's ten times the help an' comfort to Cap'n Stanwood than Jim is. Everybody lkes 'er, too. Everybody likes Jim, fer that matter; but he's goin' to the dogs. 'r I miss my guess. It's a shame, that's what I say—good-natured feller like Jim. He's too darned good-natured, that's one thing that ails 'im! The Cap'n's worth thousands, but Jim 'd run through with it in ten years—'r less time—if he had control of it.

"Amy'll git married to that young druggist, Hugh Connor, one o' these long-come-shorts. That'll feather his nest! Seems 's though some fellers 's born to be lucky—an' he's one of 'em.

"Jim ought to git married—mebby he'd settle down: but no danger o' him marryin'! He's too lazy to court the gals, even! He's the han'somest man in town—great, strappin', big, good-lookin' feller. Well, well! money don't alluz make folks happy, does it? The ol' Cap'n ain't happy—not by a jugful!"

Captain Stanwood lived on the second floor of the large frame building before mentioned. The first floor was used as storeroom and warehouse, and the third floor as the public hall. Two stairways led to the second floor, one from the street and the other from the storeroom. The Captain had a small room on the first floor fitted up for office purposes. It contained the usual office furniture, including two desks, a bookcase, and a large old-fashioned safe.

On this hot June day Captain Stanwood set in his stuffy little office, poring over his ledger's. A lusty bumble-bee buzzed and boomed against the upper panes in the dusty and cobwebbed window, and the hum of voices from the storeroom beyond floated drowsily in. Throwing down his pen at last the old gentleman arose, yawned, and paced up and down the narrow room nervously. He was a straight, well proportioned man with iron gray hair and a drooping white mustache. He paused at the open window, thrust his hands deep into his trousers pockets and stared out into vacancy, a puzzled, worried look on his handsome face.

"I don't know what to do with Jim," he muttered, shaking his head; "I have offered him every chance in the world, but he don't seem to care for anything but downright foolishness. He is drifting to the bad as fast as he can. I have spent all the money on him that I intend to spend. If he don't straighten up and go to work, I'll let him shift for himself. He's discontented—says he wants to go away and study art and music. Such nonsense! I'll never waste money on him in that way—never. He could be of great help to me in my business, if he only *would.* Amy has always been a contented and dutiful child. I *do wish* that Jim were like *her.*"

He sauntered out of the office and up the stairs to the living apartments, still musing. As he entered the room, at the window of which Amy sat, he noted the woebegone[1] expression on the girl's face.

"Amy, child, what is the matter?" he inquired kindly.

His daughter turned toward him, the unshed tears shining in her brown eyes, and answered: "Father, I am thoroughly sick of all this—the place, the people, the life we are leading, and everything."

"What!" was all Captain Stanwood could ejaculate, surprise and consternation in his tone.

"It is true, father; I have suppressed my feelings as long as I can. I do not wish to worry you. But I can stand this life no longer. There is no church, no society, no anything here. What is the good of all our riches? You work like a slave day after day—and—wish Jim to do the same. But he has no taste for business, and in this miserable little town he's going to ruin for want of congenial employment. Oh! Father, do sell out and let us move away from here. We have enough money, let us go away somewhere and enjoy it."

The Captain's jaw dropped and he simply stood and looked at her. Was this the girl that he had thought so well satisfied with her surroundings?

"Why, Amy," he began, at last recovering from his amazement, "I never suspected that you felt so."

"No, as I said, I have suppressed my feelings and smothered my desires and longings, because I knew that Jim was a source of trouble to you, and I did not want to add to the burden that you already bore."

"But, Amy, I thought you were looking forward to your marriage with Hugh Connor with pleasure, and that you would be perfectly satisfied to spend your days here as his wife. Hugh's business is here, you know, as well as mine."

"Yes, yes, I know all that," returned the girl, following up the temporary advantage that she fancied she had gained, "but he can go

---

1 **woebegone** - affected with or marked by deep sorrow, grief, or wretchedness

into business elsewhere. He would not care—he would not stay here if it were not for me. He has told me so many times."

And she smiled through her tears.

"Tut, Tut! Amy, you do not know what you ask. I would be compelled to sacrifice half that I am worth. I cannot do it; it is out of the question. I have spent a lifetime to gain what I have in this village, and now my children ask me to give it all up, to gratify a mere whim."

Captain Stanwood sank into a chair and bowed his head upon his hands. Amy came over from the window, put her white arms around his neck and kissed him tenderly.

"Father," she whispered, "you have toiled for wealth long enough. For Jim's sake—for my sake—let us leave here. If Hugh Connors cares for me, he will follow."

The father lifted his head and took his daughter in his arms. "It is for Jim's sake more than for your own, then, that you wish to go," he said, smiling sadly. "You are a good girl and a faithful and true sister. Amy, but your love and sympathy is not appreciated by your brother. There is nothing in him, I began to fear. He antagonizes my wishes in every way, and I cannot and will not stand it much longer. No, you marry Hugh and be happy, and let Jim look after himself. If you wish to go away after you are married, why—why, I will see about it then. There will be plenty of time to consider the matter then. I hear someone calling me, and I must go down."

As her father descended the stairs, Amy leaned her head upon the window sill, her whole frame convulsed with sobs. She dearly loved both her brother and father, and could not blind herself to the fact that the gap between the two was ever widening.

Presently she wiped her eyes and composed her features. Lifting her head, she gazed up the long reach of bright water, the old dreamy, far-away look again on her face.

Her attention was attracted by the sound of voices down by the river.

A little above the Stanwood building was the ferry landing, and moored to the shore was the ancient ferryboat with a half-dozen bare-legged boys fishing from the outer apron. They had set their

poles and were lolling about in all manner of careless and pictur-
esque attitudes, and chattering like so many blackbirds.

"No, 'taint Timms's sailboat," said a freckled faced boy, dangling his sunburned legs in the water, and shading his eyes with his
chubby hand. "Timms went down to Center Bend fishin', day before
yisterday."

"Then it's Manley's" replied a black headed boy positively, as
he lifted his line from the water and impaled a wriggling worm there
on the dripping hook.

"'Tain't Manley's neither," returned the freckled faced boy,
scornfully. "Manley's boat's a layin' down below the dam. I saw it
there a little bit ago."

"It's a boat from some'rs else," broke in another youthful disciple of Isaak Walton. "Don't you see it's bigger'n any boat we got
here?"

By this time Amy had grown interested in the conversation
of the ragged rascal's on the ferryboat; and listening intently, she
watched the approach of the snowy sail glistening in the sunlight.

The warm musky breeze laden with the smell of ripening wheat
and blossoming clover swept lazily down the river, rippling its dark
green surface here and there and bearing the stranger craft nearer.
The gentle ripples lapped and kissed the weatherbeaten sides of the
old ferryboat, and ran lightly up the yellow sands of the landing. The
hush of noon began to fall. Out across the brown and barren fields on
the opposite side of the river, the heat rays shimmered and danced
in the glaring sunlight; and the wild camomile along the river bank
sent up its pungent and penetrating incense. The fisher lads rolled
up their lines—and rolled down their trouser legs—and gaped and
stared at the oncoming boat.

The vessel rounded to and landed at the dock in front of the
Stanwood building, and its occupants, two in number, disembarked.
Amy saw that they were both young men, fairly well-dressed and
not unprepossessing in appearance. They made the boat fast to a piling and sauntered up the village street out of sight, followed by the
fisher lads. Amy turned from the window wondering who they were
and what brought them to Dartmore.

And the hush of noon was over all—and silence reigned.

Part II

When Jim Stanwood came to supper that evening he threw his big, manly form into an easy chair and said airily: "Amy, get on your ascension robe. There's going to be a revival in town, preparatory to a journey to the New Jerusalem with its golden streets, and all that sort of nonsense. The prophet evangelist has just arrived. 'Put your baggage on the raft, don't forget to get your check,' *et cetera., et cetera ad infinitum—ad nauseum!*"

"Jim, Jim, you ought to be ashamed to speak in that light way of sacred things," returned Amy reprovingly, but smiling in spite of herself. "What do you mean, though?"

"Just what I say," answered Jim yawning, "but to speak down to the level of your comprehension, Amy, a traveling evangelist has deigned to visit our godforsaken little burgh. He has obtained permission of the grave and reverent elders of the tabernacle—better known as the Methodist church—to hold a series of meetings within its sacred walls; and he starts the fiery ball of religious arder rolling, this evening. You have been longing for church services here, Amy, me darling, and behold! your prayers have been answered in a miraculous way. So put your house in order, and prepare to aid the good brother in his most holy work."

"Oh! Jim, if you *would* be serious for once"—began his sister, but Jim interrupted her.

"And it's serious you'd have me! Sure, I was never more serious in my life."

"I can readily believe that," said Amy quickly. Then she asked in a breath: "Who is this evangelist, where is he from, and when did he come?"

Jim threw up his hands in mock horror. "One at a time, sister mine, one at a time," he laughed. "Don't overwhelm me in that cold-blooded manner. Now, to take your numerous questions in order, he styles himself the Rev. Merton Sawlus, and according to his most reliable statement, he has been instrumental in returning so many stray lambs to the Master's fold that they have been compelled to enlarge the pasture to accommodate them all. Yea, verily!"

Jim said all this in such a droll, singsong tone that Amy had to laugh.

He went on: "As to your second question, little sister, the great and good man has, as yet, vouchsafed[2] no exact information on the subject. Now for the third and last. He and his worthy companion arrived at high noon today. They came in a sailboat and were received by a number of disciples, who were fishing as the disciples of old were wont[3] to do—"

"Why, Jim, I *saw* them!" broke in Amy, clasping her hands and nodding her head vigorously.

"Oh! you did, did you? You have that advantage over me, then. But where is father? Let's have supper." And the irrepressible Jim arose and spun around the room, whistling a bit of a waltz tune.

"Father will be here soon," replied Amy. Then after a short pause she went on: "I spoke to him about leaving here, Jim."

The young Apollo paused in his gyrations, surprise and pleasure in his look, and said: "You did! When?"

"Today."

"What reply did my lord and master—"

"Jim, you must *not* speak disrespectfully of father. You *shall* not!"

"There, there! little vixen, what did he say?"

"Why, I told him that I wanted to leave, and I begged him for my sake and yours—"

"There you made a mistake."

"For my sake and yours, sell out and go; that you might find an occupation congenial to your tastes—, and that all of us might know something of life outside of this humdrum[4] little village. He did not promise definitely, but—"

"I know what he said. I can tell you his exact words, almost," cried Jim impatiently. "He said for you to marry Hugh, and live

---

2 **vouchsafe** - bestow, confer, accord

3 **wont** - one's customary behavior in a particular situation

4 **humdrum** - lacking excitement or variety; dull; monotonous

here and be happy—and all that kind of stuff. And he told you not to bother your head about me—that I am a bad egg and not worth saving. Oh! I can hear him say it."

"Hush!" said Amy, warningly, "father is coming."

Captain Stanwood ascended the stairs and the three went into their suppers.

Very little was said during the meal, each feeling that an icy constraint was upon him. After supper Amy said to Jim: "I believe I will go to church tonight. Will you not go with me?"

"Where's Hugh Connor?" replied her brother, pursing his lips and lifting his eyebrows.

"How provoking you are, Jim," answered Amy, slightly irritated. "You know that Hugh cannot leave the drug store until it is too late for church. But we will have him call at the church to come home with us."

"No, thank you—not any of that, if you please," and Jim lengthened his face and rolled his eyes in a lugubrious[5] manner. "I don't propose to take a young lady to church, just to accommodate a rival—"

"Jim, you silly thing, will you go, or will you *not*?"

"Decidedly 'not,'" mimicked her brother, and ran down the stairs laughing. This was a sample of Amy's daily experience with Jim.

She went to church that evening. A fair sized congregation greeted Rev. Sawlus, and listened with pleased attention to his discourse. He was an athletic man of thirty years, dark complexioned, smooth faced, with piercing eyes and heavy jaws. He was a ready and forcible speaker, seemed to have an intimate knowledge of the subject, and—although his language was a little too slipshod and flowery—succeeded in pleasing his hearers very well, indeed. After the sermon he announced that the meetings would continue from night to night, as long as an interest in them was manifested.

Hugh Connor called at the church when the services were half through, and accompanied Amy home. Shortly after their arrival at the house, Jim came in. He had spent the evening at Tarbell's saloon,

---

5 **lugubrious** - mournful, dismal, or gloomy, especially to an exaggerated degree

and was in a mellow mood. Hugh and Amy were discussing the new evangelist when he arrived.

"I can't help it, Amy," Hugh was saying. "I don't like the appearance of the man."

Jim took his seat at the piano and began to drum the keys absent-mindedly.

"Hugh," replied Amy, "I thought chemistry and pharmacy exact sciences, and that they taught one not to jump at conclusions."

"You forget, Amy, that I have studied medicine, also. One of its branches is physical diagnosis; and it teaches one to study the face—the mental and moral characteristics and there expressed— and to draw conclusions therefrom."

You may have a scientific and medical mind, but you have not a legal mind," returned Amy. "You would not make a good judge— you would condemn before trial."

"Great Sakes! What a learned discussion," broke in Jim, and resumed his drumming at the keys of the piano.

Without heeding the interruption Hugh said: "I have not condemned Rev. Merton Sawlus. I have said simply that he has not a good face and that I do not like him. It is a sort of mental and physical antagonism, perhaps. He may be a very good man."

"He is a very good *looking* man, at least," insisted Amy.

"Whew!" said Jim without turning around, "you would better look sharp, Connor. The Reverand seems to have made a wonderful impression on little sister, here. She is badly smitten."

Amy laughed lightly, but Hugh was gravely silent; noticing which the girl leaned toward him and whispered softly:

"Foolish boy! You are not jealous?"

"Say!" bawled Jim whirling about on the stool, "Don't you people know that it is ill-bred to whisper when company is present?"

"The company came unbidden," replied Amy testily. It was Jim's turn to laugh and he improved the opportunity.

"Why didn't *you* go to church tonight, Jim?" asked Hugh presently.

"I am out of practice—I am not working at it now," was the reply.

Amy started into reprove her brother but he held up his hand and said: "By jocks! I *was* at church, though. We had church at Tarbell's."

"Oh! Jim—" began his sister.

"It's a fact! That other evangelist—what's his name—dropped in and spent the evening with us. I mean the Reverend right bower, Wilmer Smartley he calls himself. He's a jolly dog, too. Much more companionable than Sawlus, I've no doubt: and just as good morally."

"You don't mean to say, Jim, that Rev. Merton Sawlus' traveling companion spent the evening at Tarbell's saloon?" asked Hugh in surprise.

"That's just what I do—and it's just what he did!"

Hugh looked at Amy and said: "What do you think of that?"

"I think that it's *true*," answered the girl earnestly, "for I never knew Jim to tell a lie—*in earnest*. But what if he did spend the evening there? That proves nothing against the evangelist. Jim spent the evening there, too; and he's my brother. That does not prove that I am in sympathy with the place and its wickedness. I have tried to keep Jim from frequenting such places: doubtless Mr. Sawlus has tried to do the same with his companion, Wilmer Smartley. I understand that he is a young man that the evangelist has hired to sail the boat—nothing more. *His* immorality proves nothing against Rev. Sawlus."

"That is true," admitted Hugh reluctantly, "but still I can but wonder that a minister would tolerate such a companion."

Then turning to Jim, he said: "Why will you persist in degrading yourself, worrying your father and hurting your sister—to say nothing of your friends—by frequenting that disreputable place and associating with your inferiors in every way? The habit is growing on you, Jim. Everybody realizes that but yourself. It will be your ruin, if you do not break off. You are half intoxicated tonight. You are gambling away your money and your morals at one and the same time. I say this as your friend—you know that I am your sincere friend—and you must not feel hard toward me."

"Hold on!" cried Jim, rising. His eyes were moist and his lips were trembling. "I can't stand that, Hugh. I hear it from Amy and father every day. I sometimes wish I were dead. I really do! I'm going to bed—good night."

He left the room, closing the door after him.

Hugh and Amy sat and stared after him, and then at each other. They had never seen him so visibly affected before.

Jim Stanwood and Hugh Connor were old-time college chums. Hugh had become acquainted with Amy through her brother bringing him to Dartmore to spend the college holidays. Hugh was Jim's senior by a year. After his graduation he had taken a course in pharmacy, and had come to Dartmore and started in the retail drug business. He was of a scientific bent of mind and his chosen profession suited him exactly. At the present time he was studying medicine, not with a view to practicing, but because he had a desire to know the science.

Hugh Connor was not the Apollo that his friend, Jim Stanwood, was. He was of medium height and rather slightly built. This was not a handsome face, but it shone with intelligence and innate nobility of character.

After Jim's abrupt departure, Hugh and Amy sat and talked over the matter. They came to the conclusion that there was still hope for Jim, if he could have congenial employment; and they resolved to make an earnest endeavor to influence his father in his favor.

Part III

The revival meetings held in the Methodist church at Dartmore, by Rev. Merton Sawlus, progressed favorably. The religious enthusiasm grew and spread until not only the village, but the surrounding country as well, was in a white heat of excitement. The old ferryman, Lish Finley, summed up the situation as follows:

"Ther's somethin' strange 'bout that preacher, sure's you're born. The first night I went to church, I'd made up my mind not to like 'im; but it didn't pan out that way. He jest seemed to git me into the boat with 'im, an' I let 'im row wherever he wanted to—an' was glad of it. He's captured the whole town—that's what he's done—an' people can't *help* but like 'im. At first that scallywag pardner o' his was a kin' o' drawback to 'im; but land sakes! he soon explained all that. Said he picked 'im up in the lumber regions, up north o' here, an' that he's much better *now* than he was *then*. Said he's goin' to stick to 'im, no matter what people says, an' try to make a man of 'im. Said he had a soul to save jest as much as anybody.

"Everybody goes to church right along, but them drinkin' and loafin' chaps down at Tarbell's. Even ol' John Sanders, the pettifogger[6], was down at the mourner's bench, 'tother night, prayin' an' shoutin' like a good feller. An' ther's Cap'n Stanwood—hadn't been inside of the church fer ten years. I guess—he's takin' a part, an' boardin' an' housin' the preacher, to boot. The comin' o' this Evangelist is the best thing that's happened to the communerty fer twenty years. W'y, we didn't *have* no church till he came, an' hadn't had fer a long time. Nearly all the ol' members was dead, an' no new ones comin' on—an' now look at it!

"Jim Stanwood an' Hugh Connor's about all the decent ones in the town that don't go to hear 'im preach. Jim don't go, because he'd rather drink an' gamble; an' Hugh don't go, because he's jealous o' the preacher. 'Fraid he'll git Amy Stanwood to lovin' 'im—least that's what everybody says."

The revival lasted several weeks. Summer as it was—the busiest time of all the year to the village inhabitants—the interest and attendance kept up to the last.

Rev. Sawlus reorganized the church, and the people engaged him for a year at a fair salary. When he first came to Dartmore he boarded at the village hotel, but his followers soon put a stop to that. They took him to their homes and treated him as a kingly guest—a sacred thing.

When Captain Stanwood was "converted" he took the preacher home with him to stay an indefinite length of time. He fitted up a private room for him, and gave him liberty to go and come, as he pleased.

Wilmer Smartley still boarded at the hotel. He and Jim Stanwood spent much of their time together, but Jim's seldom brought

---

6 **pettifogger** - an inferior legal practitioner, esp. one who deals with petty cases or employs dubious practices

him to the house. Rev. Sawlus and Jim treated each other with cool civility. They ate at the same table and exchange casual remarks; but that was all. At first Sawlus tried to win Jim's favor, but a few trials convinced him that it was of no use to make the attempt.

Amy and her father took him to task for his lack of cordiality and religious feeling. They accomplished nothing. His answer was: "Father, you and Amy go to church as often as you please. I have not the slightest objection. Mr. Sawlus is *your* guest, not *mine*. You believe in him, I do *not*; and I do not mean to act the hypocrite by pretending that I do. Of the two men, *I* prefer Smartley!"

The result was that Jim and the Captain were further and further estranged.

Hugh Connor still called upon the Stanwoods, but not so frequently as of yore[7]. Things were not to his liking. Amy frequently went out sailing with Rev. Sawlus. To this Hugh strongly objected. He spoke to the girl about the matter, and was snubbed for his pains. Then he appealed the case to her father.

"You and Amy must settle your own differences, Hugh; I do not care to interfere. Mr. Sawlus is a very nice man; and if you trust Amy, I cannot imagine why you should object to her going out sailing with him."

This was but poor comfort to Hugh, whose heart was afire with jealousy.

✳ ✳ ✳ ✳

Thus the summer passed and the autumn came. As the moral atmosphere of the village grew clearer, the foul blot in the shape of Tarbell's saloon became more apparent. Rev. Sawlus preached against it. He did not mince matters, but called things and people by their right names. He said: "Christian friends, this saloon must go. It is blighting your brightest and best. God *cannot* and *will not* bless you as long as it remains in your midst. I have nothing but love for Mr. Tarbell, but I will make everlasting war on his business. If I ruin it, so much the better for him and all concerned. He is a young man, and can do honest and honorable work at something else. And

---

7 **yore** - of long ago or former times

I say here, publicly and without fear of the consequences, this saloon shall go—peaceably, if possible; forcibly, if necessary!"

And the people said "amen" and "amen."

Along in September the villagers were startled by the report that the postoffice had been burglarized. The safe, an antiquated, rust-eaten one, had been blown open and several hundred dollars in money and stamps had been taken. There was no clue to the guilty parties. Rev. Sawlus used the unlawful occurrence as the subject of his discourse on the Sunday following, and the tide of public opinion was turned more strongly than ever against Tarbell's saloon and its habitués[8].

"Brethren," said the preacher, "my words are coming true. There is not a shadow of doubt that some of the frequenters of this den of iniquity committed the unlawful act. Young men who never work, who drink and gamble daily and nightly, wear good clothes and jewelry, must have money—some source of income. Some of them are becoming desperate and reckless—hence, this burglary. It is only the first of the many unlawful deeds that will occur if you do not root out this foul and evil resort."

Captain Stanwood took the opportunity to have an understanding with his son. He said to him: "Jim, you are bringing disgrace upon us all. I can no longer permit it. If you continue to spend your days in idleness and your nights in carousal, you must find another home—you cannot stay here."

"Do you suspect, father, that I had anything to do with this burglary?" asked Jim, his face white and twitching.

"Not in the least," was the reply, "but you *will* be suspected of such crimes if you associate with those who commit them."

"Then you think it was some of the village loafers—as you are pleased to call them—who committed the burglary."

"Of course I do."

"Well, I *don't!* I know better."

"What do you mean, Jim?" asked his father in great surprise.

"It is not worthwhile to tell you; you would hoot at my statement. But I know that it was not one of my village companions."

---

8 **habitués** - one who habitually frequents a place

With that Jim turned and walked away. He had not said that he *would* or would not do better.

The same day Rev. Sawlus met Wilmer Smartley and accosted him thus: "if you expect to be my friend and companion longer you must do differently. I can tolerate your immorality no longer. Break off from your bad habits and evil associates or I shall publicly denounce you. You are bringing me into disrepute. I have tried hard to make a man of you, but it seems that I have failed utterly."

Several of the church members heard this and reported it to the community at large, much to Mr. Sawlus' credit.

But Jim Stanwood and Wilmer Smartley made no change in their habits. They were inseparable companions. Jim's association with Smartley had done the former no good. He was fast going from bad to worse.

One Sunday morning in November the town was thrown into a fever of excitement by the finding of the dead body of a man in the river near the Stanwood building. The body was discovered by some persons who were crossing the river on their way to church. It lay in a few feet of water, near the shore, and showed no marks of violence. The dead man proved to be a young stock dealer who had spent Saturday evening at Tarbell's, gambling and drinking. Was it murder, suicide or accident? No one could say.

A coroner's inquest was held, but little light was thrown on the black affair. Witnesses testified that the unfortunate man had been at Tarbell's until a late hour, and that he had left by himself, saying that he was going to the hotel to spend the night. He had lost a large sum of money gambling, but still had a roll of bills when he left the saloon. Only a small amount of silver change was found on his person. Nothing more definite than this could be learned. Many believed that the man had been murdered; others held that it was suicide or accident.

The storm of public indignation, that had been gathering for so many months, broke at last, and it swept Tarbell's place out of existence. Tarbell left for parts unknown, to escape the righteous wrath of the citizens. Wilmer Smartley likewise disappeared.

Rev. Sawlus preached a Thanksgiving sermon in which he thanked God that the death of the young stockman had not been in vain.

Jim Stanwood seemed to have learned the lesson; at least he began to do better. He worked steadily in the store and office and spent his nights at home.

So the months rolled by. The midwinter holidays came and went, and the little village of Dartmore remained peaceful and prosperous.

Part IV

Amy was in an ecstasy of delight over Jim's reformation, but her father did not appear greatly elated. "He has disappointed me so often and so much, Amy that I have lost all confidence in him," said Captain Stanwood.

"You should not speak so, father; I am sure Jim means to be a better man," was Amy's reply. But her father only shook his head sadly and said: "we shall see."

Hugh almost ceased to call upon Amy, and their engagement was postponed indefinitely. She would brook no interference with what she considered her rights, and would hear no word against the character of Rev. Sawlus. Hugh told her that he did not believe the man to be what he represented himself, and that she ought not to make an intimate of him. He said in conclusion: "I do not care to call here or consider our engagement further so long as this man Sawlus is in the house. If you prefer him to me, well and good. Both you and your father appeared to be infatuated with him."

Amy's reply was characteristic of herself. "You speak 'as one having authority,'" she said tauntingly. "However, you may come to see us or not, as you like. It makes little difference to me."

And thus they parted; but Hugh did not sleep that night, and Amy's pillow was wet with tears.

March came and Rev. Sawlus was still at Captain Stanwood's. One day in the early part of the month some oil prospectors called upon the Captain and negotiated for the purchase of one of his farms, and two days later they consummated the deal and paid him the first payment—five thousand dollars in cash. He locked the money in a safe, intending to send it to the bank in the city as soon as possible.

Rev. Sawlus and Jim were in the office when the money was received, and the former said: "It is just as well that no one knows of this but us. There might be another burglary." and he looked square-ly at Jim.

This was early in the morning. When Jim went to the village postoffice, for the mail, at nine o'clock, he was surprised and dis-pleased to see Wilmer Smartley standing on the hotel steps.

"Hullo! Jim," called that worthy, "I'm back again. I'm here with these oilmen. How's my dearly beloved friend, Sawlus? Say! Come up to the hotel tonight, I've got something good to show you."

He winked in a mysterious manner as he said this. Jim knew what he meant, and resolved in his heart of hearts that he would not be there.

But when evening came he sauntered up that way. The old ap-petite was upon him again, and by half past eight o'clock he was in an advanced stage of intoxication. He resolved to go home; so he arose and staggered down the street and into his father's office where the latter was at work.

Jim had returned with the intention of cautioning his father about the money in the safe. Captain Stanwood seen his condition cried out: "Leave the office—go to bed. In the morning, pack your clothes and quit my house forever. I have borne this too long, al-ready. You are no son of mine."

A furious quarrel ensued; and Jim Stanwood left his father's presence, his brain on fire and his feet like lead. He tottered up the stairs and into his room then he threw himself upon the bed with his clothes on and in a few minutes he was in a drunken stupor.

The next morning at six o'clock the clerk who opened the store found Captain Stanwood dead in his office—stabbed through the heart!

The young man gave the alarm and the crowd quickly gathered. The coroner was notified, and came and took charge of the body. Jim was found asleep in his room, his face and hands smeared with blood. In the outside pocket of his sack coat, which he had not re-moved, was found a long bladed knife encrusted with dried blood.

He was arrested and placed in confinement, pending the coroner's investigation.

Hugh Connor was among the first on the scene and bent his energies toward soothing Amy, who is almost wild with grief and fear. He gave her a nervine[9] and sat by her side, holding her hand until she dropped asleep. Then he joined Dr. Barnes and the coroner in their examination of the body.

Jim Stanwood was confined in the village bastile, a diminutive and uncomfortable little structure on a back street. Here Hugh visited him in the afternoon and had a long talk with him. Jim was completely prostrated, and at first had but little to say, except to deny that he committed the awful deed.

"I am in a bad box, Hugh—I know that," he said despondently. "I can explain nothing—I recollect nothing. I have been a fool— a dissipated, ungrateful wretch, and I shall stretch hemp[10] for it probably. But you know as well as I do that I never murdered my father—never!"

After a time he became more composed and answered the question that Hugh put to him, in a straightforward way. Hugh left him, promising to do all he could to clear him of the terrible charge that hung over him.

The inquest was set for ten o'clock the next day. A jury was empanneled and witnesses were summoned.

At the appointed time the coroner's investigation began. The clerk who opened the store in the morning was the first witness examined. He testified that he opened the store at six o'clock; that he found Captain Stanwood dead in the office, lying on his back in a pool of blood; that the safe door stood wide open, and that it had been rifled of its contents; and that a part of the contents of the safe, consisting of books and papers, was scattered about the floor of the office.

Several witnesses were then called who testified that they saw Jim Stanwood, at half past eight o'clock of the night on which his father was killed, and that he was intoxicated.

____

9 **nervine** – a medicine acting on or relieving disorders of the nerves; soothing the nerves

10 **stretch hemp** – hanged from the neck by a rope

Wilmer Smartley was wanted, but could not be found. He had again disappeared; and it is well to say here that he was not seen nor heard of afterward.

Then Rev. Sawlus was placed on the stand. His testimony was as follows: "I was in my room in the Stanwood building, at nine o'clock last Wednesday night—the night on which Captain Stanwood was killed—and heard James Stanwood entered his father's office. Both stair doors were open and I could hear their conversation distinctly. The father and son quarreled, and I heard sounds of a scuffle—then all was silent. Shortly afterward James Stanwood staggered up the stairs and went to his room. I heard him open and close the door. I did not go down to the office because I did not wish to interfere in a family affair. Captain Stanwood did not come up the stairs—I am positive of that, because I lay awake all the fore part of the night."

Amy Stanwood's testimony—given with sobs and tears—corroborated that of Rev. Sawlus, except that she heard no sounds of a scuffle in the office, and she thought she heard her father ascended the stairs about ten o'clock and go to his sleeping room. She went to sleep then and heard nothing more.

Dr. Barnes and Hugh Connor testified that the wound in Captain Stanwood's chest was made by a knife, and that the wound penetrated the heart. Several witnesses saw blood on the hands and face of the son, and saw the bloody knife taken from his pocket.

The case was ready to go to the jury, when Hugh Connor created somewhat of the sensation by asking if he would be permitted to point out some facts in the case, that had not been called out when he was on the stand.

The coroner granted permission and he began: "I am aware of the fact that this is but a court of inquiry to determine the cause of Captain Charles Stanwood's death, and incidentally—if a murder has been done—to point to the guilty party or parties. At the same time, the testimony here given is pointed in but one direction—toward Jim Stanwood as the murderer of his father."

The people in the room stared stupidly at the speaker, and amid breathless silence he went on: "the case is not so simple as it appears at first glance. The weight of testimony indicates that a murder was committed not later than nine o'clock on last Wednesday night; but I stand ready to prove that it was not done earlier than eleven o'clock the same night, and probably later! *Rigor mortis*, or the stiffness of death, begins in five to seven hours after death. Dr. Barnes will bear me out in this statement. Captain Stanwood and his son had their quarrel at nine o'clock in the evening, and the body was not discovered until six o'clock the following morning; and yet when found *rigor mortis* had not begun—and the body was still warm! This is discrepancy number one.

"Amy Stanwood has testified that she thinks she heard her father come up the stairs at ten o'clock that night; and Rev. Sawlus is positive that the Captain never left his office. If Captain Stanwood was stabbed at nine o'clock, and never left his office after that hour, how are we to account for the fact that his shoes, coat and hat were found in his bedroom the next morning? This is discrepancy number two.

"Again, what has become of the money stolen from the safe? If Jim Stanwood was too drunk to wash his bloody hands and face and conceal the bloody knife, why was not the money found on his person? How could he conceal it? This is discrepancy number three.

"Further, the wound in the murdered man's breast—"

Here the coroner interrupted Hugh and apprised him of the fact that it had not been decided, as yet, that a murder had been committed; and also that he was not pleading a case, but simply giving testimony.

Scarcely heeding the interruption, Hugh proceeded, his nostrils dilated and his eyes shining. "As I was saying, the wound in the dead man's breast is a penetrating one, and an inch in length. It was made by a double edged knife—Dr. Barnes knows this to be true. The knife found in Jim Stanwood's procession has a blade but *one third* inch in width, and it has but *one* cutting-edge! This is discrepancy number four."

A murmur ran around the room as Hugh Connor said this, and he heard the whisper, "He's trying to prove Jim Stanwood ain't guilty."

"No," resumed Hugh, "I am not trying to do that. Jim Stanwood is not on trial. But I *am* trying to point to the guilty party. The main discrepancy is that the blood on Jim's hand and face was *smeared* on after it had partially *coagulated*! There was not a *drop* or *splotch* of blood about his person anywhere, as there would have been had the blood spurted on him from the wound in his father's chest. The blood found on his hands, face and knife was placed there by the guilty person, while Jim lay in a drunken sleep. I stand ready to prove this, also. The whole thing is a cleverly concocted plan to shield the guilty and condemn the innocent. The instrument with which Captain Stanwood was murdered—for murdered he was— has been found, and it bears the name of the murder, etched on the blade with acid!"

At this point Hugh Connor displayed to the gaze of the astounded people an ivory-handled dirk[11] with a few bloodstains about the base of the blade. He resumed: "These stains are human blood. I have examined them under a microscope—and I know. The owner of this dirk is in this room—"

Here Rev. Sawlus arose to his feet and started toward the door, his face as pale as ashes.

"Stop that man!" cried Hugh. "This dirk bears his name; and I found it in his trunk, where I also found the missing money from the safe."

An indescribable uproar followed this bold assertment[12] of Hugh Connor's. The constable and several others ran forward to intercept Sawlus. They surrounded him and attempted to lay hands on him, but he fought like a tiger at bay. A number of his friends rushed to his rescue, and a free-for-all fight was precipitated. It was only after several men had been more or less injured that he was finally secured. The officer and his aides bore the desperate man to the lockup. All the way there he struggled and cursed like a maniac; but once inside the walls of the prison, he broke down and confessed all.

* * * *

According to his own statement, was an educated adventurer of a half dozen different aliases, who had resorted to this sort

---

11 **dirk** - a Scottish word for a short dagger; a cut-down sword blade mounted on a dagger hilt, rather than a knife blade
12 **assertment** – act of making an assertion or bold demand

of evangelistic work for several years. Wilmer Smartley was a tool of inferior caliber, whom he had picked up a short time before he came to Dartmore. Sawlus said, "I planned the postoffice robbery, and in connection with Smartley executed it. Smartley robbed the drunken stock dealer, but his death was an accident. He stumbled into the river and was drowned. I robbed and murdered Captain Stanwood. I went down into his office at three o'clock on Thursday morning, intending to rob the safe. I knew that the Captain was in his sleeping room at the time, and I supposed that he was asleep. But he was awake and followed me. He caught me in the act and I was compelled to kill him. I had learned the combination of the safe and had no trouble in opening it. No one knew I possessed this knowledge, and I was certain that the rivalry would be attributed to Jim Stanwood—even by his father. The death of Captain Stanwood complicated matters, but I did my best to lay both the robbery and murder at Jim Stanwood's door. I would have succeeded, too, had it not been for that lynx-eyed Hugh Connor. It was I who smeared Jim's face, hands and knife with his father's blood, as he lay in a drunken stupor. He slept very soundly. I think Smartley must've drugged him with the intention of robbing him at the hotel. At any rate his deep sleep served my purpose.

"After the murder I washed my hands and knife in my room, and threw the bloody water out the window. I concealed the knife, money and two bloody handkerchiefs in my trunk, intending to hide them elsewhere as soon as possible. But Hugh Connor—who always suspected and hated me—was too clever for me. After I left the house this morning he broke open my trunk and found the things. I would be perfectly willing to die, if I could kill him first!"

Jim Stanwood was of course set at liberty. Merton Sawlus was taken to the county jail on the following day, but he never came to trial. In some manner he procured a quantity of morphine, and one morning was found dead in his cell. Notwithstanding his confession and the many proofs of his guilt, there are many people in Dartmore who believe to this day that he was an innocent man. Such was the magnetic influence he had over them.

Jim Stanwood reformed, and this time his reformation was full and complete. He, like Hugh, had suspected Sawlus and Smartley from the first, but having no proofs he dared say nothing.

Hugh and Amy were married, and in company with Jim went to live in the city.

Ten years have passed, but the inhabitants of Dartmore, as they sit around their blazing hearths on long winter evenings, still talk of the coming of Sawlus.

Mamie's Prisoner

"There—there! Willie, dear—don't cry. Sister will tie it up for you; yes, she will."

And Mamie deftly tore a slip of muslin from an old pillow case, as she attempted to comfort and soothe her little brother.

"But it hurts so," sobbed Willie, covering his face with his chubby hands, "and I's 'fraid of the bleed."

Mamie smiled as she said: "Oh! the 'bleed' won't hurt Willie. Let sister wrap it up for you; that's a good boy."

Mamie gently washed the blood from the ugly gash in the sun-burned little foot, as Willie jerked and shook the injured member and uttered an occasional "ouch." Then she neatly bandaged the wound with a strip of muslin, and procuring a needle and thread stitched it in such a manner that it would not work loose.

After the blood was washed away and the bloody water disposed of, Willie regained courage enough to remove his hands from his eyes, and watch the further proceedings with the show of interest.

"Now it feels better, doesn't it?" inquired Mamie, returning the mutilated pillow case to its place in the kitchen ragbag.

"Yes," answered the brother dubiously, "but it still smarts and aches and pains and hurts some."

Mamie laughed outright. "Why, Willie," she said, "I'm afraid I'm not much of a doctor, if it still feels so badly—but how did you hurt it, pet?"

"I stepped on a broke bottle out by the smokehouse, and it just run 'way in!"

And Willie's voice trembled and he threatened to break down and cry again.

"Well—well, let's not talk about it," said the sister soothingly. "Come, I'll carry you up to the cool upstairs hall and rock you to sleep. Father and mother will be here after awhile."

"When?"

"Oh, pretty soon, I think."

"I want them now," insisted Willie, pettishly.

"There'll surely be here soon, dear," Mamie answered as she carried the sturdy little form up the broad stairway. Reaching the upper hall, she dropped into a low rocker with her burden, and in a birdlike voice began to try to sing him to sleep.

Mamie Robinson was 12 years old, and Willie was 5; and they lived on a big farm in southeastern Ohio. Mr. and Mrs. Robinson had gone to the village, about six miles away, and the little folks had been left to "keep house" in their parents' absence. There were no neighbors within a mile of the farmhouse, but the father and mother did not fear to leave the children alone for a few hours; because Mamie was a trustworthy little woman, and would let no harm befall Willie or herself. At least that was the way the parents' reasoned about the matter.

The latter had left home just after dinner, intending to return before supper time; but now it was almost sundown and they had not come back. They had been unduly delayed for the reason that the lawyer, whom they had gone to see, was absent from home and they had to wait for his return.

Mr. and Mrs. Robinson were in sore trouble. When they had bought the farm on which they lived, they had placed a mortgage upon it; and ever since had toiled and saved in a vain endeavor to pay it off. They could have succeeded in doing so, perhaps, had it not been for the fact that times were so hard, and the prices of farm products were so low. They still owed $500 of the original mortgage, and the man who held it threatened to foreclose it—as the year's interest was overdue and unpaid. It was to try to make some satisfactory arrangement in regard to the perplexing matter that they had gone to town.

Mamie rocked and sang to Willie, but he did not go to sleep. He fretted and tossed about in her tired little arms, and peevishly called for his mother. The sun sank from sight in the shadows of evening were gathering—but still the father and mother did not come. Mamie was not worried, but Willie was. Presently he said:

"I'm hungry—I want my supper, Mamie."

"All right," Mamie answered cheerily, "you lie here on the bed, and I'll run down to the kitchen and get you a piece of bread and butter. Shall I bring you a glass of milk from the cellar, too?"

"Yes, and be quick, Mamie. I'm 'most starved."

Mamie laid him upon the bed and descended the stairs upon her errand. When she returned Willie had concluded that he wanted a boiled egg in addition to the bread and butter, and milk.

"There are no eggs in the house, Willie," said his sister. "Father and mother took them all to market."

"I want one," Willie insisted.

He was monarch of all he surveyed—a little despot whose slightest wish must be granted, whose most unreasonable command must be obeyed. For was he not her baby brother?

"Shall I go to the barn and hunt you one? I shall be gone but a minute. I can boil it on the gasoline stove for you."

"Yes," Willie replied, "but put me in the chair by the window, so I can watch you. I'm 'fraid alone."

Mamie did as he requested, and nimbly tripping down the stairs, was soon out of the house and on her way to the barn. The barn was on the opposite side of the highway from the house, and about 100 yards from it. Willie, sitting at the front bedroom window, could see his sister as she ran at full speed in the gathering dusk, toward the great red building. When she was within a few feet of the barn door, he screamed to her, saying:

"Oh! hurry, Mamie—hurry; I'm 'fraid here all alone."

"Be still, Willie," she called to him. "Nothing will happen to you. I'll be back in a minute. Just lock the doors and stay upstairs till father and mother come. Yes, Willie, I'm coming." This latter sentence in reply to her brother's querulous[1] calling.

She bounded in at the front door, closing and locking it behind her; then she passed through the lower hall to the kitchen, and closed and fastened the outside doors there. Hastening upstairs she said:

---

1 **querulous** - expressing a complaint or grievance; grumbling

"Willie, you will have to do without your egg. Sister cannot cook any for you now."

"Why?" asked Willie, beginning to sniffle.

"Never mind why, pet; you eat your bread and butter and drink your milk, and then if you want the egg I will try to get it for you. Be a good boy now, and don't tease sister."

For a wonder Willie was reasonable and consented to do as she wished. When he had finished the food that she had brought him he confessed that he had had enough and did not want the egg.

"Let me rock you to sleep, now," urged Mamie.

"Light a lamp," whined Willie, "you know I'm 'fraid of the dark."

"There is no lamp up here, and you don't want sister to leave you alone to get one, do you?"

"Take me with you."

"Oh! Willie, I can't carry you and the lamp both; and you cannot walk, you know."

"Let me hide my face on your shoulder, then, Mamie, so I won't see the dark," he pleaded.

She cuddled him in her arms and rocked him to sleep; then she placed him upon the bed, and sitting down beside him she held her breath and listened—and shivered and quaked at every sound. How she longed for father and mother to come! Had anything dreadful befallen them? What if they should not come till morning! She nearly fainted at the bare thought, but bit her white lips and said not a word. She must not wake Willie!

After a time—it seemed like hours to her, but it was only minutes—she heard a step on the front portico. Then someone tried the door. It was the tramp—she was sure of that. He went around to the kitchen and presently she heard him banging and rattling at those doors. Then all was silence for quite a while; and she was beginning to breathe easier and congratulate herself that her enemy was gone, when she heard him raising a kitchen window. She almost screamed aloud in her terror, when she heard him leaping upon the kitchen floor, and mutter angrily to himself:

"Ah! the little jade thought she had me locked out—she did. Sly little girl, eh? Never let on dat she saw me, but jest scampered into de house an' locked de doors. But I know a trick 'r two—I does. Well, I should smile!"

She did not dare to move for fear the tramp would hear her and immediately come up stairs. How she regretted that she had not thought to close the bedroom door! She heard the man moving about downstairs. Presently he said:

"Well, I'll jest see w'at dere is in de cellar dat's good to eat, an' den I'll 'ave a squint fer de ol' gent's stockin' leg o' money. Wonder w'at's become o' dem kids? Upstairs under de bed I 'spect." And he chuckled audibly to himself.

Mamie heard him strike a match and light a lamp that was standing on the kitchen mantel; then the cellar door creaked on its rusty hinges, and the frightened child heard the man clomping down the cellar stairs. What prompted her to do it she never knew; but she leapt to her feet, and noiselessly tiptoeing down to the kitchen, she slammed the cellar door shut and shot the bolt into its socket. Then she fairly flew to her former place of safety upstairs, locking the bedroom door behind her.

Scarcely had she reached the room and dropped panting into a chair, when the tramp was hammering and thundering at the cellar door. He knew that the quick-witted girl had caught him like a rat in a trap, and he was furiously angry. He swore and shouted in his impotent rage:

"Come here an' open dis door, you tricky minx. Do ye hear? If ye don't do it, I'll burn de house down—See!"

"I don't believe he'll burn the house down," reasoned Mamie, "for that would burn him up, too."

Presently the tramp descended the cellar stairs again, and attempted to wrench loose the window gratings; but they were too solidly set in the stone wall, and he was forced to give it up. Then all was silent as the grave in the big house. Mamie was more frightened than ever. What would the tramp be doing? Would her father and mother never come?

After what seemed an age to the trembling little creature, the sound of rumbling wheels was borne to her ears, and she recognized her parents' voices as they drove quickly up to the front gate. Mamie threw up the window and called:

"Hurry—hurry, father and mother, I've got a tramp locked up in the cellar!" Then she sank down in a heap on the floor.

Willie awoke and began to cry; her parents came rushing into the house, and for a little while everything was hurry and confusion. Mamie nestled in her father's strong arms and told him all that occurred in his absence. When she had recovered from her fright and had regained her composure, Mr. Robinson went into the backyard and lustily rang the big dinner bell that hung on a tall post near the cistern. The neighbors, thinking it meant fire, quickly gathered in; and Mr. Robinson and several of them took a lantern, a rope and some clubs, and descended to the cellar. They found the tramp crouching behind a vinegar barrel in one corner of the room; and although he acted ugly and showed resistance, they securely tied his arms and legs and locked him up in the corncrib. In the morning they took him to the village and lodged him in the jail.

When the man was safely behind the bars, the sheriff remarked to Mamie's father:

"That fellow is Spotty Ben, the burglar, and there is a reward of $500 offered for his capture. Your little daughter is entitled to it."

When Mamie heard that the reward was hers, she fondly kissed her father and said:

"Oh! Father, I will give it all to you to pay off the mortgage."

"I would rather have lost the farm, Mamie dear," her father replied, "then to have had my little girl so badly scared; and I will never leave you alone in that way again—never!"

The Blackmer Affair

Chapter I

To begin in the good, old, orthodox way—that has been sanctioned and adopted by many a worthy scribe long since gathered to his fathers—it was the tenth day of January, eighteen hundred and ninety-two. The hour hand on the illuminated dial of the courthouse clock in Grangerville pointed to eight, while the attenuated[1] minutes hand, having outstripped its lifelong rival in the day's weary race, rested momentarily at twelve, as the bell in the steeple clanged one, two, three—eight sonorous strokes. It was eight o'clock in the evening, then, and the night was bleak, black and bitter.

Most of the stores and shops in the town were closed for the night, and the streets were deserted—save for unfortunate, belated pedestrians here and there, whose outer garments flapped and fluttered in the icy wind, as they hurriedly wended their way homeward. The earth was hard frozen and covered with several inches of snow. The wind blew a gale from the north, bearing a dense shower of frozen snow pellets that threw themselves impetuously against the frosted window panes, and knocked and hammered at the closed doors for admittance.

The town was enveloped in darkness except where an electric arc-lamp[2] swung and danced to the rhythm of the wind, and leered and peered from the faint and diminutive circle of light that it shed around, into the flickering black shadows beyond.

Out near the edge of town stood the magnificent mansion of Matthew Blackmer, retired capitalist and millionaire. It occupied a slight elevation and was surrounded by beautiful and extensive grounds, containing gravel walks, fountains, statuary, and groves of stately trees. But on this stormy midwinter night the grounds were

---

1 **attenuated** - reduced value of

2 **arc light** - a lamp that produces light when electric current flows across the gap between two electrodes

barren and uninviting; in marked contrast to the interior of the mansion, as indicated by the warm and beckoning light that streamed from its windows.

The house was a commodious[3] building of gray sandstone, with numerous towers, wings and gables. It was richly and artistically finished and furnished throughout, and its appearance outside and inside spoke of taste and refinement on the part of its possessor.

On the ground floor on the eastern wing of the house was the owner's private office and library, a large, well lighted room of cheerful aspect. A limited number of bookcases filled with valuable and rare books surrounded the room, and choice paintings and etchings adorned the walls here and there. The floor was of hardwood, waxed and polished, with rich and costly rugs scattered about it. There were office desks with all the modern conveniences and accessories, and antique carved tables. Exotic plants budded and blossomed in the deep windows, and an office safe occupied a recess in the inner wall. In other words, the room harmonized perfectly with the character and tastes of Matthew Blackmer.

On this cold January night he sat in his favorite chair, reading the evening paper and apparently chewing the cud of worldly plenty, contentment and happiness. He was a fine looking man, tall, portly, with smoothshaven, rubicund[4] face, and close-cropped iron-gray hair. His age was fifty-nine years—but he did not appear so old.

At a desk opposite sat his private secretary, a lean, sallow young man who answered to the name of Anthony Peck, assiduously opening and answering letters that had accumulated. He had been absent a few days, visiting a brother who was sick, and this accounted for his working so late. He paused occasionally in his writing to ask a question that Mr. Blackmer answered without looking up. Then nothing was heard but the subdued rustling of the elder gentleman's newspaper, and the exultant voice of the blast outside as it capered about the gables, and curvetted[5] over the treetops till they shook their lean limbs at the frowning heavens, and creaked and groaned

---

3　**commodious** - spacious; roomy
4　**rubicund** - inclined to a healthy rosiness
5　**curvetted** - pranced or frisked about

and complained in a patient, long-suffering manner.

"Midas Outdone" would be an appropriate title for the story of Matthew Blackmer's life. Truly everything he touched turned into gold, and yet he was not a king nor the son of the king. Born of a dissipated father and ignorant mother, cradled in dirt and squalor and reared in want and poverty, he crept onward inch by inch, year after year, overcoming all difficulties and gaining courage and strength by the effort. No man could have had a lowlier origin—and yet he gained the summit of worldly success financially.

As a boy he worked for farmers adjacent to the village in which he lived; as a young man he taught the village school. At the age of thirty years he was a merchant in the town of Grangerville. He grew as the village grew—in fact, he outstripped it. At forty five he was merchant, banker, real estate dealer, manufacturer and capitalist in one; and at fifty five, retired capitalist and millionaire. Midas outdone! Aladdin and his lamp forever distanced!

At the age of twenty seven, he married a loving, lovable and intelligent woman who bore him one child, a son Robert. She died when the child was five years old, and the care and education of the sturdy youngster devolved upon the father. Matthew Blackmer lavished upon this son not only the love that was due him, but the love that he had borne his mother, as well. The son returned his father's affection and they were close companions indeed. Apparently the world held for each little else but the other.

Robert Blackmer grew to young manhood and went off to college. After graduation he took active charge of his father's diverse interests, and the two resumed their old companionable life. They were very happy—this father and son—in each other's love and society, till the serpent entered their homely Eden. And a most beautiful baby-faced, blue-eyed, golden-haired bit of femininity this serpent was, too!

She presented herself and credentials at Blackmer & Son's down-town office, with a persuasive manner and winning ways that quite captivated the benevolent Matthew's heart; and he engaged her as amanuensis[6] at once.

---

6 **amanuensis** - one employed to write from dictation or to copy manuscript

Lucretia Chadwick proved to be a treasure. She was capable, refined and agreeable, and made herself almost necessary to the business of the firm, in a few months.

The young woman was happy and contented in her new place, until she suddenly discovered one day that she was desperately in love with Bob Blackmer. Then she employed all her feminine arts and wiles to kindle an answering flame in Bob's manly bosom, but in vain. She was young—but twenty seven, younger than he by three years—beautiful and accomplished, but the invulnerable Apollo was blind to her manifold charms. To tell the truth, Bob seem blind to the whole female sex.

Piqued at his want of appreciation at last, Lucretia determined to turn her guns upon the senior member of the firm. This she did so effectively—discharging broadside after broadside of loving smiles and winsome graces at the citadel of his heart—that he hauled down his flag of widower-hood independence, and ignominiously capitulated. He made a proposal of unconditional surrender on his own part, which she promptly accepted—and they were married.

Shortly after this, trouble began for all of them. Lucretia had gained a victory—but such a victory! She was not at all satisfied. It was Bob she loved; it was Bob she wanted. She still tried in every way to win little flattering attentions from him. Matthew Blackmer noticed this and became insanely jealous.

Lucretia was installed as mistress of the great house, and Bob still retained the suite of rooms there. But his father's jealousy became so pronounced that the son concluded to take up his abode at a hotel. This he did for a number of months, but Lucretia succeeded in convincing her husband that her liking for his son was but a sisterly affection and solicitude—motherly, if he preferred—so the old gentleman prevailed upon him to return to the parental roof.

After this things went along in their accustomed groove, and smoothly enough. If the elder Blackmer felt any pangs from the gnawing of the green-eyed monster he concealed it well. Bob was kind and attentive to Lucretia, playfully called her "Little Mother," and evidently enjoyed her company—but that was as far is he ever went. One day in a fit of sheer desperation she said: "Oh! Bob, if you would love me only a little—just a very little!" Tears were in her blue, baby-like eyes as she clasped her hands convulsively and looked at him desperately, longingly hopelessly.

He gazed down upon her from his towering height of six feet two—did this big, handsome Bob Blackmer—and said some solemnly, almost sternly: "Lucretia, I respect you—I like you. But the love that you desire can never be. You forget that you are my father's wife!" And he turned and left her standing like one in a trance.

She apparently gave up the quest, but the pent-up fires in her bosom were only smothered, not quenched, and they were ready to burst forth, a devastating conflagration[7], at any moment.

Mr. Blackmer seemed assured of her fidelity, Bob was polite and friendly—and again things went on in the old way.

Such was the state of affairs in the Blackmer household on that stormy January night that introduces our story.

* * * *

Matthew Blackmer finished his paper and lay back in his chair for a nap. Anthony Peck arose from his seat, placed the books in the safe and closed it, rearrange the papers on his desk and prepared to leave. He passed into the hall, donned his hat and overcoat, muffled his slender neck in a large, woolen scarf, and returning to the room, walked up to Mr. Blackmer and said: "I am going now—good night."

"Eh? Oh! well, good night," returned the latter, suddenly waking and rubbing his eyes. "You'll have a disagreeable tramp. But you're young—you'll not mind it." And he settled back for another nap.

Peck left the house and hurried toward the street. "Oh! I'll not mind," he muttered to himself, "of course not. Nothing hurts me. Not even that *you* have everything and *I* have nothing. Not even that *you* are rolling in wealth and I am ground down by poverty. No! not even that you have the woman that I would give my immortal soul to call mine—all mine. Oh, no! Nothing hurts *me*."

---

7 **conflagration** - a large destructive fire

Stopping in his walk, he turned and shook his clenched fist at the library window and hissed: "I hate you, Matthew Blackmer, although you have been kind to me. I hate you for your success, for the fact that I must subsist on your patronage; and above all, I hate you because your money bought the woman I loved before you ever saw her."

Then he passed between the tall gate post and disappeared down the black street.

Mr. Blackmer was just falling into a sound slumber when he heard the sound of tramping feet and merry voices in the hall. The library door flew open and two young men entered like a gale bringing the breath of the storm with them. They were Bob Blackmer and Dr. Will Kenshaw.

"Hullo! Uncle," cried the latter cheerily, "don't you want to take a sleigh ride this pleasant evening? I took pity on Bob and brought him up in my sleigh. I ought to have left him walk though—by Jove! The idea of a sane man being downtown on such a night without a conveyance[8]! Of course they'll tell you that I had a night call out in this direction. But don't you believe a word of it. I did it out of pure kindness of heart. Say! Uncle, you're looking first rate. I don't believe I can charge you for this visit. You'll live to be a hundred, I verily believe. Bob and I met that hatchet-faced Peck down in the yard—he'll die of consumption inside of a year. And there he stood in the cold, apostrophizing[9] the storm and gesticulating at the heavens like a third-rate actor. He didn't even see us—and we almost rubbed against him."

Mr. Blackmer smiled blandly and said: "Sit down, boys, sit down. How you do rattle on, Will! Are you getting some practice?"

"Why, uncle, I'm working like a beaver. My slate's full of calls, my pockets full of money and my heart's full of happiness—"

"And your head's full of nonsense," interrupted his uncle.

Dr. Kenshaw laughed good naturedly, and continued: "Oh! I made no mistake in coming here. I've been located but six months and my practice will pay my cigar bill already. It's a fact—just think of it!"

---

8 **conveyance** - a means of transportation; a vehicle

9 **apostrophize** – an exclamatory passage in a speech or poem addressed to a person (typically one who is dead or absent)

The elder man looked at the younger one admiringly and lovingly. Dr. Will Kenshaw was Matthew Blackmer's only nephew—the only son of and only sister—and the kind-hearted old man loved him dearly. The harum-scarum[10] boy had been left an orphan at an early age, and his uncle had educated him and looked after his welfare. And be it said to Will Kenshaw's credit, he returned his uncle's disinterested affection in ten fold measure.

The three men chatted pleasantly for some little time, and then Dr. Kenshaw looked at his watch, with a professional squint, and remarked: "It's nine o'clock—I must be off. Good night, uncle."

Bob went with him to the door. "It's a wild night," he shivered as Will was pulling on his gloves. "I'd hate to be a poor devil of a doctor on such a night as this."

"Thank you for your sympathetic complement, I'm sure," said Will smiling, and springing lightly down the steps he made his way toward the street.

Bob ran up the broad stairway to his rooms. Left to himself, Mr. Blackmer sat and dozed as old people are wont to do, his rosy face wreathed in smiles.

Chapter II

The morning of the eleventh of January dawned bright, still and cold. The wind had fallen in the night—and the mercury had fallen with it. The fierce storm had passed and the sky was clear; but snow was everywhere. It cumbered[11] the window ledges and obstructed the doorways, held possession of the streets and blockaded the country highways.

The great trees in the Blackmer grounds that had moaned and groaned through the livelong night, stood stiff and mute in their glistening coats of mail, as if attempting by this assumption of dignity to prove that they had not given way to their feelings of distress. As far as the eye could see—as far as the imagination could reach, almost—it was one dreary expanse of snow—snow. The dead and

10 **harum-scarum** - lacking a sense of responsibility; reckless
11 **cumbered** - obstructed

frozen earth was shrouded for burial—and the night wind had sung a requiem and passed on. And in the Blackmer library lay that other dead thing—left in the track of the midnight storm!

Bob Blackmer awoke at six o'clock on that frigid morning and looked out on the sheeted world. Across the street from his window a milkman muffled to the eyes was thundering at the kitchen door. Bob could just see him through a clear space in the frosted pain. He—Bob—lay there in his cozy quarters and imagined in a dreamy sort of way that the clear spot was an irregular air hole. A Sabbath like stillness rested upon the town and the milkman's ringing blows could be heard with startling distinctness. Bob looked at his watch that lay near him on a stand, and turned over for his matutinal[12] "beauty sleep," grumbling sleepily: "The trolley cars'll not be running before noon. I'll have John drive me down. Bah! This beastly cold weather. I'll not get up till late; there's—plenty—of—ti-m-e."

He had again entered the portal of the mystical castle of dreams, when a sound roused him so suddenly that he sat bolt upright in bed before he was fully awake. It was a woman's scream, but cut the crisp air like a knife and made his alarmed nerves tingle to the ends of his fingers. What could it mean—who could it be? He sprang out of bed and began to dress. Hurriedly, frantically, he reached for his garments. Again that shrill cry echoed and re-echoed through the house—and again – and again.

He heard the sound of hurrying footsteps and the babbel of startled voices, in the hall below; and over all rose those lancinating[13], nerve-rending screams.

He did not wait to complete his toilet, but thrusting his feet into a pair of slippers and donning a smoking jacket, he threw open his door and bounded along the upper hall and down the steps—two at a time. As he reached the lower floor he found that the screams came from the library. The door stood partly open and he dashed in.

The scene that met Bob Blackmer's gaze was grand in its awful simplicity. His father lay stretched upon the polished floor, dead, with a ghastly cut in his throat and a blood-crusted razor gripped in

---

12 **matutinal** - occurring in the morning; early
13 **lancinating** - piercing

his pulseless hand. And bending over him was Lucretia, kissing the mute lips and chafing the marble forehead. Her golden hair fell in an unconfined shower over her shoulders, and trailed in the crimson pool upon the floor. Rocking herself to and fro upon her bended knees, she called the dead man by endearing names and uttered scream after scream.

Bob Blackmer paused at her side, horrified—stricken dumb. His father dead! And only the evening before he had left him in health and the best of spirits, apparently. He could not realize what had occurred. His brain whirled and he felt sick and faint. He looked down upon the lump of lifeless clay and all the old memories thronged his mind—and all the old love welled up in his heart. His eyes became moist and a tear dropped upon his father's upturned face. Then the son aroused himself. Turning to the crowd of servants that stood around with blanched countenances and staring eyes, he commanded: "Leave the room, and returned to your duties. You are not needed here. John, you go for Dr. Kenshaw."

The servants departed reluctantly and Bob bent down and lifted Lucretia to her feet. She was trembling like a leaf swayed by a bitter blast, and could scarcely stand. He placed her in a chair and spoke soothingly to her. Gradually she became calmer and lay back in the chair and moaned and shuddered.

Bob scarcely knew what to do or say. "There—there, Lucretia, do not give way," he whispered gently, "you will make yourself sick. Let me take you to your room—this is no place for you."

Then turning from her he strode up and down the room, tossing his hair back from his fair brow, interlacing his strong white fingers in whispering under his breath: "Oh! God, what a horrible affair— what a horrible affair."

But Lucretia would not leave the room and Bob could only wish and wait for the arrival of his cousin.

In a short time Dr. Will Kenshaw came. John, the coachman, had apprised him of what had occurred. He threw off his wraps in the outer hall and entered the library. For once his merry face was sad and grave, and his laughing lips were drawn into a straight stern line. He took in the situation at a glance—and seemed to know what was expected of him. Going up to Lucretia, he said: "You must go to your room and lie down. Come."

She stared at him blankly but offered no resistance, and together they ascended to her apartment. Giving her a nervine[14] he left her in charge of her maid and returned to the library.

Bob was standing by the window, looking out at the wintry scene—and seeing nothing. He turned around as Will entered and their eyes met.

"For heaven's sake! Don't look at me in that way, Will," burst forth the former, "I know what you would say. Father has committed suicide and you can assign no reason except jealously. I believe you are right. But I am innocent of any wrong in the matter—I swear it. I never gave him cause for jealousy—God knows that I am telling you the truth!"

The poor fellow was evidently very much distressed. He looked pale and haggard in the morning light, as he stood there defending himself. His cousin went up to him, and taking both his hands said simply and earnestly: "I believe that you speak the truth, Bob. But this is a bad night's work—it will create no end of talk. Do you want me to take charge of affairs? I know that you do not feel like doing anything yourself. I pity you from the bottom of my heart, old boy—I really do!"

At this expression of heartfelt sympathy Bob came near to breaking down. His lips and voice trembled as he replied: "thank you for your trust and sympathy, Will. Yes, do whatever needs to be done. I leave it all to you. I am going to my room—call me if you want me."

Left to himself, Dr. Kenshaw dispatched a messenger for the coroner, and began an examination of the premises. The body of his uncle first claimed his attention. The dead man lay full upon his back, with one leg extended and the other half flexed. Both arms were partly bent and the hands were clenched—the right one holding a razor and resting upon his breast. The face was slightly contorted, and the eyes were half closed and staring. The lips were bluish pale and a little dried froth adhered to the corners of the mouth.

---

14 **nervine** – a medicine acting on or relieving disorders of the nerves; soothing the nerves

He was dressed as Will had seen him the night before, except that his collar and cravat had been removed and lay upon the table near to which the body rested. The razor was smeared with blood, and the gaping wound in his throat divided the windpipe and the great blood vessels of the neck. The crimson flood of life blood had poured over the front of his garments and a pool of it lay upon the floor on either side of his head. The blood was coagulated and partly dried the body was rigid in death.

Dr. Kenshaw noted this all without disturbing anything. Then he turned to examine the room. He found it in order—just as it had been the night before. The safe was closed and locked, the papers and books were in place upon the desks and tables. Nothing had been disturbed.

The doctor was about to sit down to await the coming of the coroner, when he espied a torn scrap of writing paper lying beneath a closed book upon the table before mentioned. He picked it up and read:

"Dear Lucretia: I offer the world no reason or excuse for what I propose to do. I owe it none. It may call the act by what name it pleases—suicide, if it will. I care not. You know my reason—that is enough. I am thoroughly sick and tired of living as I do. Try to think of me kindly, for you know how much I have suffered.

Affectionately, Matthew Blackmer."

That was all; but it was enough. It pointed indisputably to the fact that the unfortunate man had committed suicide; and made plain to those who knew his family secrets, that uncontrollable jealousy had been the cause.

Dr. Will Kenshaw sat down and covered his face with his hands.

"Poor, deluded old man!" He murmured. "His groundless suspicions have led him on to self-destruction. It is a plain case of suicide. I shudder to think of it. That note will break Lucretia's heart. And Bob—poor chap—God help him! It is a bad business—a bad business—and all uncalled for."

It must be remembered that Bob had said to his cousin: "I never gave him cause for jealousy"—referring to his father. But at the same time he had maintained a loyal and judicial silence in regard to Lucretia's words and actions. So Will Kenshaw thought that his uncle's suspicions had been utterly groundless and that the fair-haired woman upstairs was innocent and guileless.

The young physician arose at last, and locking the library door behind him, took the note to Bob's room. The latter was lying on the bed, his face buried in the pillows. He examined the note carefully, then he choked down a lump in his throat and said: "It is father's writing—there is no disputing that. It but confirms our suspicions." And he turned his face to the wall and said no more.

Will took the note to Lucretia. "It will be a shock to her," he reasoned, "and the sooner it is over the better."

He found her staring with wide, tearless eyes at the ceiling while her maid sat by the bedside and softly stroked her hands. She read the note and burst into a storm of tears and sobs.

"Oh! How could he be so cruel," she wailed. "I did so try to make him happy! And I did love him—I did—I did! Oh! The cruel—cruel note! How could he do it—how could he!"

Dr. Kenshaw was compelled to administer another nervine. He would have staid[15] with the stricken woman to console and quiet her, but a servant came to say that the coroner had arrived; so he descended to the library.

The coroner proceeded with his investigation. He called in another physician, who with Dr. Kenshaw examine the body and made out a written report. A number of the servants were questioned, but knew nothing more than had been ascertained from the examination of the body and Will's statement. Bob was interviewed, but could throw no further light on the subject.

Lucretia's statement to the coroner—given brokenly and shatteringly—was as follows: "Mr. Blackmer's rooms adjoining mine. I thought I heard him come up at a little after ten o'clock last night, but I may have been mistaken. I cannot say positively; I was half asleep. When I awoke this morning, for some reason I was uneasy about him, and I went to his room. I discovered that his bed had not been occupied, and not seeing him I went down to the library— and—and found him dead!"

---

15 **staid** – variation of stayed

Here she gave away to another violent fit of weeping, and they questioned her no further.

Peck, the private secretary, was wanted; but inquiry at his boarding house elicited the fact that he had left on the five o'clock morning train to visit his brother, who was very sick. The landlady stated that he had received a telegram asking him to come immediately.

The coroner was not long in arriving at a conclusion—suicide. It was as plain as the noon day!

* * * *

The funeral was over—the will was read. Matthew Blackmer left his wife the palatial edifice that he had called home, and an income commensurate with her tastes and needs; to his nephew, Dr. Will Kenshaw, a lump sum of one hundred thousand dollars; and the remainder of his vast estate to his son, Robert Blackmer. The son was named as executor of the estate.

On the day following the funeral, Bob again took up his residence at the hotel.

Lucretia inquired of him: "do you think it necessary?" And his answer was: "yes, certainly. There must be no occasion for further talk." When he had gone she went to her room and wrung her jeweled hands in silent, helpless despair.

Dr. Kenshaw resumed his practice as industriously as though he was not a cent richer than he had been the week before. Several weeks passed, and the sensation occasioned by the rich man's unexpected suicide began to die away. About this time Dr. Kenshaw received a letter from a medical classmate, saying that the writer was coming to pay him a visit and would arrive on a certain day.

Chapter III

In due time Dr. Kenshaw's friend, Fred Cumfrey, arrived. The two had graduated in the same medical class, one year before the opening of our story. After graduation Dr. Cumfrey had spent a year as *interne* in the hospital of his alma mater, while Dr. Kenshaw had taken a six-month ramble through Europe—and had come back to begin practice in Grangerville.

They were the warmest of friends, although as unlike as the opposite poles of a magnet. Perhaps this was the very reason that each attracted the other—who knows? Dr. Kenshaw was big, broad shouldered, suave and voluble. He was twin Apollo to his cousin, Bob Blackmer, except that he was light complexioned and Bob was dark. He had the kindliness of gray eyes, and the blondest of blonde beards—pointed in the prevailing style.

In personal appearance Dr. Cumfrey went to the opposite extreme. He was small, lithe, active and excitable. He wore no beard, and his swarthy face and beady black eyes gave him a foreign look, not at all in keeping with his language, which consisted mainly of pronounced American provincialisms and marked rhetorical blunders. He was Dr. Kenshaw's mental inferior in many ways—but his superior in a few.

Kenshaw's reasoning faculties were broad, deep and generalizing; Cumfrey's narrow, pointed and individualizing. The latter's intuitive powers were abnormally developed—and he led his class as a quick and certain diagnostician.

On the evening of Cumfrey's arrival the two friends sat in Kenshaw's office talking over old times. When the edge of their reminiscent conversation was somewhat dulled, the former remarked in his abrupt way, "I see by the papers you had a sensational suicide down here recently."

"Yes," replied Will sadly, "my uncle committed suicide. He was one of the best—"

"Your what!"

"My uncle."

"Do you mean to tell me, Will, that that rich old nabob[16] was your uncle?"

"He was."

"Well, excuse me for speaking so lightly of the affair. But—say, tell me all about it. He was rich, wasn't he?"

Dr. Kenshaw proceeded to give his friend a brief history of

---

16 **nabob** - a person of conspicuous wealth or high status

Matthew Blackmer and family, and a short account of the suicide. He did not, however, reveal any of the family secrets or enter into the details of the tragedy. Dr. Cumfrey listened with wrapt attention to the others recital. When Kenshaw touched upon the will, and spoke in a casual and careless way of the amount that he, himself, had received, Cumfrey broke in:

"One hundred thousand dollars! Great Scott! And you speak of it as calmly as if you get a windfall of that kind every day in the week, Old man, you're in luck! A kind old gent? Well, I should say! Do you know what I'd do, if I had that wad of filthy lucre[17]?"

"No—"

"Nothing! That's just what I'd do. But you'll go on writing prescriptions and setting broken bones to the end of your life. I presume—to the end of time, may be. It's just like you! By the way, what was the cause of the rash deed?"

"Is it necessary that there be a cause?"

"Of course—apparent or unapparent. There don't seem to be any apparent cause, so there must be an unapparent one. He was rich, you say?"

"Very."

"And healthy?"

"Yes."

"Had a sound mind in a sound body?"

"To be sure."

"Then there's something back of it all. You can't fool me!"

"What makes you think that?"

"I don't think so—I know so."

"How!"

"It don't make any difference how—I know it, that's enough. Go on—tell me all about it. I am interested—I want to hear. How did he look—how was he found? Go on."

"The fact is," said Will as a wave of sadness swept over his features, "I would rather not talk about the horrible thing. I am trying to forget that it ever occurred, Fred."

"Oh, stuff!" sneered Dr. Cumfrey. "It did occur—and you won't

---

17 **lucre** - money, esp. when regarded as sordid or distasteful or gained in a dishonorable way

forget it. The way to get rid of that feeling is by talking of the matter till it becomes commonplace. Now, go ahead. Give me the details—go into the minutia."

With some hesitation Kenshaw did as he was requested. After the detailed account was finished, Cumfrey remained silent for some little time, crossing his legs nervously and pulling vigorously at his cigar. Then he said musingly:

"He cut his throat—and had a razer gripped in his hand. I don't believe it. If he cut his throat, he died from hemorrhage. Look here, Will!" He cried suddenly, "where's your pathology—your surgery?"

"If you mean my knowledge of those branches of our beloved science, Fred," answered Will yawning, "they are in my head where I usually keep such merchandise; but if you refer to my textbooks on those subjects, they are in my case in the next room."

Without a word Cumfrey leaped up like a Jack-in-a-box, and running out soon returned with several large volumes. One of these he spread upon his knees and began to turn its pages feverishly. Kenshaw watched him, with an amused smile flickering about his bearded lips.

Presently Fred ceased to turn the leaves of the book, knitted his brows and looked intently at the page before him. After a moment he said:

"Listen to this—this is what the surgery says: 'The body of a person who has died from the effects of hemorrhage presents a peculiar blanched, semi transparent, waxen look; the lips, alae of the nose, and fingernails have a somewhat vivid appearance contrasting strongly with the clear yellowish-white hue of the general surface. The entire muscular system is in a relaxed and flaccid condition, and the eyes are usually well closed.' Now, Will, does that correspond to the appearance of your uncle after death?"

"I can't say that it does exactly," replied the latter without looking up. "But he cut his throat—and committed suicide. He left a note to that effect."

"I haven't said that he didn't commit suicide; but I do say that he never died from the effects of hemorrhage," insisted Dr. Cumfrey.

"You are still jumping at conclusions, as of yore[18]," returned Kenshaw slightly nettled.

"As good a manner of locomotion as any," laughed the other, "just so you 'get there.' You say that the hands were clenched; that the eyes were half open, prominent and staring; that one leg was flexed and both arms bent; that the skin had a full-blooded appearance and that there was dried froth at the corners of the mouth. And yet you try to make yourself believe that your uncle's death was caused by hemorrhage. Your description does not correspond to the appearance of the body after death from hemorrhage, in a single particular, Will!"

"There does seem to be a discrepancy," admitted the latter reluctantly.

"Discrepancy! You mean impossibility."

"What is your theory? Out with it," replied Kenshaw impatiently.

"You will laugh at me; but I believe that his death was caused by some other means, and that his throat was cut after he was dead." Cumfrey said this slowly and earnestly.

Will Kenshaw did laugh heartily and uproariously.

"So, Fred, you think that he cut his throat after he was dead? Well, that's an original thing for a dead man to do, at any rate."

"I think that someone else cut your uncle's throat."

"After death?"

"Yes."

"Then how do you account for the pools of blood upon the floor? Had his throat been cut after death, there would have been very little blood spilled. You know that, Fred."

"Yes, I know. How much blood was there, anyhow?"

"I cannot say—but quite a quantity. Much more than there would have been, were your theory the true one."

Both men relapsed into silence. At last Dr. Crenshaw said: "it is bedtime; let us retire. But before we go tell me how you think uncle Matthew killed himself. I know you have an idea."

"I believe he poisoned himself."

---

18 **yore** - of long ago or former times

Again Will smiled incredulously, and the two friends retired to the sleeping apartments in the rear of the office.

* * * *

After breakfast the next morning Dr. Kenshaw started on his professional rounds, while his friend remained in the office reading. The former returned at eleven o'clock to find the latter still poring over his books.

"What are you reading so industriously, Fred?" Was Kenshaw's greeting.

"I'm reading up on the actions of the various poisons. Where have you been?"

"I've been up to see my uncle's widow, for one place. She is suffering from nervous prostration. Poor Lucretia! It has been a severe shock to her. Then, too, she has lost her favorite pug. He disappeared about the time of the funeral, and I suppose someone stole him. His sweet little mistress is disconsolate[19]."

Cumfrey did not look up from his book. Presently he asked: "Is she pretty?"

"Yes."

"And fascinating?"

"Y-e-s. Why do you ask?"

"Oh! Nothing, only you'll be in love with her, Will; if you are not already."

Kenshaw blushed to the roots of his hair, but he deigned no reply to this impertinent assertion. He removed his overcoat and sat down before the fire. After little while he turned to Cumfrey and inquired sharply:

"Why are you so interested in the actions of poisons?"

"I am trying to find out which one killed Matthew Blackmer."

"And have you determined?"

"Yes, I have."

"Name it."

"Hydrocyanic acid!"

---

19 **disconsolate** - seeming beyond consolation; extremely dejected

Dr. Kenshaw arose, pale and agitated, and paced up and down the room.

"What's the matter, Will?" asked Cumfrey with some concern.

Will Kenshaw paused before his questioner and answered impressively:

"I noticed the peach-stone odor of that poison in the room, the morning the body was found; and I attributed the smell to the flowers in the window."

"Of course you did! Your feelings have influenced her judgment in this matter, or you would have read many things aright that you have read wrong. There is not a shadow of doubt that your uncle was killed by hydrocyanic acid. Listen to this: 'Post mortum; rigidity sets in early after death from hydrocyanic acid, and is very pronounced. The fingers are tightly closed, the toes strongly flexed, the limbs bent, the jaws rigid and the eyes prominent and staring. The blood is dark-colored, fluid, and the great veins are gorged. Froth—sometimes bloody—exudes from the corners of the mouth.' There—that is an exact description of the appearance your dead relative presented."

"I believe you are right, Fred."

"I am right."

"But a fatal dose of that poison acts very quickly—almost instantly—and he could not have cut his own throat, then."

"No."

"Then some other person did."

"Most assuredly."

"But what could be the motive for cutting a dead man's throat?"

"It was done to conceal a crime already committed."

"You believe that he was murdered?"

"I do."

"But there could have been no motive for murder—"

"It's an odd thing, Will! No motive for murder—no motive for suicide—"

"But there was a *strong* suicidal motive."

The deuce there was! Well, why in the nation didn't you say so, long ago?"

"I did not care to divulge family secrets. But I may as well put your mind at rest, and prove to you that it *was* a case of suicide, in spite of the apparent contradictions."

So Dr. Kenshaw told of his uncle's unreasonable and uncontrollable jealousy, and ended by producing the note that the suicide had left. Dr. Cumfrey glanced at it and cried: "Why, he was left-handed!"

"How can you tell that?"

"From his handwriting—a crabbed backhand."

"Yes, he was left-handed. What of it?"

Fred Cumfrey leapt to his feet and danced about the room, clapping his hands like a maniac.

"Will Kenshaw," he shouted, "You're a fool—a veritable idiot! The idea—to believe that a left-handed man would slit his neck with his right hand! Can't you see—can't you understand? The razor was in his right hand. Whoever placed it there did not know—or did not remember—that Mr. Blackmer was left-handed!"

Dr. Kenshaw was as pale as death. He burst forth: "You're a wizard, Fred Cumfrey—a devil! I wish that you had not come here. You make me afraid—afraid that an awful, awful crime has been committed! Give up the quest—I command it. You are on the wrong scent and you are dragging me along with you!"

And he shook his fist at the slender form of the other, who almost cowered before the speaker's leonine[20] gaze.

Chapter IV

For several days after the above recorded conversation took place between the two doctors, neither reverted to the subject of Matthew Blackmer's death. Cumfrey said nothing because he did not wish to incur Kenshaw's further displeasure, and the latter remained silent for reasons best known to himself. As the sequel will show, however, neither was idle.

At the end of this interval of time Cumfrey received an invitation to visit relatives in the city fifty miles away; and he left with the intention of returning in a week.

---

20 **leonine** - resembling or suggestive of a lion

On his second arrival in Grangerville, Dr. Kenshaw met him at the train, with a conveyance. As they rode up from the station Will remarked in a casual way:

"Fred, I have exploded your hydrocyanic acid theory."

If the one addressed felt any surprise that the other should voluntarily refer to the forbidden subject, he did not show it in his manner nor voice as he replied calmly:

"Have you?"

"Yes."

"How?"

"I have looked over the poison records of all the drugstores in town; and not a drop of hydrocyanic acid has been sold in the last year, except in combination with other drugs and on prescriptions of reputable physicians."

"I was already aware of that fact."

"You were!"

"Yes, I visited all the places, myself, before I went away. But that don't prove anything. Couldn't the poison have been obtained somewhere else?"

It is not at all probable that it was."

"But possible."

"Scarcely."

Dr. Cumfrey fumbled in the breast pocket of his coat, for a moment, and then he said:

"I have had better success in the city. In the third store that I visited, I copied this from their poison record. What do you think of it?"

Kenshaw took the proffered slip of paper and read:

"Jan. 8, 1892—hydrocyanic acid dilute, Two ounces—Purchased by Anthony Peck, Grangerville, Ohio—For Dr. Will Kenshaw, Grangerville, Ohio—On prescription of Dr. Kenshaw, et cetera."

The blonde giant glared at his little companion in horrified amazement. His hand shook and his face was ashen as he asked:

"But what does it all mean?"

"It seems plain enough," returned Cumfrey coolly. "It means that on the eighth day of last January—two days before your uncle's death—his trusted private secretary, Anthony Peck, bought of a well known Cleveland druggist, two ounces of dilute hydrocyanic acid. He stated to the clerk of whom he purchased it, that it was for you—a physician of Grangerville—and in proof of this statement he presented this prescription. Did you write it, Will?"

Kenshaw received the second slip of paper, glanced at it, and replied in a hoarse whisper: "I did not. But I know who did!"

"It is your prescription blank."

"Yes, and Anthony Peck wrote the prescription himself. I know his handwriting. I could swear to it."

By this time they had arrived at the office. A patient was awaiting Dr. Kenshaw. When he had gone Will turned to Fred, and taking his hand said:

"You are right—you have been right all along. There is a mystery and crime connected with the death of my uncle. It must be cleared up. Help me to do it."

They shook hands warmly and sat down.

"These papers," resumed Kenshaw, "implicate Anthony Peck."

"Yes. How could he have obtained possession of one of your prescription blanks?"

"The easiest thing in the world—I have treated him for lung trouble. He has been to my office frequently."

"Has he returned from his sick brother's bedside? I believe you said that he was there at the time of the funeral."

"He did go to see his brother the morning after the death of Uncle Matthew; that he has been back several weeks."

"What is he doing now?"

"I do not know."

"Has he changed his quarters?"

"No."

"We must keep an eye on him—and search his rooms. Do you know anything of his previous history?"

"Yes, a little. He is a distant relative of Lucretia's. I heard Bob say at one time she obtained him the position with my uncle. He also said that Peck had been in love with her, when they were both younger; but that she would not marry him on account of his poor health and poverty. I do not know how Bob knew—perhaps she told him."

"I see! And with Matthew Blackmer out-of-the-way, Peck hopes to obtain his widow and a slice of his fortune."

"For heaven's sake! Let us go slow in this matter, Fred, and make no mistakes. I must finish my calls. We will talk of it further, this evening.

* * * *

At nine o'clock that night the two physicians sat in Kenshaw's office, silently smoking—each one busy with his own thoughts.

"So you found nothing of a suspicious character in Peck's rooms," said Cumfrey at last breaking the silence.

"Nothing at all."

"You made a thorough search?"

"I did."

"How did you manage it?"

"I bribed the landlady—she's one of my patients. I told her that I wanted to look for an important paper belonging to my uncle's estate. I did not like to lie to her, but could do nothing else under the circumstances. She will keep quiet—never fear."

"And Peck is again out of town."

"Yes."

"Where does his sick brother live?"

"In Cleveland."

"Ah! And he got the poison when he was there the first time. What was his former occupation—before he was private secretary to Mr. Blackburn?"

"He has been teacher, photographer, drug clerk—"

"That accounts for the fact that he knew how to write a prescription, and that it would probably be necessary to have one to get the poison. But go on."

"Lucretia tells me that he was always a 'ne'er-do-weel.' She is helping him now. To change the subject, that woman's case puzzles me. If she does not soon recover her nervous tone, she will become mentally unbalanced."

Dr. Cumfrey remained silent, and Dr. Kenshaw inquired:

"But what are you thinking?"

"Of the two most puzzling things in this case—the blood upon the floor and the note found upon the table. I suppose that there can be no doubt that the latter is genuine—Mr. Blackburn's writing?"

"None at all."

"There may be some doubt about the former."

"So I have thought."

"It may not be human blood at all. Have you any of the bloody articles?"

"Yes, I have the razor and the bloody watchguard that was around his neck."

"We must examine some of the blood microscopically. You have a good microscope?"

"One of the best."

"Let us prepare a slide and examine it."

Kenshaw went into the room and returned with the articles that he had mentioned. Scraping a minute quantity of the dried blood from the blade of the razor, he treated it in the appropriate way, and remarked:

"There it is. You may examine it."

"All right," consented Cumfrey, "and while I am doing so, you prepare another slide from the blood upon the watchguard."

He made a careful and painstaking examination of the specimen submitted, and said:

"It is human blood. The red corpuscles are all of one size, and practically one thirty-five thousandth of an inch in diameter. Have you the other ready? Let me have it."

After quite a while spent in silent investigation, he arose and shaking his head in a disappointed manner, he grumbled:

"They are both the same, it appears. I expected to find them different. You look, Will."

The latter did as requested, while Cumfrey lighted a fresh cigar and leaned against the wall, looking on.

After a time Kenshaw announced: "There is but little difference in them—but there is a difference. The corpuscles of the specimen from the watchguard are slightly smaller than the others. I did not expect to find a marked difference, however."

"How's that?"

"I have a theory in regard to the matter, Fred."

"I'm glad to know it. It's a hopeful sign—you are improving. Let's have your theory."

"I believe that whoever poisoned my uncle, cut his throat afterword; and the blood not flowing as the murderer had expected, he sacrificed Lucretia's pug—which was probably in the room, for he often staid there—to obtain the blood he sought. And the blood corpuscles of the dog are but little smaller than those of men."

"By Jocks! You'll do, Will. You're coming out of the kinks!" shouted Cumfrey, capering about the room in infinite delight. "Why didn't I think of that? You're right—you can't be wrong!"

It was after midnight when the two retired. Kenshaw told his friend of Peck's peculiar actions in the Blackmer grounds, on the night of Matthew Blackmer's death, and both men agreed that the finger of suspicion pointed in no uncertain manner toward the private secretary as the murderer of his employer. So far as either knew no other person could have had the shadow of a motive for committing the deed.

Kenshaw made plain that Peck could have hidden in one of the outbuildings and returned to the library after he—Kenshaw—and Bob had left. Both were confident that that was what Peck had done, and that on some pretext he had induced Mr. Blackmer to take the fatal draught. Also, that after his benefactor's death he had become alarmed and had endeavored to conceal the crime as above indicated.

"It's enough to me," concluded Dr. Cumfrey, "except that bothersome note. That's a stumper! I can't make it out at all."

* * * *

Several days passed and our two amateur detectives had gotten no further in their solution of the mystery that overshadowed Matthew Blackmer's death. They had decided to tell no one—not even

Bob—of their suspicions and beliefs until they had cleared up the whole matter—if it were possible to do so.

Bob was busily engaged in executing his father's will, and frequently advised with Lucretia. Dr. Kenshaw, who is making daily professional visits to see her—and daily falling deeper and deeper in love—notice that after each of her interviews with Bob she was worse. He could not understand it. He had been called to the great house in the night several times to administer a hypodermic hypnotic to her, because she was restless and could not sleep. These attacks grew more and more frequent and more nearly uncontrollable.

One morning while taking their breakfast at the hotel, Dr. Cumfrey remarked to Dr. Kenshaw:

"We must find out the meaning of that note, Will. We can't go another step till we do. You leave it with me this forenoon; I want to examine it more closely. There's something wrong about it, or we are wrong, that's all!"

Two hours later he was pacing in and out of Kenshaw's office, impatiently awaiting the latter's return. When Kenshaw arrived Cumfrey accosted him excitedly:

"Will, I have partly solved the note mystery."

"What do you make of it?"

"Take this glass and examine that colon following the words, 'Dear Lucretia.'"

Kenshaw took the magnifying glass and silently inspected the scrap of paper.

"What do you discover?" interrogated Cumfrey, rubbing his hands gleefully.

"I see that the colon has been made with ink of a lighter shade than that used in the rest of the note."

"Exactly! And what else?"

"That there is a small and indistinct comma just before the colon, and that the paper is slightly roughened at the place."

"What do you infer from all that?"

That the comma was made when the note was written, and that it has been partially erased; has been substituted. But I cannot fathom the meaning of it."

"I can."

"Well."

"That note is a torn piece of a letter or other paper, and the murderer used it to deceive. He changed the comma to a colon to make the piece of paper look like a complete and separate document."

"It is addressed to Lucretia."

"Yes."

"Then the letter from which it has been torn was written to her by my uncle."

"Necessarily!"

"But that would identify her with a crime!"

"The letter may have been stolen from her, as your prescription blank was from you."

"It may have been—God grant that it was! I do not know what to think. I very much fear that we are at fault—that we have started with false premises and will arrive at wrong conclusions."

Cumfrey was half provoked as he replied:

"Look here! You are not going to lose your nerve, and back down; are you, Will? If we are wrong, we shall find it out in the end. I do not pretend to know who the guilty parties are, but I mean to hunt them down—and you must help me. Justice demands it. Somebody is guilty, and that somebody must be detected."

Will Kenshaw sat silent a long time, his face in his hands. When he looked up Cumfrey saw that he was much troubled.

"Poor devil!" muttered the smaller man to himself, "he is in love with that blue-eyed siren, and he is afraid that she may be connected with this black affair."

After a further interval of silence, Kenshaw roused himself and inquired:

"Fred, what do you propose that we do next?"

"We must obtain the letter from which the scrap of writing was torn, and that bottle of hydrocyanic acid—if they are yet in existence."

Chapter V

Several weeks elapsed. Dr. Cumfrey's visit was drawing to a close. He must soon be off to look after his own business. He expected to start a practice in a Western city, and felt that he ought to be completing his arrangements. But he could not gain the consent of his mind to leave Grangerville until he had probed the Blackmer affair to the bottom.

Peck's brother was dead and Peck himself had come back to town and was keeping books for a local lumber dealer. Neither the mutilated letter nor the bottle of poison had been found, although our two doctors had been unremitting in their search. Cumfrey cultivated Peck's friendship; went to the latter's rooms frequently and kept his eyes and ears open—but all to no purpose. Kenshaw searched the Blackmer library from top to bottom, and kept a close watch on Lucretia. It was all in vain. The two physicians were no wiser than before.

The nervous strain was telling on Will Kenshaw. He could hardly eat or sleep. He grew restless, haggard and thin. He would have given his fortune to have been able to dispel the mystery—to prove Lucretia innocent. And yet he did not think her guilty—far from it.

At eleven o'clock one raw blustering night in the latter part of March he was called in haste to the Blackmer mansion. The messenger said:

"Mrs. Blackmer has one of her nervous attacks and wants you right away."

When the doctor arrived at the residence he found Lucretia wakeful, wild-eyed and almost delirious. He administered the appropriate remedies, and in a half hour was gratified to see her fall into a light sleep. He sat by her bedside and watched her. Surely that frail, angelic creature could not be guilty of a heinous crime! It was wicked to harbor the thought for a moment.

Her sleep deepened and she began to moan and babble. Presently he caught the words:

"Bob, my love—my love! You will not come to me after all that

I have done. After all that I have risked, you will not love me. And I have sinned for you, dear—sinned—sinned!"

Will Kenshaw staggered to his feet and out of the room. Her words stabbed him to the heart. They were a double revelation. He called Ada, the maid, and sent her into her mistress. Then he dropped into a chair in the adjoining room, and gave himself up to thought—soul consuming thought.

At last he roused himself and went back to his patient. She was sleeping quietly and naturally, but her flushed face and the halo of fair hair around it gave her the appearance of a tired and feverish child. How enchantingly beautiful she was—and how he loved her!

He returned to his chair in the next room, picked up the book from the table and began to turn the leaves. A paper dropped from between them, and fell upon the floor. Mechanically he picked it up and opened it. He saw that it was in his uncle's handwriting, and that it was addressed to Lucretia. He was about to return it to the book, when he noticed that a part of the first page was missing. The torn edge fascinated him. He took from his pocket the note that had been found upon the library table. The torn edges of the two papers joined perfectly!

The restored letter read:

Miss Lucretia Chadwick:—when I made you a proposal of marriage a few days since, you would not give me a definite answer. I here put the proposal in writing, to show you that I am intensely in earnest. I offer you an old man's love and respect.

You hinted to me that the world might not approve of our union; that it might say unkind things; that it might call the act foolish on my part—even childish.

Dear Lucretia, I offer the world no reason or excuse for what I propose to do. I owe it none. It may call the act by what name it pleases—suicide, if it will. I care not. You know my reason—that is enough. I am thoroughly sick and tired of living as I do. Try to think of me kindly, for you know not how much I have suffered.

Affectionately,
Matthew Blackmer.

Dreamily, automatically, Will Kenshaw placed the papers in his pocket; and rising, he again entered the room where the sick woman lay. She was still resting quietly. He told the maid that he was leaving, but that he would call again, early in the morning.

Like one stricken blind he groped his way down the stairs; and securing his coat and hat he started for the office. Arriving there he awakened Cumfrey and handed him the telltale papers. The latter read the completed letter and asked:

"What will you do, Will?"

"I will lay the whole thing before Bob, tomorrow; and he may do what he likes."

The one went back to bed and to sleep, but the other sat by the fire until daylight.

* * * *

As Dr. Kenshaw entered the Blackmer abode at eight o'clock in the morning, Bob came to the library door and remarked:

"I am waiting to see Lucretia on business of importance. Step in here as you pass out, Will, and let me know if she is able to come down."

In a quarter of an hour the doctor entered the library and said:

"She is feeling much better this morning. She instructed me to say to you that she will be down in a short time. Before she arrives I want to tell you something that directly concerns you and her."

The two cousins seated themselves, and in as brief a manner as possible Kenshaw made Bob acquainted with the details of the crime that had been committed. Bob was at first incredulous; but as Will unfolded the plot step-by-step, and showed the torn letter he became convinced of the awful truth.

Both men were so interested, so fascinated with the horrible recital, that they did not hear the light footstep that paused at the library door. Inadvertently their voices rose higher and higher as they proceeded with their discussion. The minutes slipped by uncounted. At last Kenshaw arose to go. He glanced at his watch and found that they had been talking an hour—and Lucretia had not yet come down. As he turned toward the door a wan, drooping woman, with a face like a hunted ghost, glided noiselessly up the stairway. It was Lucretia—she had heard it all!

A few minutes after Kenshaw's departure, Ada, the maid, descended to the library to inform Bob that Mrs. Blackmer was not so well, and would not be able to see him that morning. He left the house, and the girl returned to her mistress. As she entered Lucretia's apartment the latter called to her:

"Ada, I am going to write a letter, and then lie down for a long nap. Do not let anyone disturb me until dinner time. You are excused for this morning."

* * * *

When they came to wake her for dinner she was dead! We draw a veil over the terrible scene, except to say that an empty two-ounce bottle stamped with that name of a Cleveland druggist, and bearing a label: "Hydrocyanotic Acid Dilute"—stood upon the dressing case; and near it lay a sealed letter addressed to Robert Blackmer.

The letter ran:

"My Lost Love:—When you read this I will be beyond all earthly censure or punishment. My love for you has brought me to this. I loved you—and you alone. I married your father not to obtain his fortune, but to spite you. Oh, you were so coldly polite!

"I respected Mr. Blackmer, but I could not love him; and when I came to realize what I had done, I was desperate. I did so want your love! When you said to me one time, that the love I desired could never be—that I was your father's wife—I was foolish enough to fancy that if I were free again, I could win you.

"From that time forward I studied and planned how I might kill your father and escape detection. I have been insane—I believe I was.

"His playful use of the word 'suicide,' in his letter of proposal gave me an idea. I saw how that part of the letter could be used to indicate that he had committed suicide.

Anthony Peck was my blind—though innocent—tool. He procured for me the bottle of hydrocyanic acid. I gave Mr. Blackmer the poison in a glass of wine. It was a half hour after you and Dr.

Kenshaw left the library that I committed the murder. The servants had retired for the night, and I had no fear of interruption.

He died in a few minutes—just dropped on the floor and gasped and struggled. I stood and watched him die—but I had no pity. I thought only that you would be mine! After he was dead I placed a note on the table, and went to my room.

There I thought over what I had done, and grew alarmed. I was afraid that his death by poison would lead to an investigation, and that I would be discovered. Then I thought that if his throat were cut and a razor placed in his hand, no question would arise as to the cause of his death.

"I procured his razor, returned to the library and cut his throat; but only a very small quantity of dark-colored blood was discharged from the wound. I knew that was unnatural; and I was in despair. My pug lay asleep on one of the rugs and I killed him to procure the blood to hide my blunder. After the dog was dead I carefully cleansed the razor of blood and hair, dipped the blade in the dark fluid that was exuding from Mr. Blackmer's neck, and placed the instrument in his clenched right hand.

"Then I wrapped the body of the dog in the light shawl that I had around my shoulders, and hid it in an old valise in the lumber attic. There it remained until Anthony Peck returned from his second visit to his sick brother; then he took the valise away and secreted it for me, I know not where. He did not know what was in it.

"I want to make plain that Anthony Peck was my innocent dupe. I deceived him all the way through. I am sure that he did not know to what use I intended to put the poison. He was blindly in love with me—and I used him to further my ends.

"After the deed was done I felt neither pity nor remorse. I was madly elated when no question was raised by the physicians or coroner; and even yet I smiled to think how cleverly I deceive them.

"I know all—I overheard Dr. Kenshaw telling you in the library. Dr. Cumfrey has been my Nemesis. It matters little. I have failed to win your love, and I am ready to die!

"I have said that I felt neither pity nor remorse. But when I found, at last, that you are never to be mine—in spite of all that I had risked to win you—in spite of the stain of murder upon my soul—I began to think. And thought begat remorse; and remorse gave birth to fear. Oh, my God! how I have suffered—how I have been punished! The apple of love has turned to ashes on my lips!

I intended to destroy the remainder of your father's letter of proposal, but I mislaid it and could never find it. The bottle of poison I locked in my cabinet, and kept it for the purpose to which I have put it this day—my own death.

"There is no more to say. Farewell! May God forgive me—and may you forget my crime!"

Lucretia Chadwick Blackmer

They laid the erring, sinful wife to rest by the side of her wronged and murdered husband. Little by little the secret of the whole fearful tragedy leaked out, and a nine days' wonder was the result. At the end of the preverbal period of time, the busy world moved on; and the Blackmer affair was consigned to the past and to oblivion.

◆◆◆

The Diversions of Dicky Dare

I'm all the time makin' rhymes — guess I can't help it; mama says I can't anyhow. She says I'm jest like my pape an' my uncle Joe was w'en they were boys; an' says they used to git into trouble jest like I do sometimes. Do I git into trouble 'bout makin' rhymes? Well, I guess so! W'y last year I purty near got expelled from school; but it all come out right in the end. It was this way. I didn't like our teacher, Mr. White, very well; he was always so grumpy an' cross with me. If he'd see me jest twitch Jack Shaner's wool — jest a little mite, he'd hoss me out on the floor an' shake me — shake me good an' hard, too. Wasn't that unreasonable. An' once he scutched[1] me jest as I wrote a little verse on my slate an' showed it to the boys an' girls 'cross the aisle. What do you say to that?

You see Mr. White was sweet on Ms. Bessie Gray, the writing teacher; an' she was takin' private lessons from him, in grammar an' hist'ry an' so on, an' he used to hear her recite at intermissions. An' sometimes I'd see 'em settin' purty close together, you know. Yum- Yum-

Well, the little verse I wrote was like this — wasn't no harm in it, as I could see:

"There's a young writing teacher quite pretty and gay,

Who — strange to relate — has always been Gray;

But — stranger by far — some sad day or night,

This pretty young teacher will surely turn White."

Say! How the boys an' girls did laugh! An' Mr. White come back an' got the slate an' read what was on it; an' his face turned all red an' puffy.

"Richard Dare." he said; splutterin' an' pantin', "you done that!"

"Yes, sir." I owned up, kind o' scared, but hardly able to keep from laughin' at that funny look on his face.

---

1 **scutched** - to beat or whip; to drub

"Come into the cloakroom," he says; "I want to interview you."

"Well, say! I don't want to be interviewed no more. It's a painful business! He scutched me like blazes; but I wouldn't 'ave cared so much for that, if he hadn't called my poetry doggerel[2]. I don't know what doggerel is exactly, but I know it's somethin' low an' mean, an' my poetry wasn't that. So I made up my mind to git even with him; an' I did. The first thing I done was to make up a verse 'bout Mr. White; an' I sung it to all the boys — an' threatened to lick the last one of 'em, if they told Mr. White.

Well, one mornin' jest 'fore Christmas I was limpin' long past the house where Mr. White boarded, on my way to school — I had sprained my ankle skatin'; an' was singin' as big as you please — not thinkin' of what I was doin':

"We've got an old teacher in our school.

An' he's a stubborn as a mule;

And he tries to make us all mind the rule —

This crabbed old teacher in our town.

His eyes are all milky, his mouth is spread

From ear to ear, and his hair is red;

An he hasn't got much on top of his head —

This grumpy old teacher from our town!"

Ah gee! There stood Mr. White on the front portico, lookin' right at me an' grinnin' a nasty grin. I know that I was in fer trouble, sure; an' I hustled on to the schoolhouse, doing some tall thinkin', I tell you. I felt sure he'd ask for another interview with me; an' he did. But I was ready for him.

He called me into the cloak-room an' says:

"Richard, didn't I hear you singin' a nice little song this mornin', as you was passing my boardin' place?"

An' he grinned an' showed his teeth.

"Y-e-s, sir," I answered, tryin' to swaller the lump in my throat.

"An' wasn't there somethin' in it 'bout me?" he asks.

"Y-e-s, sir," I says, kind of chokin' an' battin' my eyes.

"Well, Richard," he goes on, grinnin' nastier 'n ever. "you may

---

2 **doggerel** - crudely or irregularly fashioned verse, often of a humorous or burlesque nature

sing that little song for me now; an' if it suits me then I'll have you go in an' sing it for the school."

"Oh, I don't want to sing it, Mr. White!" I says, rubbing my hands an' steppin' round.

"Yes, sing it," he growls, re'l cross.

So I walked up an' down in front of him an' sung:

"We've such a good teacher in our school,

The switch to him is an unknown tool;

And truly we try to obey his rule –

For, oh, we love him so dearly!

His heart is so tender, his voice so kind,

That every pupil jest loves to mind;

A better teacher we could not find –

For, oh, we worship him nearly!"

My! You ought to have seen how surprised he looked!

"Is that the song I heard you singing?" he asks, re'l slow an' sober.

"Yes, sir," I answers; "it's the very same tune you heard me singin'."

You see, I didn't say it was the same song — jest the same tune.

"Well," he says, given me a look I couldn't quite understand, "I must 'ave misunderstood some of the words, Richard: an' I'm sorry I did — an' pleased to know you wrote such a nice song 'bout me, an' think so much of me. An' I tell you what I'm goin' to do; I'm goin' to have you sing it at our exercises on Friday afternoon jest before the holidays. There'll be quite a number of visitors present, an' you'll make a great hit."

Well, now I was scared fer sure. I didn't want to sing that verse, you bet! After all the braggin' I'd done to the boys 'bout how I was goin' to git even with the teacher. I knowed the joke would be on me; an' that the boys wouldn't never quit teasin' me. So I says:

"Oh, please don't ask me to sing it, Mr. White — please don't!"

"Why?" he asked, kind o' raisin' his eyebrows.

"'Cause," I says; "'cause I'm — so bashful."

He jest laughed — an' squinted his eyes an' nodded his head; an' then he said:

"Oh, I guess you ain't so bashful you can't sing it; an' you'll sing it. An' I'll make you a present of a copy of Robi'son Crusoe."

"You will?" says I, tryin' to look pleased. I knowed there was no getting out of it.

"Yes," he answers.

"All right," I says, "I'll sing it."

Well sir, w'en the Friday afternoon come round, the schoolhouse was jest crowded with visitors, Mr. White an' Miss Gray was both there trigged out in th'r best. Mr. White had give me the Robi'son Crusoe book that forenoon. So w'en it come my turn I marched up to the platform, as big as old Pompey, an' sung;

"I saw our dear teacher the other day,
At noon, sittin' close to Ms. Bessie Gray;
And he was teaching her grammar this way:
'Now, conjugate love with me, love!'
'Oh, I love, and you love, and we love!' said he;
He didn't know I was there to see,
And so he kissed her jest one, two, three —
With his 'I love, and you love, an' we love!'"

Say! You ought to have heard everybody laugh — visitors an' all; an' even Mr. White an' Ms. Gray had to laugh — though the'r faces was mighty red. The school-board was goin' to expel me for impudence, but Mr. White wouldn't let him. He said:

"No, you mustn't expel Richard; it was my fault. I tried to play a trick on Richard, an' he beat me at my own game."

An' me an' Mr. White's been good friends ever sence — an' so has me an' Miss Gray.

◆—◆—◆

One of Morgan's Men

Chapter I

It was Thursday, July 23, 1863, that John Morgan's band of travel-worn raiders crossed the Muskingum river at Eagleport, Ohio—five hundred strong. Or five hundred weak, rather, for this mere handful of tatterdemalion[1] adventurers was the remnant of the hopeful and enthusiastic three thousand that organized in Kentucky for a march through the Northern states—to conquest and glory and plunder. It goes without saying that they were brave men, for none but the brave would have joined so hazardous an expedition.

At about nine o'clock in the fore noon, then, they crossed the rippling river below the gray dam, and proceeded on their way eastward; and at noon, the brown country road was stirred into a cloud of dust by the advancing hoofs, at a point ten miles from the river. Here lay the magnificent three-hundred-acre farm of John Printson, farmer and stock dealer. It was hilly upland, to be sure, but the farm was well tilled and well kept.

The residence stood a few yards back from the road, and a large yard filled with rose bushes, grotesquely-trimmed evergreen trees, and flower beds. It was a large, old-fashioned frame building, painted a dull white and trimmed in garish blue; with front porches, high and narrow windows, and massive oaken doors.

One hundred yards up the road stood the big red barn, surrounded by a coterie[2] of outbuildings, shacks and sheds. The appearance of the residence and its surroundings betokened thrift, plenty and comfort. There was no deception about it, either, for John Printson was "well-to-do." He was a typical specimen of the prosperous

---

1 **tatterdemalion** - a person wearing ragged or tattered clothing; a ragamuffin
2 **coterie** - circle

northern farmer of those days, horny-handed[3], hard-faced, just and honest—but scarcely generous.

He had been born and raised on the farm, and for the forty-odd years of his life had not been twenty miles away from it more than a dozen times. It meant everything in the world to him. On the site of his residence had stood the log cabin in which he was born, and his father had chased wild animals over almost every square rod of the big farm.

John Printson was intensely loyal to the North and its cause; but he had not volunteered to go into the army, because he loved his home and family so much that he could not gain the consent of his mind to sacrifice his private interest to the public good. He was a fearless and courageous man, and it was not owing to cowardice that he "stood the draft" and sent a substitute to the front. And be it said to his credit that—well as he loved money—he did not complain of the loss of the three hundred dollars that it cost him.

His family was small, consisting only of his wife and daughter, besides himself. "Aunt Linda" was known for miles around as a "stavin' good worker an' a powerful hand in sickness." She *was* a good woman; one of those placid, motherly bodies that everyone instinctively likes.

Nettie Printson, the daughter, was a buxom, dark-haired, black-eyed lass of eighteen summers, possessing her mother's beauty and sweet disposition, coupled with her father's sturdy enterprise and native independence. She was called "the best lookin' gal on the ridge," and was considered an eligible match for anybody. She had had a number of suitors for her hand and heart, and the broad acres that would be hers, but one only had gained favor in her sight. This was Will Walters, the son of a neighboring farmer. Will and his two brothers were in the Union army, but Nettie received letters from him quite frequently, and his picture hung over the great maple bureau in her bedroom.

This much by way of explanation. On that hot twenty-third of July, a little past the noon hour, John Printson sat on the front porch steps reading the country paper, and anon[4] looking out on the field where the hired men were hauling and stacking wheat. Just as he had thrown

---

3 **horny-handed** - having the hands horny and callous from labor
4 **anon** – at once

down the paper, and arose with the intention of joining the men in the field, his attention was attracted by a cloud of dust up the highway, beyond the barn. It grew and rose; and lifted by the lazy breeze, drifted out across the stubble land toward the dark green forest beyond.

"It must be some one with a big drove of cattle," mused Printson as he took up his hat and sauntered out to the road. As he drew near the little gate that opened into the broad highway, he saw the men in the wheatfield wildly gesticulating, and heard them shouting. They were unhitching the teams, too, and seemed to be mad with excitement. What could it all mean?

He was not long in doubt, however, for one of the workmen had seen him, left the others and ran toward him bawling at the top of his voice: "It's Morgan's men, John Printson—Morgan's men—an' we'll all be killed an' robbed!" Then catching breath he continued: "Ther' won't be hoofs o' stock left on the place, an' they'll burn the buildin's over yer head."

This startling statement was sufficient to excite and alarm almost anyone, but Printson's iron nature was proof against the announcement. He calmly looked up the road to where the foremost horsemen were dimly outlined in the cloud of dust, a quarter of a mile away. He had read in the county paper, but a few minutes before, that John Morgan had crossed the Ohio river and was on a raid through the state; that he had given it little thought, believing that the entire band would be captured, bag and baggage, before they had gone a hundred miles on Union soil. Rumors had reached him, in the last few days, that Morgan was pressing eastward across Ohio but he had possessed not the faintest idea that the bold raider was in the immediate vicinity—or would ever be.

Printson was surprised but not alarmed. He placed his straw hat firmly on his head, set his square jaws hard and went into the house for his gun. When he came out again with the squirrel rifle over his shoulder, his hired men were entering the barn with the farm horses, and the raiders were riding into the barnyard.

Covering the space between the house and barn with rapid steps in swinging stride, he confronted the leader of the raiders and demanded what he wanted.

The redoubtable[5] John Morgan, himself, smiled blandly from under his slouch hat and said quietly: "I want to partake of your hospitality. In other words, I want food for my men and horses; and if you have any good horses in your stables, I shall be only too glad to exchange some of mine that are foot-sore and weary, for them."

"Who are you?" demanded Printson in his fiercest tone.

"I am called John Morgan, and I hail from Kentucky," came the reply in the same quiet tones in which he had previously spoken.

"Then," returned Printson, "I cannot accommodate you in any way. I never have aided a rebel—and I never will."

Morgan was much amused at this, evidently, for he chuckled audibly and said: "if you are so good a Union man, you should be in the army. I am sure they need you down there. But when you say that you will never aid a rebel, you are sadly mistaken—as you shall see." Then turning to his men—"I have no time to parlay. Feed your horses from his bins and mows, and search his house yonder for food for yourselves."

By this time Printson was reckless with rage. Grasping his rifle more firmly, in hands that trembled with suppressed passion, he burst forth: "the first man that dares to enter that barn without my permission 'll fall dead in his tracks."

"You poor old fool!" exclaimed Morgan, half amused, half truthful, "do you mean to defy me? You deserve to be shot. Don't you see I have the power to take whatever I want? Submit quietly and I will take only what we need; make us trouble, and I will sack your buildings and burn them to the ground. Might makes right in love and war, my good man," and he laughed softly.

John Printson was struck speechless and almost paralyzed by this audacious threat. He was pale as marble and his knees shook so that he could hardly stand, while his heart was consuming itself in helpless, fiery rage. He did not attempt to reply—just shouldered his gun and stumbled toward the house in a dazed, bewildered way.

The raiders fed their steeds from his hay and oats, looted his cellars of eatables, robbed his smokehouse of the choices hams, and made free with his plump pullets. Then they proceeded to cook their

---

5 **redoubtable** - commanding or evoking respect, reverence, or the like

meal over fires kindled from his fences, and gorged themselves to repletion. After all this, they took four of the best horses in his stable—leaving four lean and sorry steeds in their stead and departed. He watched them as they disappeared down the highway, circled by wreaths of dun-colored dust.

For a long time he sat on the front porch silent, apparently unable to speak or move. Aunt Lindy tried to console him, pointing out the fact that his buildings still stood, and that he was still alive. He made no response. Pretty Nettie wound her plump arms around his neck and kissed him, and told him that he should not grieve—that it was desperately wicked to do so—that he still had much to be thankful for. Stimulated by the double dose of sympathy, he roused himself and said: "Blamed if I don't wish't I'd a' shot one of 'em, even if they'd killed me—the infernal scoundrels!" Then firmly and fiercely—"If I ever meet one of 'em again, I'll kill him if I die the next minute."

Chapter II

At sundown that evening, as Nettie and her father were milking the cows at the barn, a stranger galloped hurriedly through the wide gate that was open at the time, and pulled rein in front of the barn door.

"Has a large body of horsemen passed this way this afternoon?" came the inquiry from the stranger. John Printson inspected him closely before replying. He saw that he was a fair-haired, athletic young man, apparently about twenty-five years old. His face was smooth, excepting a drooping blonde mustache that partially concealed a row of firm, white teeth, and lips a trifle thin. He was dressed in citizens clothes and carried no arms, unless they were concealed. The horse that he rode showed signs of hard riding. It was covered with sweat and dusted in the foam was falling in flakes from its mouth, as it nervously champed the bit. Printson's eyes told him that the horse was a good one, of excellent mettle and endurance.

It took him but a moment to observe all this; then he answered the stranger's question thus: "A body o' highway robbers an' rebels passed this way—yes. They stopped an' robbed me, an; left about two o'clock. I reckon you don't belong to the gang?" This was said with a dangerous gleam in his steel gray eyes.

"I am in pursuit of them," replied the stranger curtly. "How many"—He broke off abruptly and stared boldly and admiringly at Nettie, who had joined her father. "How many of them were there?" he continued. "Several hundred, I should say. Them an' the'r horses et up nearly everything we had on the place," answered Printson, bitterly.

Without noticing the farmer's last remark, the young man asked: "Did they keep on down the main road?" pointing with his whip in that direction. This remark was occasioned by the fact that a byroad led off to the right, opposite the barn.

"Yes, they did, an' I hope they'll keep on goin' till they're all captured 'r killed; an' I don't care how soon that is."

Without deigning[6] to make reply, the young stranger wheeled his horse and started out the gate; but just as he was about to pass through, a hog that had been dozing in a corner of the fence, awakened with a startling "bwoof," and darted under the big horse's feet. The spirited animal reared on its hind legs and whirled like a shot. The saddle girth parted and saddle and rider were thrown to the ground in a promiscuous heap.

The horse galloped to the back of the barn lot, where—recovering from its momentary fright, it stopped, and was caught by one of the hired men. The stranger made no move to arise, and Printson hurrying to him, found him unconscious and bleeding from his nose and mouth.

In his fall his head and shoulder had come in contact with the sharp edge of the great gate post, and he was evidently seriously injured. Printson and the hired hands carried the senseless man to the farm house; and one of the men, mounting the stranger's horse, went for the doctor at Rockville—a little hamlet six miles away.

In the course of three hours Dr. Medley arrived. He was a gray bearded, bustling little man, who made up in innate kindness and attention to details what he lacked in exact medical knowledge.

---

6 **deigning** - doing something that one considers to be beneath one's dignity

After examining the injured man carefully, he announced: "He's pretty badly used up. His shoulder is dislocated, his arm fractured at the wrist, and he is also suffering from concussion of the brain."

The doctor reduced the dislocation, splinted the broken arm carefully and tenderly, then he gave his orders, as follows: "Keep cold compresses to his head, hot irons to his feet, give him this medicine as I direct—and above all keep the room quiet."

"Do you think he'll git well?" inquired the sympathetic Aunt Lindy.

"That depends on the nursing and care that he receives. I think *good* nursing and unremitting care will bring him through."

"Then he'll have *that*," put in Printson earnestly; "he was after them 'ere Morgan men, an' I'm bound to do all I kin fer him."

Dr. Medley prepared the medicine, wrote the directions on the back of a buff envelope, and departed—saying that he would return on the morrow. As he rode home that balmy summer night, he mused over all that he had seen and heard.

"I'll just let Printson think that that young fellow's a Northerner, as long as he will," thought the kind old physician to himself, "for as long as he believes *that* he'll keep him there and give him the best of attention. But if he had the faintest notion that my patient was one of Morgan's men, he'd send him off to prison—injured almost onto death as he is. I know John Printson! He's a good man in many ways—but that's what he'd do. That young blood's a Kentuckian, and that horse of his is a thoroughbred from the bluegrass region, or I am a fool for the want of common sense, and spent twenty years of my youthful existence in that part of the country, in vain. I'll never tell what I think—never, even if my patient gets well. I don't want him to rot in a Northern prison pen."

Dr. Medley was a Kentuckian by birth, and since the breaking out of the war it had been hinted more than once, in this country community, that his sympathies were at least divided. The people divined more from his manner and actions than from his words, for it was seldom indeed that he said anything about the troublous affair, one way or the other.

When he called to see his patient the next morning, he found him feverish and delirious; talking and mumbling incessantly as he tossed and rolled from side to side.

"Brain fever," whispered the doctor to himself. "Following brain shock; a mighty serious condition of affairs. And just as I expected, he's chattering of Lexington and Winchester—belongs to some of those old families down there, undoubtedly."

Turning to Nettie, who had installed herself as chief nurse, Dr. Medley asked: "did you find any papers on this young man's person that would indicate his name and residence?"

"No," answered the innocent Nettie, "he had very little about him, and nothing by which he could be identified; but he has talked so much of Lexington that father thinks he must have come from Perry county—you know there is a Lexington or New Lexington over there, and Morgan's men came through that way. Father says the raiders must have stolen horses from him, as they did from us, and he was following them to try to get them back."

Dr. Medley turned away to hide the semblance of a smile that flickered about his bearded lips, and busied himself at the bedside. It was as he would have it. No harm could come of his little deception, and if the poor fellow recovered he could depart in peace.

Nettie and Aunt Lindy were unceasing in their care and devotion to the young stranger, and even rough John Printson sat up with him of night, moistening his parched lips with the cooling draught, and replacing the heated compresses with cold ones.

At the end of the week the doctor pronounced his patient better, and predicted that in from twenty-four to thirty-six hours he would be conscious. This was the coming event that Dr. Medley dreaded. He feared that the young man would reveal something to his kind nurses, that would forever damn him in their sight, and destroy his prospects of final and complete recovery. For the doctor knew that nothing but the best of care, pure air and good food would restore him to health. Realizing the danger of a revelation, Dr. Medley impressed them all with the statement that his patient must not talk at all, until he the doctor, gave permission.

This was in the morning; and the following evening as Nettie was arranging his pillow so that he would rest more comfortably, she was startled by the stranger opening his eyes to their widest capacity, and inquiring in a weak, childish voice where he was. The faithful Nettie remembering the doctor's admonition, refused to answer him, except to tell him that he must not talk and that he should try to sleep. She gave him the powder, that Dr. Medley had left for the purpose, and was pleased to see him drop into a cool, refreshing sleep.

All through the night he slept with scarcely a stir, awaking in the morning and taking his nourishment with apparent relish for the first time. When Dr. Medley came at nine o'clock, he found him wide awake and looking a dozen inquiries at once from his big, bright eyes. Sending Nettie and her mother out of the room on trivial errands, the doctor shook his finger at the prostrate Apollo and said hastily:

"You have been very sick. You remember that you were thrown from your horse—you don't? Well, you were, and you have been at this farmhouse ever since; and these good people are nursing you back to life. Your shoulder was out of place, your arm broken and your head bumped," and the good doctor smiled at his own witticism."You are much better now," he went on, "but you must keep quiet and not worry. These people think you are a Northern man, and therefore they are very kind to you. If they had an idea that you were one of Morgan's men—as I know you are—they would send you off to prison at once; that is, if I would let them; and he chuckled in an amused way. "I can't blame them much, though, they have reason enough to hate the name of Morgan—and hate is a strong incentive to do wrong. What is your name?"

"George Stoddard," answered the sick man, weakly.

"Where from?" Was the next question.

"Lexington, Kentucky."

"Well, you leave off the Kentucky part of that statement. Tell them, when they ask you, that you are from Lexington; there is a Lexington over here in Perry county, and they will think you are from that place. If it becomes necessary, you must forget things—or lie. Do you understand? You must lie! Oh! I know you can't bear the thought of doing it, but you must. It is absolutely necessary."

Here Nettie returning to the room interrupted the conversation, but Dr. Medley had gained his point, and he felt that all was safe for the time being.

From this time on Stoddard convalesced favorably but slowly, and at the end of a few weeks he could totter about the house and yard.

Chapter III

It was the middle of October—a glorious golden month—and George Stoddard sat on the back porch at Printson's, soothed by the genial sunlight and lulled by the hum of voices from the distant orchard, where the men were gathering the winter fruit. He heard Nettie singing like a bird, as she busied herself with her household cares. He was so far recovered that he could have left at any time, and yet he lingered. He had written a number of letters home, apprising his people of the main facts in regard to himself; so he felt no uneasiness on that score. These letters had been carried to the office at Eagleport by Dr. Medley, and the postmaster not knowing from whom they came, the young man's secrets had been kept.

The Printsons had manifested but little curiosity about his private affairs. They seemed to take it for granted that his home was in the neighboring county, and beyond that cared but little. Stoddard had told them of his people—all the time carefully avoiding everything that would lead them to suspect where his relatives lived—and the Printsons felt that they knew him, and knew him well. He had evaded their direct questions as best he could, and his apparent candor has confirmed their belief that he was a true and loyal son of the Buckeye state. It did violence to his conscience to have to deceive them—especially Nettie, who had been so very kind and attentive.

He had not lied to them—as Dr. Medley had said he must do if necessary—but he had deceived them, which was as bad. It made him blush but to think of it, and yet what else could he have done?

As soon as he was able to converse with John Printson, he had learned the latter's deadly and undying hatred of everything Southern, and realized what would be his fate should Printson discover that he was not what he seemed.

He and Nettie had become the best of friends, and he wondered sometimes why she did not ask him more about his home and occupation; but then he reflected that she was an unsophisticated country lass and somewhat shy—and he attributed her want of curiosity to that.

At first he had fumed and fretted that he did not recover more rapidly. He had learned of the failure and capture of Morgan and his men, and he was anxious to get back to Southern soil and into the Confederate army. But of late—he had to own to himself—that he was not nearly so anxious to be gone.

Dr. Medley had not been to see him for over a week. The last time he had called, he had said: "You are able to go at any time; and the sooner the better, perhaps, for Printson might hear something that would make him suspicious—and he would turn you over to the authorities quicker than lightning. There are rumors in the community that you are one of Morgan's men, but Printson has not heard them yet, I am sure; but he may hear them at any moment, I think you should leave at once."

Stoddard had wrung his kind and faithful friend's hand and said: "I will leave in a few days at most. When I reach home I will send you your fees. You have saved my life in a double sense, I have no doubt, and I shall never forget your fidelity and kindness. I will bid you good-bye, for I may not see you again." And there had been tears in the old physician's eyes as he rode away.

Yet Stoddard was at the Printson farmhouse still. The secret of it all was plain, to himself at least. He was desperately in love with little Nettie Printson. Her black eyes had proven too much for his susceptible, passionate heart; and that was the reason that he dallied at John Printson's, exposed to constantly increasing danger.

He had thought it all over that bright October day, sitting out there in the sunshine, and he was half angry with himself that he could not decide to go.

"I *will* go tomorrow," he resolved at last; "why should I be a fool in this matter? I do not know that she cares a straw for me, I do know that she is engaged to a Union soldier. If she knew who I really am she would despise me, probably. Sweet Nettie! It is hard to give her up; and I have half fancied of late that it is not all pity and friendship that makes her so interested in my welfare. I wish I could tell her of myself before I go. I cannot bear to leave her without doing so. It seems too despicably mean to deceive her. I will tell her, if I get a chance, even if she turns away from me and informs her father!"

The opportunity was not long in presenting itself. Even while he was resolving and re-resolving, Nettie came out the kitchen door, with a basket on her arm and her dark ringlets fluttering in the crisp breeze.

"I am going to the orchard for apples, Mr. Stoddard; do you not want to race out there with me?" She said archly and playfully.

Stoddard replied in the affirmative, and rising he took the basket from her arm, and together they sauntered away.

While they were gathering the rosy apples, he said suddenly: "Nettie, I am going away tomorrow."

He thought that she turned a trifle pale, but perhaps it was his anxious imagination.

"What—what, so soon, George?" She returned. It was the first time she had called him by his Christian name and he noted it.

"So soon!" and smiled. "I have been here since the twenty-third of July; and now that I am fully recovered, I have no further excuse for abusing your hospitality."

"I mean so—so suddenly. I—that is, we—will miss you very much. You seem like one of the family, and—and —"

The red lips were actually trembling and the bright eyes were suffused with unshed tears. Of course it was very wrong in Stoddard to do what he did, but he did it nevertheless. He caught the neat little figure to him and passionately kissed the blushing, upturned face.

"And do you really care, Nettie?" he asked, softly.

She did not answer—only the blushing face disappeared on his shoulder, and her form was shaken by violent sobs.

"I love you, Nettie darling," he whispered, bending over her. "Do you really care for me?"

The crimson face was raised for a moment and he drank in her tremulous reply: "You will never know how much."

"Oh, Nettie, Nettie, maybe you would not love me at all if you knew who I am?" This in a questioning, heart-sick way.

"But I do know."

Stoddard was a little surprised at her positive assertion, and he asked quickly: "Who am I, then?"

"George Stoddard of Lexington, Kentucky!"

The young man held her at arms length and looked at her in almost speechless amazement. When he had somewhat recovered, he burst forth:

"Why, Nettie! How long have you known this? I had discarded everything that would tend to identify me. I had done it purposefully—being a scout for Morgan, and liable at any time to fall into the hands of my enemies. How long have you known this, Nettie?"

"Ever since you came, almost"—she answered, half smiling through her tears— "I suspected that you are not a northern man, and my suspicions were strengthened by Dr. Medley's anxiety. Then I accidentally overheard you two talking one day and of course I was sure."

"Do your parents know this?"

"No, indeed! Father would not have kept you in the house an hour, had he known it."

"And you kept it from them—my loyal little girl!"

"Yes, at first I was not certain: and when I became sure that you were a Southerner, I—I had learned to love you, and I could—could not tell them, George. Oh I could not."

Again the red lips trembled and again George Stoddard caught her to his breast and rained kisses upon the tearful face. This was adding insult to injury, of course—but he did it.

"But what are we to do, Nettie?" He said at last. "You are engaged to a Union soldier and"—

"I am not," came the indignant denial.

"Are you not engaged to that young man whose picture you showed me?"

"No, I have never promised to marry him, although he has asked me many times. I like him—we are good friends; but I do not love him."

"Then there is nothing to hinder your going home with me as my dear wife?"

"Nothing but father's consent—and that we will never get for two reasons," said Nettie, sadly. "He wants me to marry Will Walters, and he would never let me marry you, George, because you are a rebel."

"Of course it would be necessary for him to know who I am," mused Stoddard, dejectedly.

"Yes."

"Well, what are we to do, Nettie?" He cried, passionately. "I will not give you up! What are we to do?"

"You must leave, George—and tomorrow. It will not do to ask father's consent now. I know what he would do. When this awful war is over, come back for me and I will marry you—with or without father's consent. Mother would not object seriously to our marriage, and if she thought my happiness depended upon it; but it is far different with father. He is desperately set in his ways. We must have been gone too long already, and must return to the house."

They pledged their troth and said their good byes under the gray old apple trees, and then journeyed back to the farmhouse as though nothing out of the ordinary had occurred.

As they reached the yard, Nettie's father coming in from the barn accosted her with:

"What do you think, Nettie, Will Walters is home on a furlough; an' he'll be out to see you tonight. Trig up in yer best, gal, he's a first-rate feller—and he's lots o' money."

George and Nettie exchanged glances of consternation and entered the house without a word.

Chapter IV

Will Walters came over to call on the Printsons that evening. Nettie introduced him to George, and the whole company spent a very pleasant evening—at least to all appearances.

Nettie played the melodeon and sang a number of war ballots in a rich, clear voice. Stoddard applauded her as heartily as the others. He could approve of her singing; as for the sentiment of the ballads, he did not care a fig—Nettie sang them.

Walters related his army experiences in agreeable narrative, and John Printson expressed his uncompromising Union sentiments. Stoddard kept up the show of sanctioning everything that was said or done. He felt that he must do so, it would not be for long; but it was hard. He felt that he was acting the trader or hypocrite, and despised himself accordingly. He would have thrown off the mask and betrayed himself a dozen times, but Nettie's watchful and reproachful eyes were upon him.

Once or twice he caught Walters looking at him in a curious, half puzzled manner. Stoddard saw that he had no ordinary country bumpkin to deal with.

Walters was a florid, heavy-set young man, and his personal appearance did not betoken any great mental acumen; but in this case, as in many others, appearances were deceptive, for he was a man of more than ordinary shrewdness. He was a good conversationalist and Stoddard found himself listening to him with a great deal of interest.

Take it all in all, then, had it not been for the ever present fear of discovery, Stoddard's last evening at Farmer Printson's would have been a very enjoyable one indeed. He felt sure of Nettie's love and fidelity, and in spite of his anxiety he was happy.

About ten o'clock Walters took his leave. The entire company went with him to the door, and Printson accompanied him as far as the gate. When the door closed upon the others, Walters turned upon Printson and said abruptly: "I motion for you to come out here because I wanted to speak to you privately. I love your daughter Nettie—but you already know—and I have flattered myself that she cared a little for me, though she has always refused to marry me, giving as a reason that she was not ready to marry anyone. I have already asked your consent to our marriage—which you have granted—and I have been living in hope that Nettie would relent and become my wife. I came home with the intention of marrying her before I return to the army, but I begin to fear that it will never be."

"Why?" came the sharp interrogation from John Printson.

"Because she is in love with another man."

"You mean George Stoddard?"

"Yes."

"Bah! you are jealous. Nettie don't care for him. She nursed him through his sickness, an' she pities an' likes him, of course; but she don't love him."

"If I know anything of women and can judge their motives by their actions, Nettie does love him—and he loves her," insisted Walters doggedly.

Printson was somewhat nettled, and he said: "I tell you she don't, an' that's enough. Even if she does, what differ'nce does it make? She shan't marry 'im."

"Who is this Stoddard, anyway?" inquired Walters, dropping the disputed subject. "Do you know anything of him?"

Printson told him the little that he knew and the much that he surmised.

"You are totally mistaken in that, too," said Walter decidedly; "that fellow is one of John Morgan's raiders."

"It can't be."

"I tell you that he is. I thought he talked and acted like a Southerner, all the time."

Printson insisted that Walters was entirely wrong, and they went over the ground again. "He is one of Morgan's men," maintained Walters, "and if you confront him he will not deny it. He has let you believe that he is a Union man, simply because you wanted to believe it."

"If I thought he was a rebel, I'd be tempted to shoot him!" hissed Printson, savagely.

"You must not think of doing that, it would be unlawful. We must capture him and send him to prison." Then Walters unfolded the following plan:

"You go into the house and say to him that you have positive proof that he is a rebel. If he owns to it—as I am confident he will—do not appear angry, but give him to understand that you will not molest him, as he leaves tomorrow. That will throw him off his guard and he will feel secure for the night. Then you slip out here and inform me, and I will go down and get Jim Springer—who is at home on a furlough—and we will come back here and capture him while he sleeps. Now don't overdo the thing—just act natural."

"All right," said Printson when Walters had concluded. "But I won't believe Stoddard's one o' them raiders till he says so hisself."

Walters moved down the road a short distance and stopped in a shadowy corner, while Printson entered the house. Aunt Lindy had already retired, and Stoddard and Nettie were chatting by the fire. Nettie looked up quickly as her father came in and read his face. She saw that he was excited and she divined the reason at once.

Stepping quickly in front of the young Kentuckian, Printson blurted out: "Looky here, Stoddard, you're one of Morgan's raiders."

The younger man arose and faced the elder one.

"Well!" was all he said. "Are you—do you own to it?"

"Yes."

"Why didn't you say so long ago? If I'd a knowed it, you never could a come into my house. I don't harbor no rebels nor copper-head[7] secesh[8]. You've played me a scurvy trick an' you must leave here. You can stay all night, but you must go tomorrow. I don't bear you no ill will, but you can't stay here no longer."

"I will go now, if you prefer," said Stoddard proudly. "I am very sorry that I have been compelled to deceive you, but I could not do otherwise. I am grateful for your hospitality, even though—as you have confessed—you would've turned me away had you known what you do now. I will go tonight." This was what Printson did not want. Now that he knew the man for one of the raiders, he felt for him an intense and bitter hatred. So he said quickly and civilly: "No, stay an' git your breakfas' an' leave like a Christian. I don't want to drive you away in the night. Nettie, it's time you was in bed. I'll go out an' see if everything's all right at the barn."

He left the room. As the door closed Nettie, with white lips and throbbing heart, through her arms about George.

"They mean to capture you," she whispered, almost inaudibly.

---

7   **copperhead** – northerner with southern sympathies
8   **secesh** – a southern sympathizer; northern term for seceders

"I know it, dear."

"You must leave at once—as soon as you can slip away."

"But how?"

"Go to your room and wait until I call you. Have everything in readiness to leave. Raise the window and descend a ladder that I shall place there. You will find your horse in the front stall of the basement stable, saddled and bridled. Hist! I hear father returning; let us go."

When John Printson left the house he went directly to Walters and reported: "It's jest as you said—he owned up to everything."

"Did you allay his suspicions?" inquired Walters breathlessly.

"Yes; I acted good as pie. I told him he must wait till morning an' git his breakfas'. He aint no idee o' what were goin' to do."

"Are you sure of that, Printson?"

"Yes, sir; he'll stay all right."

"Good! I'll be back here with Springer about three o'clock. Just go to bed as usual—but don't go to sleep, and don't make a single move to alarm him. We will soon have this Southern mockingbird in a cage."

With that Walters disappeared in the darkness and the farmer again returned to the house. As he entered the sitting room he heard Stoddard and Nettie ascending the front stairway. He shook his fist at the invisible form of Stoddard and muttered to himself: "Oh! I'll fix you. Fool me, will you, an' git me to keep you till you're well an' hearty—you copperhead secesh! I'll see if somebody else can be deceived—I'll pay you off in your own coin."

Printson shut up the house and went to bed, resolving that he would not sleep. But a lifetime's habit was too strong for him, and in an hour he was snoring. He did not hear the light step that slipped down the back stairs to the kitchen, out the door and along the stone flags to the smokehouse. It was Nettie. She procured the heavy ladder that hung under the eaves of this outbuilding, carried it beneath the window of Stoddard's room, and with bated breath and superhuman effort, almost—pausing every now and then to listen—reared it noiselessly against the house. Next she went to the barn, and saddled and bridled his horse; then she hurried back to the house.

Stoddard had not been idle in the meantime. He had carefully placed the little gold that he had in a belt around his waist; cleaned and reloaded his revolver, donned his hat and heavy coat, and was ready and waiting.

So stealthily and silently had Nettie performed her part that George would've sworn that not a soul was stirring about the premises. He was becoming impatient. He wished that he could escape unaided, and once he made up his mind to make the attempt; but the thought that he might spoil everything that Nettie designed to do, deterred him. And what would become of Nettie when her father learned that she had aided her lover to escape! Could he go and leave her? How the weary minutes did drag! He must be off—and it would not do to linger longer; his enemies might be upon him at any time. What was that? A faint scratching on the frame of his door.

"Is that you, Nettie?" he whispered through the keyhole.

"Yes." was faintly breathed in reply.

Stoddard opened the door she darted in.

"Everything is ready," she said, breathlessly. "You must hasten—there is not a moment to lose."

"And what will you do, darling? They will know that you have helped me to escape."

"Oh! I do not know. Do not mind me – go—go!"

Her teeth were chattering with fear and cold. Stoddard looked at her a moment in silence. He loved her ardently and truly, and he could not bear the thought of leaving her to the mercies of her stern father. He knew that Printson would be insanely angry. What was to be done? Presently he said:

"Nettie, you must go with me."

"I cannot—I cannot. Go—go—please go—at once."

"I will not go and leave you here to brave the anger of your father."

"George!"

"I will not. If you stay, I stay!"

She saw that he meant it. "But if you stay they will send you to prison," she wailed, wringing her hands.

"Yes."

"And you may be killed."

"Perhaps."

"George—George, will you not go without me?"

"Never!"

She said not another word. There was no time to argue. Hastening out she procured her wraps and returned.

"I am ready," was all she said.

They raised the window cautiously, descended the ladder and paused to listen. There was no moon and it was quite dark. A cock in the cedar tree crew lustily for morning. It was half past two o'clock and quite cold.

Proceeding to the stable, they saddled Nettie's little gray pacer, led the horses out, mounted them and rode out of the barnyard. All this time scarcely a word had been spoken.

"We will take the most direct course for Kentucky," whispered Stoddard.

"Then we must pass through Rockville, cross the Muskingum at Eagleport, and bear to the west," returned Nettie. "Let us take this byroad; it will save us two miles between here and Rockville, and will throw them off the scent—if they attempt to follow us."

They started off at a brisk pace. The horses were in prime condition and would cover many miles before daylight.

As they passed down the narrow lane, two shadowy figures emerged from the highway and passed in the yard at Printson's. They were Walters and Springer.

"I was sure that I heard the sound of hoofs some minutes ago, as we crossed the pasture lot," said the former. "I hope Printson has kept a sharp watch on our Southern mocker, I would not have him escape for anything. It will be feathers in our caps, Springer—eh?"

At the end of a mile the fugitive looked back at the old farmhouse, from a bare knoll, and saw lights flashing here and there about the place. "Our absence is discovered," hissed Stoddard, through his set teeth: "let us hasten."

On through the darkness and the night they urged their horses: over rough and almost impassable roads, through bits of forest where the night wind moaned and the bare trees shook their skeleton arms overhead. At half past three they reined in their panting steeds and walked them silently through the sleeping hamlet of Rockville.

Then on again like the wind they sped. Scarcely a word did either speak, they were busy with their own thoughts and fears.

At last they began to descend toward the river; and as the faint light of coming day began to peep in from the east, they reached the river road a mile from Eagleport. Here they again reined in their horses. The fog on the river was so dense that they could see but a few yards around them.

"If we once put the river between ourselves and our pursuers, I shall —" George was saying when the sound of galloping ghosts in their rear came through the fog laden air.

"They are coming," gasped Nettie.

"Yes, you ride on to the ford and wait there for me. I will soon join you."

The gray pacer at a word from Nettie sprang forward like an arrow, and was soon lost to Stoddard's sight. Whirling his horse, the young Kentuckian drew his revolver and waited the coming of his enemies.

The sound of the approaching hoofs drew nearer and nearer. Stoddard could hear the labored breathing of the horses and the voices of their riders as they urged them on. Suddenly the weird and grotesque forms loomed up in the fog not fifty feet away.

"Halt!" cried Stoddard as he arose in his stirrups, his blue eyes dilated and flashing. The approaching horsemen drew their horses back on their haunches.

"I am George Stoddard—you know me."

"We want you."

"Come and get me, then, but the consequences be on your own heads."

With threats and imprecations they dashed forward. Stoddard took deliberate aim and emptied the five chambers of his revolver at the approaching forms. He saw one horseman fall from the saddle; the horse of another rise on his hind feet, snort wildly and go over the river bank with his rider; and the third horseman turned abruptly and galloped out of range.

George Stoddard did not wait to see more. Joining Nettie, he said: "They will not follow us farther at present. Walters is wounded, and your father's horse is dead. I did not shoot to kill."

Together the fugitives forded the river—almost losing their lives in the quick-sands on the western shore, struck the hard-packed country road again, and rode on. After days of danger and nights of anxiety, they crossed the Ohio river and were safe on Kentucky soil.

Walters returned home, recovered from the flesh wound in his shoulder, reenlisted in the main army and was killed in one of the hard-fought battles of '64.

John Printson erased Nettie's name from the old family Bible and swore by things earthly and things heavenly that she was no child of his, and that her name should never be mentioned in his presence.

After the war was over, letters bearing the postmark of Lexington, Kentucky, began to come to Aunt Lindy. Printson would bring them from the post office, but he would not permit Aunt Lindy to read them to him nor say a word as to their contents. Aunt Lindy wrote letters in return and to this he raised no objections.

One day when he went to the office, there was a letter there addressd to himself—and in Nettie's handwriting. He carried it in his pocket a week before he opened it. At last he could hold out no longer, and sitting by the fire one night he took it out and read it. He said nothing, but he handed it to Aunt Lindy, with the tears running down his furrowed cheeks. The letter prayed for forgiveness, and informed him that he had a little grandchild down in old "Kaintuck," bearing the name of John Printson Stoddard.

After that he read all of Nettie's letters and frequently talked about her to Aunt Lindy—but to no one else; and in a year from that time he sold out everything and he and Aunt Lindy left for the far West—obstensively. But the neighbors smiled at his simple ruse, for they knew that his destination was south of Mason and Dixon's line and that his future address would be "Lexington, Kentucky."

Story of a Skelton

Timothy Foley was twenty-eight years old, single and wealthy. He was a graduate of an eastern university, and had just taken his final examination at the Bellevue Hospital Medical College of New York. The one question that arose in his mind, as he sat in his room at the hotel, on the day after graduation was: "what shall I do next?"

He lay back in his easy chair, stretched his long, shapely legs toward the genial blaze in the grate, and watched the filmy wreaths of blue smoke that curled upward from his Havana. He was at peace with himself and all the world—too much so, in fact. "Tim Foley's bright, but he lacks ambition and energy," was the current comment of his friends.

Throwing away his cigar, Tim arose, adjusted his smoking cap and sauntered over to the window that looked out on the busy street. It was a raw and disagreeable March day. The sky was overcast with leaden clouds, and the streets were slosh-paved and uninviting. The doctor's phaeton[1] rolled past, edging its way in and out among the heavily laden vans and drays[2] that lumbered leisurely along.

"Ugh!" shuttered Tim, "I'm not ready to settle down to that sort of thing just yet. I'm too young. I believe I like the theory of medicine much better than the practice, anyhow. And I don't have to practice unless I wish—there's one blessed consolation. I know what I'll do for the next year. I'll combine the pursuit of pleasure with the pursuit of knowledge, by running over to Europe and visiting the hospitals. By Jove; it's a happy thought—it's just the thing."

He was not long in putting his resolution into action; and a few weeks later found him in London. From there he went to Berlin and Vienna; and six months from the time he first set foot on continental soil, he was in Paris.

---

1 **phaëton** - any of various light four-wheeled horse-drawn vehicles
2 **dray** - low, heavy cart without sides, used for haulage

Here, in visiting the hospitals, he made the acquaintance of M. Roban, a keen and brilliant young surgeon. M. Roban was Tim's senior by a few years. Their acquaintance ripened, and soon they were fast friends, spending much of their time together.

One day, a short time before Tim's departure for home, the twain sat in M. Roban's office, chatting pleasantly on various medical and surgical subjects. The Frenchman's enthusiasm in his work was contagious and Tim Foley had caught it. He wanted to get back to his native land and "settle down to hard work"—as he put it.

Among other things, they had been discussing this day the comparative merits of the American and French surgeons. M. Roban had maintained the superiority of his own countrymen, and in consequence Tim was somewhat piqued. He lighted a cigar with the ease and grace of an inveterate smoker, yawned lazily and said:

"There's one thing, M. Roban, that I freely grant you—one thing in which you Frenchman excel, at least. You mount the finest skeletons in the world. Others may articulate them to a mathematical and anatomical nicety, but you do it in an artistic way as well."

M. Roban smiled, nodded his head, and pulled his cigar in silence, for some time. At last he remarked: "Ah! yes. That's true, perhaps. I see no reason why we should not excel in that, as we do in everything else pertaining to the profession. By the way, I have never shown you the skeletons in my closet. There—don't be alarmed. I speak in a literal sense. I am not going to reveal to you some musty family secret." And again he smiled in an amused manner.

"No." answered Tim, simply, not knowing what else to say.

M. Roban arose and unlocked a cabinet that stood in one corner of the room. He threw open the door, displaying to the gaze of the surprised American a finely polished, silver-mounted skeleton. It was a thing of beauty—there was no grewsomeness[3] about it.

"There it is," laughed M. Roban, enjoying his friend's look of admiration. "There is Jacques—the most perfect skeleton in Paris. And that, as you have admitted, is saying a great deal. I had it polished and mounted to suit my most fastidious taste. Is it not a beauty—a work of art and nature combined?"

---

3 **grewsome** - *variant of* gruesome

"Whew!" ejaculated Tim, gazing in open-mouthed wonder and admiration at the perfect anatomical specimen. Then the American commercial instinct in him asserted itself, and he said: "Say, Roban, how much will you take for it?"

"Do you really desire to have it?" asked M. Roban in return.

"Certainly, or I would not have asked you to name a price."

"I will not sell it to you. Oh no! I could not do that. Jacques and I are old chums. But I will give it to you, if you will accept it."

The end of the matter was that when Tim Foley sailed for home two weeks later, he had M. Roban's peculiar gift disjointed and packed in the bottom of his trunk.

Arriving in New York, he fitted up a suite of office rooms in a downtown building, and entered upon the practice of his profession in earnest. He hung out his shingle in the shape of a brass door plate that bore the words, "Timothy Foley, M. D.," in modest letters, and sat down to wait for practice.

It was not long in coming, for the young physician was well known and well connected; besides he had the leverage that wealth lends to the happy possessor in a great city.

Jacques, the artistic skeleton, occupied a cabinet in Tim's office, similar to the one it had occupied in M. Roban's office: and was a source of pride and delight to the young disciple of Esculapius[4], and of terror to his comrades who dropped in on him occasionally.

After a few months Dr. Foley's services were in great demand, and he was slaving away as though his eternal welfare depended upon it. This fact surprised and gratified his friends. They had never expected it of Tim.

One dark and rainy evening he sat in his office. It was early November and the weather was cold and disagreeable. He had lost two night's sleep in succession, and felt worn out with severe mental and physical toil. He had dismissed the office boy for the night, and had made up his mind to retire early to secure a long night's rest, of which he was greatly in need. He looked at his watch and found that it was ten o'clock. He would glance over the latest medical journal, and then go to bed.

4 **Esculapius** – Roman god of healing

Removing his shoes, he incased his feet in a pair of office slippers, lighted a cigar and gave himself up to a half hour's enjoyment of book and weed. He had read but a few minutes when he heard a peculiar grating sound issuing from the cabinet that contained his Parisian skeleton. Turning his head hurriedly he was struck dumb with amazement and horror, to see the door of the cabinet swing open and Jacques step out!

Dr. Foley could not believe his eyes; and yet it was true—there was the skeleton standing by the door of the cabinet. Tim had boasted many times that he had not a grain of superstition in his composition—that he was a stranger to all superstitious fears. He had dissected alone in the deadhouse[5] at night, with rows of sheeted corpses as his only companions, and had felt no nervous tremors. But here was something of which he could give no scientific explanation, and he sat and trembled like a vulgar coward.

The skeleton carefully closed the door of the cabinet, walked around the end of the table and took his seat opposite the doctor. Nonchalantly throwing its leg over the arm of the chair it said in plain and unmistakable English: "Good evening." Then it carefully selected a cigar from the case that lay on the table, bit off the end with a click of its grinning teeth, and remarked:

"Well, doctor, you seem a little surprised and not over and above pleased, to have me step out to keep you company this evening. It's not a very cordial reception you're giving me, I must say. You're not afraid of me, are you? Why, you've handled me and fondled me, and called me an anatomical work of art, this many a day. And all the time you thought me the skeleton of some defunct Frenchman. But I'm not—Oh, Lord, no!"

It opened its fleshless jaws in a jerking, spasmodic way, and the chilly, cackling laugh that came from between them made Tim Foley shudder. Then it rolled the unlighted cigar between its white and glistening teeth, and resumed:

"I'm in a reminiscent, autobiographical mood tonight. This is the fifth anniversary of my death. I'm going to entertain you with a bit of personal history. There— there, you need to do none of the

____

5 **deadhouse** - morgue

talking. It's seldom that I get a chance to express myself nowadays, and I mean to improve my opportunity to the utmost."

The request for Foley to keep silence was entirely unnecessary. He could not have spoken nor stirred had his life depended upon it. Jacques, the skeleton shifted its position in the chair, went through the motion of twirling an imaginary mustache, and took up the thread of its discourse as follows: "Yes, you thought me a Frenchman just because you picked me up in Paris; but I'm a pure-bred American. I said I *am*—rather, I *was*. For this polished and mounted framework that you see is but a relic of my former self, and no source of gratification to me—as it has been to you. The worst of it is it isn't all my own! The man who mounted it threw away one of my leg bones, because it was slightly curved, and substituted another that he thought more shapely. Even the teeth in my head are borrowed ones, partly. And look at the name that they gave it—Jacques—Bah! But I *was* an *American*, and my name was Charles Percy.

"I was born and reared in Ohio, and graduated at a medical college in Cincinnati. My people were wealthy and I was their only child, consequently I was spoiled. I led a fast life while at college, but graduated with fair honors. After my graduation I began practice in a Western city, but soon gave it up and devoted my time and talents to the pursuit of pleasure. My mother died and I inherited her fortune. I drifted from one city to another, and finally gravitated to Paris. There I squandered the miserable remnant of my princely fortune. Broken down in body and mind by my excesses, I was on the point of starvation or suicide when my old father came across the ocean to try to reclaim me. He had heard of my degradation and poverty from an American tourist who had recognized me, while in Paris.

"My father wished me to accompany him home, but I could not bear the thought of leaving Paris. Besides, I did not wish to reform; I was too madly fascinated with the life I had been leading. Ah! but those were glorious days. I look back on them yet with regret and longing."

Here the skeleton sadly shook his shining skull, and a sigh seemed to well up from the depths of its hollow chest.

"Well, my father pleaded with me to return, but I would not consent. At last he grew angry and said: 'Stay here, then, and starve or rot in your infamy. I will not give you a penny.' And he shook a role of bank bills in my face. The sight of the money crazed me. I must have it. With a courage and strength born of greed and desperation, I caught up a heavy chair and struck him to the floor. The single blow fractured the skull and he lay dead before me. Taking his money and valuables I departed."

"This occurred at my apartments, two small rooms in an obscure corner of the city, that I had occupied but a few days. His body was not identified and I was not detected. The body was sent to the morgue, and there on the next day I went and saw it. I wasted the ill-gotten money in a few weeks. At last when sick and starving—without money, home or friends—I was sent to the hospital. M. Roban was the physician who attended me while I was there. A few days before my death I willed him my skeleton—this that you see before you."

The osseous[6] communicant bent its eyeless sockets as though surveying itself, crossed its lower limbs with a rattling flourish, and resumed:

"I meant to confess everything to him, for he was very kind to me; but death came unexpectedly. M. Roban had my skeleton mounted, as you know. He was very proud of it. But I could not rest—I must confess to him as I had intended. So on the second anniversary of my death—just such another night as this—I rehabited what then was left of my tenement of clay, and visited him and told him all.

"After that I was content 'till you brought my skeleton here; then I began to feel the old restlessness again, and knew that I would have no peace until I had communicated to you as I had to M. Roban.

"I have finished; and will go whence I came, after I have returned this frame to your cabinet. I have but one request to make. I want you to return my skeleton to Paris. I will be better satisfied. Good night; you would better get to bed. You look nervous and exhausted. You need have no fear; I will not return again to annoy you. Once more, good night."

____

6 **osseous** - composed of, containing, or resembling bone

It arose, took the dry and unlighted cigar from between its teeth, stretched its tall form and dropped its lower jaw in an apparent yawn, and started toward the cabinet. Reaching the end of the table it turned and said: "By the way this seems like a good cigar. I wish I might smoke it—I really do. But I'll leave it on the table here. See, it bears the imprint of my teeth. You may preserve it as conclusive proof, to yourself at least, that you have not been dreaming."

Without another word it passed on to the cabinet, stepped nimbly inside and closed the door.

Dr. Timothy Foley came to his feet with a bound. The fire in the grate had burned low and the room was cold, but this did not account for the chills that were chasing each other up and down his spine. His cigar had gone out, but it still remained between his lips. The book that he had been reading was still in his hand, and his index finger separated the leaves at the article in which he had been interested.

Had he been asleep? He had no remembrance of having been sleepy, nor did he feel as though he had just wakened. He walked over to the cabinet, opened the door boldly and looked in. The innocent-looking and inanimate skeleton hung in its place, supported by a brass ring in its skull. Tim closed the door with a bang and started toward his chair. A casual glance at the table almost took his breath away. There lay the tooth indented cigar that he had seen Jacques place there! It was no dream, then, but a reality.

The next day he sent the following cablegram "Julius Roban. Paris, France:—Do you know anything of the person whose skeleton you gave me?—T. Foley."

And this was the odd and startling reply he received: "Timothy Foley, M. D., New York, U. S.—So Charles Percy has communicated with you. I expected it. Will answer in full by mail.—Jules Roban."

M. Roban's letter, that arrived a few weeks later, gave the story of Charles Percy's life, word for word, almost, as Dr. Foley had already heard it. The letter closed thus:—"Do not part with the skeleton. If you do not care to keep it longer, ship it back to me. The reason I gave it to you was that I felt that Charles Percy would communicate with you, if you had his skeleton in your possession. He had revealed himself to me on the second anniversary of his death, and I wanted to see if he would tell his story to you. I wanted my own experience confirmed. I was not at all surprised when I received your cablegram: and I am so positive that he has visited you that I am scarcely impatient to receive your letter. I have hunted up a number of his acquaintances here, and find that the story he tells is true, so far as they know. It is a very interesting case. Write me full particulars of your experience."

The communicative skeleton once more crossed the Atlantic. Its presence in his office was too much for Tim Foley's nerves, and he never rested until it was safely on shipboard, bound for France.

—◆◆◆—

Did It Pay?

Chapter I

It was October when Dr. John Jeffrys came to Smalleyville. The country roads were hard-packed and dusty, and the parched earth was panting and longing for the cool autumnal rains. The forest trees upon the river hills were clad in gold and russet garments, and the flaming crimson of the sumac bushes made bright the copses and ravines. The airy thistle seeds danced and eddied along the highway, and the plumed goldenrod nodded in a neighborly fashion to the ripening pawpaws and rustling hazelnuts across the roadside fence. One perfect golden day succeeded another, and the rosy hours slipped by uncounted, as they always do.

Long lines of farm wagons, laden with fall fruit or grain, rattled and rumbled along the dust-white road, on their way to the village to discharge their burdens; for Smalleyville lay in the center of a rich agricultural and fruit region.

The country for miles and miles around the village was a broken and hilly upland, and the hills bounding the narrow valley in which the village lay were high and precipitous, though the upland as well as the valleys were fertile.

The little town had a personality all its own. For, while being a typical western town in many respects, it lacked much of the bustle and energy of the genuine article, and had about it a mild flavor of lassitude and decay that belongs to all truly rural places.

It had a straggling and unkept appearance, too, because of the fact that it occupied both sides of the ribbon-like river zig-zagged its way through the beautiful valley in which the village was situated. The two parts of the town seemed a pair of ragged Siamese twins, connected by an old, covered wooden bridge, a vital link—as it were—that creaked and groaned in every gale and appeared in danger of breaking in two, and leaving them forever asunder[1]. The pretty little river, that kissed and embraced the feet of the crazy and moss-grown piers, was made navigable for small steamboats by means of a system of dams and locks.

These twins, however, were not of equal size nor of equal importance. Smalleyville proper, the smaller of the twins, but the more important in many ways, occupied the right bank of the river; and if not so large as its birthmate, was more compactly built and more robust and vigorous. It contained within it circumscribed limits the postoffice, the railroad station—Smalleyville had one short-line railroad—the steamboat warehouses, the principal stores and business houses, and last, but not least, the one manufacturing plant of the place.

East Smalleyville, or Castleton, as it had been called before the villages were united under one government, the larger twin, was linear, loose-jointed and ugly. It could boast of the county court-house, a dilapidated town hall, and a few grocery stores and saloons, only.

There was a marked difference, also, in the disposition and morals of these inanimate twins, or more properly, perhaps, of their inhabitants, Smalleyville was moral, religious—in a puritanical way, severe and exacting. East Smalleyville, on the other hand, was more "liberal minded," as it was pleased to call it, and more given to pleasure and good-fellowship. The society of Smalleyville was select and exclusive; that of East Smalleyville, cosmopolitan and easy-going.

A sort of bitter-sweet feud had existed between these near and dear relatives of opposite characteristics, from time out of mind. Sometimes it was of so mild a type as to show itself in the shape of good-natured rivalry, only; at other times it presented itself as the keenest jealousy and the most unreasonable and obstinate opposition, and at rare intervals degenerated into petty quarrels and personal encounters.

It was October, then, when Dr. Jeffrys came to Smalleyville, and the wag of gossiping tongues created quite a ripple of excitement in the sluggish current of the staid little place. Not that it was

---

1 **asunder -** into separate parts or piece

an unusual thing for the village to have a doctor, for it had been the fortunate possessor of quite a number in its time, three or four of whom still remained to bless it with their presence and their services. But Dr. Jeffrys was a *young* man, comparatively, and there seemed to be an air of mystery about him and his coming that was irresistibly fascinating to the average gossip—male or female.

He seemed to have dropped down as swiftly and silently as a snowflake, from nobody knew where: or to have sprung up in the night, after the manner of the proverbial toadstool—the gossips could not say. At any rate he was there, and apparently he was there to stay.

He sent no herald to announce his coming. The first intimation the community had of his presence was when a modest gilt sign, bearing the words:

JOHN JEFFRYS, M. D.
— OFFICE. —

appeared at the entrance of the stairway leading to the second floor of a large frame building on the principal street. This building was situated in the center of the business portion of Smalleyville. The lower story was occupied by a dry goods store on the one side, and by a bookstore on the other. The second story had long been vacant. It was partitioned into several rooms, two of which fronted the street. A hallway, the termination of the stairway leading from the street, separated them.

The door at the street entrance leading to the stairway had been closed and locked. When the villagers noticed that it was open and that workmen were going in and out, it occasioned some passing comments; but very little interest was taken in the matter until that modest gilt sign challenged attention and inquiry.

Then the tongues began to wag in earnest, and many were the questions asked, and the problems propounded were legion. But the answers given or guessed were very unsatisfactory. "Whence did he come? Is he married or single? How old is he? Has he ever practiced before? Is he a regular practitioner, or only a traveling quack come for a temporary stay?" These and a hundred other knotty questions were offered for solution, but only the fall wind, as it whistled about the streets and gables and twisted the smoke and dust into fantastic wreaths and clouds, made any reply and that was a mocking one.

This much was gleaned from sources more or less reliable: that his name was John Jeffrys—his sign said so, but of course the name might be an assumed one; that he slept in one of the three rooms that he had fitted up for office purposes—at least the workmen aforesaid stated that he took his meals at the "Baldwin House"—this was gleaned from the landlord himself, and was certainly reliable; that he had a diploma of some sort, for an inquisitive, bare-legged urchin had discovered it at the noon hour when the workmen were at dinner—but then it *might* be a forged one; and that he was twenty-eight to thirty-five years old.

That was all, and little enough it was; sufficient only to whet their appetites for more.

Let us arrive at once at the real truth about Dr. Jeffrys. He was thirty-two years old, single, and an orphan; a studious, rather quiet but not uncommunicative man, caring little for fashion, folly or society, but wedded to his chosen profession—and in love with his wife. He was a graduate of two high-grade medical colleges and a practical, matter-of-fact physician of five years' experience. He had a passion for science in any and all of its branches, and loved nature with a love that was inborn and beyond his control. His one relaxation—his one recreation was literature; and he devoted to it such moments as he could steal from his professional studies and duties. He indulged in no sport, neither hunted nor fished; true, he rode a wheel, but that was for business and not for pleasure.

In personal appearance he was preposessing; fair complexioned and, dark-blue eyed, and of medium height and weight. He wore his brown hair and beard neatly trimmed, and was genteelly and appropriately dressed at all times.

He was kind and forgiving in his nature, but hated a lie, a deception and an unjust deed, as the prime prince of hades is supposed to hate holy water.

In five years of practice in a far western territory he had done a great deal of hard work and gained a world of valuable experience;

but he had failed to accumulate much money. He had come to Smalleyville with the hope of bettering his material fortunes.

Such was John Jeffrys, M. D.; a quiet, self-reliant man, having a vein of quaint humor blended with natural common sense and obstinacy of purpose. He had the courage to fight his own battles and to express his own opinions; and the self-reliance and self-restraint to keep his own counsel—qualities that were sure, sooner or later, to make him cordially respected, and cordially hated, in any community.

Dr. Jeffrys had never been in Smalleyville until the morning train rolled into the station, on that fateful October day; but he had heard of the town through a friend, and fancied it would be a suitable location for a young and energetic physician.

One of his reasons for coming was, that Smalleyville being a manufacturing town in a small way, would have considerable money in circulation at all times; while being removed from the great manufacturing centers, it would not be subject to frequent strikes and consequent depressions of business. Another and more potent reason was that having a rich agricultural and fruit country at its back, it would be fed and fostered by its rural surroundings and kept at high tide of prosperity.

For a week following the doctor's arrival in the village, boxes and packing cases in respectable numbers were unloaded in front of his door, and quickly removed up the yawning stairway. The drayman[2] reported to the outside world that "that new doctor's a flingin' on a heap o' style with carpets on the rooms an' pictur's on the wall an' great big bookcases full o' books an' a chair that you can tilt anyway with a crank, an' drawers runnin' over with shiny instruments." He said all this with a wink and a deprecating shake of the head, too; and then he climbed up on his dray, clucked encouragingly to his wheezy team and drove away.

Saturday evening was a gala hour of the week in Smalleyville. It was then the Smalleyville-Cranston Plow Factory closed at four o'clock, and its workmen were on the streets and in the places of

---

2 **drayman** - the driver of a dray, a low, flat-bed wagon without sides, pulled generally by horses or mules

business, dressed in holiday attire; then, two, the neighboring farmers came to market to buy supplies for the coming week.

On a certain Saturday evening, shortly following Dr. Jeffrys' advent, a number of men were chatting on the corner, in front of Kirby's grocery.

"So you've got a new doctor in town," said Farmer Inslip, a fat, good-natured man who lived on the Quakertown road, two miles out.

"Yes," replied one of the factory hands as he squirmed himself into a comfortable position on the horse-block[3], "but he won't stay long."

"Think not, why?"

"Well, I don't see what he wanted to come here fer, in the first place. 'Taint no place fer new doctor; w'y we've got two on this side of the river and one on the other all ready. Ain't that enough? I don't see what he wanted to come fer."

"Wanted to come to practice medicine, I s'pose," said Farmer Inslip dryly.

"Course; but as I say, 'taint no place fer a new doctor. W'y there's ol' Doc Brady on the other side, been there twenty year an' only jest makes a livin'; an' ol' Doc Hooker on this side—practiced here thirty years if he has a day. H'aint got nothin' to show fer it but a house an' lot, a crippled horse an' a pair o' shiny saddlebags. Young Doc Munsey ain't doin' no good. Don't have much to do nohow, and couldn't git nothing fer it, if he did. We don't need no more doctors an' 'taint no place fer 'em."

Farmer Inslip not caring to continue the conversation longer, apparently, turned himself around and went into the grocery; but another farmer standing near took up the cudgel[4] that Inslip had dropped. "I don't see why it ain't a good place for another doctor," he ventured; "ther's a rich country 'round here an' it pays good, even if 'tis a little slow comin'."

"That may be so, fer's the country's concerned," answered the factory hand, "but us poor devils that works for Smalley-Cranston

---

3 **horse-block** - step or block of stone, wood, etc., for getting on or off a horse or in or out of a vehicle

4 **took up the cudgel** - joined in a dispute, esp to defend oneself or another

don't never have enough to make a decent livin', let alone payin' doctor bills; an' we git sick jest as often as anybody. If we git one week behind, we can't never ketch up—ther' ain't no use tryin'. Course I don't mean to say that ther' ain't some that *wouldn't* pay nothin', even if they *could*; but the most of us is honest—only we don't make enough to be honest *on*."

"Well," responded the farmer, "I don't know as we'll do much better'n you fellers, this year, about payin' our bills. You see, the p'tater crop's a total failure, a'most, on account o' the drouth; an' corn won't be worth nothin' at all. The wheat was purty good, but it don't pay to raise it no more on account o' the price." Then drifting back to the original subject, he continued: "still I contend that this ought to be a good place fer a new doctor. W'y we've only got one young doctor—that's Doc Munsey—an' our ol' ones has jest about seen the'r best day. Seems to me a young doctor ought to do well here. Them ol' fellers 'll have to quit ridin' purty soon—ought to quit now by rights."

"Yes, that's all true enough," admitted the factory hand, rising and yawning, "but the troubles right here. They've got nothin' to live on, if they quit practicin', an' so they'll go on as long as they can. An' we'll employ 'em,, too; fer they've been mighty good to us poor folks, waitin' on us and our families, time and ag'in, when we hadn't a cent to pay 'em—an' they knowed it. Most of us owes 'em big bills an' we feel like we ought to keep on employin' 'em an' pay 'em a dollar whenever we can. Young Doc Munsey's been here sever'l years now, an' people ain't took up with him no great sight, yit. I don't see how this feller expects to make a livin'."

The same evening, the drayman's wife, Mrs. Waldoner, entered the drug store to make a trifling purchase. A small, nervous, fussy woman was Mrs. Waldoner. "By the way," she broke in on the druggist, as he was extolling the merits of the article she had just bought, "has the new doctor been in to see you! If he has, he didn't buy anything, I'll be bound. My husband says he's fixing things up grand over in that old den—wouldn't know it was the same place. Says he has dead loads of instruments and books, and that he keeps his own medicines—bushels of them! Yes, and I think he will keep them in this town, that he'll not get anything to do, I am sure."

Mr. Ashmore, the druggist, a pale scant-haired man of uncertain age and rapid, jerky manner and speech, wiped his nose vigorously, and pulling savagely at his light mustache, said hurriedly: "Yes, yes—been in once or twice—came in to get some bottles and corks—green fellow, very. Keeps his own medicines—yes, yes— won't do any good here—too high-toned—too high-toned entirely. Surly-like, too—strange man, very."

"Why don't he want to write prescriptions as the others doctors do? I think they should all patronize their home store. Why, even Dr. Brady, over the river, buys his drugs from you; don't he, Mr. Ashmore?"

As Mrs. Waldoner said this, she turned to go; but the druggist followed her to the door with—"Yes, yes – Brady's all right—good practitioner, very. Dr. Jeffrys don't know enough to write prescriptions, perhaps—takes a scholar, you know. Not scholar enough, undoubtedly—not scholar enough."

Dr. Jeffrys was in blissful ignorance of the stir that he was causing in this small hive of industry, and of the fact, also, that he was viewed as a most unwelcome interloper.

He had not called on his brother physicians, as yet, although he knew that the code of ethics required him to do so. He thought he had, thus far, a valid excuse for not having done so. He had been very busy receiving his goods and arranging his office. But now that all his things were in order—that his net was set and he was waiting only for some venturesome fly to stray into it—he felt that he could postpone the disagreeable duty no longer. It was something that he disliked very much to do. He thought that they would receive him politely and bid him welcome with their lips; but he knew that, at the same time, they would wish him in Guinea—or some other climate equally warm.

He called first upon the oldest physician in the village, Dr. Samuel Hooker. The old gentleman was stooped, white-haired and in an advanced stage of senility. His office was a front room of his dwelling, a neat frame cottage on a side street, back toward the hills.

Dr. Jeffrys introduced himself, and Dr. Hooker shook his hand in a weak, childish way. He had but little to say, but expressed his willingness to give up all his practice to Dr. Jeffrys, if the latter would pay him handsomely for his "goodwill." In the same breath, almost, in answer to the question, "Has your practice proven remunerative?" He answered emphatically: "No! I have made a living—that's all. You'll do well to do as much."

This was not a flattering prospect, to be sure, but Dr. Jeffrys was not discouraged. He smiled an amused smile as he left the dingy and stuffy office, followed by the older man's parting favor. "If you get into deep water with any of your cases, let me know and I will do my best to help you out."

Jeffrys wended his way down the street and across the rickety wooden bridge, toward East Smalleyville. He was going to call upon Dr. James Brady.

Dr. Brady's office and residence were at the far end of East Smalleyville, so Dr. Jeffrys had a hot and dusty tramp. "I wish my wheel were here," he muttered to himself, "but these people, no doubt, would think it beneath the dignity of the physician to ride one." When he arrived at Dr. Brady's, he found that the gentleman was on a trip to the country. Mrs. Brady evidently mistook him for a transient patient; she said her husband would return in an hour and insisted on Jeffrys waiting. Telling her his name and requesting her to inform Dr. Brady that he had called, he retraced his steps to Smalleyville and called upon Dr. Eugene S. Munsey.

Dr. Munsey was a married man, as were Dr. Hooker and Dr. Brady. He lived just off the main street, around the corner from Dr. Jeffrys' office. He was at home. His office was a small weatherboarded building—that had at one time served as a cobbler shop— and consisted of one poorly furnished room. The residence stood somewhat back from the street, as though to give the office a chance to show off its natural and acquired ugliness to best advantage. The latter was entirely separate from the house and stood flush with the flag-paved sidewalk.

The door of the office stood wide open, and the autumn leaves that had drifted in were scattered about the bare floor.

Seeing a man inside, engaged in the apparently futile effort to extract a cork from a bottle, Jeffrys guessed that it was Dr. Munsey and walked in. The latter stood with his back to the door and was not aware of the other's presence until he coughed to attract his attention. Then he turned around and motioned Jeffrys to a seat.

"I am the new doctor," said the latter, when seated, "and have come to pay you a call that I hope may lead to a pleasant and lasting acquaintance."

"I'm glad to meet you, doctor."—and Dr. Munsey shook hands quite heartily—"wait till I get this confounded cork out and I'll talk to you. Business before pleasure, you know." Accomplishing this, he placed the bottle on an oilcloth-covered table that stood at one side of the room, sat down and resumed: "Well, how do you like Smalleyville, by this time?"

"I have been here so short a time and have seen so little of the place and the people, that I can scarcely say that I have formed an opinion. Still, I must own that my first impression is not very favorable."

"Neither was mine: and my last impression is much more unfavorable. If I had the money to get away on, I wouldn't stay here twenty-four hours. You'll soon get heart-sick of it as I have. However, I wish you success and I'm glad that you have come. Maybe both of us can do what I have failed to do alone: make it so warm for these old doctors—or rather dotards[5]—that they will be glad to give up the field and the fight. I have been trying for three years, now, to make folks understand that these old fogies don't know anything, but I can't say that my success has been very marked. Many of the people owe them and still persist in employing them, although they will admit that the old men are behind the times."

Dr. Munsey's black eyes snapped as he said this, and he toyed with his watch chain nervously. Dr. Jeffrys saw that he was very frank and very much in earnest.

"If, instead of trying to show that the old doctors do not know anything, you had spent your time in showing that *you do* know something, how would it have been, do you think?" inquired Jeffrys, with a half smile.

---

5 **dotard** - an old person, esp. one who has become weak or senile

Dr. Munsey laughed. "The people here are not inclined to give a newcomer a chance to show what he does or does not know. They are very cautious and conservative, I have found. It's hard to convince them against their will. I hope you may be more successful than I have been—I do, really; but I don't believe you will. You can't honey around people any better than I can, and you will find out that it takes lots of flattery and coaxing to get practice here."

"Then I will not get it," asserted Jeffrys hotly: "it is not in me to play the fawning sycophant[6], and I hate all double dealing."

"You'll never succeed in the practice of medicine in this place," said Dr. Munsey, with a shake of his head, as Dr. Jeffrys arose to go; "you are entirely too independent. The people will not tolerate that."

Dr. John Jeffrys returned to his office musing. If all—or half—that he had heard were true, he had located in a veritable grave-yard of dead hopes. "The choice of a physician, with most people, is a matter of preference and not of merit. Still, I hold that merit must win in the end. If I possess the requisite medical knowledge and skill, I am bound to succeed—even in Smalleyville. I am not ready to give up the fight until I'm thoroughly convinced that I am whipped; and the fight is but just begun." Resolving this, he took a book from the case and was soon lost in the intricacies of an abstruse surgical subject.

Two months winged their flight, and Dr. Jeffrys still lacked that necessary adjunct to the successful doctor—a patient.

Chapter II

The beautiful autumn waned and vanished, and with it the gorgeous fall flowers and leaves, and sunshiny weather. It was December, and one dismal, rainy day succeeded another with persistent regularity.

All through the fine fall months Dr. Jeffrys had sat in his office. Occasionally, of an evening, he had taken a spin on his wheel through the village or along the pleasant river road. He had purchased a horse and cart and—as he expressed it to himself—all he

6 **sycophant** - a person who overly flatters someone in authority for personal gain

needed was a number of paying patients. He wanted practice; he was sick of theory. He wished to get out into the field and fight disease, asking no favors and giving no quarter.

So far he had been doomed to disappointment. He had had two or three callers at his office, but none of them had come for professional advice or treatment. A life insurance agent had ventured in one evening, but owing to the frigidity that seemed to pervade the office, he had not tarried long; a countryman had put his head in the door to inquire how much the doctor charged for pulling teeth—or rather, if he pulled them for nothing; and Mr. Lane, the dry goods merchant beneath him, had called through courtesy. "Is there anything I can do to make things more pleasant for you?" Mr. Lane had inquired.

"Yes," Jeffrys had answered, with a humorous light in his blue eyes.

"What shall it be, doctor?"

"Bring me a half dozen patients of assorted sizes."

Mr. Lane had laughed heartily at this sally[7]. "I don't believe I can do it, doctor; but don't be discouraged; they'll come after a while, never fear." Then after a short pause he said: "I do believe, doctor, it would be a good thing for you to go into the church and one or more of the secret societies; you would get acquainted faster and make more friends."

"In other words, you would have me act the hypocrite in order to gain a livelihood."

"No, I do not mean that, exactly. I think it would be an advantage to you in many ways."

"But I take no interest in such matters—or but very little—and surely you would not have me become a member of the church or lodge through selfish motives, wholly. I care absolutely nothing for society; it is not my nature. I love to sit and talk to a friend or two, but a crowd I abhor. I seem to be lost in it, and always feel strange and ill at ease."

"You must overcome that feeling," Mr. Lane insisted. "Our people are a church and society people and they will expect you to come out among them."

---

7 **sally** – quick retort

Just then the clerk had come to tell Mr. Lane that he was wanted at the store, and so the conversation had dropped.

Jeffrys often thought over this conversation, but every time came to the same decision. "I cannot do it," he would resolve. "I cannot and will not belittle myself in my own estimation and sacrifice my personal independence to gain favor with this people. I have no war to make on church or secret society; they are all right, undoubtedly; but I will never join either because I think it will help me in a professional way."

In the meantime the report had been circulated that Dr. Jeffrys was an atheist and a disbeliever in secret societies. Coupled with this had gone another—much more damaging in certain circles—to the effect that he was a confirmed "woman hater." Had Jeffrys but known half the absurd tales that were going, he must have despaired utterly.

The other doctors came and went on their rounds; even old Dr. Hooker, growing more and more feeble day by day, occasionally jogged past in this cart. Jeffrys chafed inwardly, but outwardly he gave no sign.

One dark and rainy night in early December, he sat in his office reading—reading until his eyes ached and his brain whirled. He had little to do in rough weather except to eat and sleep and read. It was a lonely existence, but he was used to it.

The rain swept in sheets against the window panes, and the wind shook the loose sash as it whistled and howled down the deserted street. The sheet-iron roof overhead creaked and boomed, and the sound echoed and reverberated like successive volleys of artillery. Dr. Jeffrys threw down his book, went to the window and looked out. Nothing was visible but an unbroken wall of intense blackness. Up on the corner by the bank, a smoky street lamp winked and swayed in a drunken manner. It seemed trying to peer into the darkness beyond the diminutive circle of light that it shed around. Jeffrys looked at his watch and muttered: "What a howling wilderness of rain and darkness it is! The wind sounds like the wail of a lost soul." The courthouse clock across the river began to strike the hour; one, two—eleven times. "Enough of this, I will go to bed," and he turned from the window; but just then he caught the glimmer of a lantern coming down the street, on the opposite side. It drew nearer and nearer, crossed the street, and he saw the muffled figure that bore it stop at the entrance to his stairway. Then came a heavy tread upon the stairs and presently a knock on the door. Dr. Jeffrys advanced and opened it. "Come in," he said.

The man—for such the muffled figure proved to be—divested himself of his dripping mackintosh, and standing his umbrella in a corner, came in and took a chair. Jeffrys knew him for Col. William Cranston, president and chief stockholder of the Smalley-Cranston Plow company. He was a large, dark man, about 45 years old, of military bearing, with keen gray eyes, square and heavy lower jaw, and iron-gray hair and beard—closely cropped.

"Can I be of service to you, Col. Cranston?" inquired the doctor when the former was seated.

"So you know me, then," came the unexpected reply.

"Yes, sir, I have had you pointed out to me as Col. Cranston of the Smalley-Cranston firm, but I have never had the honor of meeting you."

"And you are Dr. John Jeffrys?"

"I am."

"How long have you been here, doctor?"

"Over two months."

"Are you succeeding in building up the practice?"

"I have not had a patient."

Col. Cranston did not seem to be surprised at the younger man's frank admission. Jeffrys did not feel like resenting the older man's catechism[8]; he did not know why. Starting suddenly, Col. Cranston arose and said: "I must not forget my errand. I want you to come up to my house. My sister is suffering from a bad attack of neuralgia."

Jeffrys tried hard to conceal his gratification. He put his case of medicines into his pocket, donned his storm coat and hat, and expressed himself as ready to go. Out into the night they went; up the

---

8 **catechism** - a series of fixed questions, answers, or precepts used for instruction in other situations

sloppy street, guiding their steps by the faint light of the swinging lantern.

Col. Bill Cranston, as he was called in a familiar way by the town people, lived in a large brick house, half way up the hill back of the factory of which he was the directing spirit. The house was an old one, but had been altered and improved to satisfy modern utility and taste. The grounds surrounding it were ample and well kept; and the interior of the house finished and furnished in keeping with wealth and refinement. The village folk facetiously called the residence "Col. Bill's mansion in the skies," because of its exalted situation; and some of the more outspoken would add: "he'd better make much of it, it's the only one he'll ever see!"

Col. Cranston's family consisted of himself; his daughter—Ms. Mabel Cranston, a lovable, intelligent girl of twenty-four; and his maiden sister—Miss. Ellen Cranston, who was his housekeeper. His wife died when Mabel was a baby, and "Aunt Ellen" was all the mother the girl had ever known.

As Col. Cranston and Dr. Jeffrys proceeded, the former gave the latter an outline of Aunt Ellen's case. Then he continued: "Dr. Hooker has been our family physician for years. He is a nice old man and all of that, and has been a good doctor, but he is worn out in the service. I have been thinking of changing doctors for some time, but could not see where I could better myself until you came. I listened to all the idle reports about you and decided that you are the man I want. I have known all about you since you came to Smalleyville, and I admire personal independence and manly courage. It is hard to give up our old doctor, I admit; he has seemed like one of the family. I started to go for him tonight, but I thought it was too stormy to call the old fellow out, and so I resolved to come for you and make the change at once. I could have sent a servant for you, but I thought I could fetch you more quickly myself."

As they entered the hall, Mabel Cranston came hurrying to them. "Oh! I am so glad you have come, father; Aunt Ellen has been suffering so terribly." Then perceiving that it was not Dr. Hooker that had accompanied her father, but a young man and a stranger, she paused and hesitated.

"Dr. Jeffrys, this is my daughter, Mabel," explained Col. Cranston, simply. Mabel held out her hand; Jeffrys shook it and hastily followed her father into the presence of the patient.

Miss Ellen Cranston was a frail, sweet-faced woman of forty, the feminine counterpart of her soldierly brother. She lay on the broad sofa in the parlor and was moaning with pain, when the doctor entered.

"How are you feeling by this time, Ellen? I have brought you the new doctor—Dr. Jeffrys," was Col. Cranston's greeting.

As Jeffrys gave her directions how the medicine was to be given, he had a chance to observe her closely, without appearing rude, and his mental comment was: "Mabel Cranston is a most beautiful woman."

When he left the house the owner followed him to the door and said: "Come up to see her in the morning. You are to be our family physician. Here! Take this lantern with you. Good night."

Dr. Jeffrys hastened toward his office, his mind in a tumult of excitement. It was raining still. Just as he crossed the street in front of his own door, a man stepped out from the shelter of the doorway, and said: "Are you Dr. Jeffrys? I was just upstairs huntin' yon. They want you out to Inslip's on the Quakertown road, right away, quick as you can come." Jeffrys understood. "'It never rains but it pours,' is true in a double sense tonight," he muttered as he went for his horse.

At four o'clock in the morning he returned, wet and weary, and went to bed for an hour or two's sleep; and while dropping off into dreamland he murmured: "A most beautiful woman!"

＊　＊　＊　＊

From this time onward Dr. Jeffrys' bowl was right side up, and it rained porridge; at first in scattered drops, anon[9] in fitful showers, and at last in a steady downpour—a deluge. The report soon went abroad in the village that Col. Bill Cranston had given up old Dr. Hooker and was employing Dr. Jeffrys. This was enough to ensure the latter a steady increasing patronage; for in Smalleyville what-

---

9　**anon** - archaic english word meaning soon; presently

ever Col. Cranston advocated was adopted, and whatever he supported, succeeded.

By the middle of January Dr. Hooker was too feeble to go longer, and dropping out of the race, was left like a worn-out cart-horse to starve by the wayside; this left the course to the younger men, Munsey and Jeffrys, and the latter had the inside track with a fair chance of winning everything in sight and out of sight.

Dr. Brady's practice was confined almost entirely to the east side, and he cut a small figure in the real struggle. Pneumonia was epidemic in the town and surrounding country, and Dr. Jeffrys was having good success in the treatment of his cases. He bought another horse and sleigh, and went day and night, often without sleep for nights in succession, and with irregular meals or none at all. His robust constitution, hardened by five years of toil and exposure in the west, stood him in good stead, and he appeared never to tire.

The stories about his religious and social beliefs were apparently forgotten; nor did any seem to question the advisability of employing him on the score that he was a single man. An entire revolution of feeling had taken place, it seemed, in this short time. The people found that Jeffrys was a well-equipped physician, and employed him; but he was not of them and they resented it. They considered him "stuck up," and hated him accordingly.

Dr. Munsey had been quite friendly to the new arrival, until he saw that Jeffrys was outstripping him in the race; then he became surly, jealous and revengeful. He attempted to injure his rival's growing reputation and practice in every way he could; but when public opinion once heads in a certain direction, it takes no small obstacle to deflect it from its course.

Dr. Munsey soon found that, so far as himself was concerned, the fight was one of *de*fense and not of *off*ense. He had all that he could do to hold what he had; and he did not care to loosen his grip for a moment, for fear of losing it entirely. But secretly he schemed and studied and planned how he might work injury to Dr. Jeffrys.

It was winter—and winter in earnest. The snow lay many inches deep in the valley, and was drifted into weird, grotesque shapes upon the hill slopes and along the country roads.

Sleds and sleighs crowded the streets of Smalleyville through the day, and the tinkle of sleigh bells was heard far into the starry night. The river had frozen over after the fall of snow, and the glassy ice was black with merry skaters of both sexes and all ages. Near the boat landing, on the Smalleyville side, the local ice-men were taking out ice; and the opening thus left frozen over each night, but hardly thick enough to bear a skater's weight. As Dr. Jeffrys was returning from the country one day, he saw the skaters congregated about the margin of the thin ice, and he knew by their gesticulations and outcries that someone had gotten into the river. Putting whip to his horse, he dashed down the steep grade and along the icy street, in his light sleigh. Reaching the river bank, he jumped out and without waiting to secure the horse, ran out on the ice to the scene of the commotion. At one glance he took in the situation; the people had lost their heads and were making no concerted effort to rescue the unfortunate skater.

"Have you a rope?" cried the doctor. "Yes, Doc, here is one, but she can't hold onto it—she's too near gone."

Jeffrys took a look at the figure clinging to the thin ice, fifty feet from any solid support. He saw that it was a woman and—Mabel Cranston! She was nearly exhausted, clinging feebly to the frail and treacherous ice. It was apt to break down with her at any time. All but her head and shoulders were submerged in the icy waters, and her teeth were chattering with cold. He must act quickly. Taking the rope proffered him, he deftly made a running noose in it, coiled it quickly, and pushing back the crowd by main force, he called out to the shivering girl: "Keep up your courage—be quiet—and do as I bid you. Hold on to the ice with your right arm without changing your position, and raise your left high above your head."

She made an effort to obey him. Up went the left arm slowly, and heavily. Her teeth were set and her face was rigid white.

"There! keep that position just a minute—your life depends on it." There was a hurtling "swish" as the wet rope flew through the air, uncoiling as it went, and the people, straining forward breathlessly, saw the noose settle gracefully over Mabel Cranston's head and shoulder. Dr. Jeffrys pulled lightly to tighten the noose, and then he said quickly, and sternly: "Put your arm to your side and keep it there." Calling two young men from the crowd he hissed through his shut teeth: "Keep cool; pull gently, firmly, steadily—whatever happens." In a minute more he had the unconscious form of the young lady in his sleigh and was driving like mad toward her home.

In a few hours Mabel was out of danger, but it was several weeks before she recovered completely from the effects of her icy bath. Dr. Jeffrys made daily visits to see her and was sorry—in one sense—when he saw that she needed no further treatment. "I think you will get along nicely now," he remarked one evening, "and shall discontinue my visits."

"You must come to see us," she answered, "even if we do not need your professional services. You saved my life and I can never tell you how grateful I am—you must come up frequently. Father and Aunt Ellen enjoy your conversations so much and"—after a pause and a slight flush—"so do I."

"Thank you," replied Jeffrys; "I appreciate your invitation very much and will surely come."

He did so; and those fleeting hours, spent in the old Cranston mansion with the beautiful dark-haired girl and her father, were the happiest he had ever known. He learned to look forward to them; they were little glimpses of paradise to his starving soul. He did not try to analyze his feelings; the experience was too sweet and precious for that.

One Sunday afternoon in conversation with Col. Cranston, Jeffrys mentioned his father's name.

"Robert Jeffrys did you say?" The Col. asked quickly.

"Yes, my father's name was Robert."

"There was a private in my regiment named Robert Jeffrys. He was a good soldier and a brave man. He saved my life on one occasion by risking his own. Poor fellow! He was killed at Missionary Ridge."

"My father was killed at that place."

"He was! To what regiment did he belong."

Dr. Jeffrys told him. "The same man, "said Col. Cranston, "and he saved my life. I am deeply indebted to your family, Jeffrys—to you as its sole representative. There is little that I would not do for you, my boy." Jeffrys saw that tears stood in the elder man's eyes. The younger man started violently; an idea had occurred to him that had never entered his mind before.

* * * *

All through the winter Dr. Jeffrys' practice grew. Whenever he could spare the time, he was rather a frequent caller at the Cranston mansion. He had made few other friends in the village, and he went out in company scarcely at all. The villagers noted his visits to the Cranston's, and in their familiar way began to link his name with that of Mable Cranston. Jeffrys heard this—for a wonder—and entered into a searching self-analysis.

The result of the matter was what he might have expected. He discovered that he loved Mabel Cranston—loved her passionately. But what was her feeling towards him? He could not tell. She seemed pleased, always, to have him come, and found fault with him when he staid away longer than usual; but perhaps it was gratitude only— a sense of duty. Perhaps she felt under obligations to him for the service he had rendered her. He would not have it so. He longed to know if she loved him. But of course she did not! Why should she?

Spring came. Hard times had prevailed through the winter, and as spring approached they grew even more stringent. The Smalley-Cranston factory was running "full time," but the wages paid were small and the workmen were compelled to practice the most rigid economy to keep the wolf from the door. Many of them were deeply in debt. There had been a great deal of sickness in their families during the cold season, and their doctor's bills remain unpaid—in the main.

Dr. Jeffrys learned all this to his surprise and sorrow. He needed money but found it impossible to collect what was due him. He knew the reason and it irritated him. He considered that the workmen were treated unfairly. The Smalley-Cranston company ought to pay them living wages. They could afford to do so, he was sure. Sometimes he was on the point of speaking to Col. Cranston about the matter; but he knew the nature of the man—knew that he would brook no interference with what he considered his private business—and feared the result. Was he becoming cowardly, then? He was afraid so.

Jeffrys had learned much of Col. Cranston's history. The colonel was a nephew of G. W. Smalley, deceased, the founder of the factory and the man for whom the village had been named. He had come out of the army with a little money, and his uncle had taken him into the business as a partner. Under the efficient management of the nephew, the factory had grown in wealth and prosperity. On the death of Mr. Smalley a stock company had been organized, and Col. Cranston had been chosen president. He was a man of endurance, energy and business sagacity; and in twenty-five years had amassed a large fortune.

He was not a hard or cruel man. In fact, he had been considered public-spirited and charitable; but he thought he had a legal and moral right to hire men at any price he could. He had followed out his belief until it had become a fixed principle with him—and he was a rod of iron, not easily bent or swayed.

Of late there had been a great deal of grumbling and dissatisfaction among the factory hands. They pointed to the fact that Col. Cranston had made a fortune in the factory and that they had made a bare living. These mutterings of the approaching storm grew and spread. Affairs were fast coming to a crisis at Smalley-Cranston's.

Chapter III

The clock of the year had made one-forth revolution and the hand upon the seasons dial pointed to early summer. The flowers were in full bloom, the trees in full leaf and the gentle breezes fragrant and balmy. The flocks were mating, the birds were courting and caressing the honeyed blossoms. It was love-time of the year.

Dame Rumor was authority for the statement that Dr. John Jeffrys and Mabel Cranston were engaged; and for once, the much aligned old lady was in the right. Jeffrys had fluttered about the dazzling light of Mabel's eyes, until his wings were sadly scorched. He realized that he must do one of two things, he must tell her of his love or he must cease to see her. He could not bear the thought of the latter alternative, so he resolved upon the former. With him to resolve was to act; and he waited and watched for an opportunity to put his resolution into action. The opportunity was not long in presenting itself, and when it did, he told her in a manly, straightforward way. Mabel received his declaration with bowed head, passive and silent.

I intended never to tell you this," he continued, "but I lose my self-control in your sweet presence. I have alarmed and pained you, perhaps; try to forgive me. I had no reason to believe that you returned my love, and ought not to have spoken."

She lifted her head for a moment. "Do you say that you have no reason to believe that I love you?" she asked.

"Mabel," he cried, as he drew near to her, "do not deceive me— do not mock a drowning man by throwing him a straw. Surely, surely, you do not mean that you love me!"

"But I do," she answered softly, as she clung to him. "I have loved you ever since you saved my life. What else could you expect, dear?"

He did not answer. He held her in his arms and kissed her passionately, again and again. His hungry heart was satisfied.

The thought never entered his mind that she was Col. William Cranston's only child—that she was rich and he was poor, and that her father might not consent to their union. He knew only that he loved her and was loved by her. When he left the house that night he felt like he had conquered the world; but on the morrow came calmer thought and with it some doubts and misgivings.

He would go to her father at once. He found Col. Cranston in his private office at the factory, and in a few blundering sentences— what with all his thirty-two years he felt very much like a big, bashful boy—he asked a momentous question.

Col. Cranston looked at him fixedly and sternly, Jeffrys thought. At last he spoke. "I have been expecting this. I am not surprised. When I said to you, one time, but there was little that I would not do for you, I foresaw that you would ask me for my child—my dearest treasure. You have come and I can but say that you have my consent to your marriage; but you must promise me that you will not take her from me. I could not stand that. You must make your home with me."

No secret was made of the engagement. The report was in the mouth of the gossips soon, and they rolled and rerolled it under their tongues as the most delicious morsel.

"Did you hear the news, Mr. Ashmore?" inquired Miss Pitkin, the dressmaker, as she called for her monthly supply of flake-white and bay-rum. "Dr. Jeffrys is engaged to Col. Bill's daughter, Mabel Cranston. Mrs. Martin told me today, when she was in to try on her dress. I guess it's so."

"Yes, yes"—and Mr. Ashmore smiled knowingly—"sly dog, that Jeffrys—very cunning fellow, yes indeed—knows what he's about. Col. Cranston has money—yes, yes—and plenty of it. Jeffrys knows on which side his bread's buttered—you bet. Sly dog, I say—very."

The opinion so concisely expressed by Mr. Ashmore was the prevailing one. According to these harpies, who had tried on every occasion to tear Jeffrys character piecemeal, Mabel Cranston was in love with him, but he was an adventurer anxious only to obtain her fortune.

For years the Smalley-Cranston firm had been in the habit of closing the factory a few weeks in mid-summer, for the annual invoice. As this period of compulsory idleness approached, the workmen became more and more outspoken in their denunciations of the niggardly[10] policy of the firm. Col. Cranston received a large share of the blame. Some of the men had worked for him ever since he had been a member of the firm; and yet they were receiving lower wages at this time than ever before. He had grown rich; they had remained poor. He could well afford to pay better wages, and he ought to do so. Little by little the secrets of the company became known, until they were common property. The officials' salaries were too high; the workingmen's wages were too low. A big dividend was declared each year; that they knew; and the building fund had been set aside the year before. The midsummer "shut down" would sink the employees still deeper in debt and their credit would be ruined.

---

10 **niggardly** - grudging and petty in giving or spending

A rumor had gone forth that their wages were to be further reduced after the "shutdown." To this they declared they would never submit—it meant starvation and slavery!

Little else was talked of in the village. One hundred and fifty families depended upon the factory for support, and the prosperity of every one in Smalleyville hinged on the scale of wages. The women took a vital interest in the subject and the children, even, babbled of it at their play.

Jeffrys saw the storm coming and felt that he would be drawn into the vortex. His sympathies were with the workmen and he did not hesitate to say so, although he knew that it was apt to bring him into disfavor with Col. Cranston.

"Doc, have you been up to see Sally Gormley?" widow Galbraith inquired, as she leaned across her front gate and fanned herself vigorously with her checked apron.

"I have not," answered Jeffrys, half pausing in his rapid walk.

"Do you know what ails her?"

"I understand that she is demented."

"That's jest what I said! Doc Munsey says she's a money maniac. The idea! She never had no money to go crazy about. Now there's old Bill Cranston—he' a money maniac fer you. The hardhearted ol' miser! Killin' off my boys in his ol' smoky an' dusty shops, an' half starvin' 'em to boot. He jest ought to be burned out o' house and home—he's too mean and stingy to live!"

Jeffrys hurried on. He had made up his mind as to what he would do. That evening he called at the Cranston mansion and sought a private interview with the colonel.

After Jeffrys had told him all that he had heard and seen, and all that he knew and feared in regard to the situation, the Colonel put his hand on the young man's shoulder and explained:

"You are needlessly alarmed, my boy. I have seen and known all this several times before, though not quite so pronounced, perhaps. It is the nature of these fellows to grumble and threaten, but I have no fear of them. The Smalley-Cranston people will look after their own interests and protect their own property. The men will quiet down when they find that their threats and growls do no good, and that the public is not in sympathy with them. The only thing liable to give us trouble is that some of the businessmen of the town may encourage and abet them, through selfish motives. It will not pay you to worry about the affair; it will come out all right in the end."

"It is not a question of pay, but of principle," replied Jeffrys boldly.

"A question of principle—I do not understand you."

"To be candid with you, Col. Cranston, I think that your workmen should receive higher wages. They do not get enough to enable them to live and pay their honest debts. You should not expect them to be happy and contented under such circumstances."

"Bah! It's simply a question of economy, Jeffrys. They always have been in debt, and they always will be—no matter what their wages. They are extravagant and waste much of their money for drink. Your sympathies are misplaced; they do not deserve them. Besides, I cannot imagine why you take so much interest in their welfare."

"I have two reasons—double interest; the common interest that any good citizen should have in the welfare of this community; and a special interest in over fifteen hundred dollars that your men already owe me and cannot pay."

At this Col. Cranston actually laughed. "So that's the quarter in which the wind lies. Well, we can remedy all that. But you mean to say that they *will not* pay you; they *could* if they *would*. There are several ways to adjust the thing, however. You hand in your bills to the company and I will see that they are paid. I will deduct it from their wages, in weekly payments. If any man objects, out he goes. Hands are plenty and two men stand ready to take the place of one that quits."

"I would rather lose it all than to collect a penny in that way," returned Jeffrys earnestly.

Col. Cranston was very much amused. "You are entirely too charitable toward them, young man. I warn you they do not deserve it. But then you need not treat them at all, if you do not choose. There is plenty of practice for you that is better pay—that can afford to pay better, if you care to put it that way. And, as a last resort, you can quit the whole thing. I have enough for Mabel and you, and you can go into business—anything you wish."

Jeffrys thanked him for his liberal offer, but said firmly: "I love my profession, Colonel, and I will not quit it under any circumstances, as long as I am able to practice it. But this is dodging the question. Your company can afford to pay these men better wages and you should do it."

Col. Cranston was slightly irritated and he showed it by his voice and manner, when he said: "Tut, tut—such quixotic[11] notions! Jeffrys, you must put them aside; they are utterly impracticable. We have a legal right to hire hands at any price to which they will consent. If they do not think it enough, let them quit; and we will hire others at the same price. It is a question of supply and demand, solely. The supply is great, here, and the demand is small; hence the low rate of wages."

Jeffrys' face was flushed and his eyes were shining. "I admit that you have the *legal* right, but I deny that you have the *moral* right. You tacitly admit, Colonel, that you can afford to pay more; then you are morally bound to pay living wages, at least; and this you do not do. I know whereof I speak. Take the average wages that you are paying your employees at the present time; no family can live on it and keep out of debt. You say that the men may quit. So they may, but it means actual want to their families. They can do no better here, because they cannot procure other work; but you should not oppress them simply because you have the power and the opportunity."

"Perhaps," interrupted the elder man with a sneer, "you think that the right to hire should be taken from the employer and placed in the hands of the state; the scale of wages should be established in each case, by a committee appointed by the state authorities?"

Jeffrys saw that Col. Cranston was growing angry, but it did not deter him from replying: "That is my idea, exactly. The state establishes a rate of interest for the protection of the unfortunate borrower; it should establish the scale of wages for the protection of the more unfortunate wage earner."

---

11 **quixotic** - extravagantly chivalrous or romantic; visionary, impractical, or impracticable

The Colonel's face grew purple with rage. "Dr. Jeffrys," he said slowly and sternly, "let us never approach the subject again. You have your ideas and I have mine. We shall never agree. If you value my friendship and esteem, never mention your communistic heresies in my presence again." Then, somewhat softened, he continued: "We have been good friends, and our happiness and the happiness of her whom we both love depends upon our having no differences of opinion. I readily overlook your rash and foolish talk. You are young. You will learn better in time. For the sake of everyone concerned do not indulge in such expressions in public. Above all, do not talk in this manner to the workmen; it will do them no good and it may incite them to some foolhardy act. Drop this whole matter; it will not pay you in any sense. Let us go out on the veranda and have a smoke."

Chapter IV

The crisis had come and the fight was on at Smalley Cranston's. When, on the first pay day after the annual "shut-down," the men discovered that their pay had been reduced, they were righteously and wildly indignant. They crowded the streets in the evening and squads of angry men held Indignation meetings[12] on the corners and in the stores and shops. There was no labor organization in Smalleyville, but at eight o'clock the workmen assembled at the town hall to determine what they should do. Some of the men had visited the saloons over the river, early in the evening, and were noisy and quarrelsome. The meeting was called to order and several speeches were made—some of them inflammatory and threatening. It was an open meeting and many citizens were present, among them Dr. Jeffrys and Dr. Munsey.

Jeffrys went to the meeting with Mr. Kirby, the grocer. As they walked along Mr. Kirby remarked: "This shut-down has cost me five hundred dollars. Now that the workmen's wages are again cut down, they can never pay it—I shall lose it all. The poor devil must

---

12 **Indignation meetings** - meetings held for the purpose of expressing and discussing grievances

live, and you and I help to keep them all because the company will not pay them decent wages. It is a burning shame! This Smalley-Cranston company is a leech that is bleeding the entire community, to fatten itself. It will never be better till the men strike; I believe that we should encourage them."

"You have voiced my opinion exactly," said Jeffrys quietly.

Mr. Kirby was a little surprised. "I hardly expected that you would go so far, doctor, sustaining the prospective relationship to the Cranston's that you do."

"I allow nothing to blunt my sense of duty; and the fact that I am engaged to Col. Cranston's daughter will not influence me in this matter, in the least." Dr. Jeffrys said this earnestly and impressively.

When he arrived at the hall he found the meeting in an uproar. A motion, that the men refuse to work at the reduced rate, had been made and was under discussion as he entered. There was not a dissenting speech. The motion was put and carried amid a storm of applause. Then a number of the businessmen of the village were called upon for an expression of opinion; among the number was Jeffrys. He arose and told them that he was heartily in sympathy with them, as they well knew; that he believed that they would win if they held together; and that he wished them success, and would aid them in any way that he could. At the same time he cautioned them to be discreet and indulge in no unlawful acts. With that he sat down. He had said very little, but coming, as it did, from Col. Cranston's prospective son-in-law, it was greeted with cheers that shook the old hall. As Jeffrys took his seat, Dr. Munsey slipped out of the hall and rapidly made his way in the direction of the Cranston residence. As he hurried along he muttered to himself: "That young man's goose will be cooked as soon as Col. Bill Cranston knows what he has done tonight. I will have the pleasure of setting the ball to rolling. This is my chance to get even with him," and he shook his fist in the darkness.

Arriving at the house he called the owner out and began: "Excuse me, Col. Cranston, but did you know that your men are holding a meeting tonight?"

"Yes," replied the Colonel curtly, for he did not like Dr. Munsey and his fawning ways.

"Did you know that they had voted to go out?"

"I did not."

"Well, they have; and that pet of yours, Dr. Jeffrys, is down there congratulating and embracing them. He has them worked up to such a pitch they are liable to burn the factory before morning. I thought I'd call and tell you; you could thank Jeffrys for it all. Good evening!"

Col. Cranston turned and went into the house for his coat and hat. Presently he emerged and started for Dr. Jeffrys office. He was in a towering passion. He met Jeffrys at the street entrance and accompanied him up stairs, without saying a word. Jeffrys knew instinctively why he had come, and waited for him to speak.

"Were you at the meeting of those idiots tonight?" blurted out the Colonel.

"I was at the meeting held by your employees."

"Did you congratulate them on their insane decision, and express sympathy for them?"

"I did."

"Then"—and the enraged man brought his fist down on the table with the mighty whack—"you are a most precious fool, and your engagement with my daughter is canceled. I do not care to hold any further intercourse with you. Never let your presence darken my door again until I send for you."

"As you please," returned Jeffrys calmly, but his lips were white and his face was drawn. "I have exercised my prerogative as a citizen and a man. If to be your friend, Col. Cranston, I must also be your slave, I prefer to do without your friendship."

The president of the Smalley-Cranston company did not wait to hear more. He stalked down the stairs and up the street in the direction of home.

On the following Monday the men did not return to work. The Smalley-Cranston officials held a meeting, and gave out to the public that they would wait one week for the men to come back to work at the reduced rate. If at the end of that time they still remained out, the company would fill their places with new men.

Toward the last of the week some of the workmen began to waver. Jeffrys went from one to another and urged them to stand firm. Orders for the fall trade were coming in, and the company was losing hundreds of dollars daily.

The week passed and not a man return to work. At one time it seemed that a stampede was imminent; but Jeffrys assumed leadership, and by mere will power held them back. The company attempted to start with new men. To this the strikers offered no resistance, apparently knowing how it would be. Everything went wrong from the start. On the afternoon of the second day word came down street that a piece of machinery had broken, and that Col. Cranston, who was superintending that part of the work himself, was desperately injured by a flying shaft. He was taken to his home and Dr. Brady and Dr. Munsey were summoned in hot haste.

That night at eleven o'clock Dr. Jeffrys was pacing his office to and fro, to and fro. He could not sleep. His mind was in a chaotic condition and his heart went out in love and sympathy to Mabel. He had not seen her since Col. Cranston had forbidden him to come to the house. Had her father told her of their disagreement and that the engagement was at an end? He longed to go to her to comfort and aid her, if it were possible.

At half past eleven a messenger came from the Cranston residence. "They want you to come up and see Col. Cranston," he said.

"Who sent for me?"

"Miss Mabel said to tell you that her father has asked for you, and that she wants you to come."

Then she knew all; her father had told her.

Jeffrys did not wait to hear anything further. He donned his hat and went. When he entered the chamber and saw the massive frame of Col. Cranston stretched full length upon the bed, and helpless; saw his pale face with the bloody foam oozing from his lips, he was touched—stoic that he was. "I am very sorry to see you thus, Col. Cranston," he said feelingly.

The injured man turned his eyes full upon Dr. Jeffrys and whispered painfully: "I have dismissed those other doctors. They told me they could do nothing for me. I sent for you hoping that you might be able to help me; not that I wish to renew our friendship, or that

I had relented in the least. Do not misinterpret my action; you have aided in bringing me to this and I can never forgive you."

Jeffrys winced, but he sat down at the bedside without making reply. He heard Mabel sobbing over by the window. He read the signs of speedy dissolution in the waxen face, and felt them in the weak and thready pulse.

"Do you think I have any chance to recover?" asked Col. Cranston faintly.

"It pains me to tell you that you will live but a few hours, at most," answered the doctor.

The dying man closed his eyes and lay silent for a few minutes; then he said: "Send these people out of the room; I want to speak to you and Mabel."

When the others were gone, Dr. Jeffrys led the trembling girl to her father's side. Col. Cranston motioned for her to bend over him and whispered almost inaudibly: "Mabel, my darling child, I am dying. Before I leave you I would exact from you a promise that you will not marry this man,"—pointing feebly at Jeffrys—"Will you promise your dying father this?" Sobs shook the frame of his daughter, and her face was as white as his own. She bent lower and kissed him but made no reply.

"Mabel, child, will you promise?"

"Oh! father, father, how can I? I love him so—I love him so!"

A pained and disappointed expression crossed his face, and he gasped: "Mabel, Mabel, can you refuse my last request?"

"No, no," she almost shrieked, "anything—anything, I promise anything!"

A flickering smile of gratification and triumph lighted his death-like features for a moment. Mabel arose, tottered, staggered, and would have fallen had not Jeffrys caught her in his arms. She had fainted. He bore her from the room, gave her into the care of the attendants and returned to his post.

All through the long hours he waited and watched for the end. Twice only Col. Cranston spoke. The first time was when Jeffrys returned to the room. "It seems cruel, but it is for the best; you would dissipate her fortune with your quixotic notions." Jeffrys saw his lips move and bending over him caught the words. At another time the patient started from a troubled sleep into which he had fallen, and mumbled to himself, slowly and indistinctively: "Perhaps, perhaps—but no—." Then he again lay quiet.

As the gray dawn came creeping in at the eastern windows, paling the night-lamp on the table in the sick chamber, the pale messenger came with it. One convulsive shudder of the great form, one gurgling respiration and all was over.

The rod of iron had remained inflexible to the end.

* * * *

After the funeral Aunt Ellen and Mabel closed the lonely house and went on a voyage to Europe. Jeffrys made no effort to see Mabel before her departure; he had heard her promise and knew that she would keep it to the death.

The Smalley-Cranston stock company was reorganized and the new president elected. Under the new regime the men receive fair compensation for their work and were prosperous and happy.

Three years have elapsed since the death of Col. Cranston. Dr. Jeffrys still practices his profession in Smalleyville, and the people have learned to love the quiet, unassuming man who is giving his life to their service. He has grown a little gray and there are care lines upon his bronzed face; but he toils on and under no regrets. What he feels no one will ever know.

Mabel Cranston has not returned to her old home. Dr. Jeffrys hears from her occasionally through her agent, Mr. Lane. She is in Italy and does not speak of coming back. The one question Dr. Jeffrys has never dared to ask himself is: "Did it pay?"

Stuff of Which Doctors Are Made

"Dr. Whiteside, I've come to tell you that I can't take care of your horses any longer. I am going away."

"What's the matter now?" inquired the doctor quickly, as he arose from his leather-seated office chair and straightened his tall, thin form.

"I am going away, sir, and— " began the first speaker, a bright eyed shabbily dressed boy of about thirteen years, but the doctor interrupted him.

"Look here, Tom Touseltop, didn't you promise me that if I would give you the job of taking care of my horses, you would go to school this season and try to make something of yourself—say, didn't you?" And the lean, angular figure shook his finger at the boy in a menacing way.

"Yes, sir,"—faltered Tom—"I did, sir, but— "

"Then what do you mean by coming to me, when school is but fairly begun, and saying that you must give up your place and that you are going away?"

Tom Touseltop seemed very much embarrassed. He thrust his hands deep into his trousers' pockets, but not finding a satisfactory explanation there, apparently, he as quickly removed them. Then he tried to force the office stove to yield an explanation by kicking it vigorously with the brass-bound toe of his cowhide boot. This failing, he once more changed tactics; and removing his white wool hat he toyed nervously with his mop of tow-colored hair. "Why— " he began.

"Speak up—out with it," insisted Dr. Whiteside.

"Why, sir—" said Tom at last recovering from his stupefaction— "It's like this, sir. Father has made a contract with the stave[1] company,

---

1 **stave** - a narrow strip of wood forming part of the sides of a barrel, tub, or similar structure

to get out timber for them up in Red Brush; and he wants me to go along to cook for him. He says that he will quit drinking, sir, and I think I ought to go, and—"

"Oh! yes, I see"—interrupted the doctor, and a half sneer played about his thin lips—"you have found an opportunity to quit school and work at the same time, and you are anxious to take it. You would rather lead a half civilized life up in Red Brush—and trap and hunt like a little savage—then go to school and become an educated young gentleman."

"No, sir—no, sir—indeed I would not," replied Tom, his chin quivering. "I would much rather go to school; but I must go with father. He says that he wants to try to do better, and I feel that I ought to help him, if I can. He says— "

"Tom!"—Dr. Whiteside spoke so abruptly that the boys fairly jumped. "Tom Touseltop, are you telling me the truth, or are you simply trying to find a suitable excuse for your own desire to be a shiftless know-nothing?"

The boy looked his-self appointed inquisitor squarely in the face, and answered manfully: "I do *not want* to go, Dr. Whiteside, but feel that I *ought* to go. I am not deceiving you."

Dr. Whiteside did not reply for a moment, and then he said: "You stay here and let your father go. I will take you to raise; and will board and clothe you, and send you to school as I would my own son, if I had one. When you are old enough, I will educate you for a physician and turn my practice over to you. I have no children—and I like you. Will you do it?"

"Oh! Dr. Whiteside, if I *only could*," Tom's cheeks were flushed and his eyes were shining. "But I cannot; I promised another on her dying bed that I would stick to father—and I *must do it*."

Dr. Whiteside looked at the small speaker, as though he would read his inmost secret. "Tom, did you promise your dying mother that?" he inquired, softly.

"Yes, sir."

"Then keep your word, no matter what the cost; but I am very sorry that you must go." Turning to a drawer the physician took out some money. "Here is what I owe you," he said sadly. "I cannot tell you how badly I feel to have you quit school. You were learning so fast. I expected great things of you. Well, good-bye—be a good boy." And he held out his firm white hand. Tom shook it warmly, and without a word turned and left the office, wiping his eyes on his ragged sleeve.

After Tom's departure the kindhearted doctor sat and pondered. "I can't determine in my own mind," he muttered to himself, "whether Tom wants to go or not. I believe that he is honest, and I *know* that he is capable. It is bad to lose him in this way; I would have done a good part by him. The boy has never had a chance; raised in poverty, his mother an invalid, his father a confirmed drunkard—one can't expect much of a thirteen-year-old boy under such circumstances." And Dr. Whiteside arose and busied himself about the office.

The village of Stoverton, in which Dr. Whiteside practiced his profession, was a small river port containing about five or six hundred inhabitants; and he was the only physician for it and the surrounding country. He was a generous, matter-of-fact man of fifty years, who by close application and rigid economy had amassed a small fortune. He had no children, and his offer to take Tom Touseltop "to raise" was a princely one—considered from Tom's standpoint; for Tom had nothing but want and squalor and wretchedness.

But in spite of the contaminating influence of poverty and ignorance, the boy was bright and honest—as Dr. Whiteside had remarked many times. Yet this day had the good doctor been grieved and irritated by him, and his mental comment was: "He will never amount to anything. I am afraid there is a streak of the Touseltop shiftlessness inbred there—I am *afraid* there is!"

When Tom left Dr. Whiteside's office he went straight home to help his father to pack their few possessions for removal to Red Brush. He was anxious to be off; he wanted to get Mr. Touseltop beyond the fascinating and seductive influence of the village saloon and boon companions as soon as possible. Tom understood his father well enough to know that the sooner they were gone the better.

The next morning a wagon backed up to the door of the miserable shanty in which the Touseltops had pretended to live. Their poor effects were loaded into it; and crossing the river, at the ferry above the dam, they proceeded on their way to Red Brush.

It was fifteen miles to their destination, over rough and almost impassable by-roads, and it was a little after midday when they arrived. The man who had brought them immediately started upon his return journey, and Tom and his father moved the things into the cabin and begin their crude housekeeping.

This cabin was a one-story log structure, consisting of but one room and having a door, a window and a fireplace. It had been built by timbermen a number of years before, and was in a fair state of preservation.

Here in the heart of the unbroken forest, fifteen miles from civilization, Tom began his new life. He liked it—of course he did. What boy would not! He cooked their simple meals, piled stave timber for his father, and hunted and trapped.

Those were long, sunshiny fall days; and every one of them had something new in it for Tom. When night came his father would retire early; but Tom often set by the huge fire far into the night, conning[2] the school books that he had brought with him, and listening to the crooning voice of the night wind among the trees.

Mr. Touseltop worked hard and—as intoxicants were beyond his reach—kept sober. So Tom was satisfied and contented, if not wholly happy. He also thought of Dr. Whiteside's kind offer and wished—sincerely wished—that he had been able to accept it.

Thus a number of months sped away. It had been early autumn when they had come to Red Brush; and it was now midwinter. The streams were frozen and the snow lay many inches deep in the surrounding woods.

Mr. Touseltop had visited the village some two or three times since their arrival, going for supplies of bacon and flour. Each time he had left the cabin in the early morning, and had returned late in the evening—duly sober. Tom was not lonely in his father's absence—for he always had plenty of work with which to busy himself—but he dreaded to have him go; he feared that his old habit would overcome them. Yet each time Mr. Touseltop had come back

____

2 **conning** – commiting to memory; to studying or examining closely

in a normal condition, and Tom began to think that perhaps he had magnified the danger.

In February came a thaw. The snow disappeared from the hills, and the brooks and rills became raging torrents. One night when Tom went to bed it was raining hard, and in the morning when he arose it was still pouring down.

While he was preparing their frugal breakfast, his father said to him: "I'm goin' to Stoverton today. Hurry up breakfas'."

"In this rain, father?" Said Tom in surprise and alarm; "we don't need anything."

"It don't make no differ'nce," was the surly response, "I'm goin'." And he did.

Tom worried about him all day. He feared the worst. His father could have no motive for going to town, unless it be for drink.

When night came and the absent man did not return, Tom was almost frantic. He was afraid to be left alone at night, to be sure, but that was not the principal cause of the boy's anxiety. He thought that some ill had befallen his father. All night long he sat by the fire, listening and longing—and praying, if ever a boy *did* pray, who had never heard a prayer in his life. He heard strange noises and quaked with fear. At one time he fancied he saw a face at the window, and almost fainted from terror. What a long, long, dreary night it was!

About noon the next day Mr. Touseltop returned—bleary-eyed and besotted, and caring a jug full of liquor. He was wet and bedraggled and evidently in a very bad humor. Tom asked him no questions; he saw that his father was in no state of mind to be questioned. After eating his dinner Mr. Touseltop fell into a drunken stupor, and did not arouse until it was coming dusk. When he arose, he took a drink from the jug, shouldered his axe and started out. In answer to Tom's inquiry he said he was going to work.

It was evident to Tom that his father scarcely knew what he was doing, so the poor boy tried to dissuade him from his purpose. His effort availed nothing; the father shook his head stubbornly and staggered out. In a short time Tom thought he heard him calling, so he opened the door and listened. Above the noise of the brawling stream that ran by he recognized the voice bawling lustily for aid. It was raining violently and fast growing dark. Directed by the sound of his father's voice in the darkness, Tom found him.

"I have cut my foot a little," said Mr. Touseltop, in a maudlin tone, "help me to the house."

Tom assisted his father to the cabin and attempted to pull the boot from the injured foot; but he could not succeed on account of the pain that it caused the groaning wretch.

So Tom took his knife and cut the boot off. He found that the foot was badly injured indeed, the keen axe had almost divided it at the base of the toes, and the wound was bleeding profusely and dangerously from the severed arteries.

What was to be done? Fifteen miles from a doctor or other aid, what could a thirteen-year-old boy do? Just this: he drew the edges of the gaping wound together as best he could; made a compress of a folded towel, and bound it firmly in place; fashioned a tourniquet out of a bit of rope and a stick, and fixed it tightly around the leg just above the ankle; elevated the wounded foot upon an old store-box that had served him for a table, and started for Dr. Whiteside, through fifteen miles of almost impenetrable darkness—without so much as a lantern to guide his footsteps.

On went Tom Touseltop, over logs and through thickets, fording swollen streams and drenched to the skin by the incessant rain. The low branches of the trees smote him in the face, and the wild wind buffeted and mocked him as it howled through the woods. His clothes were torn by the thorns and brambles, and his hands were bruised and bleeding, but he dared not pause nor falter. Once he lost his way completely and was almost ready to give up in despair. He broke down and sobbed, he could not help it. But he quickly recovered his courage, and following the course of a ravine, he came to where the path crossed it—and he went on.

After hours of exertion, terror and heartsick loneliness—it seemed years to Tom—he at last stood upon the bank of the river, opposite Stoverton. Resting a moment to quiet his tumultuously beating heart, he heard the courthouse clock in the village striking the hour of midnight. He had been five hours upon the way.

The usually placid river was a raging yellow flood, that swept far out over the lowlands, and filled the night with crash and roar. And over it all rose the boom of the great dam, sounding to the lonely and terrified boy like an oncoming avalanche.

Across the mad stream lay the dark and silent village, with a faint light twinkling here and there. Down close to the river's edge, a light somewhat brighter than the other shot its red rays across the waste of tawny waters. Tom knew that it was the lamp in the ferry house. The boats were on the village side; he must try to make some one hear him.

Placing his hands up like a funnel to his mouth, he shouted "o–o–ov–er," several times. No one heard him, he knew that, but his voice seemed to fall at his feet. Perhaps they would not take the risk of coming to him, if they *did* hear, for the river was full of logs and drift. He would find a boat. He knew where one was kept about a mile up the river. So skirting the backwaters, he painfully worked his way through the tangled willows, in that direction.

Arriving at the place, he found the boat moored in a large creek that emptied into the river a few hundred yards above the wagon bridge that spanned the mouth of the swift running stream.

The boat was not locked, and Tom untied it and climbed in. Picking up the oars he turned the frail craft around. He felt the current catch the skiff, and found himself born toward the river with frightful velocity. He had barely time to duck his head, when the boat darted under the bridge and out into the larger stream. "Whew," he remarked to himself, "that was a close shave; I could have touched that bridge with my tongue!" However, his dangerous voyage was but just begun. He strained every muscle to reach the opposite shore, knowing full well that he must put forth his best effort, or he would inevitably drift over the dam and be lost. Once the boat was caught between two drifting logs, and was carried several hundred feet downstream, before Tom could disengage it.

He came in sight of the ferry light; and realized how fast he was drifting, by the rapidity with which the light was apparently approaching.

But he was out of the main current now; and if no accident befell him, he would soon be ashore. With a few rapid strokes he shot the skiff toward land; then he dropped the oars and leaped toward the bow. He clutched frantically at the piling of the ferry dock—lost his hold—caught again—and clung with numb fingers while the boat swept from under him and disappeared over the dam a short distance below.

Gaining a foothold on the slippery timbers, he struggled to the top of the dock; and a few moments after was staggering up the black and muddy street. Reaching Dr. Whiteside's office, he knocked loudly on the door—and sank down exhausted!

*　*　*　*

As the gray and murky daylight crept across the angry river, on its way westward, it saw Dr. Whiteside and two companions in a wagon, going for the wounded man up in Red Brush.

They found him just as Tom had left him; but the fire was out and he was thoroughly chilled and almost unconscious. Dr. Whiteside litigated the severed arteries and dressed the wound, then they loaded the unfortunate man into the wagon and brought him to Stoverton.

Mr. Touseltop never recovered. His dissipation and consequent exposure brought on an attack of lung fever, from which he died in a few weeks after his return to the village.

Tom Touseltop had been true to his trust. He had stood by his father to the last.

After the funeral was over Dr. Whiteside took Tom home with him; and in a few days subsequently, formally adopted him.

In giving his reasons for so doing, the good doctor always said: "Tom Tousletop may not have in him the stuff of which heroes are made, but he has in him the stuff of which doctors are made!"

Beggars Awheel

Chapter I

The letter that Jim Hardy held in his hand read as follows:

"My Dear Nephew:—I have not seen you since you were quite a little boy, and I feel that I can wait no longer. You must come to visit me this vacation, since I cannot come to see you. I wish that your dear mother could come with you, but if she cannot do so, you must be sure to come at any rate.

"It will do you good to get out of the hot and smoky city for a few weeks; and I understand from your mother that you know very little of life in the country. We live right out near to the heart of nature, and you will enjoy yourself ever so much. If your mother cannot come with you, bring some school mate, for we have no young folks about the place and you might get lonesome and homesick.

"Urge your parents to let you come. I really must have you. Your loving Aunt,

"Margaret Lockary."

The letter was addressed to "Mr. James B. Hardy," and Jim felt that he was quite a man indeed. He lived with his parents in a large city and—as his aunt had hinted in her letter—knew little of the country, from actual observation. His parents were well-to-do people, but not wealthy by any means. His father was the proprietor of a large livery stable and Jim usually spent his vacations doing odd jobs in and about the place. He was fifteen years old, strong, intelligent and bubbling over with the effervescent spirits of boyhood. The prospect that his aunt held out to him set him almost wild with joy and anticipation.

He hurried into the house to consult his mother in regard to the matter. School had closed but a few weeks before; and he felt that he would be off at once could he gain his parents' consent.

"Would you really like to go?" asked his mother, smiling at his enthusiasm.

"Should I like to go! Why, mother, of course I should."

"Well, you have my consent—but you must ask your father. I do not know what he will say. He may think that he needs your help. Times are not very good; and money is not so plentiful with us as it used to be. The advent of the bicycle has hurt your father's business considerably."

At his mother's reference to the bicycle Jim started, and a smile irradiated his features from ear to ear.

"Oh! Mother," he exclaimed. "I can ride through on my wheel."

His mother laughed heartily, "You don't know what you are talking about, Jim. You have no idea of the distance. It is 250 miles."

"I don't care—that isn't very far. We can ride it in five days."

You have never ridden over rough country roads. It would take you a week or ten days, under the most favorable circumstances. And you might get hurt—or something dreadful happened to you; I should be uneasy about you all the time."

"Oh! we could do it, mother! and it would be such fun!"

"What do you mean by 'we'?"

"Why, Aunt Margaret says that I am to bring some school mate with me; and I am going to take Dick Manley. He's a good rider— and we like each other—and we could go through just a whizzing!" And Jim danced about the room in an ecstasy of delight.

"Well, go and ask your father. I am willing to abide by his decision; but I do not think he will let you go in that way. Be off now—I must return to my work."

Jim Hardy's father was a man of excellent judgment and few words. He listened patiently and attentively to all that his son had to say; then he remarked:

"It seems to me that there are a few obstacles in the way, that you have overlooked."

Jim's countenance fell. "What are they, father?" he inquired anxiously.

"In the first place, where is the money to come from to pay your expenses?"

"I—I don't know," stammered Jim.

"In the second place, you have not consulted Dick Manley nor his parents. You do not know that he will want to go—"

"He will – he will want to go; I know that," interrupted Jim.

Mr. Hardy did not heed the interruption, but continued: "and his parents may not give their consent."

"I will ride out on my wheel and see them right now," and Jim started to carry his resolution into practice.

"Hold—not so fast!" Commanded his father: "supposing that Dick wants to go, and that he can gain his parents consent, who is to pay your expenses? You have not answered that question."

"Dick's father can pay his way, and you can pay mine. Can you not?"

"Probably I could do so, but I do not think it the best way. But if you could earn the money, you would have a right to spend it. I will tell you what I will do. I will give you an Dick attempts to earn your expense money, by working for me in the stables. It will take you but a few weeks, and you will have plenty of time for your trip. What do you say?"

"Just the thing, father! I will go and see Dick at once."

"You had better wait until I have talked to his father; I think I can do more with him than you can."

The result of the conference between Mr. Hardy and Mr. Manley was that they determined to let the boys take their proposed journey, provided they would earn their money in the way suggested by Mr. Hardy. At first the two mothers offered some objections to their boys going by wheel; but after due consideration they readily gave their consent, and entered into the spirit of the adventure with the zest equal to that manifested by their sons.

Jim had received his aunt's letter on a Thursday about the first day of July and on the following Monday he and Dick began work for Mr. Hardy. They worked with the will, currying horses, washing vehicles, and performing the various duties assigned them, with cheerfulness and alacrity[1]. They devoted their spare moments to preparations for their trip. They thoroughly cleaned and overhauled

---

1 **alacrity** - brisk and cheerful readiness

their bicycles, repacked their tool bags and repaired their pumps. Each Saturday night, when they received their week's wages, they spent a part of it to procure themselves the things that they thought would be necessary to the success and comfort of their outing trip.

Each bought himself a traveler's case to swing in the frame of his wheel. In this he packed an extra bicycle suit—sweater, trousers, cap and stockings—and such other small articles as he thought he would need. By the time they had purchased what they wanted, and had saved money to pay their expenses, it was the first of August; so they had just one month in which to perform the journey each way, and make a short visit with Aunt Margaret.

On the last Saturday night before their departure they were at Jim's home completing their arrangements.

"Now, Dick," said Jim, "I wonder if we've forgotten anything. We'll send our Sunday suits of clothes through by express, so that we'll have something decent to wear when we get to Aunt Margaret's. Do you think of anything else?"

"We want to put in needle and thread and buttons," replied Dick earnestly.

"That's so, Dick; for we may need them badly." And then both laughed.

"I would suggest that you add a bottle of arnica[2] and a yard or two of sticking plaster," said Mr. Hardy without looking up from his paper; and again the boys laughed heartily, but they acted on the suggestion.

"How about it, Dick, shall we take our bicycle lamps? "inquired Jim.

"No, will not need them; will only ride in the daytime. We don't want to be loaded down like a pair of pack peddlers."

"All right, then; that's all I think of. But I b'lieve I'll take my lamp in case we should possibly need it."

"Well, that's enough; were not going on a voyage to the north pole; nor on a trip across the Sahara desert. You seem to think, Jim, that we're going to bid goodbye to civilization as soon as we get off

---

2 **arnica** - a preparation of this plant used medicinally, esp. for the treatment of bruises

the city pavements. There'll be towns all along the route, and we can get anything we may need."

Jim made no reply to this knock-down argument, and Dick took up his cap went home.

They were to start the following Monday, and all Sabbath day they were restless and ill at ease—they could think of nothing but the glorious free life they were going to lead for a few weeks.

Monday morning bright and early they started. They fondly kiss their mothers, shook hands with their fathers—and were off. The start was made from Jim's home, and Dick's parents and many of the neighbors were there to see them start. They were a pair of sturdy, self-reliant lads and no one had any misgivings about them. They were a pretty sight as they rapidly wheeled away in their new cycling suits. Many pairs of eyes watched them as they gradually disappeared from sight, and many hearts breathed a prayer of God-speed for them.

Along the paved streets, toward the eastern outskirts of the city they flew side-by-side. The summer morning was bright and cool, and it was the very acme[3] of existence to take a spin under the circumstances. They chatted, they joked, they laughed—the exhilaration of the motion combined with the fragrant air was intoxicating. They left the city far in the rear, they flitted through the suburbs. The paved streets ended; the well-kept lawns gave place to vacant lots overgrown with weeds. Cultivated fields and bits of woodland put in an appearance, and a white farm house glistened in the morning sunshine, here and there. They were in the country!

The roads were hard-packed clay and very smooth, but the boys began to slacken their speed and look around them. The land was gently rolling, and as far as the eyes could see was an expanse of rich farmlands, broken here and there by a clump of forest trees or lazily flowing stream. The sun was climbing step-by-step up the eastern heavens, and the day was growing warm. For the last few miles neither had scarcely spoken. Dick was the first to break the silence.

---

3 **acme** - the highest point, as of achievement or development

"Let's stop and take off our coats, Jim; I'm getting too hot, and there is no use in our riding so hard—we're not making a century run nor trying to lower a record."

"All right," returned Jim with alacrity, "that's agreeable to me."

In the shade of a large ash tree that grew near the road they dismounted.

"It's just nine o'clock." announced Jim, glancing at the little nickel-case watch that he carried.

"And we've come twenty miles," laughed Dick, after examining his cyclometer. "I told you there was no use in our riding so hard—we don't want to go through without feeding. Let sit down and rest. Say! have you got that money all right?"

Jim patted his hip pocket complacently and answered:

"Yes, indeed! It's right there."

"You're not carrying all of your worldly wealth in your hip pocket, are you? You'll lose that, sure as fate. Put it in your other pocket."

"What for? I'll not lose it."

"Yes, you will; the jolting of the wheel will work it out. And a pack of mixed pickles we should be in without it! You know I haven't got a cent. Father is to send mine by check so that we shall have it to get home with."

"Oh! There is no danger of losing it—Look at that train away over yonder! Doesn't it look small? And how slowly it appears to move."

After a brief breathing spell they remounted and went on, but much more leisurely. The country road stretched ahead of them like a gray ribbon, and the heat-waves shimmered and danced across the bare meadow fields, in a way that made their eyes ache. They pulled their caps low over their foreheads and pushed on. The dust rose in dense clouds behind them, and floated lazily across the adjacent fields. There was not the faintest breeze to rustle the tasseled corn or cool our travelers' burning faces. The boys were becoming sweat-grimed, hungry and weary.

"Hello!" Suddenly exclaimed Dick, "What does this mean? Which road do we take here?"

"I don't know, I'm sure," answered Jim; "they told us to keep the main road till we came to Kellersville; but here the road forks—and which is the main one?"

They stopped to determine if possible which road to take. There was a post standing at the junction of the two roads, but the sign board, that it had borne in days long past, had disappeared.

"Let's take to the right," Dick said, "it's always customary to keep to the right, at any rate, and that one seemed traveled the most." And they leaped to their wheels and moved on.

After they had gone about a mile they met a man with a team who informed them that they were on the right road, and they were in better spirits.

"Look at your watch, Jim, and see what time it is; I'm almost famished. We've got to spy out a place for dinner."

"It's almost 11 o'clock, Dick."

"Well, the first farm house we come to we'll try for a square meal; I have an aching void that needs to be filled."

Just then the cling-clang of a bell pulsated on the stifling air, and a few minutes later the weird notes of the horn struck upon their ears.

"What's that mean?" inquired Jim, in some alarm.

"I can't say," replied Dick, "it sounds as if it was meant for some sort of signal."

"There goes the bell again—and look yonder, you can see a girl ringing it at that farm house out the lane to the left."

Jim almost lost control of his wheel in a convulsion of laughter. "What precious city greenies we are in the country," he cried as soon as he could catch his breath, "that's the dinner bell, of course. We'll just ride out that lane, and have dinner with them. That horn was blown for the same purpose, at some farm house further on. That's the way they called the farm hands to dinner, of course."

The boys turned into the grassy lane and were soon in front of the farm house. Dick went to the front door to inquire if they could get dinner. He knocked and knocked, but received no response. "Go around to the other door—they're all in the kitchen," called Jim. Dick did as advised and soon returned with a glowing face to inform Jim that he had been successful.

They leaned their wheels against the board fence and went around the house to the cistern[4] to wash. In the meantime the farmer, his stalwart son, and two farm hands had arrived from the field, and all proceeded to wash their faces and hands. Then they went into dinner. The boys started to unstrap their coats from their wheels, but the farmer laughed at them good-naturedly and said:

"You needn't do that; shirt sleeves goes here. We ain't stuck up! Come on in an' eat; we want to get back to work."

Dinner consisted of chicken potpie, boiled green corn, string beans, hot biscuits and strong black coffee. Jim and Dick ate very heartily, and thought they had never partaken of a meal that tasted one half so good.

After dinner the men prepared to return to the field. Jim asked the lady of the house how much he owed her, and she informed him that the bill was fifty cents for the two. He reached into his hip pocket for the money, and almost fainted from surprise and consternation. The money was gone!

Chapter II

"I—I've lost my money," stammered Jim, his face red with shame and mortification.

The farmer was passing through the gate into the barnyard behind the house, but he turned back at this remark. Dick looked reproachfully at Jim, and Jim gazed hopelessly and helplessly at Dick.

"Did you say you'd lost y'r money?" interrogated the farmer.

"Yes, sir," replied Jim, fumbling in his pockets, "I had it in my hip pocket—and it's gone."

"Where do you think you lost it?"

"I had it back a few miles—Dick, look at your cyclometer and see how far we have come since we rested under the tree. It marked twenty miles then."

"We come seven miles since then," answered Dick, coming back from his examination of his wheel.

4 **cistern** - an underground reservoir for rainwater

"Well," said the farmer slowly, "some people wouldn't believe y'r story; but I do. You look like you're going to be sick. But if you intend to go on two of three hundred miles—as you said at the table—you're in a bad box. I've hear o' beggars on horseback, but this is my first experience with beggars on wheels," and he laughed uproariously at his own joke.

"You'd better ride right back over the road, an' see if you can't find the money," suggested one of the farm hands.

After a short consultation the boys determined to do so. They assured their host that, if they found the money, they would pay him as they came back. Then they leaped to their wheels and rode slowly away, with heads bent low, and carefully examining the ground as they moved along.

They traversed the weary first seven miles, speaking scarcely a word, but they discovered no trace of the missing purse. Seating themselves beneath the tree where they had made their first halt, they held a consultation as to what they should do.

"We can't go on without money," asserted Dick, "and we might just as well ride on home at once."

"Somebody has picked up that purse—I should hate to steal money in that way," grumbled Jim, pettishly. "But my address was in the pocketbook, and if any honest person found it he will return it."

"You ought not to complain, Jim; had you done as I advised you, we should have been all right. It is all your fault."

"I know that as well as you do; but that doesn't help matters—to growl at me. Let's decide what we shall do. I say go on home."

"And I say that I'll never do it—even if I have to go to Aunt Margaret's by myself."

"But we can't go on without money. And why don't you want to return home?"

Jim's eyes flashed, and he set his lips in a determined way.

"I'll never go back to being the laughing stock of everyone. I mean what I say—I'm going to Aunt Margaret's, money or no money; and I'm going to start on this very minute. If you want to return home, Dick, there's the road; if you've got the grit to go with me, jump your wheel."

"Bully for you, Jim Hardy!" shouted Dick grasping his friend's hand. "You're made of the true stuff; and I'll go with you if I have to live on air and water all the way."

It was about half past one o'clock, and the air was close and sultry. Big dun-colored clouds began to loom up in the west, as our "beggars awheel" retraced the seven miles that they had traveled twice that day already. On they sped until they again arrived at the farm house where they had eaten dinner. Dick waited at the road, while Jim pedaled out the lane to inform the good woman that he had not found the money, but that he would send fifty cents to her when he returned home.

"Well," said she, "I don't mind the pay, but you may send it and then we shall know you're honest. Your going back to hunt shows you told the truth about losing the money."

Again they proceeded on their journey. The dun clouds in the west grew blacker and blacker, and rose higher and higher in the heavens. Fitful gusts of wind rustled the leaves on the trees along the high road, and sent clouds of dust whirling and eddying in all directions. The thunder's muttering growl was borne to their ears, and the sun was blotted out. Occasional large drops of rain pattered in the dusty road like leaden bullets.

The lads were on a long descending grade, now, that led down to a broad, shallow valley through which flowed is sluggish creek. They coasted down this grade gaining in speed at every second until they "fairly flew," as Dick expressed it. But fast as they traveled the storm traveled faster. The thunder sounded nearer, the air grew darker. The wind was blowing a gale, carrying the leaves and wisps of straw and hay high over their heads.

A vivid, bluish streak of lightning rent the sky, and the thunder crashed and rattled as if the whole artillery of heaven had been discharged in a single volley. Then the rain poured down in torrents. It blew into their faces until they could scarcely discern the road.

"There is a covered bridge just ahead," shouted Jim about the tumult; "push for it!"

They gained the shelter of the wooden bridge, and panting from their exertions, leaped from their wheels. Their garments were soaked, their bicycles freely splattered with mud.

The bridge was weather-boarded at the sides, and covered with a sloping shingle roof, and afforded excellent protection from the storm. It stood upon two stone piers, and the roadway sloped up to it at each end. All around it stretched acres of low bottom lands.

The rain settled into a steady downpour and showed no signs of stopping. Dick and Jim wiped the water and mud from their machines, tested their tires, and sat down to await the pleasure of the weather.

"We've ridden forty-seven miles according to the cyclometer," mused Dick, "subtracting fourteen miles for our hunting expedition after that purse, leaves thirty-three miles that we have progressed."

"It's now 4 o'clock," Jim returned, "and this rain stops our riding for today. When the storm's over we shall hunt some place to get our suppers and stay all night. I declare! It's raining harder than ever."

A while they sat in silence listening to the rain—and each of them a little lonely and homesick. Their reverie was broken by a distant roaring, crashing sound far up the stream that grew louder every moment.

"What in the world can that be?" almost whispered Jim. Dick made no response, and both ran to the end of the bridge to look out. They listened intently, the volume of sound growing louder and more terrible every minute.

"Oh! Jim, it's water—it's a flood!" cried Dick. "Look – look! It is sweeping fences and everything before it. Isn't it a grand and awful sight."

The flood came rolling, crashing, rumbling onward, bearing rails, logs, haycocks and other debris upon its surface.

"Say!" shouted Jim in mad alarm, "we had better get out of here. It may take the bridge with it."

They ran for their wheels, and quickly returned with them to the end of the bridge; but already the flood of water was upon them. It spread in tawny billows over the lowlands on each side of the bed of the stream, and hissed and foamed around the piers of the bridge. The water rose higher and higher until it came within a few feet of the floor of the bridge; and the ancient and crazy structure tumbled on its foundation, as the drift caught against it—piled up—crashed and disappeared in the muddy torrent.

Night was rapidly approaching, and the air was growing cool. The rain had ceased to fall, but still the flood continues to rise. There had been a veritable cloud burst near the headwaters of the stream. Darkness shut down, and Jim and Dick were still prisoners on their uncertain support. The angry waters were within a foot of the bridge floor. The boys were terror-stricken and did not know what to do. What could they do? Nothing!

"What is to become of us, Jim!" whimpered Dick. "Oh! If we had only gone back home, as I wanted to do."

"You must not give up that way, Dick; there is no danger yet. If the bridge floats off with us, we will stick to it until it lands us somewhere—"

"Or goes to pieces!" completed Dick.

"There is not much danger of that; it has heavy timbers that will not easily break."

Jim spoke with much more assurance than he felt; and it had the desired effect of reassuring Dick somewhat.

"Look at that light bobbling along over yonder," Dick exclaimed, suddenly.

"That's someone with a lantern," asserted Jim. "I wonder what he is doing."

"Jim, I hear voices over in that direction."

"So do I. No doubt it's someone trying to save something from the flood."

"Let's halloo to them. Say, let's light our bicycle lamp. Ain't I glad we brought one after all."

"All right—but I don't suppose they can hear us, though they may see our light."

"We can hear them, and see their light, too."

"That's true! We'll try calling to them at any rate, and that may make them look this way and see the light."

The two boys stood as far out on the approach of the bridge as they dared, and raised their voices in one prolonged and mighty shout, and flashed their light towards the other one. Then they listened with wildly beating hearts, but no answering call came back across the troubled waters. They shouted again and again until their throats were sore and their hearts in their shoes.

"Once more, Jim; and then if they don't hear us well give it up."

Once more their voices rose in a last effort—and again they waited. A faint halloo floated to them from the faraway shore, and they capered about in delight. They felt that their troubles were over—they did not stop to ask themselves how the people on shore were to aid them.

"The light is still over there, Dick."

"Yes, they'll not leave us now. What time is it?"

"Eight o'clock," replied Jim, examining his watch by the light of the lamp. He held the lamp near the floor, and announced joyfully that the water was falling.

Our two young friends strained their eyes until they ached, watching the lantern upon the shore. Inch by inch the angry waters receded, and little by little the roaring became less. The hours dragged slowly away; and the boys,, exhausted in mind and body, lay down upon the dusty planks of the bridge and fell into fitful slumber.

Some time after midnight they were aroused by a light flashing in their faces. A gaunt form enveloped in a mud splashed "slicker" was bending over them.

"Blamed poor place to make y'r bed, youngsters." said a gruff voice from the depths of a cavernous mouth surrounded by a thicket of coarse black beard.

Jim and Dick sprang to their feet, rubbing their eyes.

"Yes." continued the gruff voice, "I heerd you holler, and seen your light; but I couldn't git to you till the water went down a good 'eal—the current was so swift. It's the biggest raise that we ever had on this bottom. I give you fellers up fer goners—thought the ol' bridge'ld go this time sure. You ain't the first ones that has been caught here; so I knowed right where you was when you hollered, even if you hadn't had no light. Come on; I've got a skiff here an' I'll take you over home an' see that you git bed an' breakfas'. Hullo! you've got bisickles, ain't you?"

The boys were almost too sleepy to make reply; but they remembered their "manners" and thanked him for his hospitable offer, and procuring their wheels they clambered into the skiff that was tied to the end of the bridge. The water had subsided to a considerable extent, but the current was still swift and dangerous. The country-man's strong arms swept the oars rapidly, and soon the trio reached shore and sprang out.

Their guide led the way along the narrow path through a grove of young trees, and the two young adventurers followed closely in his footsteps, carrying their bicycles to keep them out of the mud and water. Presently they began to ascend a slight elevation of land on the summit of which stood an old frame house. Their guide talk-ed volubly[5] as he covered the ground with long strides.

"Me an' Sally lives all alone—Sally, she's my ol' maid sister; an' I'm an ol' bach'lor." and he chuckled softly.

"You won't find things very grand, but you're welcome to all we've got. I suppose you want to take a snooze before you have any-thing to eat; an' that'll suit Sally, fer she don't like to be called up in the night. We'll just keep re'l still w'en we git to the house, an' you two can sleep in the spare bedroom on the end o' the porch."

Arriving at their destination, the long and lank rustic whispered:

"Now, put y'r carts on the porch in the dry, an' turn in. Here's y'r room. I s'pose you don't want to be called till you've had y'r sleep out? All right—good night." But in a few moments he knocked at the door, and shoving a half of a huge pumpkin pie in the door, remarked:

"After all, mebbe you'll sleep better ef ye put y'er selves outside'n this ere!" Then he vanished again.

The boys did as suggested, and then took a look at their quarters. The room in which they found themselves was a small, unplastered apartment, containing a bed and one chair. It was innocent of carpet, wash stand or dressing case. However, the lads could not afford to be over critical or fastidious after their rough experience, and they remembered that "beggars must not be choosers." And so removing their clothing they dropped upon the bed and were soon fast asleep.

The sun was several hours high when they awoke. They stretched their stiffened limbs and leisurely crawled out of bed. The

---

5 **volubly** - characterized by ready or rapid speech

window of their room looked out over the valley below, and a scene of ruin and desolation was spread out before them. As far as they could see up and down the stream was an expanse of slimy mud and drift through which ran the swollen creek. A gentle breeze was blowing and it wafted to their nostrils the disagreeable odor of stagnant water and decaying vegetation.

They heard some one moving briskly about the house; and through a crack in the thin outer wall of the room they caught sight of their rescuer working about the stable yard. Jim glanced ruefully at his soiled and mud stained garments, and remarked:

"We made a good start at roughing it, I should say. I wish I had my case in here; I would put on some clean clothes."

"We had better to save our clean suits for a future location, Jim; we can brush these up so they will look first-rate."

"You're right. If we start out this morning we shall find the roads very muddy, I suppose."

They dressed hurriedly and stepped out upon the porch. "Sally," a fat, bustling little woman of middle age, came out of the kitchen and bade them a cheery good morning.

"I'm gitting y'r breakfast—it'll be ready in a little bit. Do you want to clean up a little? Jest so; well, here's a broom-brush, an' blackin', an' shoe-brush—an' there's soap-an'-water, an' tow'l on the end o' the porch."

They brushed their clothes thoroughly, blacked their shoes, and after scrubbing their faces and hands with water and yellow bar soap, they joined Sally and her brother at breakfast.

Chapter III

A half hour later they were again ready for the road. Their host's parting injunction was: "Keep right straight on—thirteen miles'll bring you to Kellersville. You'll git there in time for dinner, I s'pect." A hearty handshake and a cheery goodbye, and they resumed their travels.

For the first few miles the road was heavy, the grade slightly ascending, and their progress necessarily slow. But breeze and sun soon did their work, and the boys reeled off mile after mile with ease and comfort. They passed through Kellersville, a bustling little town of several thousand inhabitants, without stopping. Here they again struck the railroad and felt that they were not so isolated. They were speeding through a rich and level agricultural region now. Large farms with neat white farmhouses and big red barns followed one another in quick succession, on each side of the road. The laborers were in the field, plowing for the fall sowing; the dark-green corn waved its shining tassels in the sunlight; and bushels of luscious fruit hung, ripening in the orchards. It was a beautiful scene of prosperity—prosperity as a result of honest toil.

A few miles beyond Kellersville Jim punctured his front tire on hedge thorn. He did not notice it until Dick remarked:

"There doesn't seem to be much air in your front tire, Jim."

"Goodness! I believe I've got a puncture," and Jim jumped to the ground in a jiffy.

"That's what I've got," he said after a few moments examination.

He dragged his vehicle onto a sodded bank in the shade, and Dick joined him. They opened their tool bags and went to work, and in a short time the puncture was closed. Jim mopped the sweat from his glowing visage[6], and puffed.

"My, but it is getting hot again. How far have we come, Dick?"

"Twenty-three miles this morning."

"Then we're fifty-six miles on our road. Let's go on; we'll run five or six miles and try to find some dinner."

The heat was intense, and our young wheelmen road very leisurely; and stopped frequently to cool themselves in a welcome shade, or to procure water to slake their ever-present thirst. At one place at which they stopped, Dick suggested that they ask for something to eat. A woman was peeping at them through the lattice work of the back porch, and heard Dick's words. She stepped out upon the flags and inquired:

"Do you want your dinners?"

Dick acting as spokesman, replied: "We are not particular about

____
6 **visage** - the face or facial expression of a person; countenance

a regular meal, but we should like something to eat—say a glass of milk and some bread and butter."

"All right," and the woman turned to enter the house; but Dick resumed: "I must inform you that we have no money."

She paused stiff as a statute and piercing Dick with her black eyes, she cried:

"You say you have no money?"

"That's what I said—yes, ma'am."

"Then you don't get anything—I can tell you that. You're a pretty pair o' beggars! Riding along the roads on high tone bicycles and asking honest, hard-working people to feed you. Get right out of here—get right out."

The boys did not wait for further hints!—they went, they stood not on the order of their going. When they had mounted their wheels and were riding on, Jim leaned over his handlebars and burst into a roar of laughter.

"What's so funny?" snapped Dick, a little nettled.

"Oh—oh!" gasped his companion, "I can't help but think of what you said yesterday. You resolved to go on with me, if you had to live on air and water. Well, we had enough water last night to do with the whole trip—and today, I suppose, will begin on our diet of air."

Dick's good humor returned at once, and he laughed as heartily as Jim. "You may try at the next place," he chuckled; "and I wish you better luck, for I am as hungry as a bear."

Jim was more unfortunate than Dick, if possible, at the next place where they tried to obtain food. The old farmer himself came out to meet them and was in a very bad humor evidently. He curtly told them that he had no use for tramps on foot or on wheels.

"I don't think that I feel much better," grinned Dick, as they left the second farmhouse; "in fact it appears that my symptoms are steadily growing worse. Talk about your prodigal son, Jim! I could eat husks, stalks and all. I intend to have some fruit at the next orchard, unless the bulldog is bigger than a cow. I don't mean to starve in the midst of plenty."

"This may get to be a serious matter, Dick; I am half famished, really. Hello! here's an orchard; now what shall we do—go out that little lane and ask for some of the fruit, or take it without leave?"

A parley ensued. Dick was for procuring the fruit at once and asking for it afterwards; Jim held that it would be more manly to ask permission—even if they had to steal the fruit afterward. Dick finally came around to Jim's view of the matter, and together they proceeded to the house. Here an agreeable surprise was in store for them. At their request for fruit, the farmer who was leaping off the barn floor, said:

"Certainly, you can have as much as you wish—but, have you had any dinner?"

"No, sir," answered Dick promptly.

"Well, we've had ours; but I'll tell mother to give you some bread and milk anyway."

He led the way to the house, the two hungry tourists following eagerly in his wake. His wife, a matronly woman of forty, gave them seats on the cool back porch and pulled a small table out from the wall. On this she placed nice wheat bread, a pitcher of cold, rich milk, a plate of butter and a dish of honey. Furnishing them with bowls, spoons, knives and forks, she told them to help themselves, and left them to eat all they wanted.

"Isn't this just grand!" munched Dick; "especially since we've had such a hard time to get it?"

"Grand! I should say so. Aren't you glad we came on, Dick?"

"Of course, I am! Say, Jim, we'll be full to the neck. I don't think we shall want much fruit—eh?"

Jim only smiled a reply, and rising from his chair, brushed the crumbs from his lap. The kind lady came out and urged them to have more; but for the reason that each felt that he could not hold another morsel, they declined. After thanking her many times, they took their departure. They found riding hot and disagreeable after so hearty a dinner, so they stopped quite frequently in the shade, and idled away much of the afternoon. At one place, Jim—lying on his back under a tree, and winking at a glimpse of blue sky through the branches above—said in an amusing way:

"Its too hot to ride in the middle of the day. We must start earlier of mornings, and ride later of evenings."

"That would be better," assented Dick. Then both were quiet again, through sheer lack of energy. Both dozed for a little while, then Jim took up the broken thread of conversation.

"Say! Dick, what would our parents say, if they knew that we were begging our way?"

"Do you think it wrong?"

"I don't know; but I don't believe our folks would like it, if they knew."

"It was your decision that we came on."

"I know it—I did not want to turn back; but still it may have been wrong."

"Shall we tell them all about it when we get back home?"

"Yes, indeed! It would not be right to keep it from them. I think we should write to them when we get to Aunt Margaret's, and tell them all about it."

Dick was too drowsy to argue the question—even had he felt that Jim was wrong—and both dozed off to sleep again. They had slept but a few minutes, probably, when they awoke simultaneously and leaped to their feet. The smell of coal smoke assailed with their nostrils, and a gurgling, coughing, hissing noise greeted their ears. Coming slowly up the middle of the highroad was what appeared to be a railroad locomotive, drawing behind it a strange looking car.

"Jewhilikens!" was all that Dick could ejaculate.

"It's a traction engine and thresher," explained Jim, after gazing at it a moment in silence, "and it's going to thresh some farmers crops along this road. I wish we knew where; we would stop and see them work."

The engine passed; and as the sun had dropped low in the western sky and the air was much cooler, Dick and Jim proceeded on their way. It was pleasant riding, and they rolled along at a brisk rate. The sun went down, the stars peeped out and lights began to twinkle in the houses along the road. They passed through a little hamlet containing several houses, a country store, and the blacksmith shop—at the glowing forge of which the smith was hard at work. At the barnyards that they passed the tired men were doing the evening chores. They crossed a railroad track and still sped on, but it was growing quite dark and they could not be certain of the road.

"I say we stop at the next house, Jim."

"I'm agreed—and here it is."

A large quadranglular shadow loomed up on the right side of the road. It proved to be a barn; and the great doors were wide open. A lighted lantern swung from a peg in the barn entrance, and threw its feeble rays out into the barnyard. A traction engine stood in front of the open doors, and a thresher occupied the center of the barn floor. A number of men busied themselves in and about the building, and the incessant stamp of many horses could be heard in the stables at the rear.

Jim and Dick wheeled into the yard and dismounted, "Hullo!" called a hearty voice from the blackness of the horse stables, and a stalwart figure moved toward them.

"Good evening," answered the two boys, moving forward to meet the figure. Then Jim inquired: "Can we get our suppers and bed and breakfast? We are traveling and have no money."

"Ain't got any money—eh?" said the man, peering into their faces.

"No, sir; we had plenty of money, but we lost it on the way."

"Did you lose it bettin' on hoss races or base ball?" and he guffawed at his own humor.

"I lost it out of my pocket," explained Jim.

"Well, that's all right, youngsters; I was jest teasin' you a little. You're welcome to stay, if you can put up with the fare; and I reckon you can stand it a little while for nothin' when we stand it all the time and work for 't, too." And again he paused to laugh.

Then he continued: "But I s'pect you're hungry. Run y'r bisickles into the barn, and go out to the house an' tell Nellie I said to give you somethin' to eat. You'll have to be contented with a cold bite, we've had supper two hours ago. I s'pect you'll have to sleep in the barn. You see, we've got the threshers here; but you won't mind that this hot night—it'll just be comfortable."

The lads did as they were directed. As they reached the house—a large new frame building in an unfinished condition—an old lady came out of the kitchen, and seating herself upon the stone steps, began to smoke a clay pipe composedly.

"The gentleman at the barn sent us here to get something to eat," ventured Dick.

"Hey!" shrieked the old lady holding her hand to her ear.

"Speak louder—she's deaf," said Jim in a low tone. Dick repeated his announcement.

"Oh, he's out at the barn—yes, Henry's at the barn."

It was evident that she could not understand a word that Dick said; and they did not know what move to make next—for the old lady completely and composedly blocked the doorway. The problem was solved by a young lady who emerged from the door of a smoke house near by. To her Dick repeated his message. She invited them in to the kitchen and cheerfully attended to their wants, chatting to them all the while about themselves and their trip.

After they had satisfied their hunger the young lady cleared away the things and said: "Now, Jim and Dick"—and she smiled so sweetly that both boys were half in love with her—"you need not sleep in the barn at all, unless you prefer to do so. I can make down a bed for you on the floor. But a number of the threshers will sleep in the barn, and it may be that you covet the experience, do you?"

They assured her that they did.

"Very well, you should get as much rural experience out of your trip as possible. I have taught in the city schools, and I know that you will have ever so much, that is new, to tell when you return home. When you are tired of my talk, I will send you to your sleeping apartments in the barn." And again she smiled with that sweet smile.

"Is—is your name Nellie?" timidly ventured Jim.

"Yes, that is my name."

"Are you the big man's wife—the man out of the barn?"

She broke into a silvery laugh. "No, indeed! Do I look so old?"

Jim hastened to assure her that she did not; and Dick enjoyed the joke at Jim's expense ever so much. Then she went on to tell them that she was Henry Geddes' niece, that her home was in the

city, but that she had been her uncle's housekeeper since the death
of his wife two years before.

"And who is the old lady?" asked Dick.

"She is my grandmother—Uncle Henry's mother."

"She is very old, isn't she?"

"Very old—and very deaf; and very feeble of late."

"I never saw a woman before that smoked," asserted Dick
earnestly.

Nellie laughed. "Few women smoke at the present time, I am
glad to say," she replied; "but when grandmother was young a great
many of them did. You will learn many new things on your journey,
as I said before. You must stay here tomorrow forenoon to see them
thresh. Now, you had better go to rest—I know you must be tired. I
want to talk with you more tomorrow."

When our youthful friends return to the barn the chores were all
done and the men were lounging about in various attitudes, resting
and talking after the labors of the day.

The boys threw themselves down on a pile of hay and listened
to the hum of voices. The soft, cool air stole in at the open doors
and fanned their sun-burned cheeks. Presently the men separated to
retire to sleep; some of them going to the house and others seeking
out comfortable places in the barn. Then all was still but the restless
stamping of the horses in the stables. Gradually this sound grew
fainter and more distant—ever fainter and more distant. At last it
ceased altogether, Jim and Dick were fast asleep.

Chapter IV

"Rouse up here, fellers—le's get to the chores!"

Dick popped up like a Jack-in-the-Box, and rubbed his sleepy
eyes. Where was he? Had he heard someone calling, or was it but an
uneasy dream? The first faint gray streaks of daylight were stealing
into the gloomy and cobwebbed barn. Dick's doubts were dispelled
by seeing Mr. Geddes standing in the barn door, smiling. The men
began to stir themselves and to crawl out of their nests in the hay and
straw. They yawned, and stretched their stiffened limbs; and bustled

off to attend to the feeding of the horses. Dick aroused Jim by shaking him by the shoulder.

"What do you want?" demanded Jim ill-naturedly.

"The farmers called out the men; get up, and let's see them at their work."

Jim grumbled at such early rising, but sprung up and followed Dick to the stables.

The men were already at work. Some of them were currying and rubbing down the horses, placing feed in their boxes and putting the harness upon them; others were cleaning and sweeping out the stalls and throwing hay into the mangers, from the mows. One man was starting a fire in the traction engine; another was arranging belts and bands around the thresher, and oiling the journals and bearings. Two men harnessed a team to the tank wagon, and started for the well in the orchard, to convey water to the engine. The place in a few minutes had become a busy and animated hive of industry.

For an hour the men worked without stopping; then the breakfast bell rang and they trooped out to the house. They scrubbed their grimy and dusty faces at the cistern, and hurried into breakfast. Jim and Dick were astounded at the amount that the laborers could eat; the boys, themselves, were not very hungry—it was too early a breakfast for them.

The morning meal over, the company returned to the barn. Here other men armed with forks, had congregated. The engineer tested the steam in the boiler, and finding that he had sufficient pressure, informed them that all was ready. The men took their places. The engine puffed and snorted, the black smoke rolled in volumes from the chimney, the wheels began to revolve and the thresher to vibrate and rumble—and the lads saw a threshing machine in full operation, for the first time in their lives.

To say that they watched the proceedings with a great deal of interest is indulging in a platitude. What boy ever lived who did not like to see a threshing machine in operation—or what man either, for that matter? There is something fascinating about it all—the buzzing machinery, the flying sheaves, the tumbling golden straw, and the bright grain flowing in a steady stream from the spout. What an inspiring sight—what a triumphant of ingenuity! Jim and Dick carried water for the men to drink, held sacks for the man who measured the wheat, and even took a turn at pitching straw from the tail of the machine. It was sweaty, dirty work, but Mr. Geddes had given them old clothes for it as requested. And what glorious sport to city bred boys of fifteen years!

Nellie, in a clean gingham dress and a straw hat, came out to see how they were enjoying themselves; then they abandoned all idea of leaving until after dinner. Was ever a forenoon so short?

About 11 o'clock the bandcutter made a mis-stroke and cut a terrible gash in his hand. The sight of the flowing blood made Dick a little faint. Nellie brought clean muslin from the house, and Jim bravely helped her to dress the injured hand. But this spouting blood continued to flow; and Dick promptly took his wheel and went for the doctor, who lived at the little hamlet that the wheelmen had passed the previous evening.

When the doctor arrived he found that the keen knife had divided an artery; this he tied and redressed the hand. He smilingly complemented Nellie on her attempt at surgery, and rode away. Jim and Dick noticed that he waved farewell to her as he disappeared up the road; and that she blushed. They were not long in drawing an inference—boys of that age seldom are!

After a midday meal with the threshers in the great cool kitchen of the farm house, our cross-country riders prepared for their departure. As they were oiling their wheels and inflating their tires, Nellie standing by, said:

"How far have you come?"

"Seventy-six mile," promptly responded Dick.

"Then you still have about one hundred and seventy-five miles to go."

Both responded in the affirmative.

"Well," resumed Nellie. "I dislike very much to lose your company, but of course you must go. I have learned to like you in so short a time. When I am married you shall come to visit me—say next vacation."

Dick and Jim looked at each other and smiled slyly.

"At what are you smiling?" queried Nellie.

Jim colored, that Dick broke into an uncontrollable fit of laughter. "Oh!" he said, "we were just certain that you were going to marry him—and now you've told us."

"Who do you mean by 'him'?" asked Nellie, also laughing.

"We mean that young doctor that was here this morning."

"Do you think he will make me a good husband, boys?"

"Yes, indeed!" They answered in unison.

"Very well, then; I shall rely on your judgment, and marry him. And you will come to visit us next summer. So, good-bye! be good boys—and write to me when you get back home."

They shook hands with her warmly, even affectionately; and in a minute more were out of sight down the dusty road.

The afternoon was cool and pleasant, and Jim and Dick were determined to make up for lost time. With scarcely a stop they rolled along the brown highroad bordered by fields of tasseled corn and golden stubble. They flitted past farm houses and scurried through hamlets and villages. The surface of the country through which they were passing was still rolling, but becoming a little more uneven and broken. The population was more dense, and towns and railroads appeared with greater frequency.

As evening crept on—as the sun sunk like a globe of molten red gold in the West—they observed a tall pyramidal-shaped structure of bare timbers off to the right; then another loomed up on the left—and in a few minutes several more put in an appearance far ahead of them.

The city lads speculated much as to what the strange looking structures could be. A peculiar odor pervaded the atmosphere—an oily, penetrating smell not wholly unpleasant. At last Dick solved the perplexing question.

"They are derricks," he asserted positively; "we are getting into the region of oil and gas wells."

"That's it!" coincided Jim. "Why in the world didn't we think of it sooner?"

The derricks grew more numerous until they appeared like monstrous steeples, in all directions. Some of them stood close to the road, and pipes ran from them to large oil tanks in the distance.

The shades of evening gathered, and great sheets of light flickered and darted here and there, outlining the trees and other objects in a semi-ghostly way.

Presently the boys found that they were upon a descending grade that led to a little valley. A hissing, roaring noise was wafted to their ears, and on turning a corner they beheld a column of flame twenty or more feet in hight. It swayed, and curled and gyrated; it leaped, and reached, and recoiled—only to leap forth with greater fury, and to change color in its futile rage.

It was a magnificent sight—such as the boys had never seen; a grand spectacle that caused them to stop in wonder and admiration. It was a burning gas well.

A huge derrick, standing near the pipe from which issued the gas, was lighted from base to apex; an engine in a shed near at hand puffed and snorted, and added to the pandemonium of noise that prevailed. A team of horses harnessed to a light-covered wagon stood near at hand; and human forms casting long guant shadows moved about the scene.

The two boys had stopped some distance from the well, and stood watching everything with rapt attention.

"What is that man carrying from the wagon to the derrick?" remarked Jim. "See how carefully he holds it."

"I don't know what it is," returned Dick, "let's move down there where we can see them."

"I suppose there is no danger."

"No! how could there be? We will not go close to the machinery."

"All right—let's go down."

They leaned their wheels against the fence, and climbing over, they ran down the gentle slope to the well. Once on the ground, they saw that the gas that was burning was coming through a pipe, from another well a few hundred yards away. Also, they saw that the men were emptying some substance from cans into long, bright tin tubes; and lowering the tubes into the new well beneath the derrick, near which they stood.

The men were very busy, and at first did not notice the presence of spectators. As soon as they did, however, they promptly ordered our young friends to take their departure.

"Are we in your way, or is there danger?" inquired Jim.

The man who had spoken, answered: "Danger! Do you know what we are doing?"

"No, sir."

"I thought not, from your question. Well, we are charging this well with nitroglycerin, and a slight jar is liable to blow everything into Kingdom come."

"What do you mean by charging the well?" asked Dick, very much interested.

"I mean that we are putting sixty quarts of nitroglycerin into the well—thirteen hundred feet under ground—and that we mean to explode it down in there, by means of a cap and a dropped weight. This we call shooting a well."

"But what do you do it for?"

"It is done for the purpose of opening up the crevices in the earth and rock; and the oil or gas is expected to escape through these."

This was all very interesting to the boys, but the man insisted on their moving away from the well, until it was charged or loaded. They retreated to the road, and took up their old position. In a few minutes a man sprang into the wagon standing near the well and drove rapidly away. Then someone beneath the immense derrick shouted: "Already now! Turn out that gas!"

In a moment everything was wrapped in the blackness of darkness—a darkness rendered more absolute and intense by the former brilliancy of the gaslight. The puffing of the engine, the rumbling and grinding of cogs and wheels, and the voices of the men all ceased. The stillness was oppressive. A weird loneliness seemed to pervade the atmosphere of the place; and Jim and Dick were tortured with expectancy of—they knew not what!

"All right! Let 'er go!"

The voice seemed literally to cut the darkness like a knife. Then there was the sound of scurrying footsteps, a brief interval of silence, and—boom! The sound was faint, muffled and indistinct, but the earth trembled slightly and the boys caught each other's hands convulsively.

They listened intently—held their breath and listened. What would occur? All at once a rolling, foaming, indescribable sound smote upon their ears. It grew louder and louder—they could not hear each other speak—it was around them, above them and beneath them. Then they saw a dark column of water, earth and stone outlined against the sky. It shot higher and higher; it surmounted the apex of the derrick and rained mud and debris for yards around. Then it's sank down—down—and disappeared. The shot had been a complete success—and all was over.

The two lads stood spellbound in the darkness. Jim was the first to recover the power of speech.

"Wasn't it grand?" he whispered.

"Grand and awful," assented Dick. "I suppose all danger is past; let's go down again and hear what they have found."

They had crossed the fence and were again descending the slope when a blinding glare of light caused them to stop and shade their eyes. The men had lighted the gas again. On reaching the derrick, they were informed by the workmen that the shot had developed an oil well—how good a one, no one seemed to know.

The excitement over, Dick and Jim began to feel their need of supper. They made inquiries of one of the men, as to the chances of obtaining food and bed for the night, at some neighboring farm house.

"We're jest goin' down to the shanty to have supper," replied the man. "You're welcome to go down with us—an' stay all night, too, if you can put up with the quilt on the floor. We don't put on no great style—but we'll give you plenty to eat."

The boys were only too glad to accept the man's kind invitation. The workmen arranged things for the night, donned their blouses, and together the whole company set off down the road toward the shanty, a half-mile away; the weary and hungry city lads walking and leading their wheels.

Arriving at the board shanty of two rooms, they entered and found supper awaiting them. The furnishings were few and rude—a table, a number of stools and chairs, folding cots on which to sleep, a gas stove, and kitchen utensils constituting the whole. The fare was rough but plentiful, and well-cooked by a male cook. The boys were not fastidious and ate heartily. Shortly after supper the men placed folded quilts upon the floor, and Jim and Dick lay down to rest. They dropped asleep with the smell of oil in their nostrils, and the hiss of escaping gas in their ears.

Chapter V

The next morning our youthful wheelman rose early, ate their breakfast by gaslight, bade the rough but kind-hearted workmen farewell, and were on the road again. They had traveled three days and had accomplished about half of their journey, but the topography of the country was becoming rougher and more hilly all the time, and their further progress would be slower.

They left the gas and oil region behind them; streams and bridges were more numerous, and the grades were heavier. The roads along the bottom lands were rough and stony, and in places washed into gullies.

Bad luck apparently attended them. First Jim punctured his rear tire in two places; next Dick punctured his front tire. Then Jim lost a nut from his pedal, and had to wrap the screw with string to hold it in place; and finally Dick took a header, bending his handle bar and cutting a bad gash in his arm, from which the blood flowed freely.

This latter accident occurred at a culvert just as they were nearing a village, and at about 10 o'clock in the forenoon. Jim bound up the injured member for Dick, as best he could, and they wheeled into the village. Here Jim procured a nut for his pedal from a local cyclist, and Dick went to consult the village physician about his arm.

"How did you do it?" asked the gruff old doctor, after he had unbound the arm.

"I took a header from my wheel."

"You mean you fell from a bicycle?"

"Yes, sir."

"Well, it serves you right! Anybody that's fool enough to ride one of those confounded machines ought to get hurt. You've bruised your arm like everything, too. Do you want it plastered up?"

"Yes, sir; but I have no money to pay you."

"That's nothing new—I'm used to that," grumbled the doctor. "But you cut a pretty figure—you do, young man; riding around over the country on a hundred-dollar bicycle, and not a cent in your pocket. You're wasting your time and risking your neck for nothing. You would a great deal better be at work."

Dick blushingly explained the situation more fully.

"Oh! that's somewhat different," admitted the doctor, slightly mollified. "Square around in your chair, and I'll make you as good as new in a few minutes. But you'll have a sore arm for several days—you don't mean to ride with it, do you?"

Dick informed him that he did. The old fellow grunted and growled something about boys having no judgment nowadays, and all the time went on making preparations to dress the injured arm.

He washed and cleansed the cuts and plastered and bandaged the arm neatly and dextrously. Dick bore the pain with the stoicism of an Indian, setting his teeth hard and screwing his face into grimaces to keep from crying out.

"There," said the physician when he had finished, "you are ready to be mangled again. If that arm becomes red, swollen and painful, you had better stop your riding—that's all; or you may have a serious time with it."

Dick bade the bluff old fellow good day, thanking him heartily and hurried out to hunt Jim. He found him at the livery stable across the street, washing a buggy.

"Did you get your arm dressed?" hailed Jim.

"Yes; what are you doing, Jim?"

"Canst thou not see! I'm cleaning this vehicle to earn my unfortunate friend, Dick Manley, his dinner. The gentleman who runs this stable is the proprietor of the hostelry hard by, and he has kindly agreed to give us our dinners—provided thy humble servant renders efficient service in the rejuvenating of this vehicle. Hie thee hence to the pump, and fetch a brimming pail of water;

and thus aid in earning something to tickle thy palate and comfort thy inner man."

"Have you taken leave of your senses, Jim?" cried Dick, laughing.

"Not exactly," returned Jim, "but mine host has promised to give us our prandial[7] meal and a half dollar of filthy for the rejuvenating of three vehicles; and, comrade mine, again we shall be bloated capitalists. Why should I not be in high feather?"

"You have already washed one buggy."

"Thou art in the right."

"Oh! Jim, do quit your nonsense and act like a sane being," muttered Dick, half provoked. His arm was paining him considerably and he was inclined to be irritable.

"For thy dear sake I shall repress my feelings, Dick—but, first! I'm bereft of the aqueous[8] fluid! Haste thee and fill the bucket."

When Jim's contract was completed, they brushed and washed themselves and went into dinner. After they had eaten and were ready to resume their journey, their host said:

"Here, boys, is a half dollar apiece; and I wish you all kinds of good fortune on your trip. You are plucky little fellows to undertake such a journey without money."

A few revolutions of the wheels, a cloud of dust in the village streets, two vanishing forms in the distance—and Dick and Jim were out of town, and wheeling rapidly along the road that ran through a deep narrow valley. The hills rose precipitously on either side of the valley, their summits crowned with a sparse growth of stunted oaks and pines. Tall willows bordered the stream on both banks and almost hid it from view. Here the clear water murmured and rippled over its pebble bed; and there it dashed in a cascade of foam, from a small ledge of rocks, into a clear and sparkling pool beneath.

The valley was cool and quiet, and the youngsters spun along the narrow trail with little effort. Occasionally they swung their caps and shouted from mere excess of animal spirits, until their voices echoed and re-echoed from hilltop to hilltop.

After a time the narrow vale opened out into a broader valley.

---

7 **prandial** - late breakfast

8 **acqueous** - made from, with, or by water

Here the scenery changed; the level bottom lands were dotted with farm houses and expanses of stagnant water alternated with cultivated fields. They came to a cross-road, and were at a loss which course to take.

"Let's keep to the right as usual," cried Dick; "if we are wrong we shall soon find it out."

On they went. The road bore more rapidly to the right, and they soon found themselves leaving the valley and ascending a narrow and torturous ravine. The road was rough and steep, but they toiled on. They passed no houses, and the road dwindled to a mere bridle path on a hillside covered with a dense growth of timber. They had been walking for some time, leading their machines.

"This must be the wrong road," grumbled Jim. "This all comes of your being so ready to turn to the right. You see you turned to the wrong this time. We have come five or six miles out of the way—I am sure of that."

"Well," returned to Dick hotly. "we can go back, I suppose; there is nothing to hinder our doing that. You didn't offer any objections to taking this road. Let's try it over; there's no use to cry over spilled milk!"

They laboriously retraced their course to the cross road. Just as they arrived at this point, a farmer with a yoke of oxen came from a field near by into the public highway. Of him they made inquiries.

"You ought to 'ave kept right straight ahead, and turned to the right two miles beyond Parkhurst's mill, three miles from here."

Jim and Dick did not wait to hear more. "Thank you—thank you," they shouted as they bent over their handle bars, and spurned the earth beneath their tires. They passed Parkhurst's mill—an ancient, crazy-looking structure where two or three loafers dangled their bare feet from a row of empty barrels, and gazed at them in sleepy astonishment; they reached the fork of the road and turned to the right—and still their pedals flew, and still they did not pause.

By this time the afternoon was far advanced. The air was cool and damp, and a faint musty smell was arising from the swamp lands. The tinkle of cow bells far up the grassy hill slopes sounded clearly and distinctly, and the frogs commenced their evening serenade. A home-sick feeling stole over the boys—and the shadows of evening stalked silently into the valley.

"Hark!" Dick cried all at once, his voice breaking the oppressive stillness. "What was that sound?" The two dismounted and listened, their young hearts beating a nervous rat-tat against their sweaters.

"I thought I heard something over there at the side of the road—just beyond that tree," said Dick in a half whisper.

"So did I," replied Jim.

They peered into the semi-darkness and listened intently. In a moment the sound was repeated, a moaning, grunting sound like that made by a person in distress or pain.

"There—there it is again," whispered Dick.

"I hear it," Jim returned in the same low tone; "it must be some one badly hurt."

"Drunk."

"Let's lay our wheels down and investigate the matter. Come on!"

"Wait! It may be some one that will grab us and do as an injury."

"That's true! What shall we do?"

"Let's ride on to the next house and give the alarm."

"The poor man may die in the meantime."

"I don't see what we can do to help him."

"You stay here by the wheels, Dick, and I'll slip up a few steps, and call to him."

"All right—but be very careful; it may be some one that wants to rob us." And Dick felt in his pocket to see if his half-dollar was safely in his possession.

Jim crept forward cautiously, peering into the fence corner from which issued the strange sounds; Dick awaited the result of the venture with trembling limbs and bated breath.

After advancing a dozen steps Jim called out—"hello!" There was no movement on the part of the individual addressed, but the groaning and grunting went on as before. Jim advanced a few paces further, and again called—this time in a louder tone. Still no answer was returned to his salutation; but he fancied the dark object moved uneasily.

"He's alive, Dick!"

"Well, don't you get reckless—be ready to run at any minute."

Jim had no idea of disobeying this latter suggestion, from his valiant companion in the rear! In fact, he was debating in his own mind whether he had not already gone far enough. However, after a moment's indecision he moved forward two or three steps and almost shouted:

"Hello! hello there! Are you hurt, sir? Shall I come and help you up?"

No answer was returned to Jim's vigorous salute, and turning to Dick he said:

"I believe he's unconscious, Dick. What shall I do—go over and touch him?"

Dick did not reply for a full half minute, then he answered:

"Yes; but take to your heels if he tries to catch hold of you."

Step by step, foot by foot, Jim moved forward toward the black object in the dark corner. He paused frequently to look and listen. When he had arrived within a few feet of the prostrate individual, the groaning noise suddenly ceased. Jim stood transfixed, and he felt a creepy sensation stealing up and down his spine.

"Are you awake, sir?" he inquired and tremulous tone.

Neither movement nor sound proceeded from the black and mysterious personage.

"Jim, you watch out!" Dick shouted. "He's playing 'Possum.'"

Whatever emboldened him to do it, Jim could never tell; but he leaped forward all at once and thrust out his hand. The next second he was flat upon his back, and the large black body had leaped over him with a startled growl or "bwoof," and was tearing up the road in the direction of Dick.

"It's a bear—it's a bear!" Jim cried, springing to his feet and preparing for flight. "Look out, Dick, he's coming!"

Dick needed no second warning. Leaving the bicycles to be devoured by the savage beast—should he care to make an evening meal on rubber tires and wooden rims—the thoroughly frightened boy tumbled over a low board fence, and disappeared in the neighboring corn field. The strange animal rapidly vanished up the high road, its "bwoofs" sounding fainter and fainter in the far distance.

Jim waited until the alarming sounds had died out; then he called to Dick, but got no reply. He helloed again and again with no better success. After waiting quite a long time he picked up the wheels and started down the road, leading one on each side of him.

What had become of Dick? Jim felt somewhat uneasy about him. And it was time that they were looking out for supper and bed. He paused and listened, but apparently no human being was in the vicinity. It would not do to go further without his friend. What should he do? He would hellow once more.

"Oh! Dick!" he shouted; and his own voice sounded weird and lonesome to him. What was that? A faint cry came to him from the farther side of the cornfield.

"Is that you, Jim?"

"Yes—yes, come out to the road."

"Is the bear gone?"

"Yes—come on."

"All right! I'm coming." And Jim heard a great crashing and rattling in the tall corn.

"Are you hurt, Jim?" Dick inquired earnestly as he climbed into the road.

"Not a bit."

"The bear didn't hurt you when he knocked you down?"

"No; get on and let's hunt some supper. I'm hungry."

"Very well; but I don't know that I can eat anything. I was nearly scared to death. I thought that the bear had killed you sure; and was after me. Was he very big?"

"About the size of a cow."

"Honest!"

"It appeared so to me. Hello! Here's another mill and some houses. We'll try to find some supper and a bed."

A smoky lantern stood on top of a post in front of the mill door. The mill was running and the clatter and buzz of the rickety machinery floated out on the night air. The fatigued travelers leaned their bicycles against the gray building, and entered the door. Flour was everywhere! It dusted the lamps swung at various points, recorded footprints on the uneven floor, covered the window panes, and made fleecy veils of the many cobwebs that festooned with the low ceiling. There were three stones revolving—one for corn and two for wheat—and a gigantic young man was emptying a bag of wheat into one of the hoppers.

Him Dick accosted by saying, "good evening," in an ordinary tone of voice; but he could not hear himself speak on account of the noise of the machinery. So he raised his voice to a higher pitch, and repeated his salutation. The young man threw down the empty bag, and with arms akimbo demanded:

"What do you want?"

"We want our suppers."

"Do you take this for a tavern?"

"No, sir; but perhaps you can tell us where we can get something to eat."

"You can get it over there at Widder Swipe's," pointing out the door, "if you have any money. If you haven't—you can't."

"What will she charge us?"

"A quarter apiece."

"Can we get a bed there, too?"

"No—are you travelin'?"

"Yes, sir; we are traveling on our wheels."

"Well, you can sleep in the mill office here with me, if you ain't hard to suit. I've got a bunk in here."

Jim and Dick hastened to inform him that they were easily satisfied.

"Good enough!" cried the young giant. "Go over and get your feed, and come back. I'm pretty near done for the day. Can you play checkers?"

Both boys assured him that they could. He gave each a rousing slap on the back, and capered about the floor in an ungainly way, howling: "Good enough—good enough! Hurry up, an' we'll 'ave a dozen games 'fore bedtime."

"Widder Swipes" laid out a "cold bite" to the lads—a cold bite consisting of a plentiful supply of meat and potatoes, bread and milk, and pumpkin pie. They devoured it ravenously, and were in imminent danger of losing their city table manners. When they returned to the weather-beaten old mill on the bank of the stream, all the lights were out, except one that winked and twinkled from the little window in the mill office. They were at last nearly over their fright at the narrow escape from the bear.

Chapter VI

"Now," the young miller began as the two boys entered the office, "my name is Joe Farley, what's yours?"

The boys told him their respective appellations[9], and he continued:

"Here's some chairs"—kicking the articles of furniture toward them—"set down."

They seated themselves and gazed about the apartment. It was a small, dingy, flour-dusted room containing a stove—that stood in the middle of the floor, and a box of sand,—a number of splint-bottomed chairs, and a tall upright desk. At the end of the room farthest from the door was Joe's "bunk." It consisted of a platform of boards raised a few feet from the floor, and covered with quilts and comforters.

The evening air had grown quite chilly, so Joe threw some dry corncobs into the stove, and started a fire. Then he brought an ancient wooden checker-board from the tall desk, and producing a handful of corn from his pocket counted out twelve white grains and twelve red ones.

"Now," said he, "whichever one o' you chaps can play the best, can set there an' look on while I play the other one. I ain't a very good player—I'm just learning—and I don't want to tackle the best player first."

Dick admitted that he was the less skillful of the two, and moved his chair in front of Joe. They held the board upon their laps, placed their men in position and began the game. The fire of cobs sent a pleasant spicy odor through the room, the night wind gently shook

---

9 **appellation** - a name, title, or designation

the window sash, and the water in the race under the mill gurgled and rippled in a musical manner.

Jim sat and watched them as they played. Joe sat rigid as a statue in his floury suit, his good-natured red face alight with interest and excitement. The two were about evenly matched, apparently. After a half dozen games, Joe stretched his great arms, yawned and remarked:

"That's three games apiece, Dick. This one is the rubber. If I win it, I'll play Jim a few games."

The game was hard fought on both sides—but Joe won it, and Jim took Dick's place. Strange to relate, Joe won every game. Jim could not understand it—nor could he understand the peculiar self-satisfied and confident smile that irradiated Joe's features. At last Jim remarked:

"Say! Joe, you are playing much better than you did with Dick."

"Yes, I'm learning," admitted Joe with great complacency.

"You have won four straight games, Joe; and you must give me odds, if I play anymore," insisted Jim.

"Good enough—good enough! I'll take three kings an' you may 'ave four kings and four single men—an' we'll place 'em as we please. Now, go ahead."

The result remained the same; Jim again suffered overwhelming defeat, and quit in disgust. Dick enjoyed Jim's discomforture ever so much, clapping his hands and laughing immoderately.

"Oh! Jim," he cried, "you can't play as well as I. Why, I beat him three games!"

Jim was somewhat irritated over his ill success, and the words added fuel to the claim that was torturing him.

"Well," he burst forth. "I never ran across a forty-acre corn-field to get away from a bear—and left a comrade to fight it all alone."

Dick colored to the roots of his hair, but ceased his badinage[10] and said nothing. Joe was all attention in a moment—was a bear story forthcoming? He could not contain himself, and quickly inquired:

"What about the bear—when did you see it—where was it?"

Jim and Dick together told the story, interrupting each other at

---

10 **badinage** - light, playful banter or raillery

frequent intervals, but finally succeeded in giving a detailed account of the adventure. The effect produced upon Joe was something startling to behold. At first, he turned slightly pale and listened intently; a few minutes later, he grew red in the face, pursed his lips and puffed his cheeks, and had the appearance of a man threatened with an apoplectic seizure; finally, he clapped both hands upon his stomach and went into a prolonged convulsion of laughter—rolling his head from side to side, and stamping the floor with both feet; and, as a fitting climax to the whole, he tumbled to the floor and rolled and roared until the rafters shook.

The boys could not perceive a reason for such an exorbitant manifestation of mirth, and so expressed themselves. This expression on their part appeared to galvanize Joe's funny bone, and set him going again. At last he ceased to roar, and climbed up on his chair again; but not until the two lads were seriously doubting sanity.

"So—so, you saw a bear?" he puffed when he had gained control of himself sufficiently to speak.

"Yes, sir," replied Jim positively but curtly.

"What color was it?"

"Black."

"An' about how big?"

"I don't know—big enough to knock me down, and run over me."

"An' it grunted while it laid in the corner, an' "bwoofed" wh'n it jumped out?"

"Of course it did."

All the time Joe was asking these questions he had shown unmistakable signs of going into another spasm of glee. He controlled himself, however, and continued his interrogatory thus:

"Did you know that ther' ain't a bear in a hundred miles o' here?"

"I know I saw one," answered Jim silently.

"No you didn't! You didn't see nothin' but a hog—Colburn's ol' black sow!"

Joe had restrained his risibilities[11] up to this point; but beyond this he could not go—he immediately dropped to the floor and went

---

11 **risibility** - relating to laughter or used in eliciting laughter

into another convulsion. His example was contagious. The ludi-
crousness of their blunder dawned upon the boys, and they joined
Joe in peals of hearty laughter. They roared, they whooped, they
yelled; until the gray old mill resounded with their boisterous hilar-
ity. They concluded that the boys might be as "green" in the country
as country boys are in the city.

They subsided from their laughing at last from sheer exhaus-
tion, and Dick suggested that they go to bed. It was 10 o'clock, and
the katydid's were keeping up a serenade in the tall elms outside. Joe
arranged the quilts and comforters on the "bunk," and all lay down
to sleep, without removing their clothing. The squealing of the rats
in various parts of the mill awoke the lads several times during the
night; but Joe reassured them, and they went to sleep again lulled by
the gurgling waters beneath the mill.

Bright and early the next morning they ate their breakfast at
"Widder Swipes,'" bade Joe a hearty farewell and proceeded on
their way. Not, however, until Joe had said: "Say, boys, that was a
trick o' mine 'bout the checkers. I could o' beat either of ye an' gi'in
ye any odds ye asked. Its an old trick o' gamblers to let their dupes
beat them and so lead them on. Let me jest tell ye now an' you see
that you remember it. Don't never bet on the other feller's game."

The valley roads were level, but quite sandy in places, and their
progress was not rapid. Gradually the broad and shallow valley narrowed, and at last merged at right angles into another. At the junction of the two valleys stood a large city, the smoke of which the
boys could see when five or six miles away from it.

When three miles from the city, their first adventure for the day
befell them. They were bending every energy to reach the city and
pass into the farming district beyond, before noon. As they were flying along with heads down, and disreputable red-nosed tramp stepped
into the road ahead of them, and called out sharply for them to stop.
Jim and Dick slackened speed slightly, but did not come to a stop.

"What do you suppose he wants?" asked Dick in a low, startled
tone.

"No matter what," Jim answered, "we are not going to obey his
command. Take to the left and I'll take to the right. Now—down to it!"

"Oh! you will, will you?" the tramp ejaculated as the youngsters flitted past him. Then he placed his grimy fingers to his mouth and blew a shrill whistle on them; and our wheelmen were filled with consternation to see three other tramps emerge from a clump of bushes, and blockade the road with their burly forms.

"What do you want?" demanded Jim as he and Dick stopped suddenly and sprung to the ground.

"We want to borry a half dollar o' you to buy something to eat—see?" said tramp number one coming up and acting as spokesman.

"We have no money," said Jim earnestly.

"Oh!, come off—that don't go."

"It is true; we have not a cent. We spent all the money we had for breakfast this morning."

"Don't give us no stiff o' that kind; shell out."

"I am telling you the truth—you may search us."

The tramps looked at each other in a puzzled way; but the one who had first hailed them grinned knowingly and cried:

"Turn y'r pockets wrong side out—we'll soon see."

The boys did as requested, triumphantly proving that they had spoken the truth.

"Well, if that don't beat my whiskers," shouted one of the tramps with an oath. "Tramps on wheels! Git out o' here—you're too high-toned for us to associate with!"

Jim and Dick were only too glad to escape so easily, and did not "let any grass grow under there"—wheels as they sped in the direction of the city. On reaching the suburbs they discovered that the road they were to follow bent suddenly to the right, without touching the city proper, and disappeared down the main river valley. This fact did not displease them, for they did not care to enter the city. They hurried on past factories, rolling mills and machine shops, and out into the rural district again.

Here the most beautiful scene that Dick and Jim had ever beheld opened around them. Two chains of lofty hills bordered the valley on each side, their precipitous slopes seamed and scarred by innumerable gullies and ravines, and their summits crowned with clumps of forest trees and green pasture lands. A small river, crystal clear and sparkling in the golden sunlight, wound its course among the hills. Its banks were margined by willows, elms and sycamores; and along its course at intervals were placed dams and locks, to render it navigable for small steamboats and to furnish water-power for mills and factories.

At a point three or four miles beyond the city, the boy's halted to look around them. To the north hung a great smoke cloud with lofty steeples pointing toward it like fingers of scorn at a tarnished name. To the south the silver river disappeared as completely as though it had found an underground outlet at their base. To the east and west were the hills themselves. The sumac and pawpaw bushes, dotting their sides in clumps here and there, were already turning to crimson and gold—just faintly tinged as it were. The halo of yellow sunlight that hovered over the scene was an inspiration of itself.

The two boys gazed enraptured at the beauties before them. At their feet lay the river, a greenish–blue sheet pouring in a cataract of foam and spray over the slope of a dam. In the distance a small steamboat was puffing and plowing its way up the stream, and awakening the pastoral echoes with the noise of its sturdy efforts. On the gray and moss–grown lockwalls, a number of fishermen were perched, their hats pulled low to shield their eyes from the reflected sunlight, and the columns of rising spray fondling and caressing their bare feet.

Here the stream closely hugged the base of the hills on the east, leaving a broad strip of bottom land on the west; and there it abruptly and perversely transferred its affection to the opposite side. The road that the lads were traveling was fringed and bordered by patches of golden-rod, wild sunflowers and other species of the compositae[12]. Purple asters peeped shyly from shady nooks, and, wild camomile and sassafras freighted the air with their balsamic odors.

After gazing their fill, Dick and Jim remounted and moved on. Jim was the first to speak. "Isn't it a lovely scene!" he said musingly; "but we will not make very good time along the route—there are too many pretty things to see."

---

12 **compositae** - a large family of dicotyledonous plants, with their flowers arranged in dense heads of many small florets

"Jim, we have finished two hundred miles of our journey almost," returned Dick; "how much farther have we to go?"

"About fifty or sixty miles."

"We can't quite make it today."

"No, but this will be our last night out—we can finish the trip by tomorrow noon."

"Good enough!"

Then both laughed at Dick's exclamation—it made them think of Joe Farley and the ludicrous time at the old mill.

"Say, Dick," said Jim, "that was good advice he gave us. If I'd had any money, I would have been willing to bet it all I could beat him after seeing how poorly he played with you.—But I'm getting hungry now."

"I can see the farm house just ahead, perhaps we can get dinner there," said Dick.

"Yonder goes a train! I didn't know a railroad ran along this valley."

"Don't you remember that we crossed the track, back there at the tile works?"

"That's a fact! I had forgotten."

The boys easily procured their dinners of the kind-hearted farm wife, and again took up the thread of their travels. They had been told that the road kept down the valley for about fifty miles. Judge of their surprise, then, when a mile beyond the farm house they found that it veered suddenly to the right, and began climbing the hill in a circuitous way toward the crest of the ridge.

"I neither like nor understand this," growled Jim. "If we travel over these hills, we shall have to walk two–thirds of the time."

Perhaps the road makes a circuit and comes back to the valley."

"Of course it does; but I see no advantage in walking up this terrific grade, only to walk down again. However, there seems no alternative—so, come on."

It was tiresome work pushing their bicycles up the steep winding road. A flood of noon sunshine poured down upon the white lime–rocks, and the air was close and stifling. At last their climb was finished; and for several miles they had hard-packed clay roads along the crest of the ridge. Then they began to descend toward the valley again.

"I say that we coast down this hill," suggested Dick; "it doesn't appear to be very steep, and the road bed is smooth."

"It may be steeper further down."

"We can keep in the track, at any rate."

"What if we should meet a team?"

"It is not at all probable that we shall. If we do, we can tumble off in some sort of manner."

"Very well; but I predict that we have trouble before we get to the bottom."

They were off! Their speed, slight at first, gradually increased with the rapidity of the dissent, until they fairly flew—their wheels scarcely touching the ground. By this time the venturesome twain were thoroughly frightened, but there was no way to check their headlong course. With eyes bulging and set, with muscles rigid as steel bands, and with every nerve screwed to the highest tension, they whirled down the frightful declivity[13]. They could not speak—the rapidity of motion almost robbed them of breath. Each would have given the worth of a world to have been safely off his wheel.

Just as they rounded a corner, and saw the river and the level valley road stretching away before them; just as they felt that their perilous ride was nearly at an end; they heard a cry of warning ahead of them.

Dick was riding fifty feet in advance of Jim. The sight that he saw blanched his rosy face, and sent the blood in a torrent to his heart. Four horses attached to a heavy load of lumber has stopped directly in the road! The driver was standing on top of the load gesticulating and shouting; and the horses were rearing, plunging and snorting in mad alarm. To the right of the wagon loomed a blank cliff of sandstone, and to the left lay a deep and rocky ravine.

Jim and Dick took in the full situation at a glance. There was no time to hesitate—to hesitate was to die! Their only chance lay in passing between the wagon and the wall of sandstone, on the other side of the road. "Keep to the upper side!" Jim shouted, and to the

____

13 **declivity -** a downward slope

driver: "Let us pass next to the bank!" Dick did not attempt to reply, but steered for the narrow pass. He whizzed through like a rocket—with not six inches to spare. Jim was not quite so fortunate; his leg grazed the hub of a wagon wheel, and the slight shock nearly threw him from the saddle. His arms were almost wrenched from their sockets, in controlling his wheel—but he did it. Both boys reached the level in safety, but when they dismounted they were so weak that they could hardly stand; and Jim had recourse to the court plaster, to repair his abraded knee.

Chapter VII

Dick and Jim sat down on a green bank to rest and talk over their foolhardy adventure. They were unanimous in coming to the decision that they would never indulge in such an escapade again. But young muscles are soon rested, young nerves quickly regain their tone; so the boys did not tarry a great deal while on the shady bank. Laughing and chatting, they resumed their course down the beautiful valley. It was mid-afternoon, and very pleasant riding along the shady river road.

"Look at the peaches!" Dick suddenly cried, as they turned an angle in the highway.

"Aren't they beauties—and bushels of them!" answered Jim, checking his wheel and looking longingly at the velvety fruit.

"Whew! They make my mouth water. I must have some of them, Jim."

By this time the two had come to a full stop.

"How are you going to get them, Dick?"

"Simply by climbing the fence and picking them."

"Without the permission of the owner?"

"Yes."

"That would be stealing, Dick."

"No, it wouldn't! There are bushels of them, and we should take only a few."

"Few or many makes little difference. It is stealing."

"Well, maybe you are right, Jim. But I see a house right

down among the trees. I'll ride down and ask for some of the fruit."

"That's the better way. It will take you but a minute or two."

Dick hurried off, and was back in a short time, announcing that they were welcome to as many as they wished.

"Good!" bellowed Jim, tossing his cap. "Now we can eat without fear of disturbance in the shape of cross dogs, and angry men armed with double-barreled shotguns, to say nothing of a goading conscience. Whoop! Come on."

Over the fence they went together, and were soon under the trees, eating their fill.

"Isn't this simply delightful, Jim?" mumbled Dick, with his mouth full. "Such appetites as cycling gives a fellow!"

"'Delightful' doesn't express it," Jim replied, swallowing quickly that he might speak.

"Aren't they luscious?"

"Delicious!"

"What could be better than ripe peaches?"

"Ripe peaches and cream!"

"That's true! But say—I'm full. I wish I could eat more."

"Alexander longing for more worlds to conquer?"

"Have you had enough?"

"Yes, and we both got our pockets full."

"Let's be going. We have idled away a great deal of time today."

"All right! I'm ready."

They walked leisurely back to the fence, and lazily climbed over into the road. Here they made the astounding discovery that their wheels were gone! They had left their dearly beloved machines leaning against the fence, but the vehicles had mysteriously disappeared.

"What can have become of them?" inquired Dick in trepidation and alarm.

"Are you sure we left them at this point, Dick?"

"Yes, I remember the place accurately by the old stump on one side of the road, and the pile of stone on the other side."

"Some one has hid them for the purpose of playing a joke on us."

"Or has stolen them."

"I hardly think that anyone would steal them. Some one passing has probably hidden them in the bushes along the river bank. Let's search for them."

The two boys had stepped to the edge of the river bank with the intention of beginning their search, when Jim ejaculated:

"Why, look! Yonder goes a skiff down the river with two rowers in it; and what's that shining in the bow of the boat? I declare it's our bicycles!"

The two lads gazed after the vessel, in silent consternation. It was rapidly disappearing down the stream, propelled by the strokes of two skillful oarsmen. There was no doubt about it now—their wheels had been stolen. What should they do?

"We must follow them," suggested Dick in a hollow tone.

"They have a half-mile start on us, and can travel faster in the boat then we can on foot," returned Jim, shaking his head.

"What else can we do?"

"Nothing! Come on."

Dick started off at a swift running pace, but Jim checked him with:

"Stop! Not so fast; you can't hold out ten minutes at that rate. We may have a long chase before us, and must save ourselves in the start. Lean well forward, strike a long, swinging trot, and breathe through your nose—with your mouth shut. That's the way to make a long run. Ready, now—we're off!"

As they started they saw the skiff and its occupants disappear around a bend in the river, a half-mile down the stream. On they ran. At first their breathing was labored and heavy from the unwonted exercise; but in a short time they gained their "second wind" and ran with ease, and celerity[14].

When they reached the bend of the river, around which the boat had passed, they discovered that the small craft was dancing over the water, still a long half-mile in the lead. Jim and Dick quickened their pace and rushed on, but the run was beginning to tell upon them; and they were almost ready to abandon all hope of overtaking the piratical[15] vessel.

---

14 **celerity** - swiftness of action or motion; speed
15 **piratical** – used for the purpose of robbing or plundering

Just as the pursued were passing the next bend in the river, the pursuers came into a large whitewashed barn standing near the road. A farmer with a span of fine bay horses attached to a light buckboard drove into the highway ahead of them and started down the river at a spanking gate. Jim hailed him, and the farmer pulled in his team and waited for the boys to come up.

A few words of explanation past, and the boys were seated in the buckboard, and the horses were making three-minute time in pursuit of the thieves. When the trio rounded the next bend, they had a three-mile stretch of the river before them—but no boat was in sight!

"They've landed somewe'r's," said the farmer, pulling his horses into a walk, "an' if they've landed on the other side o' the stream, you're left—that's all. There ain't a bridge within six miles of here, n'r a boat to be had 'nless at the fishin' camp right below here. Gosh! I reckon it wasn't none o' them fellers that stole y'r bisickles. They've been up to buy butter an' milk an' aigs o' me, sever'l times; an' they seemed like mighty nice, honest boys. No, it couldn't be them!"

"Where is the camp?" inquired Dick.

"Down here about a quarter of a mile."

"Have they a skiff?"

"Yes."

"What color is it painted?"

"White with a red band around the top."

Dick and Jim looked at each other and cried simultaneously:

"That's the skiff that contained our wheels!"

"You don't say!" Replied the farmer earnestly, peering into their faces. "Well"—and he set his teeth hard and hissed out the words—"them lads is campin' on my land; an' if they're a pack o' thieves, me an' them'll have a reckonin'!"

He drove on in moody silence. Presently, through a break in the wall of green leaves, the boy saw two white tents under a spreading elm tree. The wheels of the buckboard made little noise upon the dusty road; so the farmer was enabled to drive quite close to the camp, without his presence being known. He halted the team behind a clump of pawpaw bushes, where it could not be seen from the tents, and yet where the occupants of the buckboard could gain a fair view of the camp, by peering through the chinks in the leafy wall.

The farmer admonished the boys to keep quiet, and the three waited, and looked and listened. The sun had hidden itself behind the ridge of western hills, and the valley lay in shadow. The red-banded skiff that Dick and Jim had been following, lay moored to a stake near the larger tent, and their wheels—welcome sight!—rested against a sapling nearby. One of the campers was busily engaged preparing supper, while the others lolled about in pictur-esque attire and attitudes, laughing and chatting. They were boys and young men, their ages ranging from sixteen to twenty-five years, and had little about them to indicate that they were either thieves or desperados.

One of them lying at full length upon the sandy shore, mopped his flushed face with a handkerchief. He was talking, and these were the words that the farmer andour two travelers overheard:

"Oh! it's a splendid joke on Charley and Harry. You see we saw their wheels from the skiff; so we just ran up the bank, loaded them into the boat and came back to camp as fast as we could row. I think they were over in the peach orchard purloining the peaches from the farmer—and it served them just right. They'll be hopping mad when they get here, but we've got the joke on them, and they'll have to take it good-naturedly or go without their suppers."

"What if the wheels do not belong to Charley and Harry?" sug-gested another.

"Oh! but they do; they could belong to no one else. They were to come down on their wheels to join us today."

"They did not say positively that they would come down to-day. And I want to tell you two smarties something, that you may enjoy your joke first rate. Those wheels do not belong to Harry and Charley! I know the kind of wheel that each rides; and you have stolen those wheels from strangers—and gotten us all into trouble, probably."

The farmer in the buckboard did not wait to hear more. He lay back in his seat and burst into a roar of laughter, in which Dick and Jim joined. The campers sprung to their feet and came tearing through the bushes to the road.

"You're a putry set of fellers," the farmer cried as the campers swarmed into the road and surrounded the backboard, "stealin' bisickles from a couple o' travelin' youngsters. Who is the joke on now, I'd like to know?" And again he roared in great glee.

The campers were profuse in their apologies, and insisted on Jim and Dick joining them for the night. To this our young friends gladly consented, and the farmer, chuckling to himself, drove on in the direction of the village a short distance below.

The campers, ten in number, were from the city that Jim and Dick had passed before noon, and were nice, sociable young fellows. What a royal repast they all had together that night! They ate in the big white dining tent, with the shining yellow sand for a floor and with the music of the softly lapping wavelets in their ears. The supper consisted of fried fish—crisp and fresh from the river, boiled eggs, fresh from the farm, bread and golden butter, and peaches and cream. It was a meal fit for a king—or better still, fit for a free-born Yankee boy, who is better than any king living or dead.

After supper they built a fire of driftwood to keep away the gnats and mosquitoes, and lounged about it and told stories and sang songs. Jim and Dick told of their penniless trip with its amusing situations and adventures, all of which the campers enjoyed very much. Several of the young men sang quite well, and one of them played a guitar; so, taken all in all, it was the most pleasant evening the lads had spent since leaving home, though, as Dick said," the night with Joe was a close second."

The campers had a number of fishing poles set along the shore, and a trot line in the river. When bedtime came, they took up the poles, and carrying a lantern and a bucket of minnows, went down to the skiff, and Dick and Jim accompanied them. One of the campers sat in the bow of the boat, running the line hand over hand, removing the fish that were on it; and rebaiting the hooks. The other camper sat in the center of the skiff and handled the oars; while the two boys occupied the stern, and carried the lantern. It was a new experience to Dick and Jim, and they appreciated it accordingly.

With several fair-sized fish as the fruit of their water expedition, the four returned to land and prepared for bed—the other campers already having retired. The sleeping tent had platforms of boards running along the sides, on which were spread mattresses and bed clothing. Everything was neat and clean, and Jim and Dick doffed their soiled apparel and gladly sought their much needed repose.

About one o'clock in the morning they were awakened by one of the young men shouting:

"Turn out here, fellows; there is a storm coming and we must put things in ship shape!" The whole number of sleepers hastily tumbled out of bed and donned scant attire. Two lanterns suspended from the tent pole cast a sickly light over the group. Flashes of lightning in rapid succession, and muttering thunder, gave warning of warring elements that would soon be upon them.

The campers, assisted by Dick and Jim, made everything secure at the dining tent; and leaving two of their number to look after it, the others returned to the sleeping tent to be ready for whatever might come. The storm was close at hand; it's roaring could be heard in the woodlands upon the western hills. The lightning grew more vivid, the thunder peals sharper and more nearly constant. All at once the storm struck the camp. The dark river was whipped into foam, and the waves churned and dashed among the willows along the sandy beach. The wind blew a terrible gale. The tents swayed and flapped, and threatened to part their moorings and soar aloft. Three of the campers went to the aid of the two in the dining tent—dashing from one tent to the other between gusts. The great elm tossed its arms and creaked and groaned as though in mortal pain.

The gale grew stronger, the gusts more fierce and sudden. A few large drops of rain fell. Then, flash—boom! the storm was upon them in earnest. The wind blew with redoubled fury; the rain fell almost in solid sheets.

For ten minutes, perhaps, the campers had their hands full— moving articles from place to place to escape the dripping water; and hanging to the sides of the tents next to the storm to save the canvas domiciles from utter destruction. But the storm subsided as suddenly as it had arisen; and soon the ragged battalion of clouds was scurrying across the heavens in mad retreat, and the moon was smiling blandly above the western hilltops. The disgusted young men returned to bed, overslept themselves, and did not have breakfast the next morning until eight o'clock. The jolly campers insisted that Dick and Jim stay with them over Sunday, and promised them a fine ride in a steam launch that was coming down from the city; but our boys felt that they would rather spend the Sabbath at the home of Aunt Margaret, and politely but firmly declined the invitation. At half past eight o'clock they were again astride their faithful wheels—with but thirty-five miles of the journey remaining to be covered.

It was a most beautiful morning after the storm; the air was clear, crisp and cool, and the sun shone brightly. At nine o'clock the two lads passed through the little village to which the farmer had gone the night before; and at ten o'clock they reached a railroad town of considerable size. Here an incident occurred that was totally unexpected on their part.

They had stopped on the public square of the town, and were busily engaged in oiling their wheels and refilling their tires, when the town marshal sauntered across the street to them. He was a large, pompous man armed with a stout cane, and wearing a bright badge of office upon the lapel of his coat. A number of idlers were congregating about the boys, watching them at their work and asking them questions about their travels. The marshal elbowed the crowd right and left, and coughing impressively to attract the attention of our young wheelmen, inquired:

"Where do you boys hail from?"

Jim was wiping his chain, and answered without looking up.

"Did you come down the river this morning?" Pursued the marshal.

"Yes, sir."

"Didn't hear about any bicycles being stolen up that way, did you?"

Jim and Dick both looked up quickly, and inconsiderable surprise.

"Why—yes," replied Jim and some confusion—and blushing and stammering. "We heard of it; but there isn't any truth in the report. We were the fellows."

"That stole the wheels?"

"No, sir—no, sir!" And Jim went on to explain fully what he had meant, in fact told all about the campers' mistake. The group of idlers craned their necks to listen, and the officer eyed the speaker keenly. When Jim had finished, the big Marshall grinned in a knowing official manner, and said:

"Well, your little story may be true—but it doesn't hang together very well. I guess I'll just take you down and let you tell it to the mayor, and see what he thinks about it. Bring your bikes and come along."

The marshall started down the pavement toward the mayor's office, two blocks away, the crowd of idlers trooping at his heels. Jim and Dick exchanged glances and followed him, taking the middle of the street, however, and leading their wheels, and protesting that they had given the exact facts.

"This will delay us," Jim whispered to Dick. "We may be put in prison, even, until they investigate this foolish report."

"There is no need of our being delayed," Dick whispered and turned.

"What do you mean?"

"Let us give them the slip—jump on our wheels and make a break for liberty."

They stopped suddenly and looked at each other. "Come on!" called the officer starting toward them. He was much too slow in his movements. The two boys sprung into their saddles, and dashed down a cross street to the main street that ran along the river bank, the marshal and a lot of idlers yelling and howling in full pursuit. They soon gave up the chase, however, for they realized that they stood no chance of overtaking the fleet wheelman.

Chapter VIII

Dick and Jim did not check their headlong speed until they had left the town several miles behind; then they dismounted, laughing and panting, and stretched out on the grassy roadside to rest. As they lay there resting a man passed by in a cart, and of him Jim inquired:

"How far is it to Graysville?"

"About fifteen miles," replied the man, ejecting a stream of to-bacco juice and picking his teeth with a bit of straw.

"Do we keep the road down the river?"

"No, you turn to the right down here at the crick, an' go up the crick about a mile. Then the road forks, an' you take the one that turns to the left. It'll lead you up on the ridge. Then keep the main ridge fer about ten mile, when you come to a cross-roads; then you take the right hand road ag'in, an' about four 'r five miles'll bring you to Graysville."

"Where is a good place to stop for dinner?"

"Well, about the only place short o' Graysville is Granny Pier-pont's, about two mile out the ridge road. You see ther' ain't many houses along the ridge—it's mighty poor land. But Graysville is down on a crick bottom—an' there's a tavern there. Hows'ever, Granny'll give you somethin' to eat—she's a mighty good ol' wom-an. You don't 'spect to ride over them hills and ridges on them kind o' things, do you?" and he pointed to the bicycles.

The two boys laughingly assured him that that was exactly what they proposed to do, and bidding him good day, pushed on. They came to the creek and turned to the right; reached the road leading up to the ridge and climbed it afoot, pushing their wheels ahead of them. It was poor land, indeed, along this ridge. The road was a mere cart track and very rough, with a sparse and stunted growth of white oaks and cedar on both sides of it. It was a half hour after mid-day when they reached Granny Pierpont's and the two youngsters were weak and hungry.

The house in which Granny Pierpont lived was a hewed log structure, containing two rooms and with a frame kitchen at the back. It stood back from the road, as though afraid of passers-by; and peeped surreptitiously at the highway through a pair of small square windows. An ancient well "sweep" stood in front of the house, and sunflowers and prince's feathers made bright the front yard; while rank gourd vines bearing green and yellow striped gourds, ran riotously over the weather-beaten front of the building itself.

Dick and Jim dismounted, and leaning their bicycles against the fence of poles, climbed the low stile and walked up the path toward the front door. Granny stood in the doorway, shading her feeble eyes and watching their movements suspiciously. She was a quaint figure in her calico dress and gingham apron, coarse cowhide shoes and white lace cap. Her face was fat and red, and she held a short-stemmed clay pipe in her blackened teeth. She was very fat and short, and her apron strings were on intimate terms with her arm pits. Tresses of white hair strayed from under her cheap lace cap, and fluttered about her rosy, good-humored face.

"Can we get something to eat?" Dick inquired civilly, repressing a smile at her unusual appearance.

"That d'pends! mabe you can an' maybe you can't, who air you, wher'd you come from, an' whe' you goin'?"

The boys gave her the desired information. She pulled her brass-rimmed spectacles from beneath her cap, set them astride her nose, and eyed the speakers askance[16].

"You say that you're goin' to Margaret Lochary's, three mile beyond Graysville?"

"Yes, ma'am," answered Jim.

"An' you are her nephew?"

Jim again replied in the affirmative.

"Come right in then an' git y'r dinners! I know y'r Aunt Margaret, an' I us't to know y'r father wh'n he was a chunk of a boy, years ago."

She pushed forward two splint-bottomed chairs and invited the lads to sit down. Then she bustled around, setting the table, laying the cloth and talking all the while.

"Yes, yes!" she went on, "how time does fly! W'y it seems only jest a few years since y'r father an' y'r Aunt Margaret was boy an' girl. I knowed all y'r folks—knowed y'r gran'father, Hardy. He us't to spark me in my younger days. I come mighty near bein' y'r gran'mother."

She pointed her finger at Jim as she spoke, and shook it impressively. Dick was ready to explode with suppressed laughter; the

---

16 **askance** - with an attitude or look of suspicion or disapproval

idea of the quaint old countrywoman being Jim's grandmother—al-most—was too much for his gravity. Granny informed them that the meal was ready, and continued to talk:

"Yes, I know everybody 'round here for miles. I've doctored all over this entire kentry. I doctor with roots an' yarbs—the kitchen rafters is hangin' full on 'em. They're better'n any o' y'r new-fangled med'sins—they're nature's own remedies."

The free and unlimited volubility of Granny Pierpont did not abash Dick and Jim in the least. They ate heartily of the succotash, sweet potatoes, bread and butter, and milk that the table furnished. Then they caught up their caps, bade the curious old lady good day, and ran down the path to the road. The last words that they heard her say, were:

"Give my best respecks to y'r Aunt Margaret, an' tell 'er I'm a goin' to walk over an' see 'er one o' these days 'fore long. Tell 'er I'll bring 'er another bottle o' my yaller fariller fer 'er blood, an' a leetle snake-root an' ginsang an'—"

Jim and Dick were beyond earshot, and heard no more. They traveled the long ridge, dropped swiftly into the creek valley, and at three o'clock were at Graysville.

"Where does John Lockary live?" asked Jim of a man standing in a store door.

"Right on down the crick about three miles. It's the fourth house, an' on the right side o' the road—a big stylish frame house with a new barn right back of it."

On again they went until they reached a secluded spot on the lonely road. Here they sought the sparkling stream, took a good bath and changed their soiled and weather-stained garments for the clean clothing that they had with them.

A short time afterward they came in sight of the big farm house and the new barn. The place looked cool and inviting. The house stood on a little-knoll back from the highway, in a grove of sugar trees. Everything about the place indicated thrift and plenty.

"There is Aunt Margaret in the backyard—now for a surprise to her!" said Jim, his face flushing and his heart beating wildly. Through the open gate they whirled like a gale, and up the grassy slope, each striving to outstrip the other. They sprang to the ground, bowing and smiling; and the next moment the two lusty lads were wrapped in Aunt Margaret's motherly embrace; and Aunt Margaret's tears of joy were trickling upon their upturned faces...

Jim found at Aunt Margaret's a letter from his father containing a bank draft for $13, the remainder of his earnings above what he had spent on his outfit, and which his father had kept and sent him in that way lest he should lose it on the way—as Dick actually did.

But the surprise came when Dick opened his mother's letter which "Aunt Margaret" handed him. This was what it said:

"My Dear Son:—You will be surprised to see the enclosed draft for $8. The honest men and boys are not all dead yet. A boy only a little older than you, driving in from the country with a big load of potatoes for next day's market, picked up your pocketbook. You see now why I always had you mark it with your name, address, street and number. But for that the boy, Philip Harding, never could have found the owner. He came about sunset, the very day you left. He wouldn't take a cent for finding it, but by questioning him I found out that he was an orphan, "working out" for a farmer, who trusted him (only 16 years of age) to sell potatoes in the city and bring back the money, and that he was saving every cent he could of his wages, laying it up to get an education. 'Yes'm,' said finally, ''nd I'm goin' through college, too, if it takes me till I'm thirty.' So after I had taken his address and he had gone I mailed him a clean five-dollar bill in a registered letter and simply wrote on a card, 'To help you get through college before you are 30.' That leaves you $8 to pay your way home.

"At first I wanted to telegraph and intercept you and send you money by telegraph, but your father and Jim's father both said 'No, if they were men and lost their money they would have to take the consequences. Isn't it better to let them begin in the same way as boys? Will it not develop manliness in them?' Your mothers' hearts both said yes, but they were both very heavy and anxious, and of course we want to hear all about it as soon as you get this. For by your neither writing nor returning we are sure you found some way to go on through to Aunt Margaret's."

Such was the substance of the letter. Of course both of the boys wrote long letters home and told all their adventures.

They spent the rest of the vacation with "Uncle John" and "Aunt Margaret," except the last week which they spent as "bloated capitalists" awheel, returning home. They visited all who had been friendly to them on their down journey and offered them payment for what they had received, much to the surprise of some of those worthies, none of whom would take anything "from such honest boys."

They had at least learned independence, grown in manliness and gleaned a fund of information and experience that they could have gained in no other way so well; and they felt well paid for their trip as beggars awheel.

Jud Trainor's Ghost

I give this story for what it is worth, without embellishment or comment. For years it has been told and believed by the simple-minded country people of Unionville and vicinity. All through the seasons of flower and fruit—when men work from sunrise to sunset in the fields and retire early to recuperate for the next day's toil—it is never mentioned, but when the days grow short and the nights wax cold, when hoar-frost[1] silvers the stubble-fields and red flames roar in the cavernous chimneys, then is the story of Jud Trainor's ghost recalled and told.

As a youth Jud was freckle-faced, awkward and bashful. A man grown, he took the premium as the ugliest, most ungainly human being in the valley. His hair was sparse and straw colored; his eyes, small and dull. From his elongated chin projected a twist of harsh brindle beard. He was six feet four in height, and knock kneed and clumsy. Add to this description two brown and warty hands, a pair of stooped shoulders and a brace of splay[2] feet, and you have a vivid picture of Jud Trainor.

* * * *

His parents were well-to-do people, owning the best farm on Meigs creek—a farm consisting of 300 acres of rich bottom land and upland pasture, well stocked and improved. Jud was the only child, and had it not been for his extreme "homeliness," would have been considered the "catch" of the rural neighborhood. As it was he was the butt of ill-natured ridicule; and "as ugly as Jud Trainor" became a standard of comparison wherever he was known.

He was teased by his male companions and shunned by his female acquaintances, until his disposition was soured and his whole

---

1 **hoar-frost** - a grayish-white crystalline deposit of frozen water vapor formed in clear still weather on vegetation, fences, etc

2 **splay** - clumsy or clumsily formed; awkward

nature reeked with misanthropy[3]. The affable smile that had once been his deserted his rugged features, and a sinister scow occupied its place. He shut himself up within himself, seldom left the farm, and held intercourse with few except his parents.

Jud was thirty years old when his father died suddenly, leaving the sole care of the farm to his son. Two years later the mother bade goodbye to earth, and the crabbed and hardened man was left alone. People did not waste pity upon the forlorn and despised wretch, but laughingly wondered if he would assume the hopeless task of seeking a wife. Incredulous as it may seem, that is just what he did do; and the neighborhood was electrified by the report that Jud Trainor was courting pretty Dessie Fleming, the black-eyed belle and incorrigible coquette[4] of the village.

The villagers could hardly credit their senses—and yet it was true. On more occasions than one, reputable persons had seen him in company with a young woman. For the first time in their lives, they really pitied him; for, of course, Dessie was simply amusing herself at his expense. Then the climax came. One Sunday morning he appeared at church with her clad in an ill fitting suit of sober black and towering over her, like a great tailor-made stork.

* * * *

Dessie Fleming was the daughter of the village blacksmith. She was a vivacious, quick witted girl not yet out of her teens; and every gossip in the vicinity marveled that she could tolerate the presence and intentions of Jud Trainor. Every eligible swain within 3 miles of the little hamlet where she lived had laid siege to her heart— and failed to capture it. Was it possible that the despised outcast of the community was to succeed where they had failed? Their pride would not let them believe it; and all joined in saying that Dessie was selling her soul to the evil one for Trainor's land and gold.

One glorious autumn day the two were married; and dire were the predictions of the disappointed lovers and wrinkled crones. She

3   **misanthropy** - general hatred, mistrust or disdain of the human species or human nature
4   **coquette** - a flirt, a girl or woman who flatters and manipulates men with her charms in order to get what she wants

did not love him—of that they were sure; and she would not live with him a year—of course not. Everybody predicted that the two would live unhappily and that she would return to her father's roof; and as usual in such cases, everybody was mistaken.

Dessie appeared to be happy and contented in her new life. Judd bought her a pony and carriage and the couple drove about the country together, apparently understanding each other perfectly, and enjoying each other's company. Instead of being a drudge—as many farm wives were—she led a free and easy existence. Evidently Jud did not wish to mar the beauty of the jewel that now belonged to him alone.

* * * *

He was very jealous of her, though. If he found her talking to a young and handsome man, he promptly swooped down upon them like a great bird of prey and bore her off in malignant triumph. At such times he became furiously angry and swore vengeance upon the innocent object of his jealous hatred. These outbursts of passion were the only clouds in pretty Dessie's marital sky—so far as the public knew at any rate. If she ever regretted her choice, no one was the wiser, for she kept her own counsel.

Several years passed and people ceased to take more than an ordinary interest in them and their affairs. A child was born to them and another change came over Jud Trainor. He treated his wife with greater care and deference than ever, and even had an occasional smile and cheery word for a neighbor.

But he was very eccentric—very erratic—and liable to fly off at a tangent, if anyone smiled upon Dessie or showed her marked attention in any way. He was insanely jealous of her.

* * * *

The following incident illustrates this phase of his character:

A life insurance agent from the city, 20 miles away, found his way into the valley and put up at the village tavern. Among others he solicited Jud to take out the policy.

"What's it all for?" was Trainor's first question.

"It is a protection to your wife and child," explained the agent. "Should you die while carrying the insurance our company will pay your wife the sum for which you are insured."

"If I'm insured for $5000, she'll get that amount, will she?"

"When you die—yes."

"I don't get anything?"

"No."

"I just keep the premiums paid?"

"Yes."

"And she gets it all when I'm dead and gone?"

"Certainly."

Jud clawed at his brindle beard with his knotty fingers—a sure sign that his anger was rising—and snorted like a mad bull:

"Get right out of here—get off my place and never come back. I understand your scheme first rate. Die and leave $5000, eh. Just coax somebody to step into my shoes as soon as I'm gone? Not much! They'll be running after her soon enough—they'd like to take her from me right now. I don't want any of your insurance—I don't. When I die I'll leave her enough to keep her in board and clothes— and not a cent more; and if she marries again, I'll come back and haunt her. I will—so help me God! You get right out of here before I lose control of myself and do you bodily harm—and don't you ever come back."

And the agent took a hasty departure.

* * *

A few months later the great civil war broke out and Jud was greatly interested in the conflict. He was an ardent Union man and read the reports of the frequent bloody engagements with ever increasing concern. A recruiting officer came to Unionville to raise a company and Jud decided to enlist.

"I'm going to war, Dessie," he announced abruptly one evening, as they sat by the crackling wood fire in the somber sitting room.

She was reading the war news to him at the time. Looking up quickly she asked in great surprise:

"Going to war? What do you mean, Jud?"

"I've enlisted," he replied sheepishly—as though he had done a dishonorable act and was ashamed to acknowledge it.

Dessie was silent for some seconds. Then she said:

" What is done cannot be undone, I suppose. Do you feel that it is your duty to go, Jud?"

"Yes."

"But what is to become of little May and me, in your absence? And who will look after the farm?"

"I thought that all out," he answered, shifting uneasily in his chair. "The Devol boys have been wanting to buy me out for a good while. They'll give me a good price—and they've got the cash, too. I'll sell out everything to them and get you and the little girl a place in town."

"You mean to sell our home?" Dessie cried in amazement.

Yes" he muttered without looking at her.

"I can't bear the thought of it, Jud," she said pleadingly. "This is our home—no other place will seem like home to me. And when you come back from the war you'll miss your farm. You won't be able to find another to suit you."

"Suppose I don't come back?" he interrupted.

She burst into tears.

"Don't talk like that," she sobbed, "of course you'll come back. Let's keep the farm, Jud, and get someone to manage it on the shares. I can help—"

But he obstinately shook his head and said decidedly:

"No, I'll sell the place and put the money where it will be safe. I'll rent you a house in the village and give you enough to live on while I'm gone. Then if I ever come back alive, we can buy another farm."

* * *

She knew it would do no good to argue or plead with him so she said no more. A few weeks later when he was ready to depart for the seat of the war he said to her as he thrust a bag of gold into her hand:

"Dessie, there's enough cash to keep you and May till I get back; I won't be gone more than a year or so at the outside. Besides, I'll send you money from time to time, if you need it."

But what have you done with all the money you received from the farm and stock?" she inquired.

"Put it in a safe place," was the indefinite reply.

"Where?"

"It don't make any difference," he answered ungraciously. "I'll know where to find it when I come back from the war."

"But—but should you never—never return—" she faltered.

An evil smile lurked around the corners of his wide mouth as he said:

"If I don't get back alive, I won't need it."

For a full minute she stared hard at his rugged face.

"True, you'll not need it," she replied slowly and with white lips; "but have you no thought for me—or your child?"

"Humph!" he sneered, "Do you suppose I'm going to leave all that money in your hands, so you can marry some lazy fop and keep him in luxury? Not by a jugful! I'm going away to fight for my country. If I come back alive, we'll enjoy the money together. If I never return, you'll have to make your own living. Then no young and handsome man will want to marry you. I couldn't rest in my grave if you should marry another man—that's all."

"Jud, are you crazy?" she cried in anger. "If you care nothing for my welfare at least think of little May."

He stolidly shook his head and was silent for a short time then he remarked and softened tones:

"My way's the best, Dessie. It'll all come out right in the end. I'll not be killed, likely; I'll come back to you."

✻ ✻ ✻ ✻

And off to the war he went, leaving the black-eyed Dessie in tears and perplexity. She loved her bright little daughter—who was a pocket edition of her winsome self—dearly, and all through the dreary months and years that followed Jud's departure, she lived for the child alone.

It is questionable whether she had ever born her husband any love, but she had not disliked him, and they had lived peaceably together. Now she missed him as she would've missed a familiar piece of furniture; and she often looked at their child and sighed deeply, for the thought that May might be left fatherless by the remorseless game of war would intrude itself. More than she missed her husband she missed her pleasant home that was gone forever. Cooped up in two stuffy rooms in the village, she fretted and chafed against her confinement and longed for the life of ease and comparative luxury that had once been hers.

From time to time Jud wrote her brief letters, and occasionally he sent small sums of money. She did not lack the necessities and crude comforts of life, and yet she was starving—starving for a love and sympathy that she had never known. Jud's letters were full of endearing terms and reassuring promises for the future, but for some reason they did not satisfy her. She could not forget that he had not trusted her; that he had treated her cruelly; that he had been willing to sacrifice the prospects of his own child, to his unreasonable and selfish jealousy.

* * * *

The war was drawing to a close. General Sherman laid siege to Atlanta. Then came news to Dessie—a communication from his captain—that Jud Trainor was among the missing. Whether he was killed or captured was not known. Some of Dessie's neighbors were unkind enough to hint that he had deserted. She wrote to the colonel of the regiment to ascertain something more definite, but he could tell her no more than she already knew. She waited and hoped, but no further tidings of the missing man came.

At first, in a mild way, she grieved over the loss of the father of her child; but when she came to a full realization of the wrong he had done her, when she began to feel the pinch of want and poverty, she thought only of the heartless deeds and forgot that he had ever shown her a kindness.

* * * *

The war closed. Singly and in groups the bronzed veterans returned to their homes. Dessie questioned each and all of Jud's comrades-in-arms, but they professed to know nothing of his fate.

"Dead or captured," was the verdict they delivered; and the cowardly stay-at-homes who had hinted at desertion, were silenced. The wronged young wife hoped against hope that he would eventually return. She was not thinking of him but of the money she needed so badly and what should have been hers.

But the months dragged drearily by, and he came not. Dessie was too proud to return to the home of her parents. She bravely fought her own battle, eking out a scant living by doing plain sewing and helping the neighboring farmers' wives in the busy season. Persons who had fawned upon her in prosperity frowned upon her in adversity. They said cutting things of her, maliciously remarking that she had received her reward for jilting worthy young men and marrying such a scarecrow as Jud Trainor for his wealth; and a few went so far as to whisper that her character was not all that could be desired, or her husband would not have treated her as he had done.

* * * *

She was very lonely; and of all the friends she had possessed in the old days but one remained true to her and sought to aid and comfort her. Harold Price had been a suitor for her hand in the dear dead past—as she now loved to call the springtime of her life. He was a handsome, manly fellow of cheerful, helpful disposition—and he still loved her with the old love. He was a country schoolteacher and owned a house and lot in the village.

What wonder that she began to look for his coming and to feel safe and happy in his presence? The gossips wagged their vitriolic tongues, but Harold and Dessie gave little heed; and on the day that little May was eight years old they were quietly married.

But ill fortune clung to Dessie's skirts and impeded her progress along the road to happiness. Harold, exposing himself to the inclement midwinter weather, contracted inflammatory rheumatism, and for weeks lay helplessly hovering between life and death. Dessie could not leave his bedside to earn anything and they were compelled to subsist upon the charity of their relatives and neighbors.

* * * *

When spring sunshine kissed the upland and clothed them in wild flowers, Harold was not out of danger but still confined to his invalid's chair. Every day Dessie left him in the care of little May and went out to earn their daily bread. She was doomed to a life of toil and hardship, but she was measurably happy, for she was working for those she loved.

One balmy June day she was delayed longer than usual and did not start home from her place of work—a farmhouse a mile from the village—until after nightfall. The air was sweet with the smell of wild roses and the dusty road stretched away like a silver ribbon in the moonlight. As she tripped nimbly over the dewy grass of the roadside, she was thinking how Harold and the little girl were worrying over her prolonged absence. The thought lent wings to her feet and she fairly flew past the old graveyard on the gravel point and down the grade toward the straggling outskirts of the village.

Just as she came to the big bridge spanning the creek, a tall, gaunt figure stepped from the black shade and barred her path.

Bathed in the bright moonlight that flooded the highway, it stood with folded arms and bowed head before her. Something in the attitude arrested her attention. She took a second look. The figure raised its head—and the form and face of Jud Trainor were before her!

* * * *

She did not scream—she did not faint. Nameless horror seized her, and covering her face with her hands she crouched upon the ground and moaned and shivered. A thousand emotions, thoughts and fancies surge through her brain at one time.

A sudden impulse roused her. She sprang to her feet and defiantly faced the spot where she had seen the form of her former husband. Then her black eyes opened very wide and she clutched frantically at her white throat. The figure—the vision—whatever it was, was gone!

Gathering up her skirts she ran toward home at the top of her speed, panting—brokenly as she went:

"His ghost! Jud's ghost! He said—he would haunt me – if I ever married again!"

* * * *

She did not pause until she reached the gate in front of the cottage. There she stopped long enough to collect her wits and recover her breath before entering the house. The front door was open and she could see Harold in his reclining chair. As she stepped over the sill, he looked up and asked quickly:

"What is the matter, Dessie? You are pale and breathless. What has happened?"

"Oh, nothing," she replied evasively. "I hurried because I was late—and I am very tired."

"Poor girl," he murmured, the tears standing in his blue eyes. "You have to work too hard—and all for me." And he sighed deeply.

She said no more, but went about her evening's work. After supper she professed to be worn out and went to bed early. But she did not sleep. The whole night long she tossed upon her couch, a prey to conflicting emotions. Was it Jud or his ghost? She was not superstitious—and yet she must believe her own senses. She had seen something. If it was Jud in the flesh, why had he not spoken? How had he disappeared so suddenly? And if he were alive, what should she do? If it was his ghost—but then there were no such things as ghosts!

When pallid dawn crept through her window she was still in doubt. She arose and began the duties of the day, but her face was haggard and her movements were slow and listless.

During the following week, a number of persons saw the apparition—Jud Trainor's ghost.

"I tell you," said Harry Devol—one of the broad shouldered, two-fisted brothers that had bought Trainor's farm—to a group of breathless listeners at the cobbler shop. "I saw him as plain as I see you right now. It was in the lane this side of the barn. He was dressed in blue army clothes and had on a soldier cap. The moon was shining bright—it wasn't imagination."

"Was I scared?"—in answer to a question of a lounger—"Of course I was—so scared that I nearly dropped to the ground. I tell you I saw Jud Trainor's ghost."

"Maybe it was Jud himself," suggested the cobbler as he rearranged his apron and dipped a piece of sole-leather into the pail of water at his side.

Devol shook his head.

"No," he said slowly and decidedly, "live men don't disappear from sight in a second, without making a sign of a noise."

"When did you see him?" Someone inquired.

"Night before last."

"The same night I saw him," said Dr. Jordan, nodding vigorously. "I had been out to Bill Walton's to see his sick child, and just as I got to the approach of the bridge the thing stepped into the road and crossed the bridge ahead of me. Then it disappeared as suddenly as if the earth had swallowed it up.

"As all of you know, I am not at all superstitious—medical men never are—but I own that it gave me a spell of the creeps and shivers. Whatever it was, it had the form and features of Jud Trainor. I saw his wiry, brindle beard as distinctly as I ever saw anything in my life. One of two things is sure, it was Jud Trainor or his ghost."

At this point in the conversation the cobbler drove the last peg in the shoe-sole and announced:

"Your shoe is all ready, doctor."

Dr. Jordan picked it up and walked away. The others conversed for some time in hollow, awe-struck tones and then dispersed. Within a few days the report was current throughout the village and countryside, that Jud Trainor's ghost had returned to haunt Dessie.

* * * *

Benighted pedestrians kept to the middle of the road and mumbled a hymn to themselves to keep up their courage. Children would not venture out after dark and cried for a light to be left burning in their rooms when they were put to bed. Dr. Jordan and a few others held the opinion that Trainor was alive and had returned secretly to ascertain how things had gone in his absence, but the greater number were convinced that the mysterious something that had been seen was the spirit of a dead man. Dessie heard the idle chatter but said nothing until Harold broached the subject to her.

"What is the meaning of the silly talk of Trainor's ghost having been seen?" he asked her.

She was silent for a moment, then she replied:

"I have seen it—whatever it is."

"You, Dessie?" he cried in great surprise.

"Yes."

"When?"

She told him.

"That accounts for your agitation that night."

"Yes."

"What do you think?" was his next question.

"I don't know."

"If you saw anything, it was Jud himself," he declared, stoutly.

"I saw something."

"Dessie," he gasped, "if Jud be alive and here, what are we to do?"

She threw her arms around his neck, sobbing.

"Oh! don't mention such a thing, Harold: you frighten me. I would rather see his ghost than himself—a thousand times rather. Let us talk of it no more. Perhaps I was mistaken—perhaps I imagined it all."

"But others saw him," he insisted.

"Oh, I don't know what to think nor do!" she burst forth; and wringing her hands in distress she left the room.

* * * *

That evening after Harold and little May retired, Dessie stepped out upon the lawn for a breath of fresh air. Her head ached terribly, and she thought that the cool night breeze would relieve her. Throwing a light shawl around her shoulders she left the house, gently closing the door behind her.

Hardly had she reached the ground, when chancing to glance toward the gate she saw Jud Trainor standing with his long arms folded upon it and his face turned toward the house. With her hands clenched until the nails dug into her palms, she strained her eyes through the semi-gloom. She was not mistaken this time; it was Jud's form and face—it was Jud or his spirit. Acting on a sudden impulse, she sprang forward, crying:

"What is it, Jud—what do you want?"

The tall figure raised a hand and beckoned her, appearing to float away from the gate and down the deserted street as it did so. Trembling in every fiber she followed. Her teeth chattered and the cold sweat stood upon her brow—but she kept on. Her ghostly conductor turned the first corner and half pausing, still beckoned her. She followed swiftly. To her excited imagination he appeared to rise clear of the ground and float through the atmosphere, without moving his nether[5] limbs.

They left the sleeping village behind and entered the narrow lane leading to the Devol farmhouse—her old home. Before reaching the buildings at the end of the lane, her uncanny guide turned into the orchard on the right, and occasionally casting a glance over his shoulder to see that she was following him, proceeded to an old gnarled apple tree standing near the creek bank. There he stopped and pointed toward his feet. She rushed toward him, but he slowly backed away from her and waving his gaunt arms disappeared among the willows that grew along the banks of the stream.

She reached the place where he had stopped under the apple tree just as he vanished. Standing upright in the green sod was a rusty garden spade.

Like a flash she recovered her senses. For a moment she stood there irresolutely staring around her; then she turned and sped like the wind toward home. She reached the cottage and divesting herself of her dew-dampened garments, crept into bed and lay there shivering and moaning.

____

5 **nether** - located beneath or below; lower or under

Her brain was on fire—her hands were as ice—she could not think. As morning approached she grew calmer and reviewed her experience of the night. She decided that she had seen an apparition but she could not fathom the meaning of her spectral visitant's behavior.

She resolved to say nothing to Harold; she did not wish to excite and worry him to no purpose. But she must talk with someone—someone that could explain the matter and give her counsel. To whom should she go? She thought of the village solon[6], Dr. Jordan. Yes, she would go to him.

* * * *

Early in the day she sought his office and relayed to him her weird adventure of the night before. He listened eagerly but quietly to all she had to tell; then he said:

"Dessie, have you told anyone else of this?"

"No."

"Well, mention it to no one—not to Harold, even. I have an idea. I think I know what Jud wants—what is on his mind—"

"You don't think it is his ghost?" she interrupted.

"I do not know—it does not matter. Dead or alive he wants you to do something; and I believe I know what it is. When the others have gone to bed tonight, slip out of the house and meet me at the entrance of Devol's lane. You understand?"

"Yes."

"That's all—keep your experience to yourself."

* * * *

That night at ten o'clock the two met at the appointed place, and silently and cautiously proceeded to the old apple tree upon the creek bank. The rusty garden spade still stood upright in the side near the roots of the tree. The moon, rising big and bright over the rim of eastern hills, gave to surrounding objects an unreal appearance. The gurgling, moaning voice of the stream near at hand sounded like the choking cry of a drowning man.

____

6   **solon** - a lawmaker or legislator, esp. a wise one

Without a word Dr. Jordan took the spade and commenced to remove the soft earth at the foot of the tree. Dessie silently watched him—furtively glancing around her from time to time and shuddering apprehensively. A screech owl screamed from the gable of the barn in the lane.

"Oh, Doctor!" The young woman cried, suddenly gripping his arm, "I can't stand this any longer. Let's go home—I'm afraid."

* * * *

He paused with the spade uplifted as he replied:

"Don't speak so loud—someone might hear you; and I don't want anybody to know we are here. That was an owl. Nothing can harm you."

"But what are you trying to do?" she returned in a stage whisper.

"Wait and see," was the laconic[7] answer.

She said no more, but leaning against the gnarled tree trunk for support, silently watched him as he threw the dry earth right and left over the green grass. The blade of his tool struck a hard substance with a sharp, hollow ring, and Dessie with difficulties suppressed a scream.

"What—what is it?" she inquired.

Without replying the physician threw out a few more spadefuls of dirt, and bending over the hole he had made seized and dragged out an old metal tea canister with a screw top. He shook it and it gave forth a jingling sound.

"Money! Jud's money!" panted Dessie, springing forward and seizing the canister with both hands.

"Sh!" cautioned the doctor. "Yes—I think so—let's see."

The treasure-box was rust-eaten and almost ready to fall to pieces; so Dr. Jordan had little difficulty in prying off the lid.

"It is Jud's gold," he announced as he held up a handful of yellow coins. "Take it—it rightfully belongs to you. But, if I were you, I should say nothing about finding it. The Devols might give you trouble. Let us be off. This is a good night's work for you, Dessie."

---

7 **laconic** - using or involving the use of a minimum of words : concise to the point of seeming rude or mysterious

"Do—do you suppose," she asked falteringly as she stood hugging the canister to her breast, "that this is what Jud—Jud's ghost wanted to tell me?"

"Certainly," Dr. Jordan replied, a queer smile over-spreading his features. "A faint noise—little louder than the breath of a sigh—called their attention toward the bank of the creek. There, distinctly outlined in the moonlight, they again beheld the form of Jud Trainor; and even as they looked he waved his hand to them in token that his mission was accomplished and slowly faded from sight.

The story of Dessie's good fortune gradually leaked out. Whether it was Jud Trainor in the flesh or his spirit that had pointed out the hiding place of the gold, is still a subject for debate in Unionville. A week or two after recovering the hidden wealth, Dr. Jordan smiled knowingly as he read in the county paper that a man's body—clad in faded blue uniform, but mangled beyond recognition—had been found at the crossing of the mineral railroad, twenty miles down the valley.

The Mills of the Gods

Chapter I

"Can you wait faithfully, Katie dear, throughout the years that lie between now and then? It will take me two years to graduate, you know, provided I am successful in passing all my examinations; then two or three years more of you waiting for practice to come knocking at my door. I do not wish to bind you to something against which your spirit will chafe, dear. I am poor and your people do not take kindly to our union; they think that your social standing is far above mine—and I can't but admit that they are more than half right. I know and feel that I am not worthy of you, in many ways— and yet I am selfish enough to love you. After five or six years we can be married; but then, even, I shall be but a country doctor and very poor. Can you wait willingly and contentedly, or do you think it best to cancel our engagement?"

The fall wind, that had been playing hide-and-seek about the corners of the gray old farm house in front of which they were standing, ceased its whistling melody to listen; and the sunflowers in the garden—growing black in the face with plethoric seeds—bowed their heads and waited for her answer.

It was so long in coming that the stalwart young man, towering above her, reached down two brown sinewy hands and lifted her face toward his own. Her features were scarlet and her eyes suffused with tears.

"Why do you not answer me, Katie?" He inquired somewhat impatiently.

"Do you want to break off our engagement, Mark!" she returned reproachfully.

"Far from it, little one, but you know what I mean. It is a long time to wait, and I fear you may grow sick of your bargain."

"Have you so little faith in my constancy?"

"It is not that. You misunderstand me. I have all faith in your love and constancy. What I mean is this: if I am to lose you at all, it must be now. I could not bear to look forward to our marriage for two or three years, and lose you then. It would completely sour me. And you will not find it easy to be true when I am gone. Your parents want you to marry Walt Janes—that I know. He is wealthy, I am poor. When once I am away they will bring to bear all their persuasive powers. They may resort to harsh treatment even, to accomplish their purpose. Walt Janes will be your shadow—forever at your side and pleading with you. Can you withstand it all?"

"I will be true to you, Mark; you need not fear. I will gladly wait," she said with quiet determination.

Mark Standish was ecstatically happy, if not perfectly satisfied. He pressed her in his arms, and passionately kissed her upturned face. "Till death do us part," he whispered; then he muttered a hasty goodbye and was gone.

The young woman watched him hurry with the long stride of a sturdy country-man, up the grassy lane to the high road and out of sight. Then she threw her checked apron over her head and burst into an uncontrollable fit of sobbing. When the storm of grief had spent itself she uncovered her face, smoothed back her tresses and stamping her little foot impetuously, murmured to herself:

"He shall see that I can be true. He is half jealous, and does not trust me fully because I have teased him so. But I do not care a cent for Walt Janes—and I do so love Mark. It is cruel in him to doubt me, but I will be true to him in spite of everyone and everything," and her black eyes snapped angrily.

She sauntered up the sidewalk, and around the corner of the house to the well. Here she bathed her face and eyes, to hide all traces of her recent grief, and entered the house. In the kitchen she encountered her mother, who inquired:

"Is he gone?"

"Yes."

"For good, I hope! Howsomever, if he ever comes back you're to have nothin' to do with him—the low down porper."

Katie returned no answer to this, but ran upstairs to her room to think over the whole matter.

Marcus Standish and Catherine Flynn had been lovers, in a way, from childhood—ever since the days when they first lisped the alphabet beside their teachers knee, in the little white school-house on the ridge. He was her senior by three years. When they played "Johnny Bull" in the shade of the gnarled old oak on the playground, Katie always chose Mark—and Mark in turn chose Katie. He was her knight, she was his lady. As the years slipped by— as years are wont[1] to do—he escorted her home from the country spelling schools and play-parties. As boy and girl they were more like brother and sister—ought to be. As they grew older their close companionship ripened into love.

All through the juvenile comedy and youthful drama Walter Janes played the part of the rival. Low-browed, swarthy and cunning, he was Mark Standish's inferior physically and intellectually. He was idle at school and learned little. However, he possessed a certain dash—and devil-may-care manner that appealed to the thoughtless and passed current for wit and good fellowship. In addition, he was rich—that is, rich for the country community in which he lived. He was an only child, and his father owned several well-stocked farms and had money in the village bank. And wealth is only comparative, and has a leverage in the country as in the city.

Mark Standish was an orphan, and at the age of twenty one had nothing but an excellent constitution, a clear head and a noble heart. On reaching his majority he left the miserly old uncle who had given him a home, and began to teach school. How he had ever gotten enough book knowledge to be able to do so was one of the problems that the gossips could not fault.

At the time of which I write, Mark was twenty five years old, a smooth-faced, cheery young man of more than ordinary intelligence and ability. He had saved enough money from his teaching to take him through college; and had come to have a final understanding with Katie before he left. For, be it understood, Katie had that habit—possessed by pretty girls the world over—of showering her

---

1 **wont** - one's customary behavior in a particular situation

smiles and favors somewhat impartially; and Mark had made up his mind that he must know his final fate before he left.

Chapter II

Mark Standish paid his matriculation fee at the college in the great city, and settled down to the daily humdrum of a medical student. He had pleasant rooms, fair meals and an agreeable room mate, so things moved along smoothly enough.

Weekly letters came from Katie—letters full of love and encouragement that made his big heart beat ten pulsations faster a minute, and helped him over many a hard place in the laboratory and clinic. Those letters he religiously answered the day he received them, no matter how busy he was.

Harry Martin, his room mate, was a bright, companionable fellow, and he and Mark soon became fast friends indeed. Harry could but notice the many letters that Mark received, addressed in a woman's delicate handwriting, and playfully twitted him about it.

"You're in love, old man," said Harry one day, "a condition of affairs that is inexcusable in a medical student. Beware of wine and women, say I."

Mark, in a burst of confidence unusual with him, told his friend of Katie and how he loved her. The latter listened patiently to the former's rapturous description of his lady love; then he lighted a cigar, crossed his shapely legs and remarked:

"Mark, you love that girl fondly—desperately."

"Of course I do."

"More's the pity for you."

"Why?"

"Suppose she should prove false to you?"

"I shall entertain no such supposition."

"I know—but still suppose she should; other women have been trusted and have proven false. You have lost your heart, and you are just sanguine[2] enough in your nature to lose your head—should she jilt you."

---

2   **sanguine** - cheerfully optimistic, hopeful, or confident

"It would ruin me. I should not have a spark of ambition left," said Mark seriously.

"Bah! don't be a fool. Standish, if you want to get over such nonsensical sentimentality, look at me! I've been jilted a dozen times, and I simply get fat on it."

Mark looked at the speaker's smiling boyish face, and burst into a roar of hearty laughter. Then they donned their overcoats and started for the nine o'clock lecture.

Thus week after week passed away. Mark's good health did not fail him, although he studied far into the small hours of the night, and took little or no exercise. He was recognized by all as one of the best students in the class, and many predicted that he would lead his class the second year, and carry off the scholarship prize.

The six months term began to draw to a close. There were about three weeks more of lectures, and then the term would close with a week of final examinations for the year.

All at once Katie's letters stopped coming. For the first week of their non-arrival Mark was not greatly concerned. He thought that they were slow in coming because the country roads were blocked with snow, and that they would all arrive at once when they did come; and he pictured to himself what a love feast he would have when they finally arrived. But ten days passed and still no word from Katie came. What could be the matter? Was she seriously ill? He did not know what to think. During the ten endless days he had written to her almost daily.

He grew nervous and restless. He lost his appetite, and could neither study nor sleep. He paced his room as the tiger paces his cage, and a black fear began to tug at his heartstrings—a fear that he dared not own.

Harry Martin did not fail to detect the change that had come over his friend. He was not blind, and he could not help but see that something was worrying Mark badly. At last he burst forth:

"Look here, Standish, you give me the blues with your everlasting restlessness and sighing. You don't study, you don't eat, and you don't sleep. There's something wrong. Out with it."

Mark returned a snappish reply to the effect that it was nothing serious, and that Harry need not concern himself about it.

"It's all right," interrupted the latter. "I know your trouble."

"Do you?" returned Mark apathetically.

"Yes, I do. You've not got a letter from Katie for a week or ten days, and you're making an ass of yourself on account of it. Brace up—be a man. She's thrown you overboard undoubtedly, but your head's still above water and you can swim for it. You're that much better off. It's a good riddance of bad—"

Standish's eyes flashed dangerously. "Stop;" he thundered. "I will not hear such words even from you, my privileged friend."

"Oh! well, I've aroused you at any rate," chuckled Harry. "Now, look here—let's be sensible. Her letters have miscarried in the mail. When they come, they'll come in a lump. Don't give up and wear a face like an epitaph on a tombstone. You make me feel creepy. I never could endure tragedy. I was just teasing you to arouse you from your moody silence—everything is all right, and you'll be laughing at yourself in a day or two."

Somewhat comforted and reassured, Mark sat down to his books and studied as he has not done for days.

This was in the morning. When they returned from lecture at five o'clock that evening a letter awaited Mark. It was from Katie. He picked it up from the table, but his strong fingers—that had never before trembled—shook so that he could hardly open it. Harry Martin watched him intently. At last the envelope yielded to Mark's nervous pluckiness and he pulled forth the missive.

He unfolded it and began to read its contents by the light from the window near which he was standing. Gradually the color faded from his lips, and his face assumed a drawn and pinched look. His hands were steady enough now. He carefully refolded the letter, slipped it into the mutilated envelope and put the whole in his pocket. Then he mechanically sought a chair, and sat gazing into the fire.

All this time neither of the friends had spoken. The silence became unbearable to Martin.

"What is it?" He inquired almost in a whisper. "Is it all over?"

"Yes, it is all over," replied Mark huskily.

"Is she dead?"

"Married!"

Harry Martin leapt to his feet, his face aflame with rage. "I am no prophet nor the son of a prophet," he almost shouted, "but, Mark Standish, that woman will suffer for what she has done, as sure as there is the law of justice in nature. Your present suffering—great as I see it is—will be nothing to what she will have to endure in future years. 'The mills of the gods grind slowly, but they grind exceedingly fine!'"

"Hush, Harry," said Mark quietly, almost soothingly, "you do not know all—I do not know all."

"For heaven's sake, Mark, rouse up—get mad—anything but that accursed calm, look! What did she say?"

"Simply that she has married Walter Janes, my old rival, in accordance with the wishes of her parents and her own desires, and politely beg my pardon for not apprising me sooner of her purpose."

Mark Standish could never tell in after years how he went through that examination week; but he passed among the highest in his class.

* * * *

After Mark's departure for college Katie was very lonely. She had known him so long and he was so intimately associated with her whole life that she did not realize what he was to her until he was gone.

When her household duties did not engage her, she wandered listlessly about the place or sat idly in her room wondering what he was doing in the far off city. Her mother noted her fits of abstraction and said:

"You needn't go moping around about Mark Standish. He ain't coming back. He'll find some rich woman over there in the East an' marry her. He'll forget you quick enough, soon as he's a way. That's the way with all of 'em. You'd better take Walt Janes while you've got the chance."

As usual, Katie said nothing, but ran away to her room to write another letter to Mark.

Walter Janes haunted the Flynn homestead. He became Katie's shadow, as Mark had said he would. He exerted himself to the utmost to be unobtrusive and agreeable. Katie had never realized before that he could be so much of a gentleman, when he tried. His company was not wholly distasteful to her, either. She was lonely and he helped to amuse her.

For weeks he never mentioned love or marriage to her—he seemed to have forgotten his previous avowals. This piqued Katie, and unconsciously she began to exercise her little feminine arts and wiles, to win him back. She did not love him—no! But she could not bear the thought that one of her slaves should escape so easily. Her pride was hurt. She gave him every opportunity to declare his love and devotion. She took long rides with him over the country roads; she took Sunday rambles with him across the autumn-browned fields. Still he maintained a stolid silence. She determined that she would draw a proposal out of him at all hazard. Of course she intended to reject him!

"How fickle men are!" She remarked one October afternoon, as they were sitting beneath a gnarled apple tree in the orchard back of the house.

Walt stifled a yawn, folded his arms back of his head, and leaning lazily against the trunk of the tree asked in a careless manner:

"Why do you say so?"

He had been playing a shrewd and desperate game, and he did not mean to lose it now by a show of interest. He possessed too much low down cunning for that.

"Because—Oh! because"—she began in some confusion.

"Has Mark Standish played you false?" Katie started at the point blank question.

"No, indeed!" answered she; "whatever prompted you to ask such a question?"

"I hoped that he had."

"Walt!"

"I did! Then you would give me some consideration. And he will play you false in the end—you will see. The idea of him asking you to wait five or six years for him. Your father told me that he did that. Why, in that length of time your beauty will begin to fade, and he will become disenchanted—and marry another. But what is the use of talking—women are born fools!"

There was a ring of genuine passion in his voice as he said this. Katie said nothing in reply, and after a pause Walt continued quietly, almost sadly:

"I must wait. After years—after he has discarded you—you will come to me; and I shall be only too glad to receive you."

Katie was troubled. It all seemed so real—so pathetic! It tickled her vanity to hear him talk so. She had never seen him so humble before.

However, she changed the subject and no more was said about it at that time. But the subtle poison, that day instilled into her heart, began its deadly work. She became discontented and fretful. What right had Mark to ask her to wait so long? She peered into the glass and fancied that already she could detect signs of wrinkles upon her face and she always had a horror of growing old!

Why had not Mark married her and taken her to the city with him? Why was he not rich so they could be married at once? In short, why had he not done and been all the things that it was impossible for him to do and be! She felt that her anchors were dragging, that she was drifting out of the safe harbor of love into the tumultuous sea of uncertainty; and yet she lifted no prayer to God to send her favoring gale, that she might out ride the storm.

Midwinter came and still she kept up her regular correspondence with Mark. Spring was not far distant—and Mark would be back to teach a summer term of school. She must decide before he arrived. What should she do?

She cut the gordian knot—that she *would* not untie—by appealing to her father for advice. The result was that she married Walter Janes a month from that day. Then she coolly sat down and wrote Mark Standish the cruel letter before mentioned. It was all over— and she had sold a life's happiness for a paltry mess of worldly prosperity!

Chapter III

Mark did not return to spend his summer vacation. A year past—and another, and another—and still he came not. The villagers and the country folk, all of whom knew and loved him, marveled and wondered. Rumors as to his whereabouts occasionally reached the village—rumors vague and unauthenticated. It was circulated that he had graduated at the head of his class and had won fame and fortune in an eastern city; but no one seemed able to confirm the report.

Five years elapsed. One beautiful day in early June he returned, quietly and unostentatiously as he had left. He was much changed. He was a beardless young man no longer. He bore the unmistakable stamp of a bold and self-reliant professional man. He wore a close-cropped beard and glasses. The waving hair about his temples was becoming silvered. His village friends observed that his hand clasp was as warm and cordial as of yore, but the cheery, radiant smile that had illuminated his features had given place to the quiet, pacific smile that comes to those who have suffered great mental anguish. His manner was not the bubbling, effervescent manner that they had known, but one of subdued dignity. They recognized at once that this was not Mark Standish who had come back to them, but Doctor Standish.

He made no secret of his plans and intentions. He had come back to practice in his native place. Why, he did not say. He fitted up office rooms at the hotel and entered upon the duties of his profession. He seemed to have an abundance of money, and did not appear at all anxious about his future success.

Dr. Standish had not been long in the village before he learned that Katie's lot was not one to be envied. Walter Janes had always enjoyed the company of the village roysterers[3], and his marriage did not change his disposition nor alter his habits. He and Katie began their married life with his parents, on the home farm three miles from the village. As time went on Mr. Janes gave the management of his landed estate into the hands of his son; this called Walt away from home a great deal.

3 **roysterers** – those who engage in boisterous merrymaking; revel noisily

More than once he came back from town in an intoxicated condition, and rumors said that he was a heavy loser at cards. Katie un-
dertook to remonstrate with him. He flew into a passion and gave
her to understand that he could attend to his own business and would
brook no interference from her. This was but the beginning of Katie's
troubles. Walt grew jealous of her—jealous of the absent lover, Mark
Standish, and many stormy encounters ensued. His unreasoning and
unreasonable jealousy drove him on from bad to worse. He would
spend a week or two at a time on a protracted spree away from home,
and these absences became more and more frequent. Katie staid[4]
closely at home with his parents; she seldom appeared in company.

The second year of their marriage a son was born to them—a
child feeble in mind and body. After the birth of her child Katie
appeared haggard and careworn, but her appearance had no effect
upon her husband—unless it was to make him more unkind, if possible. He said the most cruel and cutting things to her. He accused
her of marrying him for his money—he accused her of still loving
Mark Standish—and frankly told her that he was sorry he had ever
seen her.

Mrs. Janes died, and the sole care of the household devolved[5]
upon Katie. She became a common drudge whose work was not
finished from sun to sun. Walter squandered money right and left.
Mr. Janes placed mortgages upon his land to pay his son's gambling
debts; and Mr. Flynn—contrary to Katie's expressed desire—went
his security to secure him money at the bank. This was about the
condition of affairs at the time of Dr. Standish's return.

The first time that Katie saw her old friend and former lover,
after his five years absence, she met him face to face on the village
street. She could scarcely lift her eyes to his face, but he greeted
her kindly and asked after her health and welfare. She noticed that
he was cool and collected through it all, while she was trembling
with—what, she could not tell.

On her way home she remarked to herself how dignified and
manly he looked, and how prosperous and contented he appeared to

---

4   **staid** – variation of stayed
5   **devolved** - passed on or delegated to another

be. And then her heart bounded with the feeling that she knew only too well. She loved him still!

"Oh! if I had only waited," she moaned, heedless of the fretful child upon her lap, and careless of the road over which she was driving. She mused on—"if I were only free—!" Then she almost leapt from the buggy in alarm. Of what was she thinking! And she bowed her head and wept of the most bitter tears that she had ever known.

As the days went by she strove earnestly to conquer herself, but in vain. The old passion burned as a consuming fire within her, and would not be quenched. She wanted to meet him again—just once—just to see his face—just to feel the clasp of his strong hand. She must see him—and she would!

She readily found an excuse—she would take her child to him for treatment. She tried to convince herself that this was her only reason for going; but her heart fluttered guiltily. She knew better; she could not deceive herself. Her soul revolted at the black lies she was acting.

She spoke to her husband of the proposed call. He sneered in her face, but to her unbounded surprise and relief he offered no objection. In fact, of late he took little interest in her or the child.

Dr. Standish received her as he would have received any other lady. He addressed her as "Mrs. Janes," and was affable and pleasant. He was carefully exact in his examination of the little sufferer, and ventured an opinion that he would improve physically, in time. As to his mental infirmity he said nothing, and she asked no questions. The doctor indicated that the interview was at an end, by asking her to return in two weeks, and she withdrew to give place to another patient.

Subsequent interviews were no more satisfactory to her; the boy grew some stronger, and she discontinued her calls.

But she would not—could not—give it up that way. Again she returned, this time to get medicine for herself—she was so weak and nervous. At one of these interviews she lost all control.

"Why do you treat me so coolly?" she asked beseechingly. "Do you not know what forgiveness means, Mark? Can you not see how I have suffered?"

He smiled sadly, placidly, as he answered: "I have forgiven you long ago, Katie."

It was the first time that he had called her by her Christian name since those dear old days, and the tone in which he said it made her pulses tingle in an ecstasy of hope. Her face became radiant and the old mischievous light shone in her eyes. Would he go on and say what her soul was starving to know? Would he say that he still loved her? She waited with bated breath.

Dr. Standish continued—"but I have forgotten, also." The half rebuke stung her like a lash. Each word seemed to fall upon her heart like a lump of ice. All colors faded from her face; all hope from her soul. She slipped out of the office like a hunted thing and hurried home. Dr. Standish did not meet her again for months.

* * * *

Ten years passed—ten years of uninterrupted professional toil to Dr. Standish. One stormy January night he sat in his office with a current magazine in his hand. The fire in the grate flickered and danced to the harsh music of the wind outside, and the shadows upon the rosy-hued walls capered in unison. Outside was a howling wilderness of blackness. Sash rattled in the windows, shutters banged and sign boards creaked. The icy rain poured down in torrents.

The doctor threw down his magazine, stretched back in his large, leather-covered chair and closing his eyes remained motionless. His hair was almost white and his beard plentifully sprinkled with gray. Care lines crossed and recrossed his brow and temples, and his shoulders had acquired much of the stoop of the habitual student.

In a short time the regular and rhythmic heaving of his chest denoted that he was slumbering. All at once came hurried footsteps upon the stair and a vigorous ring at the outer door.

The doctor leapt to his feet but half awake. He hastened to the door and unhesitatingly threw it open. A besotted wretch stood without, the water pouring in streams from his battered hat and ragged garments.

"What's wanted?" demanded the doctor brusquely.

"Doc," panted the nocturnal intruder, "they want you down to Jack Bawdy's right away."

"What's the matter down there this time?"

"There's a feller got stabbed over a game of cards."

"Where is he hurt?"

"Don't know, Doc; in the breast I think. They carried him into the back room, and he looked awful pale an' bad—guess he's dyin'."

"This is the second time within the month that I've been called there to patch up some poor sod wounded in a drunken brawl. Who is it this time?"

"Walt Janes."

The doctor started, but did not change countenance. "All right. I'll be down in a few minutes," he said; and he banged the door in the messenger's face.

He procured his emergency case, put on his heavy mackintosh and hurried down to the street. The wind blew in gusts and the rain still fell in heavy sheets. A few smoky street lamps, here and there, lighted the sloppy streets and pavements with that faint, uncertain glare.

Dr. Standish turned off at the first side street, and proceeded along it until he came to a row of one-story wooden buildings. One of these he fearlessly entered. It was a low saloon. A number of men stood around the gandy bar, conversing in low excited tones. They were an ill favored lot—this, the scum of the community.

A pool table stood in the center of the room, and along the wall were arranged a number of card tables—but no one was playing at this time. Near one of the tables was a broken chair, some torn cards and a pool of clotted blood. The room was rejoined with the smell of vile drinks and tobacco.

"Where is he?" inquired the doctor in a cool professional way, of the bartender.

"He's on the cot in the back room. Jack's in there with him."

"Who did it?"

"Joe Green—the marshal's got 'em."

Dr. Standish, without further questions, passed into the other room. It was lighted by a swinging oil lamp. It contained a chintz-covered couch, a green baize table and a number of chairs. It was Jack Bawdy's private gambling den—the one in which Walt Janes had spent many a night, bartering everything he had on earth, his immortal soul included, to satisfy his appetite for gaming and debauchery.

The injured man lay upon his back, breathing heavily. His face was pale, emaciated, cadaverous. A stertorous[6] rattle sounded in his throat, and bloody foam oozed from the corners of his mouth and blubbered from his half closed lips. His coat and vest were thrown back, and a shirt was open revealing his hairy chest. On the right side of his breast, about three inches below the collarbone, was a small puncture wound about an inch in length, from which trickled a few drops of dark-colored blood.

The doctor's practiced eye took in all these details in the fraction of a minute. He took a seat beside the cot and grasped his patient's wrist. The pulse was full but feeble and slow. Walt opened his eyes and attempted to speak. A violent fit of coughing was the result; and the bright red blood ran in a stream from his mouth and nose.

After the spasm was over he lay back exhausted. Presently he essayed to speak again. Turning his eyes full upon the doctor he panted:

"Standish, am I—hurt—very badly?"

"You are very seriously injured."

"Can—I get—well?"

Dr. Standish counted the pulse for a full half minute. Then he replied slowly and calmly:

"Janes, you have but a short time to live. You are bleeding internally."

The dying man whispered huskily: "My God! can you do nothing for me?"

"Nothing – you are beyond mortal aid. If you have any arrangements to make—any message to leave—you would better attend to the matter at once; your time is short."

Walter Janes lay quiet for some minutes. Occasionally he moaned and moved his bloodstained lips convulsively. At last he

---

6 **stertorous** - characterized by a gasping sound

again opened his fast-glazing eyes, and murmured feebly—almost inaudibly:

"It—is—all over. I—have run—my race; and—so—so—soon!"

He spoke no more. A few seconds after the last word had passed his lips, he spring halfway to a sitting position, clutching at his throat, and the blood streaming in a crimson flood over his chest. The rigid muscles gradually relaxed, and he fell back dead.

All was indeed over. He left no message; expressed no regret for the past—no hope for the future. Dr. Standish dispatched a messenger to inform his wife of her husband's death and returned to his rooms at the hotel.

After the death of Walter Janes came the deluge—the deluge that swept away the Janes and Flynn estates, and left Katie scarcely a foundation of sand beneath her feet. Mr. Janes died from shock and grief, and Katie's parents—left almost penniless—went to live with a son in the West. Katie had left from the general ruin a small cabin and a few acres of ground; and this she owed to the careful watchfulness of Dr. Standish.

She was a nervous, physical wreck. For months her health had been gradually failing, and her husband's tragic death rapidly hastened her decline. She was a broken down, broken-hearted woman, when she should have been in the prime of life. Her hair was still coal black, however, and lent pallor to her drawn and haggard features.

Through all her troubles Dr. Standish stood steadfastly by her; he was the only friend she had left, almost. The butterflies of prosperity disappeared after the delusion of adversity.

The doctor gave her treatment, offered her words of encouragement and hope, and used his own money to purchase her comforts and delicacies that were beyond her slender means. This latter fact he tactfully concealed from her, letting her rest easy in the belief that her own money paid all bills.

They had many long conversations together, but all allusions to that dead past he carefully avoided. She treated him with the faith of a child and seemed glad to lean upon his steady friendship. But in spite of all the knowledge and skill of Dr. Standish, the fell destroyer[7] was steadily at work. The bow had been bent too long—all elasticity was lost.

The end came at the little cabin on the creek one July night when the heavens were studded with burning stars, and the air was balmy with the smell of new hay and mint. The doctor rode out to see her in the dusk of the summer evening, and staid with her until she closed her eyes in death.

An oppressive stillness pervaded the little cabin, and the lamps glowed with the subdued light. Down by the creek side the frogs croak hoarsely, and a cowbell tinkled far up the stream. The bay of a distant farm dog floated down from the hilltops on the dew-laden air, and phosphorescent fireflies flitted here and there.

A number of the neighbor women moved stealthily and noiselessly from room to room about the house. On the woodpile back of the house sat the feeble-minded boy, making discordant strains from a cracked violla, and chuckling and mumbling to himself.

When the doctor arrived Katie was sleeping. He sat down at the bedside and took her hand without wakening her. For a long time he sat silent and immovable, studying her wan features intently. If any but purely professional thoughts were in his mind, a chance observer would not have perceived it in his face. At last she stirred uneasily and awoke.

"How are you feeling, Katie?" He asked, softly.

"I am easy, but tired—oh! so tired. I wish that I could sleep more."

"Shall I give you another opiate[8]?"

She hesitated a moment and then whispered faintly: "No, I want to talk to you. How long can I last?"

"It is a question of but a few hours at most."

"Then I must talk to you now. After I have said what I want to say you may give me the sleeping powder."

She rested a few moments and continued: "Oh! what a fatal mistake my life has been; it were better had I never lived. Tell me—tell

---

7 **Fell destroyer** – a reference to a poem "Trapping Woodcocks" by William Wordworth

8 **opiate** - a drug (as morphine, heroin) containing or derived from opium and tending to induce sleep and to alleviate pain

me one thing. Have you forgiven all—everything, Mark?"

"All—everything has been forgiven long, long ago, Katie."

"But do not say forgotten, Mark—Ah! that dear old name—do not say forgotten. I cannot stand it. It was cruel of you to say it as you did once. But you have been so kind to me of late—pity, that is all. Oh! Mark, Mark, what might have been but for my own inconstancy!"

She buried her thin face in the pillow and wept silently. Dr. Standish sat by her side apparently unmoved and answered not. The plaintive, wailing notes of the cracked violin floated in at the open window. They aroused the dying woman and again she spoke:

"Mark, will you not be kind to my poor boy? He has not a friend on earth to look after him."

"He shall be provided for Katie; you need not give the matter a thought."

"Ah! that I should have to ask it of you—you of all men—you whom I have so cruelly wronged. Surely 'the mills of the gods grind slowly, but they grind exceedingly fine!'"

At these words the doctor started and came near to losing his strong self-control. The muscles of his face twitched spasmodically; Harry Martin's harsh prophecy came vividly back to his mind. He rose from his chair, and walking rapidly up and down the floor he steeled himself to composure.

"Is there anything more that you want me to do?" He inquired huskily, returning to her side.

"No, that is all," she replied very feebly. "Sit here and hold my hand; I want to go to sleep."

At three o'clock the next morning he mounted his horse and rode away from the house. When he reached the summit of the hill that overlooks the little valley he paused and looked back; then he rode on in the gray dawn, his head bent forward and a hopeless, faraway look upon his face.

The Two Consultations at Mam Starling's

Mam Starling was old—very, very old! Her birth dated back to a time that was dimmed and almost obliterated by the swiftly drifting shadows of the past. Whence she had come was as little known to the good folks who were her neighbors, as whither she was going; for Mam Starling with all her senile volubility was uncommunicative in regard to herself. All that the country people knew was that for years and years she had lived all alone, in the little log cabin beside the noisy creek; and that the cabin had become a gray and antiquated ruin, as had the old woman herself. The clapboards that composed the roof of the cabin were bleached and curled like her own scant hair, and the log walls were warped and stooped like her own gaunt form; but the two small windows that peeped slyly from the front were as bright as Mam's black eyes themselves, and the mouth of the stick chimney puffed a volume of blue smoke toward the skies, that the old dame—with all her smoking—could not equal.

In this little cabin—consisting of one room—Mam Starling lived and moved and had her being. The interior was neat and clean—the hearth and floor scoured to snowy whiteness—but the furniture was not obtrusively in the way, nor were the inside walls guilty of ornamentation.

Outside the little mud-daubed domicile it was far different. Morning-glory and quarter vines climbed from foundation stone to gable, ran riotously over the low eaves, and twined themselves around the windows and doors. Pink and yellow hollyhocks nestled in the angles made by the projecting stick chimney, and staid and stately sunflowers ranged themselves, like rows of soldiers, above the low paling[1] fence; while princes lined the pathway that led down to the highroad.

---

1 **paling** - a fence made from pointed wooden or metal stakes

Back of the house rose the great hills, their sides covered with copses of sumac and hazel bushes, and their heads crowned with the virgin forest. These woods and thickets had been Mam Starling's one source of wealth and revenue. Here it was that she gathered the barks and roots from which she concocted her famous medicines—for be it known she was a "root and herb" doctor of no meager reputation.

Passersby frequently saw her nimbly descending the precipitous hill slope, her bulging and plethoric apron indicating that her search had not been a bootless[2] one; and venturesome fox-hunters had peered into her windows at night, and had seen her brewing her various magic remedies.

All the country side knew her. There was scarcely a house within a radius of twenty miles in which she had not treated some member of the family; and the farm dogs, even, knew her so well that they had long ago ceased to bark at her approach. It is impossible to say, however, whether the sight of her green sunbonnet and the smell of her clay pipe inspired more of fear or respect in the minds of the adult population. So far as the children were concerned, they considered her little less than a witch; and curly heads would dodge 'neath the bed clothes at the mention of her name or medicine, and nimble bare feet would scurry out of sight at her coming.

As I have said, she lived all alone. It was seldom indeed that anyone crossed her threshold; so it is not at all strange that when at last her strength began to fail her, and she fell ill one autumn, no one knew of it for several days. When the neighbors were apprised of her illness by a passing traveler, who had stopped at the cabin for a drink of water, they flocked in from various directions to administer to her needs and comfort. She was unable to rise from her bed, and for the greater part of the week she had had neither food nor drink. Her pinched and wrinkled features had lost all color, and her cracked and querulous voice had sunk to a husky whisper; but her keen black eyes gleamed defiantly from the pillows like two living coals of fire.

Then began the battle royal for her life. She was too well known a personage to be allowed to die in peace! At her own instigation,

---

2 **bootless** - without advantage or benefit; useless

and under her own directions, they poulticed and bathed and baked her; they deluged her with herb teas and tormented her with rude bitters—but all to no avail. She grew worse. She must have a doctor—that she must!

At first the old dame fought lustily against this suggestion; but when she found that her own idols could not save her, she lost faith in them and consented to have a physician. With this stipulation, however:

"I ain't agoin' to 'ave that ol' Doc Ferris! Me an' him has quar'led too much—he'd kill me with his strong medicine. If you send for him, I won't take nothin'. An' I won't 'ave that young upstart of a Doc Able—he don't know nothin' but to curl his mustache an' grin at the girls. If you must send for somebody, git Doc Noster, down at Hoppletown. He's all right—he don't use no p'izen miner'ls!"

So Dr. Noster came up from Hoppletown, fifteen miles away, and instituted treatment. He was a pompous, ignorant, red-faced old man, who had not a common school education, even, and who had learned all that he knew of the science of medicine, from a set of leather-bound "doctor books" fifty years out of date.

"What do you think of my case?" whispered Mam Starling anxiously.

"You're a purty sick woman," grunted the doctor, looking wise and feeling her pulse.

"Can I git well?"

"Well, that depends! You're purty old and weak, and 'bout wore out; but I'll do the best I can fer you."

"I ain't very old—not much over ninety," returned Mam in a spiteful whisper.

Dr. Noster made no reply, but went on measuring out his medicine from a pair of large leather saddlebags. When he had finished, he mounted his gray and bony nag, and dignifiedly rode away.

But in spite of his boluses[3], powders and blisters, the old woman persisted in growing worse. She could take no nourishment, and it was pitiful to see her attempting to swallow the nauseating doses. Dr. Noster visited her several times, changing his heroic treatment

---

3 **bolus -** a rounded mass of food or pharmaceutical preparation ready to swallow

each time. At last the kind-hearted neighbors decided that she should have the benefit of a consultation. They informed Dr. Noster of their decision, and he offered strenuous opposition to the measure.

"There ain't a bit o' sense in it," he snorted, "I'm a doin' all that anybody can do. If you send fer some one else, I'll quit the case. It jest looks like you hadn't any confidence in my ability!" And he strutted around the yard like an angry turkey cock.

But the neighbors were firm; and farmer Herrick from down the creek, acting as spokesman, thus replied:

"You can leave the case 'r do jest w'at you please. We're a goin' to 'ave a consultation. It ain't 'cause we're not satisfied with you. Your doctorin' may be all right—if it is, a consultation won't do you no harm. Mam Starling may be a pore an' wore out ol' creature, but she's deservin' o' the best treatment we can git fer her; an' we're a goin' to have a consultation!"

The other neighbors nodded approval to this, and Dr. Noster was compelled to swallow his ire and yield to their demands with the best grace he could muster.

And thus consultation number one came about. Messengers were dispatched posthaste for Dr. Able at Onionville and Dr. Ferris at Crooksburgh. This was the morning of a warm and sunshiny autumn day; and at two o'clock in the afternoon the three medical men were at the cabin, and the yard was filled with anxious and inquisitive country people.

Holmes has said:

"When e'er a doctor's patients are perplexed
A consultation comes in order next;
You know what that is? In a certain place
Meet certain doctors to discuss the case."

It would have been better had he said: "When e'er a patient's neighbors are perplexed," for these officious and mistaken though kind-hearted persons are the source from which emanate nine out of ten of the so-called consultations.

A half-hour after the arrival of the last physician, consultation number one was in full blast. Mam Starling was able to offer no resistance, and was at their mercy. They hovered over her, they swooped about her like birds of prey. They twisted and turned the poor emaciated body this way and that to facilitate their examinations. They percussed and palpitated and auscultated[4] to their hearts' content, and then they withdrew to talk over what each imagined that he had discovered. With stately carriage and important air each strode out the low door and down the flower-bordered walk to the paling fence. Here they paused and began their exchange of opinions. Unconsciously their voices rose higher and higher as they earnestly and angrily discussed the matter; and the country folk in and about the cabin craned their necks and strained their ears to catch the words.

"I tell you," cried young Dr. Able, "that I find that she has chronic bronchitis complicated by weak cardiac action; besides, she is suffering from acute indigestion and malassimilation[5]!" and he stroked his small brown mustache complacently, and twisted the rings upon his white fingers.

"Stuff!" hissed old Dr. Ferris, "she's dying from old **age** and nothing else—she's worn out. You've a great deal to learn yet, young man."

"Old age!" sneered Dr. Noster, "that's all you know, Ferris. She's dying from liver complaint; and she ain't got no bronkeetis n'r nothin' o' that kind, neither. You two men don't know nothin' about her case. Of course, I admit that her age is ag'in 'er, but I'd a got 'er through if—"

"You have not the slightest idea of what a scientific, physical diagnosis means," vociferated[6] Dr. Able, gesticulating wildly. "You are a pair of old fogies, and have fallen into ruts from which you cannot extricate yourselves. The old lady needs—"

"Much you know what she needs!" thundered Dr. Ferris, bristling all over with anger and excitement, "dictating to me, when you haven't been out of college a year. I've seen thirty years of practice, young fellow, and I know what I'm talking about. What you

---

4   **auscultate** - the act of listening for sounds made by internal organs, as the heart and lungs, to aid in the diagnosis of certain disorders

5   **malassimilation** - imperfect absorption of nutrients into the body

6   **vociferate** - shout, complain, or argue loudly or vehemently

say about Noster here is true, however. He always was a botanical quack—"

"I never killed anybody with arsenic an' quicksilver an' such pizens," returned Noster, his red face growing redder; "an' that's what you 'ave done, Ferris an' you know it!"

"You are an unmitigated liar!" Dr. Ferris howled.

"You're another!" wheezed Dr. Noster, "an' I can whip you!"

"You are a pair of ancient fools!" Dr. Abel interjected. "If you expect to do anything for the old woman, stop your quarreling—and let's decide on something."

"You mind your own business!" cried the older two, turning upon the younger.

"I do not propose to stay here to be insulted by a pair of old dotards[7]," answered Dr. Able sharply; and passing through the gate he untied his horse and prepared to depart.

"Come back here, you young fop!" frothed Dr. Ferris. "Do you mean to leave a veteran of your own school here, to assume the responsibility of this botanical quack's blunders and mistakes?"

"Yes, sir, you come back here," commanded Dr. Noster. "I want your help—your help—not the help of this old miner'l p'izener. Come back here, I say!"

Dr. Abel retied his horse and came back. "We cannot agree on a diagnosis," he said quietly, "so what do you propose to do?"

Dr. Ferris studied for a moment and replied: "She's dying, and there's no use in giving her anything; but I would suggest a little stimulant and a placebo—just to keep the neighbors satisfied that we are doing something."

"Of course, she's dyin'," ventured Dr. Noster, mopping his red face with a redder bandanna handkerchief, "but I think her liver needs rowsin, an' I would be in favor of giving her a little mayapple tea."

A half sneer hovered about Dr. Abel's mouth, but he suppressed it and asked;

"Why not say to the neighbors that she is dying, and that we can do nothing for her—and take our departure?"

───────────

7 **dotard** - an old person, esp. one who has become weak or senile

"Oh! that would never do," cried the older two in chorus.

"Why?" Dr. Abel insisted.

"Because," replied Dr. Ferris, "the neighbors and friends expect us to do something, and we must do it."

"That's it, exactly," assented Dr. Noster, rubbing his fat hands.

"Then," continued Dr. Abel, "let us leave a placebo of chalk and water, give them explicit directions as to its administration, impress upon their minds that it must not be given too frequently on account of its dangerous qualities, and—leave. I am sick of it all. What do you say?"

"That's all right," assented Dr. Ferris.

"I'm agreed," said Dr. Noster.

Dr. Abel resumed: "Very well, then, let us go to the house and relieve their anxiety. Who shall act as spokesman?"

"You."

"Yes, you."

They filed up the pathway to the cabin, and Dr. Abel accosted the anxious group of people—many of whom had heard snatches of the doctors stormy consultation—thus:

"Friends and neighbors, you have shown your kindness of heart and your great interest in this case by calling a consultation of physicians. I realize that you are anxious to know our joint opinion, and that you are on the tip toe of expectancy to hear the same. There is absolutely no difference of opinion in regard to this case—there can be none! Mrs. Starling is a very sick woman, but her case is not necessarily hopeless—while there is life there is always hope. We agree heartily as to the disease, and Dr. Ferris and myself wish to say to you that Dr. Noster has treated the case sensibly and scientifically, that he has done all that mortal man could do, and that we have no criticisms to make or suggestions to offer. However, we three have decided to try one more very potent and dangerous remedy. Dr. Ferris and Dr. Noster will prepare it, and you must be very careful in its administration. If it acts as we expect and hope it to act the results will be favorable; if it does not act so, then we can do no more—and Mrs. Starling must die!"

The country folk listened in open-mouthed wonder and astonishment to this flow of oratory; but when Dr. Abel had ceased, answered him with approving smiles and nods. In the meantime the other physicians had prepared the medicine and given directions as to its administration. Then the three mounted their horses and rode away in dignified and impressive silence.

Then consultation number two broke loose, and out rivaled the other in noise and bluster. Each physician was defended by hot and bitter partisan adherents, and the discussion became so animated and the participants so oblivious to all else, that they deserted Mam Starling's bedside in the cabin, and adjourned to the yard to settle the matter.

"There ain't no use a talkin'," farmer Herrick said, "that old Doc Noster don't know nothin'. We never would a knowed w'at ailed Mam if it hadn't been fer young Doc Able."

"I can't see that we know yit," sagely remarked Mrs. Hammer from back on the hill. "Doc Abel didn't tell us—and I don't believe he knowed. I'd jest as leave trust Doc Noster as any o' y'r young doctors."

"You're prejudiced!" broke in Mrs. Babcock. "Doc Ferris has more brains 'n both of 'em. He settled the matter an' give the medicine an—"

"I reckon Doc Noster helped him put out the medicine," Mrs. Hammer interrupted, and several others added their approving voices.

"Yes—oh! yes, it was easy fer them to put out the medicine after Doc Abel had told 'em jest what to do!" This from pretty Miss Miller.

"Maby you think you'll git to marry Doc Able," cried Miss Bishop, tossing her auburn curls, "but I can tell you, Maggie Miller, that y'r chances 're mighty slim."

"Oh, you spiteful thing! I'd like—" and thus it went on—and on, while the sun sank to rest behind the western hills and the shadows of evening gathered. One by one the contestants gave up the struggle and departed, until only two or three remained—and they maintained an armed peace. Night's sable garment settled down on the scene, and the two consultations were over; but the field of battle was strewn with broken friendships, blasted loves and forgotten kindnesses. And many a livid scar and festering wound still remains to tell of a day ill-spent.

It is hardly necessary to say that Mam Starling laid down the heavy burden of years, and took her departure without a sigh and without a struggle, even before the second consultation was concluded.

Wild Tom

Wild Tom he was called—and Wild Tom he was. The name he signed to the monthly pay-roll of the A. & Z. railroad was "Tom Wild," but his associates transposed the two parts of the appellation and the public knew him only as Wild Tom.

The name was no misnomer. It fairly represented the man—mentally, morally and physically.

His advent in Malconta corresponded in time to the advent of the first train on the new railroad. He made his appearance as engineer of a construction train; and the apparently reckless manner in which he would send his engine. "Old Thirty-four," bumping and groaning and swinging along the unballasted[1] and uneven track proved his right to the graphic and descriptive designation—"Wild Tom."

Nothing was known of his antecedents, relatives or former place of residence; and little was known of the man, himself.

He was not young and he was not old—just of that uncertain age that is hard to fix exactly. He was of medium size, muscular and active, with black hair and eyes.

His dark brown mustache was slightly tinged with gray, and his face—when free from soot and grime—was smooth-shaven and intelligent looking. At times he was boisterously hilarious, at other times taciturn and morose. He was not uncommunicative, yet he said but little; and when he did speak, his communication was brief, brusque and directly to the point—the sentences decapitated and chopped into bits.

In many respects he was an average railroad man—fearless, profane and prodigal. He drank and gambled when off-duty, but he met his obligations promptly and no one ever saw him unduly intoxicated. He had many acquaintances, but few friends; and

---

1 **unballasted** - unsteady; wavering

his most intimate friend knew as little of him as did any chance acquaintance.

A human paradox was Wild Tom. Apparently reckless of life and limb, he met with no accident; openly prodigal and dissipated, he was just and honest; rude and sullen externally, he had in him a heart capable of tender pity and undying love.

When the railroad was completed, Tom and Old Thirty-Four were transferred to the daily freight. Malconta was the midway station on the road and the point where the trains passed each other.

One raw and disagreeable February day Wild Tom's freight rolled into the village. After switching a number of way cars Old Thirty-Four came to a rest on the side track, and puffed and wheezed in a contented and self-satisfied way. Tom leaned out the cab window, a scowl on his blackened face. For some unapparent reason he was in a very bad humor. He removed his oil stained hat and mopped his forehead with the sleeve of his plaid blouse, from force of habit. Then he shifted his position and chewed the end of his cigar viciously.

Hank Henery, the firemen, sat on the opposite seat and said nothing. He had learned Tom's moods and knew when to maintain a judicious silence.

A ragged, dirty-faced boy of eight or nine years, bearing a basket, passed along the main track, picking the lumps of coal that had rolled from the cars. His grimy toes peeped out of the miserable shoes that he wore, and his face looked pinched and cold; but he was whistling bravely—pausing occasionally to breathe upon his blackened and benumbed fingers.

Tom's face softened slightly as he beheld the boy.

"Hullo!" he called, "hullo! there, Little Feller. What you doin'?"

The boy stopped whistling and looked around.

"What you doin'?" repeated Tom.

"Gatherin' coal! What do you s'pose?" came the saucy reply, and the lad resumed his tune and his quest.

"Say, Little Feller, don't you know you're stealing that coal? Now, you get on out of here—get out!" And in order to enforce the command, Tom gathered a number of lumps of coal from the tender and flung them one after another, at the small figure.

Judging from his actions, Tom was very angry indeed. The boy picked up his basket, whirled on his diminutive heel and dashed around the corner of the freight shed out of sight.

"See him skedaddle!" roared Tom, indulging in a fit of utterly unreasonable and uncontrollable laughter. Then he turned to Hank and began talking, his moroseness having melted away in the incident.

After the train had departed the boy returned and gathered up the lumps that Tom had thrown at him.

From that time onward the same scene was enacted daily. "The Little Feller"—for so Tom had christened him—was sure to make his appearance on the stage as soon as Old Thirty-Four was side-tracked. Tom would initiate the performance by calling "hullo," carry out his part minutely and religiously, and conclude with the advertised fit of laughter and "see him skedaddle." The Little Feller would respond to Tom's questions, and the stereotyped expression: "Gathering coal—what do you s'pose," and retire hurriedly from the stage according to program—only to return after the curtain had fallen, to procure the bouquets in the shape of coveted lumps of coal.

One change only was noticeable, and that was in the stage paraphernalia. The lumps of coal thrown by Tom grew larger and larger! Hank Henery was the person who noticed that fact—but he kept a discreet silence.

A change came over Wild Tom. He was in danger of losing his right to the distinguishing title. He swore more seldom, drank lesser quantity of whiskey, and was more companionable and agreeable. Hank Henery noted all that, too, but still said nothing.

Well, thus they played to a select audience—very select and exclusive indeed, for nine times out of ten Hank was the sole witness to the act—for a month or more.

But one day there was a hitch in the proceedings—the play did not come off. Tom was there with his lines well committed, the stage settings and paraphernalia were at hand; Hank—audience and press critic in one—was there to encore the efforts of the actors; but the

Little Feller failed to put in an appearance. Here was a dilemma, to be sure. Of course the play could not begin with one of the principal characters left out. It would have been "Hamlet with Hamlet left out." With a vengeance! Wild Tom—star actor and manager—said nothing, but Hank saw that he was very uneasy. He grew more and more angry and restless, and by the time they were ready to pull out with the train he was in a towering and glowering rage.

Old Thirty-Four was hauling a heavy train of coal that day, and when they came to the upgrade at the edge of the village "she throws up like a balky mule," as Hank expressed it.

Tom reversed the engine and ran back to the water tank, and tried again; and again he failed. He never deserved the sobriquet[2] of "Wild Tom" more than he did at that moment. Backing rapidly toward the water tank once more, he shouted to the guard at the street crossing, as he passed: "Keep this street clear. I'm coming down here in a minute, like a singed bat out of hell!"

Whether the guard had a personal knowledge of the speed with which a scorched chiropter[3] emerges from the superheated and sulphurous atmosphere of that dreaded region, does not appear: but he kept the crossing clear—there is no question about that.

The next day when Tom and his train arrived the Little Feller was still absent, so manager Tom canceled all engagements for the time and sought the whereabouts of the recanted young actor.

Dismounting from the engine and approaching half shamefacedly the station agent, he inquired:

"Where is The Little Feller?"

"How's that?" replied the agent with a puzzled look.

"The Little Feller—gathers up coal out there," and Tom pointed up the track, "where's he?"

"Oh!" said the agent, as a smile flitted across his features, "Charlie Beaumont?"

---

2 **sobriquet** - a descriptive name or epithet

3 **chiropter** - a mammal, such as the bat, that is a member of the order Chiroptera and has forelimbs modified as wings

"The Little Feller—yes!" and Tom nodded.

"Why," the agent resumed, "I heard my wife say this morning that he's down with lung fever."

"Where?" and Tom swallowed the lump that rose in his throat.

"He lives with his grandmother, up beyond the plow factory warehouse."

Tom said no more, but turned and walked away. A few minutes later he was knocking at the door of the crazy cottage in which The Little Feller lived.

He was admitted by the grandmother, a feeble old woman—and quite deaf.

"Where is The Little Feller?" was Tom's inquiry.

"Hey?" replied the old lady, in a crass and high keyed voice.

"The Little Feller—The Little Feller!" shouted the engineer.

The aged women seem to comprehend what he meant, for she answered: "Do you know him?"

"Course! I want to see him."

The grandmother led the way into the poorly furnished room in which the sick boy lay.

Tom drew a chair up to the couch and said: "Hullo, Little Feller, what you doin'?"

The flushed little face smiled up at him, and a hot, pulsing little hand sought his blackened, calloused palm.

"Gatherin' coal"—The Little Feller began but a fit of coughing interrupted him.

Tom bent tenderly over the boy and said:

"Are you pretty sick?"

"Yes," came the husky reply.

"Had a doctor?"

"No."

"N'r medicine?"

"Yes—a little."

"I'll send the doctor—don't worry – everything will be 'll right."

With that Tom departed. As he went through the kitchen he gave the old woman some money and commanded: "Git everything he needs—I'll see to a doctor."

The grandmother shaded her dim eyes with her hand, and looked after him in speechless amazement. She probably thought him an angel masquerading in plaid blouse and overalls—and a very greasy and sooty angel at that.

Calling at the doctor's office, Tom explained the situation briefly and concluded: "Bring him through; I'll foot the bill."

Well, on the following day Tom went to see The Little Feller, and on the next, and the next. For three weeks his visits were as regular as the doctor's, if not so frequent.

During the lad's sickness a more marked and remarkable change appeared in the disposition and habits of Wild Tom. His friends almost failed to recognize him. He quit drinking and swearing and was almost kind and considerate in his actions. To use another of Hank Henery's favorite expressions, "Tom was meeker than Moses."

At last The Little Feller took a turn for the better, and he and Tom improved together; he, physically—Tom, morally. Just at this time the big-hearted engineer was in imminent danger of killing his little friend, owing to the quantities of sweet-meats and other edibles that he carried to him.

One balmy April day, as Old Thirty-Four steamed in on the sidetrack and commenced wheezing and crooning to herself in a confidential and vainglorious[4] manner, The Little Feller—basket in hand—once more appeared before the footlights! He was a little paler, but cleaner and better dressed; and Tom actually smiled as he took his cue and called out "hullo."

The play had a new lease of life—and seemed fresher and better than before; but the performance became more elaborate, varying little by little—at first almost imperceptibly. Tom added a word to his lines now and then, and threw in a gesture here and there. The Little Feller did the same. So the play grew longer, and the players more sociable and friendly.

One sunshiny day an innovation of the startling character was introduced. A new personage appeared on the scene, without leave or license or previous intimation of his coming.

---

4   **vainglorious -** characterized by or exhibiting excessive vanity; boastful

It was like this: Tom had flung the lumps of coal at the retreating form of his protégé, and was making ready to indulge in his customary laugh, when a rough, overgrown lad, who had witnessed the proceedings, thought to gain the applause of the audience by coup-de-main[5]—ran across the track crying: "I'll scoot him for you, mister!" Suiting the action to the word, the big boy caught The Little Feller and was proceeding to chastise him, when Tom saw what was taking place. He was out of the cab like a flash, and off to the rescue and never before, perhaps, did a vulgar bully get such a shaking." The "audience" sat on the cab seat and approved of the forcible suggestion that manager Tom made, that no new talent need apply.

The long bright summer waned, the hazy autumn came and went, and icy winter was at hand again. All this time the play ran an uninterrupted course of triumph. One season of success only whetted manager Tom's insatiable appetite; he would have it go on forever! But the end came.

On a rainy, murky day in November, as Tom pulled out of Malconta, he waved a cheery farewell to The Little Feller standing at the end of the freight shed. It was the last time the boy ever saw him alive.

It had been raining for days and the roadbed was soft and spongy. In places along the precipitous hills that the railroads skirted, landslides were occurring.

Two miles below Malconta was a long and steep down grade. At this point the road lay between the rocky hills on the one hand and the swift-running river on the other, and just beyond was a long trestle that spanned Douda Run.

Tom and Hank were exceedingly watchful and careful that day, for both knew that there was danger of Old Thirty-Four ditching herself at any moment. Tom remarked to his companion: "Hank, somehow I feel strange—sort o' smell danger in the air." Hank said nothing in reply, but he turned a trifle pale about the mouth and his lips twitched. He knew what Tom meant.

It came, but it came in a form that neither had expected. What mysterious influence was it that warned Wild Tom of his approaching

---

5 **coup-de-main** - a sudden action undertaken to surprise an enemy

doom? One person was not surprised when it came. That person was Hank Henery.

As the great locomotive flew down the steep grade, with a long line of freight and coal cars rocking and thundering behind her, and urging her on, Hank and Tom leaned far out of the cab windows and scanned the wet track anxiously.

Just how it happened Hank Henery could never tell. Tom was on the side next to the hill. He turned his head to say: "Hank, there's a slip an' some trees"—but he never finished the sentence. Hank heard a crash, a cry; and leaped to his feet only to see Tom snatched through the window, amid a shower of limbs and broken glass and flung violetly to the earth.

Hank jumped to the lever, ran the train across the trestle at the foot of the grade, and brought it to a standstill; then he and the other trainmen ran back to look for their comrade.

They found him lying in a pool of mud and water by the side of the track. He was injured unto death but still conscious. They bore him tenderly to the caboose and made him as comfortable as possible, intending to run to Hookton, sidetrack the train, and with the engine and caboose carry the injured man back to Malconta. The nearest railroad surgeon lived at the latter village.

But Tom understood all, and he said. "It ain't no use, boys. I've run my last run—I throwed the lever for the last time. I don't much care. I'll die 'fore you get me back to Malconta. Cover me up—I'm cold."

The conductor offered him a drink of whiskey from a flask. Tom shook his head. "No," he said, hoarsely, "none o' that. The Little Feller didn't like to have me drink. I won't take it!"

Hank ran the train down to Hookton and sidetracked it. As he came into the caboose again, Tom motioned for him to come forward.

"Hank," he whispered, and Hank Henery saw strange, sweet light shining in the black eyes, "I want you to do something for me, ol' pard. Will you?"

Hank expressed his willingness to do anything that Tom wished.

"Hank, I want The Little Feller to have my life insurance. You mus' 'tend to that. Now, will you?"

Hank nodded, the tears running down his grimy cheeks.

"That's all, then," Tom resumed feebly, "It'll soon be over, boys. Goodbye to all of you—and—and—"

He was gasping for breath now. By a mighty effort he roused himself and murmured almost inaudibly, a look of intense and holy love beaming from his drawn countenance: "And give my best wishes and last farewell—to—to—The—Little Feller!" The broad, deep chest heaved and the strong limbs twitched convulsively; the bright eyes glazed and the blue lids drooped. All was over. Wild Tom was dead. The Little Feller lost the best friend he had on earth.

Part Two

Short Stories

by

James Ball Naylor

Introduction

Part Two

The seven stories that comprise Part Two appeared after the turn of the twentieth century—after Naylor had dropped the use of his pseudonym in favor of his full name, James Ball Naylor. The quality of these stories is much improved from the early ones. The time period between the two sets of stories may well have been several years. With a growing family, a medical practice, his schedule as an entertainer, and his writing, as well as other endeavors, he was an extremely busy man. With the advent of his 1901 best seller, *Ralph Marlowe*, Naylor became very well known in Ohio and beyond. In each of the next seven years, a new novel appeared, as well as three children's books. Always conscious of his "brand," he was much more careful about his work in these later stories.

Short stories in Part Two reflect Naylor's ability to observe and interpret human values in the people around him and his refined skill in describing their mannerisms, their speech, and their attire. As with the stories in Part One, Naylor relied on his life experience and people he knew as material for constructing characters, but he was much more confident in creating characters outside of his comfort zone, such as Claude Raymond, a secret service agent in "A Counterfeit Coin." Some of the personalities were composites of actual people with whom he interacted daily. Sometimes he took liberties with his pen, but few people were offended by what he wrote.

Jep Tucker was a delightful character in *Ralph Marlowe* who was always telling tales. Jim Whiss, a character in a series of these short stories, shares a similar trait. This might well be a case of Naylor using an idea from a novel in his short stories instead of the other way around. Five character sketches featuring

Jim Whiss appeared in *National Magazine* from January through October, 1903. Whiss was an eccentric character of whom Naylor was very fond. Although Whiss was merely the narrator in many of the sketches, the author's ability to describe his gestures and appearance so precisely makes him one of Naylor's more outstanding personalities. These stories include "How Tom Evans Won His Wife," "Mishaps of Ol' Andy Perdue," "The Youthful Indescretions of Jim Whiss," and "Ol' Cap Mingo." Another story that was a part of this series, "Sim Spike's Misadventures," appeared in Volume 19 of *National Magazine* in 1903, but that volume is no longer available, and the story has not been found anywhere else.

"A Lucky Opal" appeared in *National Magazine* in July, 1903, about a doctor who treats a mysterious young woman under odd circumstances. The use of an opal in this story was a special tribute to his wife, Villa. From the time he first submitted his manuscripts for publication, she copied his stories in her beautiful Spencerian handwriting before sending them off for publication. He was deeply appreciative of her assistance, and when their finances eventually permitted, he gave her the equivalent of a stenographer's pay. The first thing she bought with the money was an opal tie pin for him. She took pride in his personal appearance and in her role as his helpmate by always keeping his clothing neatly pressed. The pin added a special touch, and he wore it proudly.

In 1907 he submitted a manuscript of "A Counterfeit Coin" for serialization in the *Ohio Magazine*. It appeared in two volumes of the magazine, the first at the end of the year and the last at the beginning of 1908. The frontispiece of the first volume is a full-page portrait of the author. The original manuscript bears the same title but with S. Q. Lapius as the author, indicating that it was written at least ten years prior to its actual publication. The manuscript was revised extensively before its publication, a clear indication of the changing times and circumstances in publishing. Naylor departed from his usual style by creating a character not associated with the medical profession and one who was less of a stereotype. Many of his early stories had a romantic element or love story, but this one is one of his best. The locales are ones that he was most familiar with in his beloved Morgan County.

The main characters in both of these stories diverged from previous characterization of heroes. Actions and words make them more acceptable than was true of earlier characters, further reflecting Naylor's growth as a writer.

"The Undoing of Old John Chaney" is another touching story that appeared in the *Ohio Magazine* in 1906. The townspeople's attitude toward him and his reaction to them is much the same as the attitude of Babylon to Dr. Barwood in *Ralph Marlowe*.

Theresa Marie Flaherty

A Lucky Opal

The wind shrieked hysterically as it sped across the thoroughfare and down a side street. Then it grew angry and inquisitive—shaking doors and windows, thrusting its wet and icy fingers into crevices, and peeping down chimneys. Dr. Fred Dunbar heard its banshee voice and, stretching his shapely legs to the fire, shivered involuntarily.

It was a black and stormy December night. The raindrops froze as they fell; and a chill dampness penetrated entrances and halls.

Dr. Dunbar lighted a cigar and, leaning back in his comfortable office chair, began the perusal of a late journal. He was a man of thirty two, tall, erect and handsome. As he sat there, absentmindedly twirling his brown mustache around an index finger, a self satisfied smile crept over his face, lighting up his frank blue eyes. Knocking the ashes from his cigar, he yawned sleepily:

"Well, I'm a lucky dog, *this* night. Whew! hear that wind. Wouldn't I hate to face it! It's a wonder I don't have to go out tonight; I've been doing a deal of night work recently. Let's see. I've been here six months only; and already my income's becoming burden-some—almost pays my laundry bill. By jacks! it's a good thing for the young man in love with his profession to have something to fall back upon. Otherwise, through lack of proper nourishment, he might become his own skeleton, and—"

"Ting-a-ling-a-ling-ling!"

It was the telephone bell. The sound abruptly roused the doctor from his reverie. Springing to his feet, he crossed the room and took down the receiver. "Hello!" he called.

"Hello! Is this Dr. Dunbar?"

"Yes."

"Doctor, please come to the corner of King street and Hickory avenue, immediately."

"Who is it?"

No answer.

"Hello! Hello—I say!"

Still no answer.

"Hello! Who is it wants Dr. Dunbar?"

"King street and Hickory avenue," came faintly to the doctor's ear.

"Yes, I understand. But who is it?"

"It's all right. Will you come?"

"Yes; but—"

At that moment the other party rang off.

Dr. Dunbar hung up his receiver, muttering angrily:

"Well, don't that beat the devil! Whoever that was doesn't make a practice of calling a physician—or there's something shady about the affair."

A scowl rested upon his handsome face; and he strode up and down the room, in perplexity.

"Corner of King street and Hickory avenue," he continued musingly; "that's away in the East End. And, if my memory serves me right, a half dozen squares beyond the brickyards. There isn't a residence near there—ah!"—and he stopped and caught his breath sharply—"That's where the old icebarn stands. I understand everything now. I've heard it rumored that the sporting fraternity is in the habit of pulling off cock fights in that unused building. Some sport has got a knife thrust or a bit of cold lead. The affair *is* shady—they don't want the police to swoop down upon them. Well, here's for the sake of suffering humanity!"

He ordered his horse and hastily prepared for the disagreeable trip, all the while communing with himself.

"Thought I was to have a quiet evening with my books and magazines. Bah! This is a part of the penalty a man pays for being a philanthropic fool and studying medicine. Let's see—I think I've got everything I need. Well, here goes."

The night was intensely black, the wind blew a stiff gale, and the rain fell in sheets. At a fair speed he drove along the lighted streets. He left the street car tracks and electric lights behind and emerged into the sparsely settled suburbs. Then came the brick yards and the laborers' hovels surrounding them. The last light disappeared—he could hardly see to drive.

Of a sudden he pulled up and, peering intently into the blackness ahead of him, growled shiveringly:

"I must be near the place. Yes; there it is—right under my nose."

He shook the lines, and again moved forward. A muffled figure emerged from the shadow of the building he was nearing and called softly:

"Hello! Is that Dr. Dunbar?"

"Yes."

The man advanced and seizing the bridle said quietly but firmly:

"I'll lead your horse into the barn; it's quite dark."

"Somebody hurt?" inquired the physician, as the phaeton[1] rolled and lurched along the stone approach leading to the interior of the building.

The man made no reply; and a suspicion flashed upon Dunbar's mind that all was not right. However, he quieted himself with the thought that, owing to the rattle of the vehicle, his companion had not heard him. He wondered, though, that no light showed within the barn; and regretted that he had not brought his revolver.

The horse's hoofs thundered upon the plank floor, and the phaeton came to a stop. Dr. Dunbar caught the sound of shuffling footsteps and quick breathing, but could see nothing. Alarm seized him; and he was about to leap to the floor, when a hand was laid upon his arm and a voice whispered in his ear:

"Don't be alarmed, doctor; no harm is intended. A patient needs your services—a patient whom you mustn't know. It's a matter of life and death, and haste is necessary. Therefore you must consent to do my bidding; there's no time to get another physician."

Somewhat reassured and emboldened by the speaker's tone and words, Dr. Dunbar replied:

---

1 **phaëton:** any of various light four-wheeled horse-drawn vehicles

"I can't understand you nor your method of procuring medical aid. However, as your language indicates you're a gentleman and not a footpad[2], I'm ready to listen to you. What do you desire?"

"That you be blindfolded before you're conducted to the presence of the patient."

"Blindfolded?"

"Yes."

"Well, I'll be—what if I refuse?"

"Don't speak so loud," cautioned the man. "If you refuse, I'll force you to do as I wish. I've help at hand."

"Huh! What if I should raise an outcry?"

"Listen!" the voice said menacingly. "This is a lonely place—no one could hear you. Do my bidding, and you shall return to your office amply rewarded for your services; refuse, and—"

"And what?" Dunbar asked calmly. He had regained control of himself; and all his fears had vanished.

"And you die!" whispered the man, shoving the cold muzzle of a revolver against the doctor's temple.

Fred Dunbar's voice did not quaver though he involuntarily drew away from the cold weapon pressing his forehead. He said stoutly:

"The devil! I don't believe you'd dare to shoot me; so don't flatter yourself you're frightening me into acceding to your demands. And let up on your heroics. I'll see this thing through—I consent to be blindfolded. But I can't understand how I'm to administer to a patient with my eyes bandaged."

"Never mind that for the present," replied the mysterious personage. "Step out upon the floor."

The doctor obeyed; and immediately a muslin bag was dropped over his head and a silken scarf was wound around it a number of turns.

"It appears you don't wish me to see or hear either," he remarked chuckling, the humor of the affair appealing to him.

"True," was the terse answer. "Here is your satchel. Come on."

'The physician felt himself led across the barn floor. A side door opened, and the air blew upon him.

---

2 **footpad** - a thief who preys on pedestrians

"Is the patient near at hand," he inquired, some concern in his tone.

"No," was the curt rejoinder that came as a muffled whisper to his bandaged ears.

"Well, what's to become of my horse in my absence?"

"Have no fear; it's secure:"

At that moment Dunbar thought he heard someone within the barn speaking to the restive[3] animal in a low, guarded tone of voice. He—the doctor—was not at all alarmed over his safety now; in fact, he was rather enjoying the novelty of the experience.

"What a bugaboo[4] tale! I'll have to tell the fellows at the club," was the thought uppermost in his mind.

The man led him over the uneven ground for a few yards. Then they came to a sudden halt, and, by the sense of touch, the professional man became aware that they stood at the side of a closed cab.

"Climb in," commanded his conductor.

The doctor obeyed; and his companion followed him. The door was closed softly, and Dunbar felt rather than heard the driver scramble to his seat.

Away they rolled. The earth was soft, and the impact of the horses' feet upon it gave forth but little sound. The cab swayed and lurched fearfully; they were moving rapidly over the rough roads. Then, after some minutes, the doctor's bandaged ears caught faintly the sound of iron shoes upon paved streets.

"We're returning toward the heart of the city," was his mental comment. "What's to be the outcome of this adventure?"

Again they were upon the soft earth of the suburbs. After what seemed an age to Dunbar's overwrought imagination, the vehicle came to a stop. The two men alighted, and the conductor led the physician up the front steps of a building. Dunbar counted them as he ascended—one, two, three, four. Then the door opened and

---

3 **restive** - (of a horse) refusing to advance, stubbornly standing still, or moving backward or sideways

4 **bugaboo** - an imaginary monster used to frighten children

closed; and they were standing in a spacious hallway—so the doctor judged from the warm air and the hollow sound of the closing door.

A voice that was not the voice of his conductor came to his muffled ears, saying:

"Thank God! You're here at last. I thought you'd never come. There's not a moment to waste—take him to her at once."

"A lady patient," murmured the doctor, beneath his mask; and his heart throbbed with expectancy.

Once more his conductor's hand was laid upon his shoulder; and these words were breathed into his ear:

"I've brought you here to see a lady who has accidentally poisoned herself. For the sake of the family we don't want it noised[5] abroad—people are prone to put a wrong construction upon such accidents. I'll conduct you to her apartment at once. There you may remove the scarf from your head; you'll be able to see and hear through your mask. A servant is in attendance, who will procure you anything you need. Do for the patient everything that lies in your power; you shall be well paid. But you mustn't reveal your face nor your name to her; nor must you make an effort to discover who she is. Do you understand?"

Dr. Dunbar nodded.

"Very well. Remember the servant will report any treachery. If you attempt to deceive me, in the minutest particular, you'll never leave this house alive. No one but myself and trusted assistants know you're here."

"It may become necessary for me to see her face—" the doctor began.

"Under no circumstances are you to see her face," was the stern interruption.

"Then I may not be able to save her life—"

"You must! You'll save her life or *forfeit* your own!"

Dr. Fred Dunbar started, muttering under his breath:

"I'm beginning to believe this desperate scoundrel means what he says."

But aloud he said:

---

5 **noised** - talked about or made known publicly

"Bah! Ring down the curtain on the melodrama. What poison has she taken?"

"The attendant will answer your questions. Come on."

The physician was conducted up a broad stairway and pushed into a room. Then the door was closed and locked behind him. He placed his satchel upon the floor and removed the scarf that encircled his head. Then he became aware that there were holes in the muslin mask through which he could see clearly. He was in a large chamber richly furnished. Before him stood an aged and repulsive looking negress black as night. Upon a luxurious bed in one corner lay the patient.

A light covering hid her form, and one white hand rested upon it. The loose sleeve of her gown had slipped up, and the arm thus revealed was plump and shapely. Her face and neck were enveloped in the folds of a white scarf or mantilla; lips and teeth only were visible. The doctor noted that the latter were white and even and of nature's handiwork. All this his trained eye took in at a glance.

"Young and beautiful," was his mental ejaculation.

He advanced to the bedside and took the patient's hand, the negress watching him narrowly. He found the pulse slow and weak, and noted that the nails were blue, and the hand and arm cold. The full lips were cyanotic and the respiration was slow and labored.

"Weak circulation—heart depressant," was his quick diagnosis.

Then, bending over the prostrate form, he cried sharply:

"Are you awake? Can you hear me?" The still form did not stir.

Turning to the negress, the doctor asked:

"How long has your mistress lain so?"

"Fo' mo'n two hours."

"Too late for an emetic[6]," he muttered in an undertone. Then aloud:

"Do you know what she took?"

The negress silently handed him a folded paper containing a

---

6 **emetic** - a medication or substance given to induce vomiting

few grains of a white, crystalline powder. Dunbar gingerly tasted it, and, making a wry face, muttered half audibly:

"Acetanalid[7]—I thought so. That calls for prompt action."

Then to the negress:

"Get me some warm water, and a spoon and a glass—and be quick about it. I want warm flannel, hot water bottles, and brandy, too. Hurry!"

Someone was restlessly pacing up and down the hall outside. The negress tapped upon the door and it was opened slightly. Soon the doctor had the desired articles; and again the door was closed and locked.

He went to work with a will. He directed the negress to place the hot water bottles in the bed, and to wrap the cold form in warm flannels. In the meantime, he had loaded his hypodermic syringe with a powerful heart stimulant. Stepping to the bedside, he prepared to inject the medicine into his veiled patient's arm. He caught the glitter of a costly ring upon her finger, and paused momentarily to examine it. It was a neat band of gold set with a large Hungarian opal in which a heart of fire was blazing.

"I believe I'd know that ring again," he whispered as he slipped the loose sleeve still higher and remorselessly thrust the keen needle into the white skin.

For several minutes he sat upon the side of the bed, holding a finger over the minute puncture he had made and silently watching for the effects of the medicine. The negress scrutinized his every movement. He saw a small, shining white mark upon the patient's arm, and examined it closely. It was a vaccination scar almost effaced by time; and just above it were three small brown moles in a cluster.

"I *know* I'd recognize that arm—should I ever chance to see it again," he mused.

Again he felt the pulse. It was stronger, more rapid. The cyanotic hue was forsaking the lips. The medicine was having the desired effect. The patient stirred uneasily.

"Hand me that glass of brandy and water," the doctor said to

____
7 **acetanalid** – a poisonous heart depressant

the negress. Slowly and skillfully he poured a small quantity of the mixture between his patient's parted lips. Mechanically she swallowed. He repeated the dose; and she strangled and coughed. Then her hands and limbs began to recover their warmth; and she heaved a deep respiration.

"Are you feeling better?" he asked in a loud tone.

"Yes," was the reply, as faint as the whisper of a summer breeze.

He gave her a dose of brandy and digitalis, and leaving the bedside walked up and down the room for several minutes. Again he examined the pulse, and found it steadier and stronger.

"You're much better," he suggested.

"Yes," was the answer.

Her voice was weak, but as clear and sweet as the ripple of crystal water.

"I'm the doctor," he said.

"I can't see you," she began.

"That's all right—your eyes are bandaged," he interrupted hastily. "Lie still."

"Oh, why didn't you let me die!—" and she sighed deeply, despairingly.

"I'd know that voice again, too," he thought; but aloud he said to the negress:

"Your mistress is out of danger; I'm going. Give her a dose of this medicine in half an hour."

As he shook hands with his mysterious patient in parting, both of hers sought his in warm pressure, and the whispered words "Help me!" greeted his ears.

Then he felt a crumpled bit of paper thrust into his palm, and he adroitly transferred it to his pocket, without attracting the attention of the watchful black attendant.

"Here—arrange this scarf for me," he muttered brusquely, to divert her attention.

Then he groped his way to the door, his heart thumping in wild and exultant tumult.

Just outside, his conductor gripped his arm and inquired anxiously:

"What's her condition?"

"She's out of danger."

"You're not deceiving me?"

"No."

"Here's your reward, then." And a roll of bank bills was thrust into the doctor's hand.

Again the two were in the cab. Neither spoke during the return journey to the old ice barn.

An hour later Dunbar was sitting by his office fire, with nothing but a roll of bank bills to prove he had not dreamed it all. Yes, he had one other proof—the crumpled bit of paper; and now he spread it upon his knee and carefully examined it. It was a scrawling note, written in soft pencil upon fuzzy book paper. Evidently it had been prepared hurriedly, to escape the prying eyes of others than the writer. Many of the words were illegible, but this is what Dr. Dunbar deciphered:

"Doctor—whoever . . . . . be: taken poison . . . not so much my intention to commit suicide . . . to bring someone . . . rescue. . . virtually a prisoner . . . hands . . relatives . . . . pity . . find me alive . . not matter . . . die . . . so miserably unhappy. Elo . . . Le . . . ier."

"Whew!" whistled the doctor, as he folded the strange missive and placed it in his pocketbook. "I glean from these broken sentences that my veiled lady didn't mean to commit suicide, but took that rather heroic method of summoning aid. However, she thought it mattered little if she did die—she's so miserably unhappy. A prisoner in the hands of her relatives, eh? What the mischief can it all mean? She thought to bring a physician and give him this note: then she expected him to take steps to deliver her from the clutches of her relatives. But they trumped her trick neatly! I don't know her face, nor where she lives; I can't make out her name, even—Eloise something, of course. French, maybe—pshaw!"

He sat and thought until the fire went out and the room grew cold. Then he retired; but he could not sleep. The tinkle of that silvery voice was in his ears; the fiery heart of the Hungarian opal flashed before his closed eyes.

"Stuff!" he muttered at last, in deep disgust. "Why should I lose sleep over the matter? Doubtless she's some romantic and lovelorn maiden subject to attacks of hysteria."

But he could not believe his own peevish statement, and it was almost daylight ere he finally fell asleep.

After he had made his morning visits, he called upon his friend, the corner druggist. To the man of the mortar and pestle he related his adventure of the previous night in detail, producing the roll of bank bills and crumpled note in evidence. When he had finished he detected an incredulous smile upon his friend's face.

"Don't you believe what I've told you, Mr. Lucas?" he demanded irritably. "Of course," laughed Mr. Lucus. "Why don't you write it out and sell it to a newspaper syndicate."

"What do you mean?"

"Just what I say. Write out your dream in full—"

"Dream!" Dr. Dunbar broke in hotly. "It's an actual occurrence. I swear—"

"Swear not!"—And the druggist grinned inanely.—"I'm one of the most credulous mortals, Dunbar, but I can't swallow that yarn. Let's have no more of it. How's Mr. Marsden this morning?"

In a tiff the doctor left the drug store, without replying to his friend's solicitious inquiry. Then and there he resolved not to mention the matter to another human being. If Mr. Lucus—his most intimate associate—could not give credence to his tale, who would?

The days and weeks slipped by. Dr. Dunbar kept his resolve—kept his own counsel. Much connected with his nocturnal adventure grew hazy and indistinct; but a few things kept a fixed place in his memory. The soft, clear, well-moulded tones of his mysterious patient's voice became more and more insistent. He heard her words—"Help me!" on the crowded thoroughfare and in the privacy of his own rooms. At last he knew what it meant; he was in love—in love with a voice.

Six months passed. One balmy June morning he was called to the North Side. His horse was lame, and he took an electric car. At the viaduct[8] a gentleman and lady came aboard and took seats opposite. The man was swarthy, of middle age and foreign and sinister aspect. The woman was tall and willowy, but so closely veiled Dunbar could not get a glimpse of her face. Her escort stared hard at the physician from time to time, and appeared ill at ease.

When the conductor came to collect their fares, the foreign looking gentleman could not produce the requisite change and he appealed to his companion.

"Have you any small coins," he asked. Dunhar pricked up his ears; the man's voice sounded strangely familiar.

"I think so—yes," was the young woman's reply.

Dunbar started visibly. It was the voice he loved—the voice of his waking dreams, but stronger and fuller than he had ever heard it. On the instant the cool and reasoning physician vanished, and the hot and impulsive lover was there in his stead. He quivered with excitement. He saw the black eyes of the foreigner fixed full upon him, but he could not control his agitation. The young woman quietly removed her glove to procure the necessary change from her purse; and Fred Dunbar almost sprang to his feet. Upon her finger was the opal ring that had haunted his sight for months!

It was *she!* With an effort he regained control of himself, and looked away from her. The car reached the suburbs and came to a stop, and the couple alighted. The physician forgot all about his professional visit and, leaping to the ground, followed them at a distance—without pausing to question his motive or action. They proceeded along a shady street, for three or four blocks, and entered a big brick house. Dr. Dunbar counted the steps leading up to the front door. There were four of them.

For the next few days, he was in a fever of unrest and uncertainty. By inquiries, he learned that the family consisted of an old man, Henri De Voire, his son, Jean, and a young relative, Eloise Le Villier. They had occupied the house about a year and no one knew whence they came. They were exclusive, entertaining no company

---

8 **viaduct -** a series of spans or arches used to carry a road or railroad over a wide valley or over other roads or railroads

and making few acquaintances. Miss Le Villier never went out un-
accompanied by one of her male relatives, and few people had seen
her unveiled.

Dunbar at last resolved that he must know the true status of
affairs in that household. Should he write Miss Le Villier? No;
if she were under the malign control and espionage of her relatives, they would intercept any written communication. In a fit of
desperation he resolved to call at the house, and impetuously he
carried out his resolution. As he drove up to the somber-looking
residence, he cursed himself for a lovesick idiot—but did not
hold back.

An old man was spraying the front lawn. Of him the doctor
inquired: "Is Mr. De Voire at home?"

"The De Voires don't live here now," was the unexpected and
disconcerting reply.

"Don't live here?" the doctor exclaimed incredulously.

"No sir; they left day before yesterday.

"The young lady—Miss Le Villier, too?"

"Of course. They went to the lakes for her health."

"Is she ill?"

"No; just a little off in her mind, you know. They never
'lowed her out of their sight. She's been better of late; but they
took a sudden notion to go—and they went.

Dr. Dunbar returned to his office, in a perplexed and de-
pressed state of mind. So this was the end of his love dream. He
had been in love with the voice of a half demented nonentity! He
tried to despise himself, but could not. He vowed that he would
root the whole affair from his mind—and deliberately sat down to
think it over. In the end he came back to his original conviction—
that Eloise Le Villier was a wronged and suffering young woman.
And her voice continued to haunt him.

Summer sped and winter came. Again Dr. Dunbar sat alone
in his office, after a day of hard work, and again the telephone
bell broke in upon his reverie. It was a call from the Hostlerie, an
aristocratic boarding house on Vaughan street.

The landlady met him in the parlor, and said:

"Miss Lindsay in number eight was taken with a severe chill and pain in her chest, about noon, and now she's feverish and delirious. Sarah, show Dr. Dunbar up to number eight."

Number eight was a suite of three rooms. A beautiful young woman, her face flushed with fever and framed in a tumbled mass of raven hair, turned toward the door, as the doctor entered, and two black eyes stared wildly at him. He advanced to the bed and spoke soothingly to the delirious sufferer. Her lips moved tremulously, but no sound came forth, and she kept her gaze fixed upon his face. His strong, warm fingers sought her wrist, as he stood studying her countenance. His touch appeared to soothe and reassure her, and she wearily dropped her jetty lashes.

The respiration was hurried and jerky, the pulse was rapid and bounding.

"Pnuemonia," was his decision when he had finished his examination.

Just as he turned to give a command to the attendant, the patient's other hand fluttered restlessly from beneath the coverlet. Again the fateful opal revealed itself to Dr. Dunbar's startled gaze! He sprang to the bedside—unheeding the presence of the astounded servant—and, pushing up the flowing sleeve, examined the white and shapely arm. The marks were before him—"Miss Lindsey" was Eloise Le Villier.

Blessing the fates that had at last thrown them together, Dr. Dunbar set to work to save the life that was oscillating in the balance. He installed a trained nurse and made frequent visits. In two weeks his patient was convalescent, and a few days after, when he entered her apartments one morning, he found her smiling at him from the cushioned depths of an armchair. She was thin and pale—but very beautiful, he thought.

"Good morning, Doctor," was her pleasant greeting. "I feel so much better this morning, that I must perform a duty I've neglected. I desire to thank you for your skillful and unremitting care."

She paused for breath—her bosom rising and falling. Seating himself at her side, he replied hurriedly:

"Don't thank me. I'm rewarded to find you so much improved."

"You've been very kind to me—a total stranger," she went on slowly; "and very successful in your treatment. I can't realize how you understood me—my case, so well; you never treated me before—"

He resolved upon a bold stroke, and interrupted with "But I have treated you before, Miss—"

He hesitated—paused, in embarrassment. All through her illness he had called her "Miss Lindsey." What should he call her now? She turned her black eyes full upon him, in silent inquiry. He was considering whether it would be well to let her know all—whether the surprise would be too much for her weakened nerves.

"You say you've treated me before, doctor?"

He had gone too far; his retreat was barred.

"Yes," he answered quietly, "I've treated you *once* before, Miss Le Villier." He expected her to be startled—alarmed; to faint or have a nervous attack. But she did nothing of the kind. Instead, she coolly leaned back in her chair, half closing her eyes, and returned smilingly:

"So you know me, Dr. Dunbar?"

"I do."

"Then you must be the physician who attended me when I—I took acetanalid; for this is the second time in my life that I've been under a doctor's care."

He nodded gravely.

"That explains, then," she murmured musingly. "Many times during my present illness, I've striven to recall where I had heard your voice. Your face did not appear familiar, but your voice seemed like that of an old friend—that is—"

She broke off abruptly, her breast heaving, her cheeks flushed. Noticing her agitation, the doctor remarked:

"You're exciting yourself; you'll be worse. You must talk no more at present."

"I'm stronger than you think, doctor; and I'm not tiring myself," she answered pleadingly. "How did you discover my identity? You didn't see my face the night you—you saved my life."

And again the pink flush suffused her cheeks. Dr. Dunbar was eyeing her keenly, and attributed her agitation to embarrassment and nervous excitement. Now he said positively:

"We'll drop the subject for the time. I'm not going to allow you to work injury to yourself."

"No—no!" she pleaded prettily, laying her hand upon his sleeve. "Tell me how you knew me."

With her slender white fingers caressing his arm and her soulful black eyes turned beseechingly to his, he could not refuse her request—especially as he desired to do just what she requested, so he told her of the opal ring and the marks upon her arm.

"How interesting—how romantic!" she cried in genuine delight, laughing merrily.

Then, with instant gravity:

"But you haven't informed me how you learned my name. Surely Jean didn't tell you—after all the pains he took to conceal my identity? You see he tauntingly told me all—after I recovered—how he had brought you to the house and kept you in ignorance of who we were."

Dr. Dunbar made her acquainted with the street car episode and his subsequent inquiries. She clapped her hands in mercurial ecstacy, crying:

"You should be a detective, doctor." Again looking pensively grave, she continued:

"But you *were* the knight errant I thought you; you *did* try to come to my rescue."

"Did you think me a knight errant?" And he laughed uneasily— "How could you? You didn't know me—you hadn't seen me."

"I know," she replied with a bewitching show of embarrassment, "but I'd heard your voice, and—and I remembered it. And a number of days ago the suspicion flashed upon me that you were the physician who attended me in my previous illness."

"And you *were* in need of help?"

She drew herself up stiffly as she replied:

"Certainly! Did you doubt it?"

"I—I didn't know what to think," he stammered confusedly. "I couldn't decipher all of your note, you know; and—"

"I know what you thought," she broke in indignantly; "you thought me a hysterical young miss crossed in love. Oh, I know you cold and heartless professional men!"

He laughed heartily at her keen intuition; and she joined him.

"I *did* try to make myself believe something of the kind," he confessed, "but could not. Can you forgive me?"

"Readily." And once more the hot blood rushed to her face.

"Tell me of yourself," he said suddenly.

"What do you want to know?"

"Everything."

"Which is very little. I'm French. My parents died when I was quite young; and I was left to the care of my father's cousin, Henri De Voire. He brought me and Jean to America, and we lived in one city after another. Jean's mother died before we left France. Two years ago he professed to love me and asked me to marry him. I refused. His father joined him in his pleading; they wished to gain full control of my fortune. Still I refused; and at last they made a prisoner of me—would let me see no one unless they were present. They gave out that I was demented and tried to force me to accede to their demands, but I was firm—obstinate, if you please. I didn't love Jean, and I couldn't marry him. A little over a year ago we came to this city. I was growing desperate; and, in casting about for an avenue of escape from their persecutions, I hit upon the plan—romantic and silly, perhaps—of which you know. After that, they ceased to torment me, in a measure, with their importunities; but last summer, of a sudden, they took me to Canada. I know now that they left here to escape your interference in my behalf. By mere chance I eluded their vigilance and—selling my mother's jewels to obtain money—returned to this city. Here I've lived under an assumed name, teaching music to eke out an existence. You know the rest. I haven't tried to obtain possession of my fortune, for fear of them. The bare thought of Jean and his horrible temper terrorizes me. Many times he threatened to place me in a private madhouse, and at times I feared he would soon have just reason for so doing. You've been very kind to me, Dr. Dunbar; I feel grateful—I trust you. Oh, won't you protect and aid me?"

Tears were in her eyes. He took the slim, white hand, that rested so confidingly upon his arm, and, looking intently at the opal's heart of fire, made answer:

"If you'll give me the right, Eloise—yes."

Ol' Cap Mingo

He drops in to see me almost every evening—and always and invariably at a time when I am busy at something that I consider of extreme importance. In this he manifests a genius and perspicuity[1] occult, malevolent and diabolical. He reads and claws over my papers, cuts my magazines—an unpardonable offense in my eyes—and smokes my cigars. And yet I tolerate him. Why? 1 don't know; I *do*—that's all. Perhaps I like the voluble and tiresome old eccentric, in spite of his persistent intrusiveness and unforgivable shortcomings. Again, I don't know.

I hear his heavy step upon the stairs; I recognize his clumsy shuffle in the hall. Then the door opens softly, a few inches; and he peeps in—two bright blue eyes gleaming under bushy brows. Not a word does he say; nor do I. The door opens wider; a foot and leg intrudes—a big, shaggy head, and round shoulders. He's within the room; and the door closed. The manner of his entrance savors of dark intentions—deeds of violence; and in any other would be disconcerting, uncanny, alarming. Still he offers no grunt of greeting; nor do I offer a hint or gesture of welcome. He waddles to his accustomed chair, rolling his eyes in my direction, as he drags his feet across the floor. In his great, rough, brown overcoat he resembles nothing so much as a portly cinnamon bear. Once seated, he quietly removes his cap of threadbare velvet, places it upon the floor beside him, picks up a newspaper from my desk, extends his feet to the blazing gas, deliberately produces and adjusts a pair of spectacles and lolls back in his chair—emitting a long drawn grunt of satisfaction as he collapses into a rotund heap.

Invariably this is the manner of his coming, the method of his arrival, and always he takes the same chair, hitches it to one exact and identical spot, and settles himself after the prescribed fashion. The light from my study lamp shadows his shaggy head—his iron gray mane and beard and massive shoulders upon a blank space of wall near him—a lamplight silhouette, a veritable Viking.

---

1 **perspicuity** - expressing oneself clearly and effectively

I go on with my writing; he goes on with his reading. When I have come to a convenient stopping place, I look up and say:

"Good evening, Jim."

He was christened James Madison Whissen. That is, if ever he *was* christened, which I rather doubt. At any rate, that's his name. But he never gets it.

His friends—and the term includes all who know him—call him "Jim Whiss."

"G'd evenin'," he grunts surily, from whiskered depths, in reply to my delayed greeting. Then, somehow, we drift into conversation; and I always learn something from him.

"Keer 'f I smoke in here?" he jerked out one evening not long ago, after conscientiously going through the stereotyped preliminaries I have just described.

"You *have* smoked in here," I answered somewhat tartly, "and ought to *know* whether I care or not."

"Umph!" he grunted. Then, with a series of jabs into his overcoat pocket, he produced an ill-smelling pipe, fondled it between finger and thumb, and remarked, "Got nothin' to smoke but this ol' pipe; an' it smells louder'n a steam boat a-puffin'!"

The hint was so ingenious—and so palpable—that I silently opened the drawer of my desk, took out a cigar, and handed it to him. Without a word he accepted it, bit off the tip, lighted the satiny roll of tobacco and puffed away luxuriously and dreamily for some minutes. I philosophically accepted the inevitable and patiently awaited his pleasure.

At last he rolled his eyes in my direction and muttered:

"Died last night—'bout 'leven o'clock."

"Who?" I asked, stretching my legs and yawning.

"Who!" in a tone of deep disgust—"Ol' Cap Mingo."

"I never knew him, I guess."

"S'pose not," Jim growled; "seems you never *do* know anybody of any *consequence*."

"Who was he?"

"Who was he! Ol' Cap Mingo, of course; I told you once. Lived in the big brick house near t'other end o' the bridge. Great ol' feller—

funny old codger."

"Tell me about him."

"Re'ly want me to?"

"Certainly."

"Humph! All right. Ol' steamboat captain an' river man—must 'ave been up'ard of eighty. Been in all kinds o' business, though; made an' lost two 'r three fortunes—an' finally died poor as a nigger's houn'.

"Some folks says he was educated fer a preacher but fell from grace w'en he was young, an' went to steamboatin'. One thing's certain—he could quote more scripture in the way o' cuss words, 'n any feller 'long the valley. Yes, Sir! Curious critter— was Ol' Cap Mingo; big an' hairy as a bear—an' had a voice like a towboat's whistle. Years an' years ago, he used to run the Otter, from here to Zanesville, up in the mornin' an' back in the evenin'. An' you bet she alluz left the wharf here on time—five o'clock, to the tick o' the watch! He wouldn't wait a second on nobody n'r nothin'. People set the'r clocks by the whistle o' his boat. Some folks, w'en they'd be a minute late, an' git left, 'd snort an' rip around an' raise cain gener'ly; but it didn't do no good. All ol' Cap 'd say was:

"'The Otter b'longs to Captain Sam Mingo; an' he runs 'er to suit hisself. She leaves at five o'clock—wind 'r calm, rain 'r shine; an' folks that ain't on board by *that* time, can *walk*!'

"Ol' Aunt M'lissy, his wife, was a good, easy-goin' soul, an' a Christian; an' Cap's ways an' doin's was a great cross to 'er sometimes.

"One evenin' she says to him: 'Sam, I'm thinkin' o' goin' up to Zanesville with you, tomorrer.'

"'You're talkin' to Captain Mingo, mam,' he answers, swellin' out his chist.

"'Well, Captain Mingo,' she laughs, humorin' him as she alluz done, 'can y'r wife ride on y'r boat, tomorrer?'

"'If you're on board at five o'clock, Mrs. Mingo,' he answers, without crackin' a smile.

"'S'pose I'm a few minutes late?' She says.

"'The Otter leaves the wharf at five o'clock, Mrs. Mingo.'

"'But, maybe I won't wake up in time,' she complains.

"'The Otter blows her whistle at half past four, Mrs. Mingo.'

"An' that was all she could get out o' him.

"Well, the next morning w'en she got to the wharf, the Otter was jest pulling out. Aunt M'lissy waved 'er han'kerchief an' screamed:

"'Sam Mingo, what d' you mean? Come back in here!'

"'Who is it? ol' Cap bellers from the hurricane deck—fer it was still dark as a nigger pray'r meetin'.

"'It's me—M'lissy!' she yells.

"'Well, Mrs. Mingo,' he answers, as the boat swings 'er nose out an' starts up the river, 'you're just thirty-three seconds too late. The Otter leaves at five o'clock.'"

Jim's cigar had gone out, through neglect. He stooped, grunting dismally, and relighted the charred stump, at the gas fire.

"An odd character, indeed," I remarked by way of suggestion.

"Odder'n a white blackbird," he muttered, his course voice rumbling up from what seemed immeasurable depths.

Then, after a few vigorous pulls at his cigar, and a dubious glance or two from the tail of his eye at its glowing end, he resumed reminiscently:

"Finally broke up in the steamboatin' business an' took a gover'ment contract down on the public works, at the end o' the river. Sent his wife home a certain 'mount o' money ev'ry month, to live on. Was down there some three years; an' w'en he come back he hadn't saved a cent.

"One rainy day he was loafin' 'round the house, an' doin' a good 'eal o' grumblin' 'bout his bad luck, an' M'lissy says to him: 'Captain Mingo, what's the matter with you, anyhow?'

"'Sam Mingo, now, if you please, mam,' he answers way down in his boots. 'A man that hain't got no money n'r nothin', n'r no luck neither hain't got no right to a handle to his name. Plain *Sam* Mingo, from this on, mam.'

"'Well, what's the matter with you, anyhow?' she wants to know.

"'Broke—busted—that's all,' he growls. 'Been workin' three years, an' hain't got a penny—not a red. Won't never git another start, that way. 'F I had a thousan' dollars 'r so, right now, I would git a sheer in that new boat that's bein' built at Marietta, an' soon be on my feet ag'in.'

"'You don't read y'r Bible often 'nough, Sam,' M'lissy says, smilin'. 'You might have more money if—'

"'Oh, the devil!' he snorts. 'Religion don't make money fer nobody but preachers!'

"'How do you know?' his wife laughs. 'You've never tried it.'

"'N'r I ain't goin' to,' he answers, marchin' over to the winder an' lookin' out at the pourin' rain.

"'Well,' she says kind o' slow, an' 'er voice a-tremblin', 'it wouldn't do you no harm to read y'r Bible once in a while, anyhow. It'll please me; an' you might find somethin' in it that'll comfort you an' cheer you up.'

"'Humph,' he snorts, shruggin' his big shoulders.

"M'lissy went out of the room; an' ol' Cap stood at the winder, a mumblin' fer quite a spell. But his wife's words had stuck in his craw; an' he couldn't git rid of 'em. Finally, bein' lonesome an' havin' the blues so bad, an' not havin' anything else to do, he sets down, takes the big family Bible on his lap, and opens it up.

"Well, sir, there laid a fifty dollar bill, snuggled in between the leaves! Ol' Cap took it out an' turned over another leaf 'r two; an' there was another one. An' 'fore he got up from his chair he took some seventeen hundred out o' that Bible. His wife had saved ev'ry cent of it out o' the money he'd sent 'er to live on."

Jim yawned, stretched, and struggled to his feet, his cigar stub showing red between his bearded lips.

"Going?" I asked.

He bobbed an affirmative.

"And the old fellow's dead, eh?"

"Died last night, 'bout 'leven o'clock," he answered as he closed the door.

How Tom Evans Won His Wife

Jim Whiss, my eccentric old Viking, was in to see me again a few nights ago. He entered after the fashion he has prescribed for himself—which I have described in a previous sketch—with stealthy shuffle, glowering countenance, and furtive look, and seated himself according to rule.

I scribbled away silently and industriously for a half hour or more; he sat and stared at the fire, according me an occasional side glance and contemptuous shrug. I felt his presence—otherwise I was oblivious to everything but the work before me. He disturbed me no more than a dozing dog would have done—not so much, perhaps, for the best-mannered cur will sometimes make himself obnoxious, by dreaming of the pleasures of the chase and whining and scratching in his sleep.

At last I exhausted the love of my own thought, and threw down pad and pencil. He gave his undivided attention to the greenish-red blaze of the gas fire; I leaned back in my chair, and fell to studying the silhouette of a shaggy head upon the wall—wishing I were an artist and wondering what was the nature of the cargo the piratical looking old craft had drifted in to unload. The room was so still I could hear the ticking of my watch in my pocket. The unwonted silence roused him.

"Out o' fix tonight?" he growled, fidgeting, but not looking up.

"No," I yawned behind my hand.

"Thought maybe you was; you're so pesky grumpy," and he shot me a glance half surly, half humorous.

"It's damp out tonight, Jim," I remarked by way of reply.

"Damper'n ol Niobe's han'kerch'ef."

Silence again. I nodded; and brought up with a jerk at the ragged edge of dreamland, I caught the mumbled words:

"Back here on a visit."

"Who?" I asked, with a fine show of interest.

"Hadn't been asleep, you'd 'ave heard," he muttered testily.

"I wasn't asleep," I lied.

"Tom Evans an' his wife."

"Ah?"

"Uh-huh," he went on. "Seen 'em down at the depot today. Purty fine lookin' woman he's got. Purty *is* as purty *does*, though. Don't know nothin' 'bout 'er. They was dressed up sniptious[1]; an' had a whole drayload[2] o' baggage."

"Who is he?"

"Him?"

"Yes."

"Tom Evans?"

I nodded, smiling.

"Huh!"—with pitying contempt for my ignorance—"Ol' Doc Evan's son—the black sheep o' the family; but, like a good many other black sheep, he sheers the best an' biggest fleece of any o' the flock now. Was raised down at Babylon, ten miles below here. Wouldn't do nothin' but fish an' hunt an' chaw tobacker, till he was purty nigh of age. Then, all that once, he took a notion to go to school an' soon blossomed out as a school teacher. Finally got in with the big lumber concern up in Cleveland; an' now he's richer'n Jersey cream."

He stopped.

"Indeed!" I ejaculated to set him going again.

"Ever hear how he captured his wife?" he inquired.

"*Captured* his wife?" I echoed.

"Well, *got 'er*, then!" He snapped.

"I never did."

"Want to hear 'bout it?"

"Of course."

"I can alluz talk better when I smoke,"—his eyes twinkling slyly under his bushy brows.

I gave him the coveted cigar. He deliberately lighted it, lovingly rolled and fondled it between thumb and fingers, and continued:

---

1   **sniptious** - attractive, smart, fine
2   **drayload** – a load hauled by means of a low, heavy sideless cart

"After Tom got his position with the Cleveland lumber concern—some eight'r ten years ago, now—he traveled all over the country fer 'em, buyin' up tracks o' timber an' settin' mills to work, an' all that sort o' thing. Them fellers up there in Cleveland got to thinkin' he was a purty slick young chap—fer he was makin' scads o' money fer 'em; an' *Tom* got to thinkin' right smart of *hisself,* I thank you. Still he could alluz find a hat big enough fer his head; an' his eyesight wasn't ever so bad but what he could see an ol' friend.

"Some—let me see—yes, some four'r five years ago, Tom was 'way down in Tennessee, in a little town in the woods; an' he got a letter from the president o' the company he worked fer, tellin' him to drop everything an' come on the first train to Columbus, Ohio. The letter went on to say—Tom showed it to me when he told me the story—that the president would meet him at the Neill House in Columbus on important business on such an' such a date.

Well, of course there wasn't nothin' for Tom to do but cut loose and go; an' he went. But he went a-puzzlin' his brain an' a-scratchin' his head, I tell you; fer, in all the years he worked for the company, he'd never met the president—an' he couldn't 'magine what was up. Then, there was another thing that made him feel a little shaky—but that'll come out as I go along.

"When he got to Columbus, ther' was a big state convention goin' on. Brass bands an' pr'cessions was paradin' the streets; an' Tom couldn't hear hisself think, fer the whoopin' an' shoutin'. At last he got up to the Neill House, an' registered an' asked for a room.

"'Sorry,' says the clerk, 'but we're full up an' runnin' over—can't give you no room.'

"'The devil!' says Tom.

"Then a hand big as a ham o' meat was clapped on his shoulder an' somebody haw-shawed in his ear:

"'So you're here, are you? Well, you can roost with me!'

"Tom squirmed 'round, and faced a big man with a red face an' a white goatee.

"'Who are you?' he asked, drawin' hisself up stiffer'n a gun-bar'l.

"'William Howland, president o' the Erie Lumber Comp'ny,' the ol' chap answers, smilin' all over his face.

"Tom felt cheaper'n two-fer-a-cent, of course, an' didn't know what to do'r say; an' the ol' feller jest stood an' laughed at him. Then some politicians come along an' drawed the ol' man to one side, an' talked to him in whispers—him a-noddin' an' shakin' his head, but not sayin' much. Tom leaned 'ginst the counter an' stud-ied his boss—an' done some tall thinkin'. He saw that the ol' chap was trigged out in broadcloth, wore a number eight hat an' half-past-eleven shoes, an' had a di'mon' big as a hick'rynut in his shirt front. That di'mon' helped to make Tom feel all wabbly—that an' the way the ol' feller treated them politicians—kind o' lookin' over the'r heads, like he had a spell o' the stiff-neck an' couldn't git his chin down.

"Well, to sort o' double-an'-twist my yarn, so's 'twon't be so long, Tom an' his boss roomed together that night. They had cigars an' wine an' so on; an' talked over business till purty near midnight.

"The ol' feller finally pulled out his big gold watch an' looks at it an' says:

"'I guess that's all then, Evans; we understand one another—an' might as well go to bed. You're to finish up y'r work in Tennessee an' then go over to Arkansas. 'F you do these two jobs as well's you've done all y'r others, you may ask y'r own reward—an' the comp'ny'll grant it.'

"The ol' feller was feelin' his liquor a little likely an' that made him resky. An' Tom was a-feelin' purty much at home with his boss by this time—an' a-feelin' his oats some, too; so he speaks up chip-per's you please, an' says:

"'I guess I'll name my reward right now.'

"'All right,' laughs his boss, gapin' and rubbin' his hands.

"'I'll take y'r daughter,' says Tom.

"'My daughter?' gasps the ol' man, droppin' his jaw and gittin' pale 'round the gills.

"'Yes,' answers Tom.

"'W'y, w'y, what do you mean?' says ol' Howland; 'you don't even know 'er.'

"'Oh, yes, I do,' Tom explains; 'I've knowed 'er fer purty nigh two years. Got acquainted with 'er up in Michigan, when she was spendin' 'er vacation; an' we've been correspondin' ever since.'

"'The devil you say!' the ol' man snorted, jumpin' to his feet.

"Tom jest nodded; he saw the storm was comin' an' he braced hisself to face it.

"'An' you want to marry 'er, eh?' ol' Howland says, kind o' sneerin' like.

"'I do,' answers Tom.

"'You impudent pup!' bellers his boss, jumpin' up an' down an' crackin' his fists, 'I've a notion to slap y'r face, I have!'

"'Tom's mad got up at that—an' he got up with it; an' was surprised to find he was every bit as big as his boss—fer Tom is a big, two-fisted cuss.

"'You'd better change y'r notion 'bout slappin' my face, Mr. Howland,' he says, cool's a cucumber outside an' meltin' hot inside. 'Don't you try that, 'r I'll pitch you through the winder.'

"The ol' man suddenly set down—an' didn't say nothin' fer a good little bit. Then, at last, he remarks sort o' soft an' quiet:

"'You've been a good man fer us, Evans, an' we owe you a good 'eal; but you're expectin' too much, an' let me say right now, an' once fer all, you can't have my daughter. An' if you ever hint at the matter ag'in, 'r pen her another line, I'll give y'r walkin' papers.'"

"'You won't git the chance to discharge me,' says Tom; 'I've resigned.'

"'When?' asks the ol' man, liftin' his eyebrows.

"'Right now,' answers Tom.

"'If that suits you, it suits me,' was all the boss had to say.

"'An' both of 'em begun to git ready fer bed, puffin' an' blowin' an' throwin' the'r clo'es ev'ry which way. In a few minutes they was both asleep—an snorin', likely."

Jim's cigar had gone out. As he relighted the blackened stub, he remaked whimsically: "Maybe I'd better do like you story-writin' fellers, an' say—'to be continued.'"

"No," I mumbled drowsily, "go on."

He proceeded:

"Well, a squad o' them politicians come an' called Tom's boss out, 'bout three o'clock in the mornin'; an' he got up, gapin' an' stretchin', an' dressed an' went down stairs with 'em. The bang o' the door waked Tom up; an' he looked at his watch, an' come to a sudden c'nclusion that he'd run down home here—an' that he jest barely had time to jump into his clo'es an' ketch the train. Five minutes later, he was out on the street an' a-goin' like a dog with a can to his tail.

"Jest 'bout the time he' got half way to the depot, I reckon, ol' Howland was dancin' up an' down in front o' the clerk's counter, at the Neill house, an' bellerin'—like a bull in a brier patch.

"'I tell you I've been robbed—robbed o' the di'mon' I had in my shirt—robbed by the young feller that roomed with me! 'Phone fer the p'lice! The rascal's traps is gone from the room; he's made fer the station! 'Phone fer the p'lice to head him off there!'

"The upshot o' the whole matter was, that jest as Tom was boardin' his train, a couple o' p'licemen roped him in, and they toted him back to the hotel, an' brought him face to face with his boss.

"Tom hadn't the least idée what was up—fer the p'licemen wouldn't tell him nothin'; and he was mightily surprised when ol' Howland yells:

"'There it is—the impurdent cuss! Got it stuck in his shirt—bold as the devil hisself!'

"Tom looked where the ol' man was p'intin'—and fer the first time saw the di'mon' shinin' on his own bosom; an' he turned paler'n putty. He thought it was a put-up job to ruin him. Then he looked up at the ol' man—an turned red in the face, an' stood bitin' his lips.

"'What 'ave you got to say, young man?' says one of the p'licemen.

"'Nothin',' answers Tom.

"'You stole my di'mon'!' snorts ol' Howland.

"'Yes, I did,' Tom answers, bustin' into a laugh; 'but not till *you'd* stole *my shirt*!'

"Well, sir, the ol' man's eyes bulged out till they looked like peeled onions. An' then, all at once, he commenced to laugh; an' purty soon the p'licemen an' ev'rybody was laughin'.

"Finally the ol' gent sobered down, an' sidlin' up to Tom, whispers:

"'Evans, come upstairs; I want to see you.'

"When they was alone in the'r room, he says kind o' sad and solemn:

"'Tom, do you re'ly want to marry Alice?'

"'Certainly,' Tom answers.

"'Well, Tom, I've changed my mind; you can have her—but on one condition.'

"'Name it,' says Tom.

"'An' that is,' the ol' man went on, 'that you don't never say a word 'bout this affair to her n'r her mother. I'd never hear the last of it; an'—'"

I awoke with a start. Jim was gone from his place by the fire; but I heard his shuffling steps descending the stairs.

◆◆◆

The Mishaps of Ol' Andy Perdue

Evidently I had dropped asleep—lulled by the genial warmth of my office fire, and the low, moaning voice of the winter wind outside. For, when I suddenly shook myself, yawned, and sat erect in my chair, I became aware of the presence of Jim Whiss—seated in his accustomed place, and calmly and contentedly pulling at one of my cigars; and I had not heard him enter. He was leaning forward, his elbows upon his knees, his eyes fixed upon the gas blaze, as though he were striving to stare it out of countenance.

Hearing me stir he swept me a piercing glance from under his jutting brows, and remarked:

"Been snoozin', ain't you?"

I nodded—and again yawned.

"Didn't hear me come in, did you?"

I shook my head—once more yawning.

"Say, look here!" he growled testily.

"Seems to me I'm goin' to find you mighty poor company, to-night. You're gapin' like a mudcat out o' water; must be sleepier'n ol' Andy Perdue was the time he rolled off'n his kitchen roof."

"How was that, Jim?" I asked—clapping my hand over my mouth to stifle another yawn.

"Never told you, didn't I?"

"No."

"Never told you nothin' 'bout ol' Andy?"—with his shy glance—half incredulous.

"Never—not that I recall."

"Well, I *will*—if you'll promise not to go to sleep on my hands, like you're in the habit o' doin'."

"I promise."

"All right, then—an' here goes."

He proceeded with his rambling reminiscences of old Andy Perdue, punctuating his tiresome drivel with measured puffs at his shortening cigar—and an occasional sigh of regret, as he noted the rapidly accumulating ash on the lighted end. I listened with what interest I could summon, studying his profile upon the wall—as usual—and offering a nod or grunt, at intervals, to keep him going. For I have learned that Jim Whiss is like a perverse and erratic clock that insists on striking out of all order and precedent; there is no stopping him until he has run down.

"Ol' Andy Perdue," he began, "was a Quaker by birth, an' lived out at Foxtown, some thirty 'r forty years ago. Was a kin' o' carpenter an' cabinet maker—an' the slowest, sleepiest, laziest, dilatoriest[1] mortal that ever drawed the breath of life. W'y, he was so darned lazy he didn't want to die—'feared he might have to kick an' struggle a little, right at the end. His wife an' boy went off on a visit one time, an' was gone a week. Andy was too lazy to cook his own meals; an' jest turned in an' slept the whole seven days an' nights. The time he fell off'm his own kitchen he was patchin' the shingle roof; an' he went to sleep in the bilin' sun, an' rolled off. Jest waked up long enough, as he flopped over the eave trough, to holler, —'I say dead!; an' then hit the ground kerslap—and went to sleep ag'in.

"And slow—he was slower'n the seven year itch! Feller took a baby cradle to him, one time, to have a new rocker put on it. Well, sir, that p'rtic'lar piece o' furniture was kicked 'round the shop for over twenty years. Then one day Andy gits in a splutter an drawls:

"'By the way, I've neglected to fix Solomon Rafter's baby crib, thee knows; an' I must do it right away.'

"The blamed lazy ol' scamp pitched in an' put on a new rocker, shouldered the cradle, an' toted it home. An' what do you s'pose?"

"I can't form a supposition, Jim," I smiled.

"Well, sir," he resumed with an air of convincing earnestness, "maybe you won't believe it, but ol' Sol met him at the door, a-bowin' an' a-smilin', an' says:

"'I'm mighty glad you've got that cradle done an' brung it home, Andy; we're needin' it—an' I was jest startin' to come over after it. The gal we wanted to rock in it has got a baby of 'er own,

---

1 **dilatoriest** – tending to delay or postpone

now, an' we was wantin' this cradle pow'rful bad. Thank you ever so much for bein' so prompt an' accommodatin'.'

"W'y, the ol' poke was so slow people used to leave standin' orders fer coffins, years ahead. I worked fer ol' Andy one winter; an' I know all about it. Feller from Stoneburry come into the shop one day, an' says:

"'Where's Andy?'

"'Out,'" says I.

"'Be back soon?' says he.

"'Can't say. Nobody knows but him; an' the chances is that *he* don't. Want to see him on business?'"

"'Yes,' he answers. 'Wanted to trade him some cherry lumber fer furniture.'

"'S'pect we can trade,'" says I.

"'How much lumber you got?'

"'Don't know how much, yit.'

"'Seasoned?'" I asks.

"'W-e-e-l, no,' he answers, kin o' slow like. 'Fact is I jest set out the cherry sprouts this spring; but I 'lowed they'd be growed into trees big enough fer lumber by the time Andy had the furniture ready.'"

Whiss threw away the stump of the cigar, chuckling asthmatically. Then he ran his chubby fingers through his shock of hair and remarked reflectively;

"Seems most men have a certain gait an' speed—a' ain't capable of no other. Ol' Andy never got in a hurry but twice in his life; an' both times it got him into trouble. The first time was when he was askin' a silent blessin' at the breakfast table one morning. Jest as he was in the middle of his squirmin' agony he happened to hear the ol' cow smashin' down the gate that led from the barnyard into the garden patch, an' he jumps up, tippin' over his chair, an' purty near upsettin' the table, an' he hollers loud enough to keel the bark off'm a tree:

"'There's that durned ol' heifer gittin' into the sweet corn ag'in, thee knows! Call the dog, David! Dad rot her pesky ol' hide—I'll stove her ribs in.'

"An' out the door he went—like a skeered rabbit out of its squat. The whole neighborhood heerd his violent language, an' was scandalized, of course; an' ol' Andy come mighty nigh gittin' churched[2] fer his hasty words an' temper.

"The other time him an' his son David was ridin' 'long the road one Sunday mornin' on the'r way to Quaker meetin'. Jest beyond Jim Furniss's place on the ol' Roosterville road, they come upon a squir'l gatherin' nuts under a hick'ry tree. The squir'l saw them 'bout the time they saw it; an' it give a flirt to its tail, jumped onto the rail fence an' lit out fer tall timber like a streak o' moonshine. Ol' Andy got excited to once, an' hollered:

"'After him, David! We will run the little rascal down, thee knows!'

"Then both of 'em dug the'r heels into th'r pokey ol' plow-nags, an' went gallopin' down the road—leavin' a cloud of dust behind 'em, so thick you couldn't cut it with a knife.

"Well, sir, the squir'l kept the fence, fer 'bout a quarter of a mile; then it jumped off onto a tobaker house close to the road, an' skinned 'round the corner of it.

"'Jump off an' tie thee horse, David—an' git thee a club!' ol' Andy shouted. 'We've got the little varmint cornered, thee knows!'

"An' off they both tumbled. Andy went 'round the tobacker house, one way, an' David went 'round t'other. Andy come upon the squir'l jest 'round the first corner, an' cracked a lick at it with a tobacker stick, that would 'ave jolted a meetin' house. Away went the squir'l 'round the next corner, whiskin' its tail an' a-chatterin' like all-possessed; an' after it went ol' Andy—jest a-whoopin' an' yellin':

"'Here he comes, David—head him off! Crack it to him as he turns the next corner, thee understands!'

"Well, David done jest as ol' Andy advised. He struck a ton at that squir'l; but missed it slick an' clean—an' fetched his daddy a blow that purty near laid the ol' sinner out. Andy dropped his club, clapped both hands to his head an' hopped 'round on one leg, bawlin' like a yearlin' bull:

2　**churched** – re-educated in church practices

"'Gee-bush-theeself, David! Thee's killed thee father—thee's killed thee only father!'

"Other people was goin' to Quaker meetin', an' a big crowd of 'em had c'lected in the road in front of the tobacker house, an' was watchin' the whole p'rformance. They was so shocked an' mortified by the pr'cedin' that they rode away in silence, leavin' the ol' scamp a-howlin' bloody murder. An' the upshot of the matter was that ol' Andy an' his boy both got turned out o' meetin'.

"What did he do then?" I asked, feeling intuitively that there was more to come.

Jim stiffly got upon his feet, and, while buttoning his shaggy coat and winding endless folds of a red comforter around his neck, concluded:

"J'ined the Methodists down to Mount Hebron; but didn't stay with 'em long, 'n finally died a common backslider. Might 'ave stayed with the Methodists if it hadn't been fer his pesky laziness an' consumin' dilatoriness. He was so dodrotted lazy he wouldn't go to the exertion an' trouble of wearin' specs—too much work, you know, to be c'ntinually puttin' 'em on and takin' 'em off; and one time at Sunday school that verse come to him to read, where the angel troubled the water—mixed it up someway so it'd cure sick folks. If you know anything 'bout the bible, which y'r actions n' conduct don't show that you do, you'll remember that the verse reads somethin' like this—don't know that I can quote it exactly myself:

"'At certain seasons o' the year an angel went down to the pool an' troubled the water."

"Well, as I said, that verse come to ol' Andy, an' squintin' his eyes an' puckerin' his ol' saddle-flap face, he drawls out:

"'At certain seasons of the year an angel went down to the pool—'

"Right there he stuck for a minute. Then he took a deep breath an' a final squint an' finished with a jerk:

"'An'—an' *tumbled into the water!*'

"You ort to 'ave been there—to hear them people yell an' laugh. An' ol' Andy got mad, an' was never back in that church agin, an—"

Jim broke off suddenly and shuffled toward the door, grumbling thoroughly to himself, as he went. He had heard a caller's steps ascending the stairs.

The Youthful Indescretions of Jim Whiss

Jim Whiss is a devout disciple of Isaak Walton, a worshiper, a devotee at the shrine of the gentle art of angling. Unlike the worldly and sinful who fish for the mere pleasure of the pastime, Jim fishes through a sense of religious duty. He is an idolater at the altar of the sport. With muttered incantations—and objurgatons[1], he digs the bait; with persistent and praiseworthy fixity of purpose, he makes daily pilgrimages to the dam just below town—a Mecca of cool and murmurous solitude; with ecstatic exclamations and frequent quotations, he fishes and fishes, and dreams daydreams, and lets nature's benison[2] sink deep into his being. To him, the ripple of the clear water is an angel chorus; and the fishy flavor of the pebbled shore is heavenly incense.

When it's early spring in the Valley of the Muskingum, then Whiss is one of the sure harbingers of the season of sunshine and flowers. His bait can is an hourglass—telling off the hours drowsily sweet with strange woodsy odors; and his fishing rod points to summer as unerringly as the north pole points to his guiding star. When I observe him making his first pilgrimage of the year, I know that dandelions are peeping from the roadside sod and that violets are springing from the leafy mound upon the wooded hillside.

One day last spring I encountered him at his trysting place with nature, just below the dam. Seating myself upon the mossy rocks, at his side, I asked:

"Getting any bites, Jim?"

"Not many," he growled; "an' I won't git any now."

"Why?"

"Why!"—testily. "'Cause fish won't bite when they hear a fool a-gabbin'."

---

1 **objurgatons** - harsh rebukes
2 **benison** - a blessing; a benediction

I laughed softly; and Jim frowned, his eye immovably fixed upon his bobbing cork. Then I inquired with genuine interest, "Won't fish bite when they hear voices, Jim?"

"Won't bite when they hear some voices," he grumbled, reeling in his line, "voices that skeers 'em."

"Do you think that my voice would be more apt to frighten fish, then yours, Jim?"

"Know it would," he said with a surly grunt, "more likely to frighten these fish, anyhow."

"Explain." I said.

"Explain!"—snappishly. "Ther' ain't nothin' to explain. These fish is 'quainted with my voice, that's all."

And he laid his rod at his side, and gazed moodily into the depth of the water at his feet.

"Going to quit?" I ventured.

"Of course," he snorted. "Ain't fish within a mile, by this time."

"I'm sorry I spoiled your sport," I said contritely.

"Yes, awfully sorry, I s'pect," he answered sarcastically.

It was an idle hour with me; and I went about the task of placating him and drawing a yarn from him, if possible.

"Don't you think you credit your finny friends with too much intelligence, Jim?" I asked tentatively.

"No, I don't," he replied positively, according me a swift, glowering glance. "Fish, like other animals, knows a heap more than such fellers as you believes. They're smart enough to know jest what they want to eat, an' at what season o' the year they want to eat it; an' that's a heap more'n some fishermen knows.

He interlocked his fingers over his knees and leaned back against the mossy rock behind him, smiling benignly, his erstwhile irritation lost in the interest he had in his subject.

I judiciously kept quiet, and he went on, "Men feel so big cause they can gabble and tell all they know—an' a good 'eal more sometimes—they won't give up that animals knows anything. But animals have feelings; and they think just as you and me does, only they can't tell their thoughts. Still if you've got eyes and ears and a few grains of gumption, you can make out to understand 'em. W'y, a dog smiles with his tail an' frowns with his bristles, an' the horse 'll play lame when he don't want to work. If that ain't reason, I'd like fer some o' you smart chaps to tell me what it is. I s'pose a sheep has 'bout as little sense as anything on four legs—'cept a work bench; but I've seen an ol' ram git all the ewes an' lambs behind him in a fence corner, an' down his head an' fight off a sheep-killing dog. No man could reason out a thing better 'n that. I guess them scientists is right, though, when they say an elephant is the smartest of all animals. W'y,"—brightening perceptibly and warming to the task he had set himself,—"when I was a lad of 12 years, over in Pennsylvania, a circus show come to town. I was one o' the boys that earned a ticket by carryin' water to the elephant—ol' Hannibal. Ever see that beast?"

I gave a negative shake of the head.

"Well, he was a beauty. That ain't hardly the word I want to use, either. But he was so danged big an' lumpy an' wrinkled an' homely, he was purty. And I said, I got a ticket to the circus by carryin' water to ol' Hannibal. But a country feller come 'long and offered me a quarter fer the ticket; an' I made up my mind I'd sell it an' run the risk o' seein' the show in some other way. I wasn't makin' no blind bargain—not a bit of it; fer I'd had my peepers skinned an' had noticed a walnut tree standin' right outside the big tent, jest back o' where the band set. The side wall o' the tent was lowered a bit at that place, to let in the air to the band, an' I calkylated I could climb that tree, straddle a limb, an'—peakin' over the heads o' them music-makers—see all that was worth seein'.

"Well, I waited till nearly ever'body had gone into the show, then I slipped round an' skinned up that tree an' hid among the thick leaves. Nobody seen me, an' I was all hunky; an' I could see all that was goin' on inside—an' laughed to think I had a whole quarter to squander on popcorn-balls an' lemonade.

"I got so interested in watchin' the show that I didn't notice nothin' else. But, after the people had all got through lookin' at the animals an' had gone into the circus part o' the tent, the keeper of ol' Hannibal brung him out an' fastened him to that walnut tree; an' the first thing I knowed the ol' feller was rattlin' his chain an' makin' the tree shake.

I looked down—an' great an' adorable! Ol' Hannibal was standin' right under me, his big head purty near touchin' my feet. I'll bet my liver turned pale."—A rattling chuckle arose in Jim's throat, at thought of his predicament.—"I fetched a squirm an' commenced to coon higher up that tree—like a tomcat gittin' away from a brindle dog. Ol' Hannibal heerd me, an' lifted his head an' give me a squint with his little black wicked eyes, I'd got as high as I could; but I knowed he could reach me, if he tried—an', somehow, I don't know why, I felt that he was goin' to try. And he did. I'm confident the ol' feller recognized me as one o' the boys that had carried water to him—the way he used me showed that; but he knowed I hadn't no business to be up that tree an' a-peekin' in at the show. So he jest stuck his trunk up among the limbs, an' shut his eyes an' begun to feel for me. I thought I was a goner. Then he touched me, and pretty soon he wrapped his squirmin' pr'boscis round my body—an' I knowed I was a goner. I was so darned bad skeered I couldn't say a word, couldn't make a noise, even—couldn't swaller the spit in my mouth. I jest shut my eyes an' slobbered an' shivered.

"But the ol' elephant didn't mean to hurt me; I soon found that out. He lifted me down slow an' careful-like, an' set me on the ground as easy as if I was a soap bubble he was afraid o' bustin'. Then he let loose o' me, an' give a 'bwoof,' as much as to say, 'Now, youngster, you skeedaddle, an' don't let me ketch you up to no such tricks ag'in.'

"An' you bet I didn't fail to take his advice. I didn't see no more of that show—not muchy. I run home faster 'n a skeered rabbit; didn't wait to spend my quarter, even. An' that was somethin' remarkable fer me; fer if I've one talent I've never hid under a bushel, it's the talent o' alluz spending more 'n I could earn."

Whiss stopped and filled and lighted his pipe. The soft, musical gurgle of the clear, cool water at our feet was as sweet and soothing as the laughter of children in the dusk of evening. Jim had dropped into reminiscent reverie. I heartlessly roused him, by saying:

"And you think old Hannibal recognized you, Jim, and felt that you were surreptitiously enjoying what you hadn't paid for?"

"Uh-huh."—And he nodded vigorously.—"As I said, animals knows a heap. An' they have feelin's, same as people, an' they're mighty all-fired touchy sometimes, too. I remember another time when I was a boy, a couple o' men with a bear come to town, an' put up at the tavern. They give a kind of a show on the street—had the bear turnin' sumnersets, an' walkin' on his hind legs, an' all that sort o' thing. An' then, when they went to supper, they took the animal an' chained him up in a stall o' the stable back o' the tavern. I'd tagged 'em all over town, an' road on the bear's back, an' pulled his wool—an' showed off 'fore the other boys, in ev'ry way I could think of, till I'd got to feelin' bigger 'n all out doors an' was jest itchin' to do somethin' re'l smart an' devilish. So, when the men had gone into the tavern, I coaxed the boys to go round to the stable with me, promisin' to show 'em some fun. An' I did; but not jest 'xactly as I calkylated on.

"The door o' the stable was shut an' locked an' the bear—all tuckered out with the tomfoolery he'd been goin' through with—was layin' down and in his stall, an' a-dozin' an' a-gruntin' as c'ntented as a swillfed shoat[3]. I slipped round to the hole in the wall an' tried to crawl in, but I was too big—'r the hole was too little, which 'mounted to the same thing—an' I couldn't make it, could jest git my head an' one shoulder in. So I gits a long stick an' begins to punch the bear. He don't pay no 'tention—jest grunts a little louder like a drunk feller snorin' in his sleep.

"'You'd better let that bear alone, Jim,' says one o' the bigger boys; 'he'll get his mad up purty soon, an' snatch you through that hole an' chaw you into mincemeat.'

"'Pshaw!' I answers, swellin' out my chist an' lookin' wiser'n Solerman. 'That bear hain't got no grit. A bear that'll be led round by a chain won't fight. They keep a muzzle on him when he's on the street, jest fer show. He's a big coward, you can bet, an' if he was loose an' you'd go 'boo' at him, he'd never stop runnin'. I wouldn't be 'fraid to—'

"Well, I never got no further with my long-winded blowin'. My punchin' the brute with a stick didn't hurt him an' didn't stir him up

3   **shoat** - young pig, esp. one that is newly weaned

a mite; but when I begun to speak disrespectful of him—slander his reputation, as it was—he gits mad all over. An' he wasn't long 'bout it, either. I was standin' with one arm an' shoulder through the hole, an' a-braggin' an' a-blowin' like all git out, when scat! That bear bounces off the floor, like a rubber ball, an' reaches a paw fer me. An' he got me, too; that is, he got my ol' rotten wammus[4]. An' it was a dern good thing fer me that it was rotten. He skinned it off'm me slicker'n a robin can seed a cherry—an' a blamed sight quicker. You ort to 'ave seen the dust fly. Oh, cracky!"

Whiss lay back and chuckled and wheezed and gurgled. Then he stiffly arose, picked up his fishing rod and set off along the shore.

"Is that all, Jim?" I called after him.

"All but this," he muttered without turning his head, "I hain't been on re'l intimate terms with bears sence."

◆◆◆

---

4 **wammus** - a warm knitted jacket resembling a cardigan

A Counterfeit Coin

Chapter I

"Show him in"

The speaker leaned back in his leather-covered chair and interlocked his strong, white fingers behind his head, all the while puffing vigorously at a short, fat cigar and gazing fixedly toward the outer door. He was a man at whom one would turn to take a second look—tall, broad-shouldered, deep-chested and sinewy. It was not his form, however, but his face, that exercised so subtle an attraction that the casual observer would hasten to make a closer study of it. It was not a face beaming with kindness or in separate and weekly virtue, nor one in which were reflected the nobler of human passions and emotions; but one dark with the shadows of stern determination and inflexible purpose—but flickeringly radiant with the sidelights of justice and mercy. The close-cropped iron-gray hair and beard were indicative of bulldog tenacity and fixity of will; and the small, bright and ever-shifting gray eyes denoted fox-like cunning and native shrewdness. The man's age was about sixty; but his firm and elastic tread and other indications of robust health and youthful vigor gave the lie to the figures.

Such was John Travis, chief of the Secret Service of the United States.

It was midsummer in Washington City, and the hour was two-thirty in the afternoon. A flood of blinding sunshine poured upon broad streets and avenues, and suffocating heat waves radiated from tall buildings of brick and stone and shimmered and danced above the broad expanses of asphalt pavement. Not a breath of air stirred, not a leaf fluttered, not a bird chirped; on the contrary, the leaves hung in a half-wilted condition upon the dust-covered branches, the birds hopped listlessly from limb to limb, with wings drooped and eyes half closed, or drowsed waiting for the breath of cool air that did not come.

The windows of the room in which John Travis sat were raised to the highest point possible, and the shutters were flung wide open. This fact, however, did not discommode[1] the occupant of the room by interfering in any way with his privacy; for Travis's office was on the shady side of the street, in the rear of the building, and on the second floor.

The chief, suffering from the oppressive heat, had flung dignity to the dogs. He had discarded his coat, removed his tie and unbuttoned his collar, and now sat idly smoking as he awaited the coming of the person who had been announced by the factotum[2].

The private office of the head of the Secret Service was furnished to suit his needs and tastes. It was richly carpeted; a large baize-covered table occupied the center of the room, a number of chairs stood against the walls, and a leather-tufted couch had a place in one corner. The most notable piece of furniture was one—half bookcase, half cabinet—that stood between the windows and, judging from its contents, was a veritable curiosity-shop in itself. It contained a diminutive and delicate pair of scales, a number of books— many of them musty with age—glass-stoppered bottles holding colorless liquid, a microscope, boxes of counterfeit coins, and odds and ends innumerable.

Travis threw his cigar out of the window and arose to his feet, as the door opened and a man entered the apartment.

"Sit down, Raymond, and cool off," said the chief, motioning to a chair; "you look as hot as a furnace. Here's a fan. Say! Do you know I'm awfully glad to see you?"

"Want to use me, I suppose," replied the newcomer, as he seated himself and mopped the perspiration from his glowing countenance.

Travis laughed softly and said: "I think I've taught you in the past not to act upon suppositions, but to wait for certainties."

"I'm not acting on a supposition," the visitor returned, coolly; "I simply had remarked that I *had* a supposition."

---

1 **discommode** - to put to inconvenience; trouble
2 **factotum** - any employee or official having many different responsibilities

Travis went to the cabinet between the windows, and returned with a box of cigars.

"Here,"—smiling good-naturedly,—"take a cigar; it'll brace you up and put you in better humor. You seem a little bit out of sorts."

"I'm not feeling very well, Travis; I need a rest." However, he took the proffered cigar, lighted it and leaned back in his chair, puffing serenely. Travis looked upon the athletic figure before him and remarked satirically, "You look like a very sick man, Raymond—a mere shadow of your former self. Shall I call an ambulance to take you to the hospital?"

Claude Raymond removed the cigar from between his lips and laughed softly. His smooth-shaven, swarthy face puckered into a mass of merry dimples and wrinkles, and his steel-blue eyes danced humorously.

"Travis," he said, "you wouldn't think me sick, if you saw me upon my deathbed."

"I would, if you looked sick,"—chuckling.

"Don't I look sick?"

"Not a bit."

"I want a vacation, at any rate; I haven't had one in four years."

"I thought the wind was blowing from that quarter. Well, you can't have it. I've got a beautiful job for you; that's why I was so glad to see you."

"Of course!"

"I want you to go over to New York and run down a gang. They're flooding the city with bogus ten-dollar bills, and the case demands immediate attention. You ought to feel flattered over the trust and confidence I place in you; lots of the boys would give their two eyes for the case I now offer you."

"Let one of 'em have it, then—with my complimemts."

"What?"

"I don't want it."

"Why?"

"Because I'm going off on a vacation."

"Suppose I won't grant you the permission?"

"You've taught me not to act on supposition, Chief, but to await the proofs."

"The proofs are forthcoming. You can't go."

"Look here, Travis,"—earnestly—"you've promised me a vacation."

"I know I have."

"Well, don't you think I've earned it? And don't you mean to keep your promise?"

"Yes—to both your questions; but I hate to let you off now. Where do you think of going?"

Raymond leaned back in his chair, heaved a sigh of relief and satisfaction, and answered, "There's a little nook of paradise—a little bit of Eden—lodged down among the hills of southeastern Ohio. I was born in that part of the country, but I haven't seen the old place in years and years. Well, I'm going out there to rest and dream for a few weeks."

"What's the young lady's name?" inquired Travis, his eyes twinkling merrily.

Claude Raymond, detective, stared at his honored chief in blank amazement. "What on earth are you talking about?" he asked at last.

"I want to know the young woman's name," was the reply, calm and provoking.

"What young woman?"—irritably.

"The one you are going out there to see—the angel of your pastoral paradise."

"Look here, Travis!"—Raymond was slightly nettled, which fact amused his chief not a little. "You seem to think I'm a liar or a fool—or both. The idea of me—a confirmed bachelor and thirty-eight years old—being in love! No, sir! I'm wedded to my profession—and a very exacting mistress I've found her; so much so that I don't care to risk another. Slightly altering the scriptural text—a man can't serve two mistresses. But I must be off; I want to get out of the city as soon as possible."

With the concluding words he arose to his feet; but Travis pointed to the empty chair, saying, "Sit down; I'm not through with you yet. This place you're going to—how far is it from Pittsburgh?"

"A hundred miles or so."

"Do you go through that city on your way?"

"Yes."

"Well, I've got a case out there for you, then."

"I don't want it."

"I know; but you'll have to take it."

"Say, Travis! This is a little too much—this asking a fellow to take a case on his vacation trip. It's like asking a man to court the acquaintance of a nightmare, or to take a nauseous drug for sick stomach."

"You rebel, eh?"

"I rebel."

"Let me explain. This job won't take much of your precious time, as you're going right through the city, anyhow. You can give a few hours to it and report. It's yet in its incipiency. Let me show you." The chief arose, went to the cabinet and returned with two letters, a number of silver coins and a magnifying glass.

"Now," he went on, "these letters are of little importance. They're from two Pittsburgh banks and state that within the last few days the writers have detected a number of counterfeit silver dollars in circulation. Here are the coins that came with the letters. Examine them and tell me what you think of them."

Raymond's professional curiosity was aroused at once; his professional instinct was excited and he became interested in spite of himself. For the moment he forgot all about his summer vacation, as he knitted his brows and toyed with the coins before him. He weighed them in his hands, carefully inspected them with the glass, rang them upon the table and counted the mills around their edges. At last he placed them in a neat pile and looked up at the chief without speaking.

"Well?" Travis said interrogatively.

"What do I think of them?"

"Of course."

"Three of them are counterfeit, one is genuine."

"Yes, I added a genuine coin of the lot. Which is it?"

"This one," Raymond said, positively, as he touched the top coin of the pile.

"You're right, of course. But how did you determine?"

"In the old rough and ready way. First, the false coins are a few grains lighter than the true one; second, the final letter in the phrase—'In God We Trust'—is an 'f,' not a 't;' third, the notches around the middle rim are five or six short of the usual number. Then, there are only 18 distinct feathers in the eagle's right wing; besides—"

"That'll do!" Travis cried, smiling. "But what have you got to say as to the age of the false coins?"

"The're freshly minted."

"Each bears the date '1889,' and has a pocket-worn appearance."

"Yes; but they're fresh-minted pieces."

"Sure?"

"Of course, I am. They've been aged artificially."

"How?"

"By scouring, a dilute acid bath, and the use of a little grease and plumbago[3]."

"I guess you're onto your job," the chief remarked, leaning back and lighting a fresh cigar.

"I ought to be by this time, if ever—after ten years in the service."

"One thing more. How much short in weight do you think they are?"

"A few grains—eight or ten, perhaps."

"You're close. And I've tested them; and the're nearly up to standard silver."

"That so?" remarked Raymond. "That shows one thing, then."

"What?"

"That it's a gang of old hands at the work."

"Making them nearly standard to render them difficult to detect?"

"Certainly."

The chief nodded, and said: "I saw you glancing at the acids in the cabinet, just now. But I've weighed and melted and tested one of these spurious pieces, in every way. However, you may repeat the process, if you care to do so."

---

3   **plumbago** - graphite , an allotropic form of carbon, known also as black lead

"I'm fully satisfied."

"Well, are you interested? That's more to the point."

"A little," Raymond confessed with a laugh.

"A little!" Travis snorted in a tone of disgust. "In a case like this! Raymond, I'm ashamed of you. But here's what I want you to do: I want you to stop a few days in Pittsburgh, on your way out to Ohio, and run these rascals to earth. They're right there in the city."

"I don't think so."

"You have a different opinion?"

"Yes."

"Out with it."

"I have a theory in regard to these coins. If it's true, then the makers of them are not in Pittsburgh—nor any other large city, for that matter. Let's reason on the thing. The coins are almost up to standard silver and they're the very best counterfeits I've ever seen. They are dated '1889,' and have been aged artificially. All this renders them very difficult to detect. You speak of the case being in its incipiency. So far as we're concerned, that's true; so far as the counterfeiters are concerned, I hold that it's false. Stuff so hard to detect has probably been in circulation for months. The skill with which they have been made and aged shows, as I said, that old hands are at the business of shoving them. As unpleasant as you made it for counterfeiters in the large places in the last few years, no gang of old jail-birds would think of doing the work in one of the big cities, though they might shove the stuff there. Then, another thing, these coins being nearly pure silver, indicates that they may come from the mining regions of the west. The low price of bullion is a great temptation to some of the mine owners to coin it into dollars, without consulting Uncle Sam. This is a mere guess, however, but as good as any other guess."

Travis was disgusted, and his voice and manner showed it as he said, "How many times have I told you, Raymond, that your proneness to theorize, to act on suppositions and to jump to conclusions, will one day get you into trouble?"

"You think that the makers of this stuff are in Pittsburgh?"

"Of course I do."

"And I think they have their plant located in some rural district—in a cave or in old barn, for instance. Well, time alone will tell who's right. I may be wrong; I lay no claim to infallibility. I'll give the matter some attention when I get to Pittsburgh; but I don't mean to sacrifice my vacation upon the government's altar of mammon. If the case proves complex and shows a tendency to consume time and nerve tissues, I'll wire you to send on another man."

"Raymond," the chief said earnestly, "I want you to have your vacation alright enough; but you are the very man to look after this case."

Raymond smiled indulgently as he answered, "And the case in New York, too?"

"Yes, and the case in New York!" was the emphatic reply. "You are the best man in the service; but—confound you!—you know it and are too deuced independent and hard to manage."

The two shook hands, both smiling; and Raymond turned to go, but stopped suddenly, saying: "Give me one of those coins; I may need it. Good-bye, Chief, till I see you again."

"Good-bye—and say! Give my respects to the little Buckeye woman."

The detective shook a finger at his superior and replied fiercely: "Travis, if you ever hint another word about my getting married, I'll quit the service. Now!"

When the sound of Raymond's receding footsteps had died out, Travis muttered to himself: "A jolly good fellow is Raymond, and the keenest and most trustworthy man in the service; but he's too conceited, too independent. He ought to have a wife; it would tame him down a bit."

Then he lighted a fresh cigar, leaned back in his chair and closed his eyes, smiling inscrutability.

Chapter II

Claude Raymond made hurried preparations for his trip. He was in a fever to be off. The city had never seemed so hot and disagreeable, the country so cool and inviting. He felt like a big boy just out of school, off to his aunt's on the farm. Memory sped ahead of him to the hills of the blue Muskingum, where he had played as a lad; and recollection was busy with the thousand and one things and places he had seen and known when a child.

Would he recognize the scenes and the people? Perhaps not; for years had passed since he had visited his birthplace. It did not matter; he wanted to go. He would exchange the man-made city for the God-made solitudes—

Swap the dust fer fresh-mowed hay,
Dandeli'ns an' fields o' green;
Change September back to May—
Jest like tradin' sight-on-scene!

He whistled softly to himself, as he packed his trunk and hand bag, and was surprised to note that he was whistling the tune of an old song his mother had sung to him in his youth. Then he heaved a deep sigh and moved about softly and silently; for his mother—the only woman he had ever loved, that had ever been more to him than a casual friend or acquaintance—lay sleeping beneath the sod of the far western prairies.

"Let's see," he muttered as he went on with his packing, "I must take my gun and fishing-tackle. I don't suppose there's any game out there worth the hunting, but I can give rein to my savage instincts by shooting chipmunks. I remember they used to be a pest to the farmers out there. As for the fishing, a fish is a fish—no matter how small and insignificant; and it's a jolly thing to pretend one's having sport, at any rate. It's been a long, long while since I felt as carefree as I do today. I very much fear the Pittsburgh counterfeiters will be unmolested, so far as I am concerned."

A few hours later he was rolling swiftly westward. Arriving in Pittsburgh, he went to one of the principal hotels and registered under an assumed name. The next morning, refreshed by a night's sleep, a cold bath, and a hearty breakfast, he set about the business in hand, having in mind the resolve to keep his promise to his chief, but to perform the duty in a merely perfunctory way.

He first called at one of the banks that had written to the Treasury Department.

Stopping at one of the side wickets[4], he said to the young man bending over a big ledger:

"Is the president or teller in?"

"The teller hasn't come in yet," the young man answered, without looking up; "he's a little late this morning. But the president's in his private office, I think."

"Can I get in to see him?"

"Card?" answered the pasty-faced youth.

Then glancing at the bit of pasteboard he had received:

"Secret Service! All right; I'll be back in a minute, sir."

He retreated to the president's private office and in a few moments returned and announced, "The president will see you at once, Mr. Raymond. Step this way, please."

When the detective had entered the bank president's room, he found himself in the presence of a corpulent[5], well-preserved man of fifty years. Raymond wasted no time, but entered upon his business as soon as he was seated.

"You're the president of this bank?" was his opening remark.

"Yes, sir," replied the president, in a dignified and somewhat pompous manner.

"You sent a letter to the Treasury Department," Raymond went on, "stating that your bank had discovered a number of counterfeit silver coins in circulation. That letter was referred to the Secret Service, and in answer to it I am here to confer with you. Do you wish to see my commission before we proceed to business?"

The banker had been studying the detective's face and, apparently impressed in his favor, now answered graciously, "It's not at all necessary, Mr. Raymond. The fact that you're aware of the letter sent

---

4 **wicket** - an opening in a door or wall, often fitted with glass or a grille and used for selling tickets or as a teller's cage in a bank

5 **corpulent** - bulkiness or largeness of body; excessively fat

to the Treasury Department satisfies me that you're in the service of the government. What can I do for you? What do you want to know?"

"Everything," was the smiling reply.

"Everything I can tell you in regard to the counterfeit coins?"

"Yes."

"Well, to be brief, I know little more than was contained in the letter—which you undoubtedly saw. My attention was called to one of the false pieces about a week ago by the teller. We examined the silver dollars we had on hand and discovered two or three more that were spurious. Since writing the department, we have found four or five others that are bogus."

"Are the false pieces all alike?"

"I think they are."

"Have you got them here?

"All but the one or two sent to Washington."

"May I see them?"

"Certainly."

The banker unlocked a drawer in the desk at his elbow and produced the coins. Raymond looked them over critically and remarked: "Yes, they're all right—that is, all wrong—all counterfeit and all alike. You have a very clever teller, Mr. Baldwin."

"How's that?"

"I say you have a very clever teller."

"Well, yes—perhaps; but I fail to catch your meaning."

"My meaning is this: not one bank teller in ten would have suspected even, that these coins are counterfeits."

"The teller called your attention to them, you said?"

"Yes."

"Did you detect *wherein* they are counterfeits?"

The banker gave a start, shook his head, and answered with a short laugh: "No, I didn't. Mr. Gimp, the teller, pointed it all out to me. I understand what you mean now. It's easy to tell a certain counterfeit, after some one has shown you wherein it *is* counterfeit; but very hard to tell if a coin's good or bad, that you have no reason to suspect. Isn't that it?"

"Exactly," the detective replied, smiling. "One naturally accepts money on faith and at its face value. A bank teller, even, does not usually inspect every piece that passes through his hands and does not detect a counterfeit as nearly perfect as the one we have been considering."

"Mr. Gimp has been with us for quite a number of years," the banker said, with a show of hauteur[6], "and we have always considered him a trustworthy and efficient officer. But I don't know that he has ever paid particular attention to the detection of counterfeits. However, he may have done so. At any rate, he *did* detect these."

"True," Raymond said, musingly; "and he's above suspicion, of course."

The banker nodded stiffly, smiling.

"Would you mind calling him?"

"Not at all."

A minute later the teller entered the apartment. He was a large, handsome man of middle age, wearing a neatly trimmed blonde beard and gold-rimmed glasses. He was fashionably dressed and had about him an air of genteel prosperity.

"Mr. Gimp," said the president, "this is Mr. Raymond, of the Secret Service, here in answer to our letter to the Treasury Department. He desires to talk with you in reference to those counterfeit silver dollars."

The two men honored the introduction with a hand-shake, and Gimp remarked pleasantly, "Very glad to meet you, Mr. Raymond; and I'm ready to help you in any way I can."

"Thank you," the detective replied, simply. "Have I the privilege of asking you a few questions?"

"Assuredly."

"How was your attention first called to these coins?"

"I hardly know. Of course you understand that a part of my duties is to keep a sharp outlook for all kinds of counterfeits. Well, I was running over a number of silver dollars and found one of these. Then I began to search for others."

---

6 **hauteur** - haughtiness in bearing and attitude; arrogance

"What called your attention to the first one?"

"I don't remember—yes, I think I noticed that it was of light weight."

Raymond asked quickly: "You notice that while running the coins over in your hands?"

"I—I think so, yes." Gimp appeared a little confused.

"What did you do then?" the detective questioned smoothly.

"I examined it with a pocket-glass, and assured myself that it was false."

"I see. And what did you find?"

Gimp's face suddenly flushed; and he replied with considerable spirit. "You know what I found. Why do you ask such questions?"

Raymond smiled blandly and reassuringly as he made answer: "Mr. Gimp, I'm simply trying to determine how hard these particular coins are to detect. If they are difficult to detect, probably they have been in circulation for some time, but if they are easy to detect, they may have been out but a short time. It's important that I know how long they've been in the channels of trade. Do you understand?"

The teller had recovered his equanimity and replied with a laugh: "Oh, that's all! Well, go ahead with your questions."

The detective continued, "What did you discover with the pocket-glass?"

"That there was a mistake in the spelling of the word 'trust'— the final 't' being an 'f;' that the number of notches around the milled edge was short of the requisite and that there were eighteen feathers only in the eagle's right wing."

"You discovered all this on your examination?"

"Yes. You see after my suspicions were aroused I naturally made a careful examination."

"Naturally. What did you think of the age of the coin?"

"I saw at once that it had been made to look older than it really was."

"You had no trouble in determining that the piece was spurious, then?"

"None whatever."

"Mr. Gimp," the detective said, with an expression of countenance and intonation of voice indicative of open admiration or covert irony, "you're a pretty shrewd man, and invaluable to the institution in whose employ you are. You ought to be in the Secret Service,"—smiling blandly. "It will surprise you, no doubt, when I tell you that we of the Department have looked upon this particular coin as a very dangerous counterfeit and one very hard to detect. Now, here are two dollars I happen to have with me. One is a counterfeit; the other is genuine. Be kind enough to tell me—if you will, Mr. Gimp—which of the two is the bogus piece. I don't mind telling you, in all candor, that I consider this counterfeit a clumsy makeshift, compared with the other." And Raymond laughingly presented the coins to the teller.

Gimp's face immediately became a study. He nervously stroked his beard, bit his lips and turned red of countenance. However, he took the coins and carefully inspected them. Then, with a rather sickly smile, he remarked, "It's unfair to ask me to determine in this offhand fashion, you know."

The president and Raymond laughed outright. Then the latter said, "You had no trouble in detecting the other, you say?"

"No, but—"

"How about this one, then?"

Gimp studied the two coins for a minute or two longer, minutely, weighed them in his hands, and rang them up on the desk. At last he answered, "This is the genuine coin, and this is the counterfeit." And he handed them one at a time to the detective.

"Right you are!" laughed Raymond, as he jingled them and dropped them into his pocket. Then he continued soberly, "Of course, you've no idea who's shoving this stuff, Mr. Gimp?"

"None whatever."

"And you don't know whether they're made in the city?"

"I do not, indeed; I have no idea."

"Well," Raymond said, rising, "I thank you, gentlemen, for your promptness in reporting the case and for your courtesy. If you discover anything worth reporting, wire the Department. Hope I may be successful in running the fellows down. Good-bye."

He cordially shook hands with the two and left. On reaching the street he halted as though in doubt as to what he should do next. A peculiar smile hovered about his straight, firm lips, as he stood in momentary hesitation. Consulting his watch, he found that it was almost ten o'clock.

"I'll do it," he resolved, and started down the street at a rapid pace. At the next corner he entered a drugstore and spent a few minutes consulting a directory. Then he closed the book with a bang, hurried to the street and leaped aboard an electric car; and a few minutes later was rolling away toward the suburbs.

Far out on one of the principal residence streets, he alighted at a large and handsome house standing in the center of beautiful and extensive grounds. Critically he inspected it from two sides and entered a few notes in his memorandum-book. Then he boarded a returning car and was soon in the business portion of the city again. Here he entered another drugstore, made a trifling purchase and thumbed over a directory. Once more on the street, he sought the office of a prominent real-estate broker; and when closeted with him made brisk inquiry, "Mr. Edson, can you tell me who owns the fine residence at the corner of Blank and Incog streets?"

The broker referred to a large map upon the wall, muttered a number under his breath, and began to turn the pages of a large canvas-bound book. Presently he answered, "Harold P. Gimp, teller of the Capitalists' Bank."

"Is the place for sale?"

"I don't know; but I can find out for you. However, I don't suppose it is; I see Gimp bought it within the last year."

"I presume he'd sell, if his price was offered him."

"Probably."

"I wish I knew," Raymond said, musingly, "whether his financial affairs are such that he can afford to own the property, or whether they are such that the place might be bought at a bargain. Does he own stock in the bank?"

"No, I'm sure he doesn't. I know all of the principal stockholders, and Gimp isn't one of them. But I believe I've heard it rumored lately that he's made a pile, within the last year or so, by shrewd speculation. Shall I look the matter up for you?"

"Yes, but do it very quietly. I'm going out of the city for a few weeks; have everything in readiness upon my return. Here's ten dollars to pay you for your trouble—until I see you."

"All right," assented the broker, briskly. "But what's the name, please?"

"Howard C. Curtis," Raymond answered, promptly, "but I'm not a resident of the city and don't care to be known in the deal, for the present. Keep things dark."

Mr. Edson nodded knowingly, and the detective passed out the door.

His next call was at the other bank that had written the Treasury Department. Here he learned nothing new except that the attention of the officers of this bank had been called to the counterfeits by Gimp.

"It was at our club," remarked the president, "that he showed me one of the counterfeits. Being interested, I of course made search and found a few, one or two of which I sent to Washington. I didn't know the Capitalists' Bank had done likewise."

"Is Mr. Gimp a stockholder in the Capitalists' Bank?" Raymond inquired, in an offhand way.

"No, sir."

"You say he's a member of your club?"

"Yes, he's belonged to the club about three months, I think. He's made some lucky speculations of late and has bought him a fine property."

The detective thanked the officials and returned to his hotel.

Chapter III

After dinner Raymond retired to his room and sat down with the intention of quietly and systematically joining and weaving the disconnected and broken threads of information into a whole piece of tangible and certain truth. He lighted a cigar, placed a pitcher of lemonade upon the table within easy reach, lolled back in his chair and gave himself up to concentrated thought.

The air was close and hot, and the mutterings of a distant thunderstorm came to his ears. Heavy drays[7] and vans rumbled up and down the superheated thoroughfair, and a parrot in front of a saloon across the street cursed the passerby and screamed discordantly. Raymond fumed and sweat and mentally condemned the bird, the weather and everybody and everything—himself especially—for agreeing to stop in the city at all.

"I ought to have gone on without meddling in this complicated affair at all," he muttered, savagely biting his cigar. "I'll waste half my vacation—and accomplish nothing, more than likely. But the devil of it is I've become *interested*! It's a most fascinating case. Let's see what I have: Gimp is the one person who discovered the counterfeits. His president *believes* him to be an expert, and I *know* him to be an arrant fraud; for he failed signally[8] to detect the counterfeits of the two coins I submitted to him, although, as I warned him, it was a bold and based makeshift compared with the one he claims to have detected so easily. Of course, I let him believe he was right and disarmed him of suspicion, I hope."

He took a drink of lemonade, relighted his cigar, and continued his cogitations[9], "Gimp has purchased a fine residence within the last few months and quite recently joined an aristocratic and expensive club. His salary doesn't warrant him in doing these things, but he tells his friends he's made some lucky speculations. On whose money does he speculate, I wonder? One thing's sure: Gimp's either a smooth scoundrel or an egregious[10] and egotistical ass!"

He threw aside his half-smoked cigar, wiped the perspiration from his countenance, and mused on: "I am possessed of the fool idea that Gimp is in some way connected with this case. He may be shoving the stuff through the bank; more unlikely things have happened in my experience. If so, why does he tell his president and the officials

---

7 **dray** - low, heavy cart without sides, used for haulage

8 **signally** - to a conspicuous degree; notably

9 **cogitations** - a serious thought; a carefully considered reflection

10 **egregious** - extraordinary in some bad way; glaring; flagrant

of the other bank that it's bogus? Is it a case of over caution—the case of a drunken man proving himself drunk, by striving to appear sober? I believe it is. Gimp has sense enough to know the thing can't go on forever, and he's fortifying himself again suspicion. He shoving out this stuff to those who come to get checks cashed or bills changed—a dollar here and a dollar there. If detected, he'll be in a position to say: 'It's an oversight; I was the first to discover these counterfeits—and promptly informed the authorities.' Of course, this spurious stuff is being shoved in other ways, probably. Now, where is it being made—and who's making it? The case must be worked from this end. I must determine more of Gimp's habits, haunts and associates; also, I must look up his family and relatives."

Raymond arose, yawned, donned coat and hat and left the hotel. In the course of the afternoon and evening, by means of shrewd and careful inquiries directed to various business and professional men who did business at the Capitalists' Bank, he learned much of what he desired to know. He accomplished all this, too, without revealing his identity or arousing the curiosity of those with whom he talked. He learned that Gimp was married, but had no children; that he had no relatives in the city, but that his wife's sister had made her home with them until a few months back; that he was a careful, methodical man of strict probity[11] and untarnished honor; that he had never been known to drink nor gamble, but that of late he had been a more or less successful speculator.

All this did not upset the detective's theory; it but added to his suspicions. He reasoned that this was just the sort of man to do the things he suspected Gimp of doing—with little chance of being apprehended.

The next day Raymond instituted proceedings to catch the teller in the very act of shoving the bogus coin. Within a half square of the bank he bought a paper of a newsboy, tendering the gamin a ten-dollar bill in payment.

"Can't change it, Mister," said the lad, eyeing the bill suspiciously.

"Run into the Capitalists' Bank and get the teller to change it," Raymond made answer. "Front wicket—man with the beard. And

---

11 **probity** - adherence to the highest principles and ideals : uprightness

no tricks! I'll be at the door—with an eye upon you."

"Oh, I'll bring y'r change back all right!" replied the urchin, skurrying away.

A minute later the boy had returned and Raymond had the change in his hand. He paid the lad and sauntered from the spot, and when secure from observation made examination of the money. As he did so he smiled grimly, and shook his head in half-pitying contempt. Two of the counterfeit silver dollars were in the lot.

The detective suspicions were confirmed. He was convinced but not fully satisfied. So a few minutes later he repeated the test by tendering a twenty-dollar bill at a fruit stand. Again the bill went to the bank to be changed, and again a number of the counterfeits put in an appearance.

"I'll leave the city tomorrow morning," Raymond resolved, on his way to his hotel. "There is no need of my staying here longer at present. Thus far the case is absurdly plain. Gimp shoves the stuff at the bank; of course he may have confederates who are doing the same in other parts of the city and in other places. That doesn't matter, however; Gimp is the central figure in the farce-comedy, thus far. Of course he doesn't receive this spurious stuff at the bank; he brings it there in small amounts, secretes it in a handy receptacle and pushes it into the hands of the unsuspecting. Then he pockets good money for the bad. The silver in a dollar is worth about fifty cents; the government stamp does the rest. It's the case of fifty cents invested winning a dollar—a clean profit of one hundred percent on each and every transaction. And he runs little risk—or did so long as he kept his head. But now his days of freedom and unlawful prosperity are about numbered; for when I return I'll unravel the whole affair. It'll be comparatively easy to shadow him and find out where the coin's made. I guess Travis was right, though—the plant's in Pittsburgh, or near."

That evening Raymond was standing at the clerk's desk in the hotel lobby, when a drummer[12] came out to settle his account. The man deliberately set down his bag, flung the key to his room upon the desk, and asked with a yawn:

---

12 **drummer** - a commercial traveler or traveling sales representative

"What's my bill?"

"Three dollars," answered the clerk.

The drummer leisurely put his hand into his trousers pocket, brought out the money, and threw it upon the desk. Then he sauntered over to the cigar stand and lighted a cheroot. The clerk was in the act of transferring the coins to the till when the detectives hand interfered with his design.

"Wait a moment, please," said Raymond. "Will you let me see those coins?"

"Certainly,"—in obvious wonnder.

The detective took them and carefully looked them over. When through, he smilingly returned them to the clerk's palm, satisfying the latter's apparent curiosity, with the words, "I'm just a numismatic crank. Thank you."

Evidently the unusual word mystified the clerk, for he inquired quickly: "Do you mean you're a coin collector?"

"No—not exactly; I'm just interested in them."

"Guess we all are," laughed the young man, as he dropped the money into the till.

Raymond approached the drummer at once who was making a pretense of lighting a cigar and said in a low tone, "Pardon me; but would you mind telling me where you got the money you just now gave to the clerk?"

"How's that?" the commercial man exclaimed, a puzzled expression upon his fat face.

"The money you just now gave to the clerk," Raymond repeated—"where did you get it?"

The drummer stared hard—half in anger, half in surprise.

"Where did I get the money I gave to the clerk?" he repeated.

"Yes."

"Well, that's a hell of a question!"

"I know, but I have a reason for asking it."

"Well, I've no reason to answer it,"—haughtily.

"I think you have."

"You do, eh? Well, I *won't*."

"No?"

"No!"

The chuffy drummer was growing excited. His face flushed and his puffy white hand trembled. But the detective maintained an unruffled composure. He stood looking into the cigar case and drumming upon it with his knuckles.

"One of the coins you gave to the clerk is peculiar," he remarked quietly.

"Peculiar?"

Raymond nodded, and added, "Entirely out of the ordinary."

"That's so?"—with aroused interest in voice and manner.

"Yes."

"Has—has it got any special value?"—native cupidity[13] alert.

"No; it's a counterfeit."

"The devil!"

Raymond nodded, smiling.

"And I suppose you had to go and tell the clerk?"

"No; I didn't tell him. Where did you get it?"

"Good; I'm glad you didn't tell him!"—in a tone of exultation.

"Did you mean to pass it on him?"

The drummer indulged in a smart laugh. "Suppose I did?" he said.

"I'd have to arrest you."

"What!"—in unqualified amazement.

"I'm from Missouri," sneered the commercial man; you'll have to show *me*."

"By arresting you?"

The drummer brought up with a sudden jerk. Then his assurance returning: "But where's your badge?"

"I'm not parading it."

"Well, why didn't you say you was a detective, in the start?"

"I don't shout that fact from the house tops when I'm working on a case."

"I see."

"Now, will you tell me where you got that counterfeit coin?"

"Yes. I got it from a drayman[14] in Zanesville, Ohio, yesterday.

---

13 **cupidity** - greed for money or possessions
14 **drayman** - the driver of a dray, a low, flat-bed wagon without sides

He hauled my trunks to the depot. I gave him a five dollar bill, and he gave me back the three silver dollars I handed to the clerk."

"You're sure?"

"Absolutely."

"Thank you. You don't wish to be held as a witness in the case, I presume?"

"Heavens, no!"

"Just keep quiet about our little talk, then. You understand?"

"Yes—and I must be off to catch my train. Good-bye."

"Good-bye."

Raymond went to his room and penned the following cipher letter:

"Secret Service Department, Washington, D. C.

"Travis:

"I'm off for Zanesville. Have found shovers of stuff in city. Will close up case on my return from Ohio. You need send no one on here till I advise you.

"Raymond."

Then he retired, and as he was dropping asleep he muttered, "Lucky I encountered that drummer. Wonder if his picking up that dollar in Zanesville means anything?"

The next morning he set out for the city of his thoughts.

Chapter IV

On arrival in Zanesville Raymond called at several of the principal houses and on one pretext or another succeeded in examining quite a number of silver dollars. To his surprise he discovered not one counterfeit.

"I don't understand the thing," he muttered, as he sat resting in the lobby of the Clarendon hotel; "that counterfeit the drummer had came from this city. Of course it may have strayed in here and out again—a mere accident; but I can hardly believe it. I was in hope of finding something definite here—something that would indicate the whereabouts of the plant. I thought, after my meeting with the drummer, that I might find this place flooded with this stuff. I guess old Travis is right in his intuitions, after all, and that I'll have to abandon my theory. I don't like to do it, though; something keeps telling me that I'm on the right scent. Well, I won't bother my brain any more about it for the present. I'll take the afternoon boat down the river and give my-self up to a few weeks of rest and unalloyed bliss. The counterfeiters may go on their way rejoicing, until I'm through with green fields and babbling brooks."

He arose, yawned and walked up to the clerk's desk and asked, "What time does the boat start down the Muskingum?"

"About one o'clock."

"It goes through to Marietta?"

"No, sir; only to McConnelsville."

"That's about halfway down the valley?"

"Almost—yes, sir."

"Well, that's probably as far as I want to go."

"The train goes through to the Ohio River."

"The train?"

The clerk simply stared in answer to the question.

"Is there a railroad down the valley now?" Raymond asked, sharply.

"Yes, sir; has been for several years."

"Then I don't know whether I want to go down the river or not," the detective murmured, as if to himself, genuine pathos in his voice. "If the iron horse has invaded the old valley I knew when a boy, there's little of its beauty left, probably. No doubt the woods are all cleared away, the hunting and fishing gone, and the leafy grass-grown solitudes changed to busy marts of trade."

"Hardly so bad as that," the clerk laughed. "The valley is still quite wild in places and very beautiful all the way down. It's becoming somewhat of a summer resort, though; and you won't find it as quiet as it used to be. Still, it's a delightful place to spend a few weeks of the hot weather."

"Where's the boat landing?" Raymond inquired.

"At the foot of Fifth street."

The detective glanced at his watch, saw that it was twelve-thirty and resolved to go down to the boat. On reaching the street the thought came to him that he ought to have a book to while away the time, should it chance to hang heavy on his hands. He went into Edmiston's and looked over a number of paper-bound novels. Selecting one at random, he threw down a bill in payment and, on receiving his change, was startled to find himself in possession of two more of the counterfeit silver dollars.

He jingled them in his hand and stood irresolute for a few seconds, pondering what to do. He was irritated to think that the pieces should thrust themselves upon him—and just at a time when he was trying to forget that they were in existence, or ever had been. But his professional pride asserted itself and his indecision was but momentary. Instantly he mapped out a course of proceedure.

"Are you sure these coins are all right?" he asked, carelessly, smiling at the young man behind the counter.

The salesman looked at the detective in surprise and wonder, as he replied: "I've no reason to think them otherwise, sir."

"Of course not," Raymond laughed, "and you wouldn't know if they were counterfeit, probably."

"No."

"Which only goes to show how much bogus money may be in circulation."

"That's so."

"And you wouldn't know where you got them, either—eh?"

"Yes, I know where I got them."

"Indeed! That's rather remarkable. A shopkeeper so seldom knows where he gets any certain piece of money."

"A lady gave me those a half hour ago, in payment for a number of bound books. The way I'm sure is that, when she came in, I had changed a number of bills and the till was empty of coin."

"I see. Is it the usual thing here to sell several bound books to one individual, in mid-summer?"

"Hardly the usual thing; but these were standard works that sell in any season."

"Of whose books do you sell most?"

"Of current fiction, you mean?"

"No, of standard works."

"That's a hard question. This lady bought 'Vanity Fair,' 'Heine's Poems,' and a finely illustrated copy of 'Lucile.'"

"Ah! A woman of superior literary taste, evidently."

"Oh! I don't know," the young salesman laughed, "a good many people buy books they have no intention of reading."

"I suppose so," he said musingly. "Probably this particular purchaser wished to add to her library in her suburban home."

"I don't think she lives in the city."

"From the country, eh?"

"Yes, sir—at present, at any rate. She mentioned several things that made me aware of the fact. Besides I saw her railroad ticket; she took it from her purse and laid it upon the counter when she was fishing for the bill she gave me."

"So this paragon of excellent literary taste is a simple country maid, after all and not a high-bread city dame," Raymond remarked, with assumed lack of definite interest in the talk, lounging upon the counter and stifling a yawn.

The salesman was not busy and seemed to be enjoying the gossipy conversation, for he rattled on: "I'm not so sure of that. She was a well-bred, stylish-looking woman, probably about twenty-eight or thirty years old; and I'm inclined to think she's rusticating[15] down the Muskingum somewhere, though she may be from Marietta."

"Uh-huh," again yawning. "What makes you think she's stopping down the river?"

"Her ticket was over the O. and L. K."

"I see."

The detective started for the door, but stopped and said, with a laugh, "Well, I'm going down the river, and perhaps I'll fall in with her. I hope so, at any rate; I enjoy talking with cultured people. You couldn't give me a description of her, could you—that I might know her, should I meet her on the train?"

---

15 **rusticating** – to go to live in, or spend time in the country

"I don't know; I'll try. She's of medium height, has on a gray traveling suit and wears gold glasses."

"All right—but say! Don't give me away, if you see her again. She'd think me a most impudent cur—talking of her as I've been doing."

"I won't mention it."

"Thank you; good day."

"Good day, sir."

The detective left the store, turned the corner and looked at his watch.

"Confound the luck!" he muttered. "Just when I think I'm to be free from work and worry, a clue bobs up to torment me. Two o'clock, and I can't go by boat, drifting and dreaming, but must ride twenty-five or thirty miles in a stuffy cross-road train. And instead of having the pleasure of viewing the scenery and ruminating on the joys of childhood, I must be on the *qui vive*[16] for a female counterfeiter—an oldish spinster of literary taste, who shoves the stuff."

He was walking rapidly, hardly knowing or heeding where he was going. Suddenly he brought up with a jerk and muttered half aloud, "I wonder if this does mean anything; or whether it's a mere circumstance—an accident. By Jove! I must find out what time that train leaves, or I'll miss it—and lose track of the woman. There were two bad dollars in that bunch of change; she's probably shoved quite a lot of it in the city today. Of course she may be an innocent victim—like the drummer—and the whole clue may prove to be only a puff of smoke; but I'll soon know, if I can run across her."

He hurried down to the station of the O. and L. K., and, going up to the ticket-seller's window, inquired, "When does the train leave for Marietta?"

"One-forty."

"Give me a ticket."

Shoving the bit of pasteboard into his pocket, he sauntered out upon the platform and stood watching the travelers coming and

---

16 **qui vive** - on the alert; attentive

going—a restless stream of humanity, reminding him of trains of ants he had observed when a boy. His train pulled into the station, and the conductor leaped off. Raymond approached him, saying, "You came up the Valley this morning?"

"Yes."

"I'm looking for a lady from down the river—dressed in a gray traveling dress and wearing gold-rimmed glasses, of medium height, a little under middle-age, intelligent looking—and rather pretty."

He added the last as an after-thought, with the idea that if the woman he sought chanced to be attractive a conductor would the more readily recall her.

Then he finished, "Did she come up on your train?"

"From what point were you expecting her?" asked the conductor, in turn.

Raymond didn't know, of course; but answered at a venture: "Beverly."

"No lady got on at that place."

"Well, did a lady of that description get on at any point?"

"No."

"Sure?"

"Yes."

Then the conductor went on in explanation: "We were light this morning, and no lady of that description was on the train. A good-looking young woman got on at Malta—in fact a number of them; but the one I'm speaking of was very good-looking. I've seen her a number of times before. She's not the one you're looking for, though; she wore a linen traveling wrap, and had no glasses."

"Thank you," said Raymond as he turned away. "Probably she didn't come."

He entered one of the coaches and took a seat. Several lady passengers came aboard, but the woman he sought did not put in an appearance. The train drew out of the station, crossed the bridge to the west side of the river, left Putnam and Fair Oaks behind and thundered off down the valley. Raymond arose and strolled through the cars but returned to his seat no wiser.

"This infernally hot weather!" he grumbled. "And just as I predicted, I've had all my stew and worry for nothing. I could murder that hair-brain clerk at the bookstore; he's bungled things for me terribly. Said he saw her have an O. and L. K. ticket; and no such woman came up on the train, or is going back on it now. He has tripped up on the description of the woman or—"

He had been lolling against the back of the seat, his eyes half closed. With a jerk he sat stiffly erect, so suddenly and vividly had an idea presented itself.

"Sure!" he growled audibly. "That's it exactly. The ticket that young putty-face saw was a B. and O. ticket—instead of an O. and L. K. The woman came over from Pittsburgh, on the same train I did—there's no doubt of it. She'll shove the stuff and return—no! I saw the very woman in my car. She was dressed in a gray traveling suit and wore glasses. But great and adorable common sense! No stretch of the imagination would enable a sane man to call her either young or pretty. By the way, though the bookstore chap didn't say she *was* pretty; I just fancied that part, I guess, and used it in my description to the conductor. Young Putty Face *did* say that she was about twenty-eight or thirty years old. The woman I saw was past forty, I'm sure. Well, the young fellow's more gallant then keen of observation—that's all. I wish I'd questioned him closer; but I didn't dare to, for fear of arousing his suspicions. Confound the luck—all cry and no wool! The woman I saw and the woman he saw are one and the same, undoubtedly. She's a good old grandmother of fifty, come over to visit in the country some place—and innocent of all wrong-doing. Perhaps she had a bill changed at the Capitalists' Bank, before leaving Pittsburgh." He smiled grimly, as he again lolled back in the cushioned seat and watched the ever-shifting panorama through the open window.

The afternoon was excessively hot. The river, along whose bank the railroad ran, shimmered and glanced in the rays of the declining sun, and the stubble-fields shown like great stretches of burnished gold. The wooded hillslopes and verdant pasture lands looked cool and inviting, and the dark-green corn smiled at the blazing sun and nodded to each fickle breeze that loitered by.

Raymond hungrily drank in the beauties of the scene—the river, the hills, the cliffs—and made a heroic attempt to throw aside all thought of the case that had been perplexing him; and he succeeded to the extent that a smile lighted his handsome features at last, and he whispered drowsily, "Good-bye to Secret Service affairs till I get back to Pittsburgh! Travis is right—has been right all along; the dens near that city, somewhere. Hello! Here's Eagleport. The old place looks familiar and as dilapidated as ever. I'll get off at Malta, I guess, and seek out a quiet spot for a few weeks of bliss. I want to find a place where there's not another boarder—no young women to set me crazy with their everlasting chatter, anyhow. Humph! I conjured up a rather pretty face and figure for my imagined counterfeitress. If Travis knew, he'd have the laugh on me. The idea of the old man teasing me about a woman—me, of all men! No—no, I'm too old; I'll never meet a—"

"Malta!" shouted the brakeman, thrusting his head in the door. "Malta and McConnelsville!"

The train came to a stop, and Raymond stepped off upon the platform.

Chapter V

The detective arrived in Malta upon a Saturday and took up temporary lodging. Sunday was a most beautiful midsummer day, and Raymond—worldly sinner that he was—spent it upon the hilltops back of the village. He had the unexampled temerity and hardihood to turn a deaf ear to the united peals and appeals of the clanging bells and to direct his wayward steps toward forbidden paths—paths leading to Nature's secret haunts and God's own trysting places.

Under a spreading beech, in whose branches the birds sang and nested, unmindful of the Scriptural text to keep the day holy, he lay wrapped in calm content and blissful reverie, as one golden hour succeeded another. He was one of those who—

"Jest stretch out an' bat the'r eyes
At the depths o' summer skies"

And imagine in their sinful ignorance, that they are worshiping the true and living God by admiring and enjoying His handiwork. Of course, according to strict Orthodox belief, they shall be condemned to everlasting punishment for their wilful negligence; but they are a calloused lot and give little heed to the pratings of the elect and have little care for the terrors of a fabulous future, when saturated with the joys and pleasures of an established present.

Monday came; and Raymond, desirous of securing a boarding place nearer to the solitude he craved, made inquiries of his host to that end. The unctuous[17] boniface[18] made answer:

"Let's see—there are a few people who keep boarders here in town. In fact, I could board you quite cheap myself; but you want to get right out into the country, as I understand you."

Raymond assured him that he did.

"Well, there's a place out on the hills two or three miles, where they sometimes board people. How would that suit you?"

"Not at all. I want a place along the river, where there's boating, fishing and bathing, and all that sort of thing."

"I see. Well, there's only one place close to town; and that's Jake Cassell's."

"How far is it from the village?"

"A mile or so down the river."

"He's a farmer?"

"Yes—and a good one. It's a pleasant place—shady and comfortable and quiet. You'll get good board—fresh milk, vegetables and fruit. They call the place 'Maple Grove Farm.' I know you'd like it."

"Any little children in the family?"

"No, just Jake and his wife, a grown-up son, and the hired help."

"Any other boarders?"

"No—yes, there is; an old maid school teacher. But she won't bother you; she's all the time busy hunting shells and stones and plants and things. It's better than a circus to hear her talk of botany and geology and conchology and so on. She's quiet and ladylike,

---

17 **unctuous** - characterized by affected, exaggerated, or insincere earnestness
18 **boniface** - the proprietor of a hotel, nightclub, or restaurant

though, and won't disturb you. You see, Jake sells me milk and butter, so I know all about the place.

Acting on the landlord's information and advice, Raymond called upon the Cassell's, with the result that by the middle of the afternoon he found himself comfortably installed in the commodious farm house. It was a beautiful, shady place, commanding a fine view of the winding river and the broad acres of bottom land surrounding it. The residence stood upon a slight knoll midway between the river and the base of the range of hills skirting the valley, in a grove of magnificent maples. The farm consisted of several hundred acres of rich bottom and hill pasture; and the air of prosperity about it, the condition of orchards, fences, and out-buildings indicated that the Cassells were energetic, well-to-do people.

The house was of greystone—a quaint, square building with a wide veranda running along two sides of it. The highway followed the bank of the river, and a narrow, tree-bordered lane led from it to the farm house. Back of the residence were the barns and orchard, and at the foot of the lane was the boat landing.

The room assigned to the detective was on the second floor and at the southeast corner of the building. It's low, wide windows opened just above the roof of the veranda and from them could be caught a glimpse of the tree-fringed river, a full view of the range of hills walling the valley on the east, and—from the southern two—sight of the break in the western range of hills, where the turbulent waters of Douda Run joined with the larger stream.

The Cassell farm was composed of what at one time had been several homesteads; but the present owner had, by enterprise and economy, gained possession of them one at a time and amalgamated[19] them into one extensive tract. Of the original dwellings, one or two were occupied by tenants; the others stood empty or were used for the storage of grain or fodder.

The Cassell household—as the village landlord had informed Raymond—consisted of husband and wife; the son, Frank, a young man of twenty-five; the hired man, Jap; the two servant girls, Janey

---

19 **amalgamate** - to combine into a unified or integrated whole; unite

and Ruth; and Miss Myra Haskins, a boarder. The Cassells were simple-minded country folks, neither knowing nor caring much for the twin follies, society and style.

Raymond on his arrival at the farm house immediately unpacked his trunk and bag, donned a suit of gray flannel and a neglige shirt[20] and went out into the grounds to find a place to hang his hammock. It was then that he realized for the first time that there was another pleasure seeker about the place; for he came plump upon another hammock suspended between two of the big maples just in front of the house. He brought up with a jerk, and the expression of child-like gladness faded from his countenance and was replaced by one of surprise and disgust mingled. He scratched his head in genuine perplexity, shifted uneasily from one foot to the other and eyed this swinging nest of fringe and ribbons with frank disapproval.

"I've made another of my innumerable blunders," he growled, with all the fervor of a confirmed bachelor. "This one is the crowning glory of them all. An old maid, forsooth! A school mistress, bah! I know exactly what she's like—painted cheeks, goggles, false teeth and a wig; forty years old, and trying to look like a miss in her teens; talks science for show, and is all the time dreaming day dreams of love in a cottage. She'll lay systematic siege to the citadel of my susceptible heart, and I'll be forced to act the boor to get rid of her. Curse the fates that sent me here!"

He heaved a lugubrious[21] sigh, shook his fist at the offending hammock, as though he considered it responsible for all of life's ills, present, past and future, and continued his "book of the lamentations."

"She's pre-empted the best place in the whole yard, too—of course; and I'll be compelled to go down to the river or back upon the hills, likely, to find a place where I can have a minute's peace. And this is the paradise I dreamed of!"

However, he paced on and selected a spot some twenty yards to the left of the object of his apostrophe[22]. There he made fast his hammock ropes to two of the sturdy maples, dropped into this swing-

---

20 **neglige shirt** - informal or incomplete attire
21 **lugubrious** - mournful, dismal, or gloomy, especially to an exaggerated degree
22 **apostrophe** - an exclamatory passage in a speech or poem addressed to a person (typically one who is dead or absent)

ing net, and, pulling his straw hat low over his eyes, grumblingly composed himself for a siesta. But just as he was dropping into a doze he heard, or thought he heard, a half-suppressed, rippling peal of laughter, issuing from the open window of the upstairs room in the northeastern corner of the house—the room just across the hall from his own.

"Those giddy little housemaids are up there peeping at me," he muttered, irritably, and immediately dropped off to sleep.

He slept two hours and was awakened by the clanging of the big bell at the top of a tall post near the side gate leading to the barn yard.

"Supper, I suppose," he yawned, and he arose and sauntered around the corner toward the kitchen.

A sight met his gaze that caused him to smile broadly. Clinging to the bell rope with both hands and leaping fully two feet into the air at every swing of the brazen instrument of torture, was the diminutive and mercurial Janey. Her shock of flaxen hair danced and bobbed about her bony neck and shoulders, and her shoe soles beat a quick tattoo upon the hard-packed earth. She was ringing the bell to call the men from the field and was all unconscious of the presence of the new boarder. When she became aware she was observed, she clattered along the flagstones and into the kitchen, at a speed little short of a run.

The detective continued to smile as he ascended the stairs and kept on smiling, as he bathed his flushed face and smoothed his tousled hair. Janey's performance and her consequent embarrassment and flight appealed to his sense of the ludicrous, and he was ready to burst forth laughing at any moment.

When he again descended the stairs, the men had come in from the fields, and scrubbed their faces and hands, and were ready for supper. The long dining table was spread upon the south veranda, and everything about it looked neat and inviting. The combined odors of rose and honeysuckle made sweet the evening air, and the birds in the tall maples were chirping a musical medley. The soft breeze stole along the wide veranda and dallied with the leaves of the honeysuckle and playfully shook the petals from the full blown

                    A Counterfeit Coin

roses.

They were just ready to sit down to the table, when Mrs. Cassell exclaimed, "W'y, Miss Haskins ain't here! Janey—Janey, you run up to her room an' tell her supper's ready. No, you needn't; I hear her comin' down the stairs now."

Raymond turned his head, as light footfalls stole through the door and sounded upon the veranda. Immediately his keen eyes opened wide and his pulse quickened. Where was the old maid he had pictured—the painted cheeks, goggles, and hollow smirk? Surely this vision of female beauty was a delusion and a cheat. Old maid wrapped up in pedagogics[23] and lavender—ah, no! He had a confused consciousness that Mrs. Cassell was presenting Miss Haskins, in a quaint, countrified way; and mechanically he acknowledged the introduction and seated himself at the table.

Miss Haskins sat opposite to Raymond. He glanced at her from time to time, as the meal went on and answered the common-place remarks directed to himself; but he was absorbed and distraut and took but little part in the conversation.

Miss Haskins was anything but what the detective had reason to expect from the village landlord's well meant but misleading description of her. She did not look to be more than twenty-five, he decided, though she may have been; she was one of those women who seem to be blessed with perennial youth. Her dress was of some soft, white, clinging fabric; and her red-brown hair lay in natural waves about her broad, fair brow and was gathered into a Psych knot[24] at the back of her well-poised head. She had the most wondrous eyes Raymond had ever seen—deep violet-blue, fascinating, with an opaline fire in their fathomless depths; and her skin was of that milk-white, satiny kind that defies the sun to produce more damaging effect than a few pin-point freckles. She was of medium height, plump but pliant, with the arched instep and taper fingers of a patrician; and—no mean consideration—her white, even teeth were of nature's handiwork.

"And this is the spinster school mistress I was dreading to

---

23 **pedagogics** - the art of teaching
24 **psych knot** - a woman's hairdo in which a knot or coil of hair projects from the back of the head

meet!" was Raymond's mental comment. "She's a well-groomed little aristocrat—that's evident; and a consummate flirt, in all probability. She might prove more dangerous to a man's peace of mind than a dry-as-dust old school marm. Well, *I'm* immune, thank heaven!"

In answer to some question of Mr. Cassell's, the detective made a humorous rejoinder. Miss Haskins laughed merrily—a silver, rippling laugh that made Raymond look up quickly. It was so very like the one he had heard issuing from the upstairs window.

"Miss Haskins," he said with mock gravity, "I know now who it was laughing at me a while ago, while I was putting up my hammock."

For a moment she was slightly embarrassed, apparently. She flushed faintly, and her eyes fell before his steady gaze. Then she lifted her long lashes and answered, with the tremulous smile:

"I plead guilty, Mr. Raymond. It was very wrong, I know; please pardon me. I offer as an extenuating circumstance, however, the fact that your actions were really amusing."

And she continued to look at him, soberly, pleadingly. It was the detective's turn to be confused—why, he could not tell. He wondered if she was in earnest—if she meant anything of what she said. He could not tell; and he was a little displeased, a little nettled. He possessed an easy-going dignity of which he was justly proud; and it hurt his vanity—it piqued him—to have a young and beautiful woman claim to have discovered something monkey-like in his actions. Then, that she had succeeded in irritating him made him downright angry. So he replied rather stiffly, "I wasn't aware that I was observed, until you laughed, Miss Haskins. I'm truly sorry I presented so ludicrous—so ridiculous a spectacle."

"Now, don't say that," she murmured, genuine distress in her voice; "I didn't mean anything of the kind."

"Well," he persisted, obstinately, "what was there in the simple act of hanging a hammock, to excite your risiabilities[25]?"

"Oh!" she exclaimed, in a tone of infinite relief. "You've entirely misunderstood me, Mr. Raymond; it wasn't the hang-

---

25 **risiabilities** - having the ability, disposition, or readiness to laugh

ing of *your* hammock that amused me, but the manner in which you apostrophized *mine*. Your face was a study; and I knew just what you were thinking—that I had pre-empted the best place in the yard, and—and that your vacation was to be spoiled by—by my intrusiveness."

And she smiled at him frankly, her countenance clear of shadows.

Raymond didn't know what to think, and his confusion increased to add to his irritation, a half-suppressed giggle emanated from the irrepressible Janey, standing in the door. The Cassells grinned broadly, and Miss Haskins bit her lips, evidently struggling with a laugh. The soul-melting influence of her bewitching dimples, of her dancing eyes, was too much for the detective's gravity; and he smiled—a smile that widened, grew, and ended in an outburst of merriment. All around the table joined him in the laugh at his own expense; and Janey fled to the kitchen, to inform Ruth of the joke on the new boarder.

When Raymond had retired that night, he lay for a long time thinking of Miss Haskins; and he dropped asleep muttering to himself, "Haskins—an unusual name; and yet it seems to me I've heard it somewhere—and recently."

Chapter VI

Raymond thoroughly enjoyed the next few days. The weather was ideal—left nothing to be desired. The air was warm but not sultry; the skies were blue and cloudless. The perfume of flowers and the song of birds lulled his senses into grateful repose and his mind into blissful reverie; and he began to get into intimate touch with his surroundings. The substratum[26] of poetical thought and feeling in his soul was stirred to its most profound depths, and it had lain in a quiescent state for many, many years.

He finished, boated, swam and took long rambles over the hill tops and up and down the rocky ravines, with his gun upon his shoulder. His fishing consisted in setting his pole and line with

---

26 **substratum -** a foundation or basis of something

a baited hook dangling idly in the limpid stream, while he lolled upon the grassy bank, in the shade of the willows, gazing half dreamily, half ecstatically, at the tiny wavelets kissing and caressing the golden sands. He boated—that is, he drifted with the current when he could, and rowed when he must—drinking in the redbirds liquid melody, as that feathered voluptuarys [27]swayed upon the topmost bough of a spreading elm and poured forth its tinkling notes in a cataract of song. He went gunning, but his fowling piece[28] served only to entice him to spend hour after hour in the dark, green forest, soporific[29] with the smell of sassafras and pennyroyal.

He found himself growing poetical—sentimental, almost; and bits of verse and snatches of song came into his mind and fell from his lips, with ever recurring insistency. He quoted:

"Those Summer days of long ago—
I seem to feel and know them still."

He was living his boyhood over again. And yet not so; a new element has crept into his life—a new force—a something he had never known before. What was it? He did not know—he could not say; yet he was conscious of it. It made the skies brighter, the fields greener, the flowers fairer. No doubt it was the legitimate result of a carefree life he was leading, he decided at last; but he was not satisfied with his decision, and continued to let his mind revert to the matter many times each day. In fact, he seemed to have little to do with the thing; his mind acted subconsciously, as it were. He felt the mysterious influence at all times, but felt it most when in the presence of Miss Haskins! What could it be?

The two had become well acquainted in those few days—so he thought, at least. Their acquaintance, in the genial glow of the summer sun, quickly ripened into friendship. The unconventional life they led, their unrestricted dealings and conversations, had the effect of bringing them into closer companionship than a whole season in

---

27 **voluptuarys** - a person (or thing) whose life is given over to luxury and sensual pleasures; a sensualist
28 **fowling piece** - a light shotgun for shooting birds and small animals
29 **soporific** - causing or tending to cause sleep

polite society could have done.

Sitting upon the broad and cool veranda, one evening a week after his advent of the farmhouse, he said to her with a candor foreign to his secretive nature, "When they told me at the village hotel that an old maid school teacher was boarding here, I pictured to myself a snuffy, scientific, old body who would not accord me a good morning even; and I was satisfied that it should be so. But when I saw your bedecked and bedizzened hammock, I changed my opinion. I was dismayed and feared that my vacation was to be spoiled by the presence of a faded female of uncertain age, with painted cheeks and false hair."

Miss Haskins was sitting upon the edge of the veranda, half leaning against one of the pillars, and she smiled serenely as she answered, "There! I told you I read your face that day; and now you confess to just what I said. And you haven't found me a snuffy, scientific old body?"

"No, indeed."

"Nor an old maid school mistress, even?"

"Far from it," he answered, earnestly, dangerously expressing with his eyes and voice much more than he knew. "I've found you most congenial—most companionable, if I may say so."

"But I *am* a teacher," she laughed; "and an old maid—almost, at any rate—and I am addicted to the study of science."

"Yes," he admitted, "but you know what I mean. You're not at all what I imaged. How long have you been teaching?"

Miss Haskins closed her eyes; and a thoughtful little frown corrugated her brows.

"Let me see," she said; "I think it's about seven years."

"So long?"

"Yes; I began quite young, you see—at the age of eighteen, in fact."

"Eighteen and seven are twenty-five."

"Oh"—with an assumed start—"I didn't mean to tell you my age."

"But you have."

"So it appears."

"Where have you taught, Miss Haskins?"

"In Pittsburg."

"Indeed?"

"Yes, seven consecutive years. This year my health failed me, and I quit at the beginning of the spring term and came out here for a rest."

"You appear to have fully recovered." And Raymond smiled skeptically, yet admiringly.

"Oh! I wasn't really ill, you know," she explained; "just nervous and worn out from the constant grind and worry of the school room. But this quiet, restful life has done wonders for me. I've been here since the first spring beauties peeped through the half-frozen earth on the sunny hillsides in April."

"And you added one more to the number—and the fairest of them all," Raymond returned quickly.

Then he stopped suddenly, surprised and embarrassed at his own temerity, and half wishing he had not voiced his admiration so boldly. But Miss Haskins smiled in a gratified, self-possessed way, and said demurely, "Thank you. You could not pay me a higher compliment. I love those sweet, modest little flowers."

"What have you done all these months, to put in the time and occupy yourself?" asked Raymond, to relieve his embarrassment. Somehow, he felt like a big, green school boy in her presence, in spite of his eight and thirty years of life varied experience.

Miss Haskins shifted her position ever so slightly, readjusted her skirts, and replied, "I've not suffered from *ennui*[30]—I've not wanted for employment, I assure you. I've pled guilty of being addicted to the study of science. Well, out here I've indulged in the pleasurable side of geology, botany and conchology; and I've found the place a field rich in specimens. This entire section of country is seamed and scarred with marks of the glacial period; I've found the drift on the highest hill tops. Then, there are fossiliferous and other rocks found here, that are not found in most other localities. As to botany, the flora is rich and varied—especially the summer and autumn flowers of the compositae[31]. Besides, I've been making up collections of

---

30 **ennui** - listlessness and dissatisfaction resulting from lack of interest; boredom
31 **compositae** - a large family of dicotyledonous plants, having their flowers arranged in dense heads of many small florets

woods, shells, rocks and flowers, and sending them to my friends. Come up to my room, and I'll show you that I haven't been idle."

Raymond arose with alacrity[32] and preceded her up the broad stairway. Together they entered her apartments. He accepted the chair she proffered him and gazed about the room. It was richly carpeted and curtained and an open door led to a sleeping chamber beyond. The furniture consisted of two or three easy chairs, a small table, a bookcase and writing desk combined, and easel and a shelved cabinet with a silken curtain drawn in front of it.

A number of etchings, water colors, and charcoal sketches decorated the walls, and a mandolin lay upon the table in the center of the room.

The detective took it all in and remarked: "You have very cozy quarters here, Miss Haskins. Did you fit them up yourself?"

"Yes—that is, I had it done. You see I expected to stay some time, and I wanted things homelike. I couldn't bear the stiff, old-fashioned furniture and faded carpets, so I furnished the rooms at my own expense and to my own taste. I'm not at all sorry for it has made my stay much more pleasant—in fact, I dislike the thought of leaving."

Apparently she did not resent his patient curiosity—seemed to invite it, rather. So he went on: "Do you expect to stay here long?"

"I can't tell," she answered; "I've engaged no school for the coming year, and I presume I'd enjoy myself here as much as I would anywhere. I have my horse and cart and can come and go as I please, and I like personal freedom; so I may stay another year. However, I can't tell what notion may seize me; I may leave at any time."

"I see you have an easel; of course you draw or paint?"

"I do a very little of both, in a very bad way. You can judge for yourself; that's my work upon the wall."

"Both the water colors and the black and white sketches?"

"Yes."

He arose and walked around the room, examining them one by one. At last he remarked: "I don't pretend to be a critic, but I like

---

32 **alacrity** - brisk and cheerful readiness

your work—I think it shows genius. You did it under the direction of a teacher, of course?"

She showed resentment and she replied, "Indeed, I did *not*!"

"Pardon me," he laughed; "I told you I was no critic. The fact that you did the work unaided renders it the more meritorious. I like the charcoal sketches; there is so much character—so much individuality, in them. And you play the mandolin?"

Without reply she took up the instrument and played a simple air, as she lay back in her chair, with eyes half closed. He silently watched her flying fingers. When she was through he thanked her, and said, "You brought me here to show me something in particular. What was it?"

She started from the reverie into which she had fallen, saying, "So I did. But first I desire to show you the picture I've been working on recently. Here it is. What do you think of it?"

As she spoke she went to the easel and turned the picture upon it toward Raymond. It was a bold, unfinished sketch of his own head, done in charcoal. He did not know what to say; it had come upon him so suddenly. The picture was little more than an outline, but the likeness was plain enough. It was evident that it would be a fair portrait when finished.

"What do you think of it?" she repeated.

"When did you do it?" he countered.

"Yesterday—when you were sitting out under the trees."

"It's a very good beginning," he said, slowly, "considering the subject."

The merest semblance of a sneer was in her voice, as she returned: "Perhaps you think I show a woeful lack of maidenly reserve and womanly discretion, in thus choosing a new-found acquaintance for my subject."

"Not at all," he answered quickly. "You must know I meant nothing of the kind. But surely one has the privilege of speaking disparagingly of oneself."

"And of getting angry, if any one else says the same things of him."

"*I* shouldn't."

"Yes, you would; you're but human. Come over to the cabinet, and I'll show you some of the specimens I've been collecting. Draw your chair over here."

He complied with her request. She drew back the curtain of the cabinet, revealing a number of shelves laden with specimens of various kinds that she had collected in her rambles about the neighborhood. There were pressed flowers and leaves, pieces of woods and barks, bits of stone and odd-looking pebbles, shells, flint arrow heads and stone axes. All were correctly labeled and neatly arranged in the cabinet.

"Am I not an industrious body?" she smiled. "I gather these things for my own information and amusement; then, when I'm tired of looking at them, I box them up and ship them off to some of my city friends—thus earning the infinite pleasure of collecting more."

"I know little of science as a study—as a pursuit," Raymond remarked, musingly. Then, picking up a bit of rock, "What's this?"

"That's a piece of fossiliferous limestone," she replied readily. "See the minute shells embedded in it? And this is a piece of red granite from the glacial drift. I found it upon the hilltop back of the house."

"Do you know all these woods and barks when you see them in the forest?"

"Of course."

"And you learned it all from books?"

"Yes."

"I know the names—that is, their common names—of most of them, too; but I got my lore from the book of Nature. You have no specimen of the black dogwood."

"No. Does it grow about here?"

"Yes; I saw a clump of it down the river, yesterday. I'll go with you to get a specimen anytime you desire. That is, if my company and services are acceptable."

"I'll be only too pleased," she replied, unassumed pleasure in her voice and manner. "We can go in the cart."

They went on examining the specimens. In handing them

to her, her white and delicate fingers occasionally fluttered into his brawny palm; and at such times his whole being thrilled in a manner inexpressibly sweet.

At last she said, "There, that's all." Then smiling archly, "Now, I mean to turn inquisitor. You have quizzed me to your heart's content; and I thirst for revenge."

The detective started guiltily. Had he been acting the boor—making an intolerable nuisance of himself? His profession had fixed upon him the habit of exacting, as a right, the privilege of putting direct questions to those with whom he came in contact. He was not used to associating with refined and sensitive women—he cared so little for society; and he had not realized until now that his conduct had been audaciously rude. No doubt he had grievously offended her. What should he do?

She appeared to read his thoughts; for she went on hastily, "There—don't be worried. I really enjoyed your transparent curiosity and frank questions. You haven't offended me in the least; I like inquisitive people—I'm rather inquisitive myself, as you'll find. And now I want to know all about you. You are a lawyer or physician."

Her eyes danced as she smilingly awaited his replied. He smiled in turn, and answered, "No."

"Neither?"

"Neither. What led you to think so?"

"Because you are so dignified—so self-possessed,"—he wondered if she meant it, or if she were laughing at him—"and, above all, because you are so fond of interrogative forms of expression."

"You're mistaken," he replied stiffly.

"You're not a business man?" she continued.

"I'm not."

"Nor a minister?"

"By no means!" and he laughed outright.

"What are you?"

"I'm a Government employee."

"At Washington?"

"Yes."

"Which department?"

"Secret Service."

"Ah!"

"Yes; and I'm thirty-eight years old. I was born in this valley and I've been in the employee of the Government quite a number of years. And, like yourself, I'm still enjoying single blessedness."

"How do you know I'm unmarried?"

He bit his lips, and was silent for a moment. Then he said, "You told me you're single, didn't you?"

"It's my turn to ask questions," she answered, with provoking coolness.

"Very well—go on." His voice showed irritation, and she was quick to notice it.

"Are you angry with me?" she asked. Her beautiful eyes had a grieved look in them and her voice was vibrant with emotion.

"That's not the question you meant to ask," he replied, looking her full in the face.

"N-o; but are you angry with me?"

"Not in the least. Will you answer me one question, though?"

"Perhaps. Let me hear the question."

"Are you married or single?"

"Single."

Then they went down to supper.

Chapter VII

A week passed, and Raymond and Miss Haskins were close companions and friends, indeed. As has been said, no restrictions were thrown about them—no barriers were erected between them; the men were in the fields, from morn till night, and the women were equally busy in kitchen and dairy. So the two boarders amused themselves as they saw fit and spent a great deal of time in each other's company. They boated and fished, rode and drove along the shady lanes and highroads and rambled here and there through the fields and woods.

To be sure, they were not inseparable. Miss Haskins occasionally took a drive by herself, and the detective sometimes played the lone fisherman or solitary hunter. But they managed to spend a few hours together each day.

It was all very pleasant to Claude Raymond. He felt that he had not enjoyed himself so well in years. At first he did not pause to ask himself the reason why but accepted it as due to the care-free life he was leading—and that alone. At last he awoke to a full realization of what had taken place; and then he was rapturously happy and immeasurably miserable, at one and the same time—happy that he loved her, fearful that she did not love him.

Mr. and Mrs. Cassell were kind and indulgent to their boarders; the hired help left little to be desired in the way of services, but Frank Cassell was a thorn in the detective's flesh. The young man treated Raymond with scant courtesy bordering on downright rudeness. The latter could not understand why this should be so and spent some time puzzling his wits over the matter. As he could explain it by no hypothesis he could bring to bear, he gave up in disgust.

However, the two were not thrown much in each other's society, as the younger spent most of his time at hard labor in the fields. But one day young Cassell was indisposed and passed the afternoon lounging about the verandas. It was here that Raymond encountered him and, desiring to be sociable, said, "Won't you come out under the maples, Cassell? Miss Haskins is going to read a story aloud, and I'd be glad to have you share the pleasure."

"It wouldn't be any pleasure to me," was the surly reply.

"No?"—in frank surprise.

"No, it wouldn't."

"You're not feeling well, eh?"

"It isn't that."

"You don't like stories, perhaps."

"I like stories better than I like some people's company."

"Ah!" Raymond replied, with lifted brows, somewhat amused at the exhibition of boyish petulance. "And it's *my* company you dislike?"

"If you want to know—yes. Besides, I don't want to hinder you in your lovemaking. All the good luck I wish you is that she'll make a fool of you, as she did me, and then throw you over."

The brief conversation had brought up the subject Raymond did not care to discuss; so he simply turned upon his heel and walked away. But, as he went, he thought, "So that's the reason of my young gentleman's marked aversion. He's jealous, eh? I wonder if Myra— Miss Haskins—did encourage his juvenile attention. I can't believe it. The young greenhorn's simply let his imagination run riot. She has treated him civilly, and he has fallen head-over-ears in love with her. I can hardly blame him, though; I've done little better myself. I wonder if she cares for me. What *would* Travis say, if he saw me now? I'm ashamed of myself—almost, not quite. I must know my fate; I can't bear this uncertainty very long."

Miss Haskins was half-reclining in her hammock, a magazine in her lap. She looked up at him as he drew near, and said reproachfully, "You've been a long while in coming; surely you were itching to have me read to you."

"I beg your pardon," he answered humbly; "but I came as soon as I could. I stopped to speak with young Cassell."

"Were you talking of fat shoats or of turnips?" she asked, with a merry laugh. "I can't imagine his talking of anything else."

"We were talking of something far removed from the idea, even, of fat shoats or turnips."

"Indeed. Of what, or whom?"

"Of yourself."

"Of me?"

"Yes."

For a moment she was silent. Her eyelids droop, she toyed nervously with the magazine in her lap. Presently she looked up and asked, "Was he telling you I'm a desperate flirt?"

"He intimated as much."

"And what did *you* say?"

"Not a word; I simply refused to discuss the subject."

"Did he tell you that he forced his attention upon me—mere boy that he is—thus making himself an unbearable nuisance, and became so infatuated that he made me a proposal before I had been here a month? If he didn't tell you that, he didn't tell you the whole truth."

"He told me very little; he simply insinuated."

"What did he insinuate?"

"That you made him love you and then threw him over."

"I had nothing to do with his foolish infatuation—not a thing; but I did have to reject him—to snub him. However, it doesn't matter. Shall we begin the story?"

"If you please."

He seated himself with his back against the trunk of one of the maples and, partly closing his eyes, listened closely to her clear, well-modulated tones, as she read the little story to him. It was the autobiography of a counterfeit bill—how it paid the minister's salary, bought a starving man a Christmas dinner, saved a young girl from shame and ruin and did many other praiseworthy and wonderful things. It was an interesting story well-told.

"How do you like it?" she asked, when she had finished.

"It's all right—in its way. But read me something more."

"No; let's talk of the story I've read. Do you think it overdrawn?"

"No—I think not. But the whole thing rings false."

"Explain."

"A counterfeit's a counterfeit—a sham—a cheat."

"Of course; but—"

"You can make nothing else of it. It *may* work good but it deserves no credit, for its intent is to work evil. If that bill did all that is recorded in its favor, it swindled somebody in the end."

"You don't take kindly to counterfeits," and her eyes danced in the mischievous way that was so becoming to their possessor. "You hate all shams—people as well as coins?"

"To be sure I do."

"How positively you say that."

"Why shouldn't I? *You* don't love the false, the untrue, the counterfeit."

"I don't know,"—reflectively—"I never had much experience. But it seems to me that counterfeit money is like an assumed virtue; if it answers all the purposes of the real, it is as good and deserves as much credit."

"You don't believe that," he said, with feeling. "The only person benefited by counterfeit is out the goods and passes it. The unfortunate possessor of it, on the day it is discovered to *be* counterfeit, is out of the goods he gave for it and may consider himself fortunate if he is not arrested for having it in his possession." She maintained a thoughtful silence.

"Did you ever see any counterfeit money?" he asked suddenly, his keen eyes fixed full upon her face.

"I—I—" she stammered in evident confusion at the unexpected question.

He came to her relief with: "Let me show you a piece." And he took from his pocket one of the spurious coins that had caused him so much thought and worry and handed it to her.

Secretly, he was displeased that the story had led to the discussion—that she had insisted on it; he did not desire to "talk shop," nor think it, even. Miss Haskins took the proffered peace and turned it over and over in her dainty fingers.

"It looks just like any other dollar," she remarked. "Do you mean to tell me it's counterfeit?"

"Yes."

"How do you tell?"

He took a true coin from his pocket and pointed out to her the differences in the two. She manifested a passive interest and asked a number of questions.

"What is the punishment for passing counterfeit money?" was one.

"A term of imprisonment," he answered.

"But the authorities have to prove that the person accused *knew* it was counterfeit, do they not?"

"No; the accused must prove his innocence."

"Suppose you should give me that bogus dollar, and that I, not knowing it to be such, should pass it; would I be sent to prison?"

"No; you wouldn't be arrested, even, on so flimsy a charge. But should you pass a number of the coins, and should other circumstances go to prove you were aware that they were spurious, then the Government would have a case against you. Do you think of going into the business?"

"I've a wholesome fear of the penitentiary," she laughed. "Changing the subject, I wish to tell you that I have some of the most beautiful mussel shells upstairs. I found them on the bar at the mouth of Douda Run. I'm going to ship them to my friends. Will you come up and see them?"

"I'll be pleased to do so."

On reaching her apartment, she brought a wooden box from the inner room and, removing the lid, showed him the contents. The box was about a foot square, and appeared to be packed with pink-tinted shells.

Raymond lifted it from the floor, and remarked: "I never realized before that shells were so heavy."

She replied laughingly, "You would have realized the fact more forcibly, had you carried them up the stairs, as I did."

"Are these shells what you had in that tin box with a bail[33] to it, that I saw you bringing in this morning?"

"Yes; I had just returned from my morning drive."

"Do you want the lid nailed on the box?"

"If you please."

He arose and went down to the woodshed, returned with hammer and nails, and proceeded to fasten the lid in place. Then, arising from his knees and mopping the perspiration from his face, he asked:

"What's become of some of your pebbles and bits of wood? I see a number of them are missing from the cabinet."

"I sent them away yesterday."

"Do you ship all your curios—your specimens—by express?"

"Yes," then quickly, "why do you ask?"

"Why don't you send them as freight?" he countered.

"I value them too highly."

"Ah!"

For a moment they stood staring at each other in silence, each striving to read the other's thoughts.

Presently he said: "What are you thinking?"

"What are *you* thinking?"

"How beautiful you are."

These words escaped him involuntarily, almost, and he was

____

33 **bail** - a bar that holds something in place, in particular

startled at his own temerity. His face flushed; he was embarrassed.

"You indulge in flattery," she answered, a blush mantling her temples.

"I'm perfectly sincere," he hastened to say, with a boldness that surprised him. "Does it displease you to tell you that you're beautiful?"

"No—that is—but you were thinking of something else, too."

Perhaps. But what were *you* thinking?"

"Of you."

"What of me?"

"I was thinking what an admirable detective you are."

"Indeed!"

"Yes, you are so keen, so far-seeing—so—so suspicious."

He started. What did she mean? He could not fathom it; he was nonplussed.

"*You* are indulging in flattery—or evasion," he said.

"Far from it."

"In irony, then."

"No, indeed. You *are* a detective, aren't you? You told me you belonged to the Secret Service."

"Did I? Well, what of it?"

"What a gallant you are," she cried, petulantly, "praising a lady's beauty, and all the while thinking you've discovered a counterfeit coin."

"I fail to catch your meaning, Miss Haskins."

"Oh, no you don't! You understand me only too well. You think I'm not what I would have you believe—that I'm masquerading."

"And you think the same of me?"

"Well—hardly. You've admitted that you're a detective."

"Have I?"

"Haven't you?"

"I said I'm in the employ of the Government, in the Secret Service department. I might be a mere clerk."

"But you're not."

"No?"

"No."

"And you think it's a case of Greek meeting Greek, eh?"

"Perhaps—yes."

"Each suspicious of the other."

She nodded slowly, then added, "And both mistaken, it may be; at least I sincerely hope so."

There was the ring of sincerity in her voice, and her beautiful eyes fixed full upon his face, were moist with unshed tears. He found it hard to resist the temptation to take her in his arms and tell her that he loved her.

"I must go and write a letter," he muttered huskily, and turned and left the room abruptly.

She seated herself by the window, a curious smile upon her lips—a smile not wholly pleasant to see.

"I thought that little story would start him to talking," she murmured, half aloud. "I was suspicious of him from the first; and now my suspicions are confirmed—in part, at least. He suspects me, I suspect him; he plots, I counterplot. What will come of it all? I must wait—and be wary; and, evidently, he has resolved to do the same. But I'll bring him to my feet, or he's more or less than mortal. He's slowly but surely yielding, still—still—"

She burst into a flood of tears—did this bit of inconsistent femininity!—and, covering her face with her hands, rocked herself to and fro, murmuring brokenly, "I love him—I love him! Spy—detective—whatever he may be, I love him!"

That evening Raymond took the letter he had written to the village. As he walked slowly up the dusty highway, he mused, "It's most provoking; I wish she hadn't read the story. The case had slipped from my mind, and I was content to have it so; but now it's back to perplex and torment me. I hadn't suspected her. But what am I to think now? She reads me a counterfeit bill's defense of itself, manifests an undue interest in the criminal business and asks me many questions. Then, she packs and ships away boxes, by express—boxes that she *says* contains specimens. But the box holding the shells had something *heavier in it*, also."

He lighted a cigar and sauntered on, continuing his cogitations, "Can there be a plant in this vicinity? It's absurd! Where could it be located, and the people not know of it? The place is too thickly settled for anything of the kind. Stuff! What am I thinking of? Miss Haskins a common criminal—educated, refined lady that she is? And yet the woman who passed the coin in the bookstore in Zanesville came down from this valley—at least that's the information I got. But that woman wore glasses; Miss Haskins doesn't. No, it's out of reason. The conductor saw no such woman as the clerk at the bookstore described; and I *know* she didn't come down on the train. Still she may have come by boat. Nonsense! I believe I'm losing my mind; and it all comes of letting the mind run in one groove for years. Here am I suspecting the woman I love of a base crime. I'm worse than the doctor who sacrifices his wife upon the altar of scientific research. I'll drop the whole matter."

It was quite dusk when the detective returned toward Maple Grove Farm. Just as he reached the foot of the lane leading up to the house, he saw two figures standing in the road ahead of him. He noted that one of the two was a woman, but the gloom was too dense to distinguish form or features clearly.

The two were conversing in low, earnest tones and did not become aware of Raymond's approach until he coughed to attract their attention. Then the man hastened down the river road, out of sight; and the woman scurried up the lane, toward the house.

"One of the housemaids keeping tryst with a lover," Raymond thought.

He passed on to the house and on the veranda met Mr. Cassell. "Was that Janey that came in just now?" he inquired of the old gentleman.

"No."

"Ruth?"

"No, Janey an' Ruth's both abed. They was dog-tired, an' went to bed early. That was Miss Haskins that came in. I guess she's been down to the river."

Raymond ascended the stairs to his room. There he flung himself into an easy chair by the window. For hours he sat oblivious to everything but his own burning thoughts. The inmates of the house retired, and the ever busy insects swarmed into the room. Still he sat there, his chin upon his breast. Sometime during the silent watch-es of the night he arose and dragged himself to bed; and the last thought in his mind was of Miss Haskins, and the last word that dropped from his lips was "Myra."

Chapter VIII

The detective arose early next morning. It had rained during the latter part of the night, and the grass was sparkling with thousands of diamond-like drops. He peeked from the window, sniffed the moist, odor-laden air and blinked at the sun peering over the eastern hills. Then he dressed hurriedly and descended to the yard, passed into the lane and walked rapidly toward the river. On reaching the point where the lane opened into the highway, he carefully surveyed the scene, to make sure that he was not observed; then he stooped and pains-takingly examined the ground at his feet.

"The rain's packed the dust and made the tracks more distinct," he muttered. With a small tape-line he took the dimensions of several. "A big man—a number nine shoe;" and he retraced his steps toward the house.

At the gate he saw Janey passing from the kitchen toward the barn yard, with milk-pails in her hand.

"Hello, Janey!" he cried, cheerily, catching up with her. "Going out to milk?"

"Yes, sir," answered the bashful Janey, without looking up.

"May I go along, and help you with the milking?"

"Oh, you can't milk," giggled the girl.

"Can't I! How do you know?"

Janey glanced shyly at him, and tittered: "You're too much of a city dude; it takes country Jakes to know how to milk."

By this time the two had reached the barn yard. Janey began her task, and Raymond stood and watched her. Presently he remarked casually, "Janey, I saw you talking to your beau last night."

"No, you didn't; I hain't got no beau."

"It was Ruth, then."

"Ruth's feller ain't in this part of the country; she writes to him."

"'Though lost to sight, to memory dear.'" Raymond quoted,

laughing.

The girl gave him a puzzled look; evidently she did not catch his meaning.

"I *do* deny it," she answered indignantly. "It wasn't me n'r Ruth; we went to bed re'l early."

"Who could it have been, then?"

"Miss Haskins an' her beau, likely."

Raymond gave a start. "Has Miss Haskins a beau?" he inquired eagerly.

"Of course she has."

"Do you know him?"

"Yes; it's you."

"Me?"

"Yes, sir,"—and Janey tittered at her own witticism.

"Has she any other beau?"

"You'd better ask her—an' not be pryin' 'round me to find out."

The detective's face flushed. He felt that the rebuke was more than half merited. But he did not relinquish his quest; he continued, "She likes Mr. Frank—don't you think so, Janey?"

"I don't know an' I don't care," she replied, sullenly. Then it seemed to dawn upon her that the detective deserved to be teased a little; and she added, "I guess she likes him some."

"Does she talk to him much—of evenings after work?"

"Some, but not as much as she does to Bud Fogle."

Raymond stared hard for a moment; then, asked: "Who's Bud Fogle?"

"One o' the fellers that lives down in the old Chalkly Grafton house."

"Is he a farmer?"

"I ain't a-goin' to tell you no more," she answered, shutting her jaws with a snap. "If you're jealous o' Miss Haskins an' want to spy on her, you can do it; but I won't tell you nothin' more."

A sense of shame assailed the detective, that he should be thus prying into Miss Haskins private affairs; but he parried the assault and sought to move the obstinate Janey from her resolution. His efforts were vain; so he sauntered off to the house, in a dissatisfied frame of mind. While seated upon the southern veranda, he observed a man passing from the back of the house, across the lawn, to the lane leading to the river. He was tall, swarthy and of middle age, apparently. His garb was rough, and a slouch hat and fierce-looking mustache gave him a bandit-like appearance. Upon his arm he carried a basket.

Raymond watched the fellow's broad shoulders disappear over the river bank. A few seconds later the rattle of a chain and the dip of oars came to the detective ears. "Who is the fellow—and what's he doing here?" the officer mused. "I never saw him before—but say! His back and shoulders remind me of those of the man I saw at the foot of the lane, last night. What's he doing here with a basket? I must find out about him."

The farmer came in from the barn, to wash for breakfast, and Raymond accosted him cheerily:

"Good morning, Mr. Cassell. It's a bright and beautiful morning, after the rain."

"Y-e-s," the old man replied dubiously; "but it'll take sever'l hours to dry off enough so's a feller can cut weeds out of the corn."

"But don't you admire the beauty of a morning like this?"

"The morning's purty an' all that," Mr. Cassell admitted; "but the rain makes me lose time—an' I have hands hired, an' want 'em to earn the'r wages."

"I see. Was that one of your men that went down the lane, with a basket, just now?"

"N-o, I guess not. I didn't see him; but I s'pect it was Bud Fogle. He comes here for butter an' milk an' eggs an' such things."

"Bud Fogle?"

"Yes. I'll talk to you soon's I git washed fer breakfast."

Mr. Cassell clumped into the kitchen, and Raymond smiled involuntarily at the sound of spluttering and splashing that soon emanated from the region of the kitchen sink. In a few minutes the old gentleman reappeared, his round face shining like the sunrise. Seating himself upon the edge of the veranda, he took a piece of horn comb from the pocket of his blouse and began to disentangle the snarls in his grizzled beard.

"We was speakin' o' Bud Fogle," he remarked, screwing his

features awry at each stroke of the comb.

Raymond curbed his eagerness, and replied with assumed lack of interest, "Bud Fogle? Oh! yes, so we were. Who is he?"

"I don't hardly know, myself. Him an' two other fellers lives down in the Chalkly Grafton house, an' he comes here to buy some o' their grub."

"Where is this house you speak of?"

"On the lower end o' my place, 'bout a half-mile up Douda Run. You see an ol' man by the name o' Chalkly Grafton used to live in the house—he owned a little piece o' land down there; but he died a long time ago an' the place had to be sold, an' I bought it. The house is a big frame affair an' stands way up at the mouth o' the gulch, and off the road; and nobody, hardly wants to live in it. So it stood empty fer years, till these fellers come along last January an' wanted to rent it. They offered me a fair rent an' I let 'em have it.

"Where are the men from?"

"I don't know—they never said. Fact is they don't say much 'bout the'r affairs, to nobody."

"What's their business, Mr. Cassell?"

"They're inventors. I s'pose that's what you'd call 'em."

"Inventors?"

"Yes."

"What do they invent?" Raymond asked, with a laugh.

The older gentleman leaned over and whispered confidentially: "They're workin' on a new kind o' automobile, they tell me—tryin' to git one that'll run *up* hill with the power it gits runnin' *down* hill. But they're keepin' the matter mighty still—'fraid somebody'll steal the'r idees, they say."

"Are all of them inventors?"

"I guess so. Fogle come first an' rented the house; then, after a week 'r two, the other two come, an' brung a lot o' machin'ry an' stuff with 'em. They must be spendin' a whole lot o' money on the'r c'ntrivance, fer they have stuff shipped to 'em every once in a while. It comes by boat an' is unloaded at the mouth o' the run. They've paid me fer havin' sever'l loads hauled fer 'em; an' I know it must be costly truck, 'cause one load was put off the boat in the night an' they wouldn't leave it lay out but must have it hauled up right away."

"Have you ever called upon them, Mr. Cassell?"

The old man chuckled: "Jest once. Guess from the way they act an' have from what they say, they ain't anxious to have visitors; don't want to be bothered, I reckon. But one day I was over on the run huntin' some sheep that had got out o' the hill pastor, and Fogle saw me an' invited me in."

"Did you see their tools and machinery?"

"Yes, but two other fellers was at work when me an' Fogle went in. They had one room fixed up fer a workshop an' was workin' at their automobile. They had lots o' tools an' things that I didn't know the use n'r names of, an' wheels an' chains an' belts till you couldn't rest."

"Were they *making* an auto?"

"Well, no—not right then they wasn't, anyhow. They said they's experimentin' to git a wheel that would overcome the dead-center; but I ain't no more idee'n the man in the moon what they meant."

"I understand. Were the other two men young or old?"

"Oldish like, both of 'em. The one that Fogle called George was a little hump-shouldered, bow-legged feller with a stubby gray mustache an' a bald head. I don't think he often leaves the place, 'cause I ain't seen him sence. The other one Fogle called Bob, an' he has long gray whiskers an' wears specs. Him an' Fogle fishes an' hunts a good 'eal; but the other one must work *all* the time."

Ruth, the black-eyed, buxum hired-girl, was spreading the cloth for breakfast and casting admiring, coquettish glances at the detective, every time she came out upon the veranda; but he— hardened sinner! was so much interested in what his host was telling that he was not aware, even, of the pretty young thing's presence. This want of appreciation on Raymond's part seemed inexcusable to the rosy-cheeked Ruth; and, tossing her black curls disdainfully, she vowed:, "The stuckup! I'll get even with him. He's so stuck on Miss Haskins he doesn't know there's anybody else in the world. I'll get even with them both, some day—the haunty, distant things!"

Raymond wanted to ask Mr. Cassell a few direct questions in

regard to the tools and machinery in the workshop at the Grafton house; but he feared he might arouse suspicion in the old gentleman's mind, so he curbed his ardent desire and changed the subject.

Miss Haskins came down to breakfast, looking as cool and fresh as the morning. She and Raymond greeted each other pleasantly, at which the buxom Ruth tilted her little nose aloft and Frank Cassell scowled darkly.

"What are you going to do this forenoon, Miss Haskins?" Raymond asked, as they seated themselves at the table.

"I've an errand to the village. I'll be at your service this afternoon, however."

"All right," he laughed. "If I can't have what I desire, I must desire what I have."

"What do you think of doing until noon?" she asked.

"I hardly know; I think I'll take a ramble down the river." And he bent a searching look upon her, but she appeared unconscious of it and went on stirring her chocolate.

An hour after breakfast Raymond sauntered down the lane toward the river. On reaching the highway he paused long enough to take the measurement of Bud Fogle's fresh footprints. Then, with bent head and thoughtful face, he set off *up* the river. Barely had the detective disappeared around a bend in the road, when a crouching form arose from the corner of a neighboring corn-field. It was Frank Cassell.

"Confound you!" He muttered. "If you had staid[34] away, I might have won her. And you're a sneaking dog! You were measuring Bud Fogle's tracks, eh! I wonder what for. Well, I'll take great pleasure in telling him about it; and, if I'm not badly mistaken, he'll call you to account. I'd like to stand by and see him hammer the life out of you. If I had *my* way you wouldn't stay here another day." Then the angry young man picked up the scythe he had dropped and resumed his task of cutting the tall weeds in the fence-corners.

Raymond proceeded up the dusty road at a dilatory[35] pace. The highway was shaded by trees upon the river-bank; and the atmo-

---

34 **staid** – variation of stayed
35 **dilatory** - inclined to waste time and lag behind

sphere, cleared and purified by the night's rain, was deliciously cool and sweet. Birds were singing in the trees near at hand and the roar of the distant dam was a subdued and soothing sound. Reaching a point where a spreading beech sheltered the bank of green sod, Raymond stopped and cast a hasty glance around.

The branches of the tree drooped in such a manner as to form a canopy around the gnarled trunk, and into the shady retreat the detective crept. Seating himself with his back to the tree and his face to the road, he patiently waited and watched, absorbed in thought.

"I might have had some doubt," he muttered, half aloud, "if Cassell hadn't described Fogle's companions to me—and told me their names. But now the thing's absurdly plain; I almost wish it wasn't. The two are George Crogan and Bob Stoneman—'Denver George' and 'Professor Bob'— two of the sharpest, most desperate crooks we've ever had to deal with. I've thought for months it was a little odd those two were keeping so quiet."

He made a move to light a cigar but returned it to his pocket, smiling. "'Twon't do," he muttered. "Somebody might smell me out. Let's see! Stoneman was discharged from Sing-Sing, not quite a year ago; and Crogan is still wanted for the part he took in that affair down at Nashville. That accounts for his sticking so close to the plant over at Douda Run; he's afraid of being nipped. But who is this man Fogle? He's a new one—to me, at least. It's a good thing for me that I never worked on a case that Crogan and Stoneman were connected with; it wouldn't be safe for me to stay here twenty-four hours. They'd murder me on sight."

He sat staring at the ground for some time. At last he sadly shook his head, murmuring, "Too bad—too bad! Such a splendid creature—such a talented and refined woman! I can hardly believe my senses; yet the case is as plain as the sun above me. I wish I hadn't come here—I wish I'd never met her. My God! I love her, and she is in league with those I must bring to justice. Can I love such a woman? Can I! I *do*—with my whole soul. What am I to do? She meets Fogle at dusk and holds a secret conference with him. She's one of the go-betweens to place the stuff in circulation. I can't disguise the truth, if I would. I don't know what to do.

Shall I leave, and turn the case over to others? No, that won't do! She'd be apprehended and sent to the penitentiary. I must save her. But can I—will she *be* saved? I wish I knew whether she loves me. Was ever a poor devil in such a predicament? I must and *will* do my duty—and yet—and yet—oh, curse the luck! What *am* I to do?

For more than an hour he sat there, pondering, resolving—and re-resolving; constructing plans of procedure, only to tear them piece-meal and fashion others. A scowl was upon his handsome face; his heart was sorely troubled. He was an honest, conscientious mortal, was Claude Raymond; and the debate in his mind was giving him the keenest of mental anguish.

At last he was aroused by the sound of wheels upon the dust-white road.

Chapter IX

The detective peered from his leafy retreat and saw Miss Haskins approaching in her cart. Her red-brown hair shone like burnished copper in the sunlight, and her opaline eyes, gazing straight ahead of her, were fixed upon vacancy. Evidently she was busy with her own thoughts and oblivious to her surroundings. Raymond's heart beat with unwanted rapidity, as he looked upon her; he thought he had never seen her so enchantingly lovely.

This sleek little mare jogged along at an easy trot, and the cart and its occupant disappeared from sight. Then Raymond stretched himself full length upon the moist sod and, burying his face upon his folded arms, lay silent and motionless. In the course of an hour the young woman repassed his hiding place, at the same gentle speed.

The detective crawled from his shady nook and, stretching his cramped limbs, muttered, "She took that box to the express office. I know she had it in the cart; her skirts didn't completely conceal it. I'll walk up to the village and learn where she sent it."

A few minutes later he walked into the express office and asked brusquely, "Any package for Claude Raymond?"

"I *think* not; let me look," the agent replied affably, as he fluttered the bunch of bills in his hand.

Raymond took the opportunity to gaze about him and soon discovered the object of his concern—the box in which he had seen the mussel shells, on which he had nailed the lid. It was sitting upon the scales—the shipping direction not yet dry upon it. Raymond read as follows:

"Mrs. Sarah H. Ormsby.

Pittsburgh, Penn.

No. 471 Blank St."

Turning to the agent, impatience in his voice, the detective asked, "Nothing for me?"

"Nothing for you."

Raymond immediately left the office, a bitter smile flickering about his lips.

"They are playing a bold game," he murmured, as he directed his steps toward the telegraph office. "Mrs. Ormsby is another link in the chain of evidence. Four seventy-one Blank Street is near Gimp's home, or a fictitious personage. It doesn't matter; the box is meant for Gimp. I'll let it go through; it'll allay suspicion. But I'll *know* what's in the next one before it starts. I know where I heard the name Haskins now, and I know who Miss Haskins is. She's Gimp's sister-in-law; and that slick scoundrel's got her into this thing. He's fooled her, or forced her; I can't believe she's a criminal from choice—I *won't* believe it. And I must save her in some way—in spite of herself if necessary, but I must make no mistake; I've got a bad lot to deal with."

He reached the telegraph office and sent the following cipher dispatch.

"Secret Service Department,

Washington, D. C.

Travis:

Send good man to Pittsburgh at once—Kennard, if possible. He will await instructions at Bloxom House. Hot trail.

Raymond."

Then he wrote a letter of instructions for the man whom Travis would send to Pittsburgh, mailed it, and set out upon his return to the farmhouse.

Sometime after Raymond and Miss Haskins had left the place, Frank Cassell threw down his scythe and sauntered around to the kitchen, for a drink of water. Ruth was scalding milk-pans at the sink and singing as she worked. Young Cassell, after slaking his thirst, turned to her; and, playfully chucking her under the chin, cried, "Come, Ruthie, let's have a kiss."

The girl's black eyes flashed fire. "No, you don't, Mr. Frank Cassell. You can't sawder me. You're awful good right now, since Miss Haskins has throwed you over for that city chap. Before she done that you couldn't *see* me." And the pretty Ruth pouted her rosy lips scornfully.

"That's all right," young Cassell laughed. "I wanted Miss Haskins, and you was sweet on Mr. Raymond; and we both got left. Now let's be sensible, and make up. What do you say?"

Ruth gave him a searching look, and replied, "You're tryin' to fool me."

"I'm not!"

"You love Miss Haskins."

"I *hate* her—and I hate Raymond more. There's nothing I wouldn't do—that I dare to do—to get even with them."

A pleased expression crept into the girl's face; and she answered, "I'm just like you, I despise both of 'em—the proud and stuckup things!"

Young Cassell came close to her and, putting his arms around her lissome waist, whispered: "Ruth, I love you better than anyone else on earth—that's the solemn truth; and I want to get even with that sneak, Raymond, and you can help me. Will you?"

A shade of suspicion spread over Ruth's features. Disengaging herself from his embrace, she said, "You want me to help you do somethin' mean ag'inst Mr. Raymond, so's you can have Miss Haskins all to yourself. You can't fool me—I know you!"

He caught her to him again, crying sharply: "Listen, you little fool! I tell you I hate both of them, like poison. I want to get rid of them—and you can help me. Raymond's here for no good. I don't know what his business is, but he's a sneak of *some* kind; for I caught him measuring Bud Fogle's tracks this morning, and he went *up* the river, just after telling Miss Haskins at the breakfast table that he was going *down* the river. He's spying on her and Fogle, for some purpose."

Ruth's black eyes sparkled; and, clapping her hands, she cried, "Oh! An' he was askin' questions of Janey, this mornin', 'bout Miss Haskins; wanted to know if Miss Haskins had a beau an' all that. Janey told me when we was washin' the dishes. An' he just asked the most questions of y'r father, too—about Bud Fogle an' the other men down at the Chalkly Grafton House."

Frank Cassell was elated. He kissed Ruth—who did not offer serious objections—and said to her, in low, cautious tones, "Look here, Ruth! There's something rotten about this whole affair. I've had my suspicions about those fellows down on Douda Run, for some time. They claim to be inventors—but stuff! They're up to no good. I believe this Raymond's a detective; and I want to spoil his little game. At the same time, you—we want to get rid of Miss Haskins. Now, I'll tell you how we'll work it. I'll let Fogle know about Raymond's mysterious maneuvers; and you let Miss Haskins know. Then things will come to a crisis. If Fogle and his men ain't all straight, they'll take the alarm and leave; and Raymond will follow them. Miss Haskins is connected with Fogle, in some way—I know that—and she'll skip, too. Sh! Here comes mother. Will you do what I want you to? Say quick!"

"Y-e-s," Ruth whispered; and Cassell kissed her again. He returned to his work, chuckling to himself, "The little fool! I can wind her around my finger. Ah! my friend Raymond, when Bud Fogle becomes aware of your true mission here, he'll make it warm for you—too warm for you to stay in these parts. Then I'll have sweet Myra all to myself; and I know enough of her doings to *force* her to do as I desire. I've not been asleep all these months; it's not specimens alone my sweet lady ships away. And why has she visited Douda Run so many times, with that convenient tin box? I *know* a few things!"

When Miss Haskins returned from the village, she went straight to her room and sat down to peruse a letter she had received. There

Ruth, making a pitcher of water an excuse for her presence, came to deliver the bundle of information with which Frank Cassell had commissioned her. Miss Haskins calmly waited until the girl had finished her rambling recital; then she replied, icily, "You're expressing concern over something that doesn't interest me, in the least. *I* have nothing to do with Mr. Raymond's words or actions; and I don't care to hear anything further. You may retire."

And the discomfited Ruth descended the stairs, humiliated and enraged.

Raymond returned at eleven o'clock, and the entire company assembled at dinner and chatted as pleasantly as though nothing out of the ordinary was in the mind of any one of them. The surface of the stream of conversation flowed bright and sparkling, and gave no hint of the mad undercurrent—black with hate and jealousy—surging beneath.

After dinner the elder Cassell said to his son, "Frank, did you get them weeds all cut?"

The son gave an affirmative answer, and the father continued, "Well, I want you to go down to the lower bottom this afternoon, an' fix that fence along the road. Ther's danger o' stock gitting in the corn."

"All right," was the mumbled reply. And young Cassell procured hachet and nails, and set out.

The mouth of the Douda Run was about a mile down the river from the Cassell homestead, and the fence Frank Cassell went to repair was near there. In the course of an hour he had completed his task and was just setting out upon his return journey, when he became aware of two men sitting under the willows along the river bank. Cassell immediately recognized the two as Fogle and Stoneman, and sauntered in their direction.

"Hello, Bud," he cried cheerily. "Catching anything?"

Fogle silently shook his head, his eyes fixed upon his line.

"Pretty warm," Cassell ventured next.

"Yes," was the curt reply.

"I know a fellow who can beat you fishing, Bud."

"Do you?" Fogle answered carelessly, as he arose and began to wind up his line.

"Yes, our new boarder, Raymond. He's fishing to catch Miss Haskins, and it seems he's in a fair way to succeed."

Fogel gave the speaker a searching look but made no reply; and Cassell was disconcerted. He had expected the inventor to take some interest in Raymond's doings. However, he went on: "You don't appear to care much about Raymond's business; but he does about yours, I can tell you."

"Does he?" answered Fogle, with so little animation as to suggest the idea that he asked the question simply to have something to say.

Cassell was puzzled. He could not understand Fogle's lack of interest in a subject so directly concerning him. So the incautious youngster continued, "Yes, he does. He measured your footprints, and asked all kinds of questions about you and your business."

"If it does him any good, let him do it; it does me no harm." And Fogel moved along the bank to a more favorable spot for fishing, thus intimating that the interview was at an end. But Cassell was not easily rebuffed; and he followed, saying, "I wouldn't have a fellow meddling in my business in that way. If I were you I'd call him to account."

Fogle dropped his pole and stood motionless for a moment. Then he turned upon the speaker, his black mustache bristling, and his eyes blazing wrathfully. "You wouldn't do anything of the kind, you cowardly cur!" he snarled. "If you've a quarrel to settle with Raymond go settle it, like a man. *I've* nothing against him—I don't even know him. Now, get away from here."

Crestfallen and thoroughly angry, Cassell slunk away; and Fogle resumed his fishing.

In the meantime a more animated conversation was taking place upon the lawn at the farmhouse—one that for a time promised to have as dramatic an ending. As Raymond and Miss Haskins quit the dinner table, she inquired, "Can I help to amuse you this afternoon?"

"Yes."

"In what way? Shall we take a ramble or a boat ride?"

"It's too hot."

"For once our views coincide. What shall we do?"

"Will you read to me?"

"Will I?" with lifted brows. "Did I ever refuse to inflict such punishment upon you?"

"Punish me again," he laughed. "Read me something soul-searching and soul-satisfying; I've had a bad attack of the blue-devils today."

"You're beset by the blue-devils? So am I. But I'll act as exorcist. What shall I read, now, as part of the rite?"

"How would something from Heine do?"

She started perceptibly; and their eyes met.

"Or something from *Lucile*?" she said slowly—a world of expression in her beautiful eyes searching his face.

"Either will please me," he answered, unflinchingly meeting her direct gaze.

Then a painful silence fell upon them, during which each strove to scare the other out of countenance, apparently. She was the first to speak.

"I'll read you some of Heine's poems," she murmured, with dry lips.

"Very well," he managed to say.

She went to her room for the book, and on her return joined him under the maples in front of the house. After she had read a number of poems, he remarked suddenly, "Does the book contain a portrait of the author?"

"Yes," and she handed him the book, open at the frontispiece.

He took the volume, glanced at the author's picture, and said, "He looks like a fancy poet *should* look." Then he returned the book to her hand. But he had seen the Zanesville bookseller's stamp upon a fly-leaf.

"Now, let's talk," she said. "Where were you this before noon?"

"Down at the river."

"You went *up* the road, after telling me you were going *down*."

"Yes."

"Why did you?"

"I had business in that direction."

"Why did you tell me you were going down the river?"

"Well," he said, slowly, "I didn't want you to know *where* I was going."

"I found out."

"So it appears. How?"

"In the same way I found out that you measured Bud Fogle's footprints."

Raymond opened wide his eyes and stared blankly. He was taken completely aback. Miss Haskins appeared to enjoy his amazement; she clapped her soft white hands and laughed merrily. But the stern line of the detective's message did not relax.

"Will you tell me how you came to know all this?" he asked.

"No," she declared, flatly. Then she countered: "Why did you measure Fogle's footprints?"

"I wanted to know if he was the man you were talking to at the foot of the lane last night."

Miss Haskins sat erect in the hammock, her eyes flashing: "You dared!" she cried. "Are you my keeper?"

"No," he answered coolly; "I wish I were, though. I wouldn't tolerate another lover."

"Another lover?"

"Yes."

"I have *none.*"

"You have *one.*"

"Who—who is it?"

"I."

"Mr. Raymond!" was all she could say.

"Yes, I love you, Myra."

This he said with a ring of true passion in his voice. Her eyes were wet with tears as she replied tremulously, "Don't—please don't say that; don't say anything more of the kind, or I'll go into the house."

"I'll say no more, if it displeases you; but the truth's out. Will you answer me one question?"

She nodded.

"What is Bud Fogle to you?"

"Absolutely nothing."

"Why did you meet him?"

"How did you know I did?" She had recovered her composure in part and asked the question with a show of her usual cool self-possession.

"Well, I *know* it," he replied; "know it as well as I know you have a copy of 'Vanity Fair' in your room."

"And how—how do you know *that*?" she faltered.

"Perhaps I saw it in your bookcase."

"No, you didn't. It has been in the drawer of my dressing-case, ever since the day I bought it—along with a copy of *Lucile* and this book of Heine's poems. Now, tell me how you knew I had them. Did you ransack my apartment?"

"You don't think that," he said reproachfully.

"No, I don't. But answer my question."

"At another time."

"Well, answer this, *now*. *Are* you a detective?"

"Yes."

She paled to the lips, and a hunted look crept into her eyes.

"I—I believe I'll go to my room," she murmured, almost in audibly.

He did not seek to detain her; and she turned away and entered the house.

Chapter X

The Chalkly Granfton house was a barn-like structure and in a dilapidated condition, standing on the bank of Douda Run, about a half-mile from the river. At the point where the house stood the little valley narrowed to a deep and dark ravine or gulch, and rock-ribbed, precipitous hills rose on both sides. The building was old—very old; and time and elements had sportively[36] twisted and warped it, curled shingles and weather-boards and played havoc with windows and doors.

It was a two-story structure, with three or four rooms on each floor and flag-paved cellar extending under the whole of it. An immense stone chimney had its origin in the basement and overtopped the comb by three feet. The building was upon a gently sloping elevation, a few hundred yards from the high road, which at this point

------

36 **sportively** - fond of or full of sport or merriment; playful

left the valley and climbed the hill on the opposite side of the brook.

It was evening, and Bud Fogle and his two companions sat in one of the rooms on the first floor, engaged in earnest conversation. The soft night air stole in at the open casement, bringing with it the moist odor of the woodland and the babble of the purling[37] brook. The condition of the atmosphere indicated rain; distant sounds could be heard with startling distinctiveness. Bullfrogs down at the brook-side croaked dolorously[38], and a katydid in the big elm at the corner of the house made night hideous with its rasping complaint. A small lamp upon the table where the men had eaten their evening meal dimly lighted the room, leaving the remote corners in dense shadow. The three men were puffing away at short black pipes, and the smell of rank tobacco smoke overpowered all other odors and scared away all venturesome nocturnal insects.

"When did young Cassell tell you this, Bud?" Stoneman was asking.

"Today," Fogle answered, filling his pipe, which had burned out.

"His communication, taken in connection with the letter Ms. Haskins received from Gimp, leaves no room for doubt. Raymond is a detective and is here to make us trouble."

"Professor Bob" readjusted his spectacles, thoughtfully stroked his long gray beard and was silent.

Crogan removed his pipe from his half-toothless gums, spat upon the floor, and meditatively passing his hand over his bald head, said, "Right you are, Pr'fessor. Gimp says in de letter to de young woman dat de feller w'at was nosin' round de bank was named Raymond. Cuss Gimp! If he hadn't overshot de mark by being too smart, dere wouldn't 'ave been nobody *nosin'* round. But Gimp wants to save hisself in case anythin' happens. *I* can read Gimp!"

Crogan relighted his pipe, which had gone out through neglect, and continued, "I'll bet ten as good dollars as was ever shoved by de perfesh dat dis Raymond is de same chap dat run down Mickey Clayton an' Bill Godfrey, up at Portland, a few

---

37 **purling** - flowing with a swirling motion and babbling sound
38 **dolorous** - mournful

years ago. An' if he *is*, he's one o' de slickest men dere is on de force—dat's all. Raymond—Raymond; it sounds to me like de same name. Its' de same man—course it is. An' he's a houn' to smell ou t'ings an' a bulldog to hang on w'en he gits a holt; so de best t'ing *we* can do is to send in his resignation fer him—an' do it soon an' quick."

"That's my opinion, exactly," Stoneman mumbled, without removing his pipe from his lips.

"What do you mean?" Fogle inquired in a hard, cold tone.

Crogan and Stoneman exchanged glances, and the Irishman facetiously winked one of his red and watery eyes. Then he remarked, "Bob, let me have another nip from dat bottle. I can talk better w'en my whistle's wet."

"It seems to require a good deal of wetting to keep it in order," Fogle grumbled. "But I want to know what you two mean by 'handing in Raymond's resignation.' Speak out."

Stoneman did not offer a reply. Crogan took a drink of liquor, wiped his lips upon the back of his rough hand, coughed apologetically and said, "We mean just dis: Raymond's a detective; he's onto our game, an' he's here to give us trouble. Dere's no scarin' him off—he ain't built dat way; an' de best t'ing we can do is help him let loose right quick."

"Do you mean we must persuade him to abandon the 'case?'" Fogle asked.

"Persuade!" Crogan chuckled hoarsely. "Come—dat's *too* good."

"Then what the hell *do* you mean—that we shall frighten him off?" Fogle cried, irritably.

At this both Crogan and Stoneman laughed uproariously; and the former said sneeringly:

"Oh, yes; we mean to frighten him, we do! Let's start right out tonight an' tell him we mean to take a stick to him. He'll never stop runnin'—*he* won't!"

Fogle brought his hand down upon the table, with a crash that made the dishes dance and jingle, shouting, "I don't want any more of your cursed fooling! What do you *mean*?"

"We mean to *kill* him," Crogan answered coolly.

Fogle sprang to his feet, his eyes ablaze; and shaking his fist in Crogan's face, thundered, "No, you don't—not while I'm around! I told you two scoundrels—"

Crogan also leapt to his feet, a dangerous light in his red eyes, and interrupted, "Draw it mild dere, pardner—none o' y'r hard names! Dey don't go, see?"

But Fogle drew himself to full height, stiffened his muscles, struggled a moment with his tempestuous temper, and said quietly—but without a tremor of fear, "You are infernal scoundrels—and I'm not afraid to fling it in your teeth! There—none of your threatening gestures; just wait till I'm through. Then, if you want satisfaction, you can have your fill of it."

He dropped his voice to a lower and milder tone, and went on: "I told you when I joined you in this enterprise, I was willing to give up my honor, my manhood, my position as master pattern-maker in the Pittsburgh shops and take the risk of serving a term in the penitentiary. I was discouraged with hard work and poor pay, and I was hungry for a chance to make money—and lots of it. But I plainly told you that I wouldn't stand for any crime but counterfeiting; and I meant what I said. I'm willing to defraud the government; but I won't have murder done—not if the last one of us spends his days in the penitentiary."

Crogan sat dumbfounded, offering not a word in reply; but Stoneman took a pull at the bottle, smacked his bearded lips, and said softly and soothingly, "Come, Fogle, don't be sentimental and squeamish. Sentiment and business don't go well together—especially in *this* business. Look at me! I used to be a professor in the schools, years ago; but like you I grew tired of the drudgery, and made up my mind to make money— literally *make* it. Well, I've been in prison a number of times and maybe again before I die; but I learned that the way to keep out is to let nobody meddle with my business. Our safety depends upon having this man Raymond out of our way; and there's no way of getting him out, but to *kill* him—and hide the job."

Fogle's voice was again cold and inflexible, as he answered:

"You'll never kill him—or anyone else—with *my* help or consent; and if I learn of your doing such a thing, I'll help to bring you to justice, if I swing for it. Do you suppose for a moment that Miss Haskins would countenance such a thing? You know as well as I that Gimp deceived her to get her into this thing and that he has resorted to the threat of exposure and imprisonment to keep her at it. Kill Raymond and she'll have us hung—that's all. Besides, what good will it do to kill the detective?"

"Just dis," Crogan snarled: "Put Raymond out of de way, an' we can go on shovin' de stuff, fer quite a spell, w'ile de gover'ment's wonderin' w'at's become o' him. Dey know where he is, but dey *don't* know w'at he's found out; 'cause it ain't de habit o' dem chaps to blow dere game till de trap's all ready to spring. Over dere in Washin'ton dey'll t'ink he's lost de scent an' is huntin' it some'rs else; an' dey won't make no move fer quite a spell, waitin' to hear from him. It'll give us plenty o' time to shape up ev'ryt'ing wid Gimp an' cut loose from him an' de gal an' start in a new place. An' I's had enough o' Gimp's way o' doin' business; he's all fer Gimp an' nobody else."

"I can't see what good can come of the killing," Fogle insisted, stubbornly. "In the first place, Raymond don't know we have a plant here—"

"Oh, don't he?" Crogan interrupted with a sneer.

"No."

"W'at's he here fer, den?"

"He's here taking an outing."

"Seems to be workin' purty hard durin' his vacation." And Crogan and Stoneman both laughed.

Fogle bit his lip, and continued, "He may *suspicion* what we have here, but he don't know; and while he's trying to find out, we can gather up our stuff and slip away."

"Oh, yes—course we can!" Crogan sneered. "De detective's here fer his health, an' he ain't watchin' ev'ry move we make—oh, no! Don't you t'ink it fer a minute; he knows w'at he's doin'—dat bloke does. You ain't had de experience wid dem fellers dat I's had. By dis time he's got a pal in Pittsburg shadderin' Gimp—Raymond has; an' he's only waitin' to make de connections an' den he'll bag de whole outfit—Gimp, de gal, an' all. Naw, Fogle, me boy, you's got to leave dis job to older hands at de biz, we'll all do time fer it. An' wid one term starin' me in de face I ain't takin' no chances. I's tired o' runnn'; an' I'll do some fightin' 'fore I give in dis time."

"And you mean to kill Raymond?" Fogle asked, quietly.

"Of course," Crogan answered, coolly.

Fogle's eyes flashed dangerously.

"If there's any killing done, I'll take no part," he said.

"All right," Crogan replied, carelessly. "It's a game more'n one can play at." Then, his anger rising, "but if you set in dat game, you want to keep y'r eyes on de dealer—dat's all."

"Here—here!" Stoneman called out. "We can't afford to be fighting among ourselves. Fogle, you must give in; our safety depends upon this step."

The younger man was silent for some moments. Then he exclaimed passionately: "I wish to God I had never seen any of you!"

"An' I wish dat I'd never seen you—n'r Gimp, n'r de gal," Crogan cried, with an oath. "Dis trouble all comes of de perfesh associatin' wid amatoors. You ain't got no blood in y'r veins, Fogle—it's just milk an' water. I's goin' to save my own napper, I is, an' de rest o' you can do w'at you pleases."

"And I'm going to save myself and the plant, too—if the killing of the detective will do it," Stoneman remarked in a matter of fact way.

"And as for me," Fogle said in a low, suppressed tone of voice, "I'll shoot the man through the heart who kills Raymond. I'll—"

"Hist!" whispered Crogan. "I hear someone 'r somethin' movin' in de weeds out dere."

Fogle walked over to the window and looked out. The room in which the three were seated was at the back of the house and the window opened out upon the steep hillside. Presently the younger man returned to his companions, and whispered; "I saw something moving up the hillside, and I'm going out to see who or what it is."

With those words he passed through the door, disappearing in the darkness. Crogan leaned toward Stoneman, muttering, "W'at's de matter wid dat cuss, anyhow?"

"He possesses one of those wholly useless inconveniences known as a conscience," Stoneman chuckled in reply. Then, soberly: "We're going to have no end of trouble with him, if we don't let him have his way; and if we *do* let him have it, we'll land in the penitentiary."

"Let him have his way—an' play checkers wid our noses?" Crogan snarled, ending with an oath. "Not by a plenty! I'll kill him an' de detective both an' burn dere bodies in dis ol' shackletrap, 'fore I'l be took. Dere ain't no use a-talkin'—"

"Sh!" cautioned Stoneman, his finger on his lips. "Not so loud; I think I hear Bud coming back. Now, I'll tell you what we must do, Crogan. We must do away with Raymond without Fogal knowing it—if that's possible. Then, if he finds out what we've done and kicks up a rumpus, we'll—we'll know what to do. Not another word! Here he comes."

Fogle stepped into the room and, seating himself, remarked, "There was somebody out there; and he disappeared over the hill, in the direction of the village."

"The detective!" his companions exclaimed, in a breath.

"I don't know," Fogle answered; "I saw nothing of him but his back."

"Course it was him," Crogan cried irritably. "But 'cordin' to you he was just takin' an evenin' stroll for his health. Oh, no; we ain't got not'ing to fear from him!"

A half hour later the three had retired and the big house was wrapped in darkness.

The man Fogle had seen prowling upon the hillside was indeed Raymond. As he passed Miss Haskins' door on his return to the farmhouse, he saw her sitting at her table, writing. She was clad in a loose wrapper, and her hair fell in a rippling cascades about her shoulders and waist. One daintily slippered foot peeped from the folds of her skirt, and one bejeweled hand shielded her eyes from the light, as she wrote. Raymond paused, attracted by her beauty. She was unaware of his presence, apparently, and wrote on. He stood watching her for several minutes, all the love and passion of his strong nature ablaze. At last he coughed to attract her attention, and she sprang up, with a startled cry: "Why, Claude—Mr. Raymond! How you frightened me!" He walked into the room, unbidden and taking a chair, motioned her to be seated. Then he said, "I'm sorry I startled you. But whom are you writing to?"

"Mr. Raymond! What a question!"

"Say 'Claude,'— then,"—with a jerky laugh.

"Myra, you're writing to your brother-in-law, Harold P. Gimp, of Pittsburgh."

She stared hard at him, wonder and admiration in her eyes.

At last she murmured, almost inaudibly: "Yes, I'm writing to my brother-in-law, Harold P. Gimp, of Pittsburgh."

"Myra," he went on, earnestly, "I told you today that I love you." She put up her hand in protest; but he continued: "I wanted to save you from yourself—from your own rash folly. But tonight I know more of the true state of affairs, and I change my plea. Let me save you from Gimp. The inevitable is rapidly approaching; and Gimp and the others will pay the penalty of their crime. But I would save *you*—I love you! Won't you let me?"

She turned very white; and, hiding her face in her hands, moaned, "Don't say anymore—please don't! I've gone too far; I—I can't turn back. Please, please leave me! You must not be seen in my room, at this time of night."

"Pardon my thoughtlessness," he answered quietly, almost coldly. "I didn't think of that. Good night."

She made no further replies, and he withdrew.

Chapter XI

Several days passed, and Raymond did not spring his trap. He had two good and sufficient reasons for his delay. He desired to save Miss Haskins, and he desired to make sure of his evidence against the others. He had seen very little of Myra since the evening interview in her room. She held aloof; but he noted, when they did meet, that she was less buoyant than usual and that her face wore a distressed and haggard expression.

"Curse the luck!" he muttered, grumblingly, as he sat alone in the dusk of his room one evening. "Things get worse instead of better. I'm a fool, no doubt, to delay matters on her account. Probably she doesn't care a straw for me; but I care for her—and that's the worst of it. I can't bear the idea of ruining her life, since I have learned what I have. I flatter myself that I played it pretty cunningly upon Fogle and his pals, the other night; they hadn't the least idea that I was hid in those tall weeds back of the house, and overheard all they said. It appears that Fogle was honey-fugled[39] into the business, too, and that his soul revolts at the thought of violence and bloodshed. So much the better for me; there's one less to fear and avoid. But look out for Crogan and Stoneman! No conscientious scruples keep that pair of worthies awake of nights. They'll kill me at the first opportunity; and they'll not rest easy till the opportunity presents itself. Well, fore-warned is fore-armed."

He lighted a cigar, elevated his feet upon the window-sill, and mused on, "But there's no use in fuming and fretting, I can't strike the blow till things are ready at both ends of the line. I must wait till I hear from Kennard—or whoever Travis has sent to Pittsburg. If Kennard is there, then everything is all right; I've worked with him before. Well, I won't have long to wait; Miss Haskins sent her letter to 'Mrs. Sarah H Ormsby,' three days ago; and this morning she sent another box to the same mysterious personage. As soon as Kennard has determined the contents of box and letter, I shall hear from him—probably tomorrow or the next day. Then things must come to a crisis. The only thing that concerns me about the Pittsburg work is that I'm afraid Travis may not have sent Kennard to do it."

He knocked the ashes from his cigar, and continued, "I must come to an understanding with Myra—and at once. I'm sure she isn't in sympathy with the dirty work she's helping to do; she *can't* be—the thought is preposterous! But Gimp has her in his power, and she fears him. Does she love me—or *doesn't* she? I wish I knew— and I *must* know!" Then, with sudden resolve: "I'll go and ask her

---

39 **honey-fugled** - duped, deceived, or swindled

at once."

With Raymond, to resolve was to act. He arose, crossed the hall, and knocked upon Miss Haskins' door. Receiving no response, he turned the knob and entered the room. It was in perfect order, but Miss Haskins was not there.

"How thoughtless of me not to remember that she went to the village," he muttered, and turned to retire.

At the door he paused irresolutely, murmuring: "It's a detestable act to contemplate; but it's in the line of duty—and for her good. I'll do it!"

He returned to the room and began a thorough search of it. He examined the things upon the table, peeked into the cabinet, tried the drawers of the bookcase and chiffonier[40] and looked under the bed in the sleeping apartment. The drawers were locked, and he discovered nothing unusual. Of a sudden he heard footsteps ascending the stairs; and he started, and mentally began to frame an excuse for being in the room.

"This will do," he muttered, taking a book from the table.

In the hall he came face to face with the black-eyed Ruth.

"I've been in Miss Haskins' room, to borrow a book," he remarked, carelessly, as he passed her.

He went on to his own quarters, dropped into a chair and listlessly turned the leaves of the volume—wondering why Miss Haskins had not yet returned from the village. An envelope dropped from the book and fell upon the floor. In a preoccupied, mechanical way, he recovered it, returned it to its place, and went on turning the pages. Suddenly, however, he stopped—and turned back to the envelope. It bore the Pittsburg postmark and was addressed, "Miss Myra Haskins, Malta, Ohio," in the crabbed handwriting of one unaccustomed to wielding a pen. Raymond withdrew the enclosure and found it typewritten throughout—even to the signature. It ran:

Pittsburg, Penn., July 7, 18—.

"Miss Myra Haskins, Malta, Ohio:

Let's have an understanding, once for all. You say I deceived you, that you're sick of the whole thing, and that you're going to quit. I've heard all

---

40 **chiffonier** - a tall chest of drawers, often with a mirror on top

that before—and have answered it too. However, I'll answer it again.

"In regard to my deceiving you: I told you the truth in the beginning, and if you have blindly misinterpreted my words, I am not to blame. I told you the silver dollars you were to help put in circulation were genuine dollars. So they are—almost. They contain within a few grains of the requisite amount of silver, they are of the usual size and appearance, and to all intents and purposes they are as good as any dollar. Many good people believe that the government should again grant free-coinage privileges to the owners of silver bullion; we have *taken* the privilege that the government has not seen fit to *grant*. You say the coins are counterfeit. That's an ethical question that it would be idle to discuss.

"As to your being sick of the work: If I remember right, at the time I offered you the position—and persuaded you to take it, if you wish to put it that way—you were sick of the drudgery of school work. Now you are anxious to return to it. It seems to me that you are just a little over particular—just a little uncertain in your mind about what you really desire to do.

"You say you are going to quit the business. I would impress upon your mind that you are absolutely in my power and that you *dare not quit*. I have laid my plans too well to protect myself; I can send you to the penitentiary anytime I choose, but you have no hold at all on me. Let me show you: No coin is shipped to me; no letters come to me, except your letters of sisterly affection; no crookedness can be traced to me; I stand well in business circles; I have been the first to call attention to the counterfeits, as you are pleased to call them; 'Sarah H Ormsby,' to whom all stuff is shipped and all business letters sent, has no existence, yet my connection with the convenient number on Blank Street cannot be traced. Do you see? Even should you keep this letter—which you will not, but will return to me in the next box of 'specimens,' as hereto for—you could not use it against me. The whole thing is typewritten and in a court of law would have no weight.

"No, there is but one thing for you to do. If you try any of your tricks with me! I'll show you no mercy, but will send you to the penitentiary, even if I have to go myself. But if you will go on attending to business, we'll be rich in a short time. I mean to do the handsome by you. Then, if anything *should* occur, I'll stand by you and do my best to clear you; and with the help of wealth and influence that would not be hard to do.

"Don't be worried over the presence of the detective. Leave the management of him to the others; they'll know what to do.

As Ever,

G.

"P. S. You will note that 'Sarah' addressed this letter—as she has all others of the kind. Now, what scrap of evidence could you bring against *me*?"

"A combination of slick scoundrel and egregious ass!" Raymond muttered, in a tone of deep disgust. "He holds the poor girl in his power, he makes her think, and he fancies himself secure from detection. Well, he has worked the thing pretty shrewdly; but we'll see how it all comes out. I guess I'll take a ramble over towards Douda, and see how things are coming on over there. I wish I could get a peek inside that old rookery. I wonder why Myra doesn't come back."

He returned the letter and book to Miss Haskins' table. Then he took up his hat and field-glass and set out. As he passed through the front gate he observed Frank Cassell and the two house-maids in earnest conversation near the corner of the house. Smiling superiority, he proceeded to the river, embarked in a rowboat, and pulled away in the direction of Douda Run.

As Raymond was passing down the lane to the river, Janey was saying to her companions, in vixenish tone, "Jest to see the way she carries on with Mr. Raymond! If one of us girls 'ld traipse 'round over the country with a man, like *she* does—oh, my! but *wouldn't* folks talk! An' I saw him in her room t'other night when I went to the head o' the stairs to put down the hall winder—*that's* what *I* saw!"

"It's scanderlous!" echoed Ruth, with a shocked expression of countenance. "And her so stuck up an' mighty!"

"You say she wouldn't listen to you, Ruth, when you went to tell her of Raymond's sneaking actions?" young Cassell asked.

"No, she wouldn't—jest ordered me out o' the room."

"Well, you'll tell her about seeing him in her room this morning, won't you?"

"N'deed I won't!" Ruth answered, with a positive toss of her pretty head. "If *you* want to snoop around the'r business, you can do it; *I'm* through."

"Of course you don't care anything for me, then," he said, in as plaintive a tone as he could command; "and I'll devote myself to some other girl."

He thought to wheedle her into doing what he desired; but in that he was mistaken. She replied promptly—snappishly, "You can do jest as you please, Mr. Frank Cassell! I know you don't care for me; you're jest tryin' to git Miss Haskins mad at Mr. Raymond, so's you can have her all to y'rself. An' you can't fool me no more—I'm on to y'r tricks. You needn't think I'm goin' to pine away an' die 'bout you neither; I've got another feller that I'm writin' to all the time. So there!"

And Ruth with a defiant toss of her head that set her black curls a-dancing, bounced into the house. The irrepressible Janey giggled at the young man's discomfiture; and, with an angry light in his eyes and an oath upon his lips, he strode off to the barn, muttering, "The cursed little minx! I thought I could move her into helping me out in the matter, but she is too suspicious. I have a notion to go over on Douda for a little walk; I saw Miss Haskins returned from town and drive on down that way. Maybe I can find out what she goes over there for. I think I know, though; and if I make sure I'll have a club to hold over her."

Thus musing, he passed through the barnyard and took the shortest route across the hills, toward the old house on Douda Run.

Chapter XII

On reaching of the mouth of Douda Run, Raymond concealed his boat beneath the drooping limbs of a willow in such a manner that it could not be seen from the bosom of the stream nor from the road along the river bank. Then he ascended the hill on the south side of the little valley, till he reached a broad bench or terrace. Following a path along this, through the woods, he came to a point where he could look down upon the narrow valley spread out beneath him. Douda Run was at his feet, and across it—and a little way up the hillside—was the house of the counterfeiters. The highway, shimmering white in the hot rays of the summer sun, wriggled along the sparkling brook and crawled off into the grateful shade of the wooded hillside.

Seating himself upon a mossy rock, Raymond unslung his field-glass and leveled it upon the house in the valley. He was heated from the climb he had made and from the close air of the forest. The stings of buzzing insects added to his discomfort. He gave little heed, however; his mind was fixed upon more important things than his own small troubles.

"Smoke pouring from that big stone chimney," he muttered. Then, shifting his position; "I can see through the open doors and windows, and there's not a soul in sight. The plant must be in the cellar; and they're down there at work."

He lowered the glass and wiped the sweat from his eyes. "Whose horse and cart is that standing at the side of the road—just where it starts up the hill?"

He pointed the glass at the spot.

"Miss Haskins' rig, I declare! But where is she? Ah—I see her now, in that clump of trees and bushes halfway up the hill, toward the house. What can she be—"

He did not finish the sentence but caught his breath sharply, and silently watched the figure on whom his interest was centered. His glass was a strong one and he could note every movement. He saw her place her tin box upon the ground and look about her in a cautious, half-fearful manner. Then she drew from a crevice in a small ledge of rocks a canvas bag, and quickly transferred its contents to the tin box; after which she threw the empty bag back into its hiding place.

The glass was so powerful—the illusion was so perfect—that Raymond felt he could reach out and touch her, almost. He saw the silver dollars as she dropped them into the receptacle, as plain as though the whole scene was not ten feet from him.

He continued to observe her. She was screened from the high-road by intervening trees and bushes; but because he was so far above, he could overlook them. She closed and fastened the lid of the box, picked it up and began the descent of the slope toward her conveyance but had gone but a few paces when a man sprang from the underbrush and confronted her.

"Frank Cassell!" muttered the detective, without lowering the glass from his eye. "Here's a complication."

Young Cassell and Miss Haskins held an animated conversation for some moments. This Raymond could see by their attitudes and gestures, though he could not catch the sound of their voices. The young woman appeared pale and worried; the young man, flushed and triumphant. Presently Cassell sprank forward and caught Miss Haskins in his arms.

"The presumptious, cowardly puppy!" cried Raymond, dropping the glass and leaping to his feet, as one long piercing scream for help came to his ears.

The detective shoved the field-glass into the case that hung at his side and—leaping, scrambling, sliding—he descended the precipitous slope, at breakneck speed. On reaching the road he ran swiftly toward the scene of the struggle. His clothing was torn and disarranged, his hands and face were scratched and bleeding; but he gave no heed. He reached the turn of the road, where Miss Haskins horse was tied, leaped over the low rail-fence and dashed up the slope.

Miss Haskins was still struggling in the arms of young Cassell, and neither was aware of the presence of the detective until the older man had the younger by the collar and was soundly kicking him. With a final cuff Raymond flung the youngster to the ground and turned just in time to catch Miss Haskins in his arms—to save her from falling. She was white and trembling and could not speak; and, after a few vain attempts at composure, she broke down and wept— her head upon Raymond's shoulder. As for him, although his heart was filled with righteous indignation toward her tormentor and with pity for her, he was ecstatically and foolishly happy.

"I'm so glad you were near," she found her voice to say, at last.

Then she attempted to disengage herself from his arms; but he held her fast.

"Myra, do you love me?" he whispered.

"Can you ask?" was the blushing reply.

They looked into each other's eyes and forgot the slinking wretch upon the ground, forgot where they were, forgot that she was a criminal—he, a sworn officer of the law; forgot everything but that they loved each other and were happy for one brief moment, at least.

"I must go," she said.

"Let me help you down to the cart," he replied. Then, turning to Cassell, he ordered, "Stay here till I come back; I want to talk with you."

The younger man answered with a nod and a scowl. Raymond picked up the tin box and led the way to the conveyance, Miss Haskins silently following. He assisted her into the cart, and handed her the tin box, with the words, "Here is your box of *specimens*, Myra."

Again she shivered as she replied, "Put it in the bottom of the vehicle."

After a moment of embarrassing silence, he asked: "Shall I drive you home?"

"No," she answered, quickly; "I'm feeling much better, I can go alone. When shall I see you—to thank you, you understand?"

"This evening, if you're feeling well enough. There's a number of things I desire to discuss with you—some arrangements to make. Drive home now and lie down for a rest. And lose this box on your way. Do you understand?"

"Y-e-s."

"The bottom of the river will be a good place for it."

"I understand."

"All right. Good-bye till I see you again. I want to devote a little time to your too ardent admirer—Mr. Frank Cassell."

"Claude!"

"Well—Myra?"

"You won't—won't punish him any further?"

"I ought to thrash the life out of him."

"Don't—please don't!"

"Didn't he insult you?"

"Y-e-s, but—"

"Then I won't promise anything."

"Please—for my sake!" And she bent towards him until their lips met.

"Very well," he said, smiling. "Go, now; and do what I told you—lie down and take a rest."

He stood watching her as she drove away. When she had disappeared around a bend in the road, he returned to the place where he had left Cassell. The younger man stood leaning against a tree, in a nonchalant attitude, a half-sullen, half-defiant expression upon his face.

"Why did you assault Miss Haskins?" Raymond asked.

"None of your business," was the bold but indiscreet reply.

The detective made a move to seize the youngster by the collar again but remembered his promise to Miss Haskins and checked himself. Cassell retreated out of reach; but kept up his show of defiance by asking: "Why did *you* attack *me*?"

"Because you insulted Miss Haskins," Raymond answered, coolly.

"You lie," was the hot retort. "I didn't. You're just jealous—you are a meddlesome—"

"Hold on!" commanded the detective, sternly. "I promised Miss Haskins that I would not chastise you further. Be careful how you fling around your epitaphs, though, or I may forget my promise and give you the hammering you so richly deserve. You followed her here; you forced your presence and attention upon her; you insulted her. I was watching and saw you. Now, you're going to answer some questions for me; or I'll take you across my knee and *spank* you."

Cassell simply glowered and offered no reply.

"Why did you insult Miss Haskins?" Raymond again asked.

"I didn't—I didn't mean to, anyhow. I was just—just"

"Well?"

"I was just trying to kiss her."

"Indeed! That was all! You followed her over here for that

purpose?"

"No, I didn't."

"You followed her."

"Yes."

"What for?"

"I wanted to see what she came over here so much for."

"Oh, you did! And you found out, I suppose."

"Yes, I did,"—a ring of malicious triumph in his voice,—"and you're welcome to her, if you want her. You don't know all *I* do. She's a counterfeiter, and I'll help to send her to the penitentiary."

Raymond turned pale. His suspicions in regard to Cassell's real mission to the place were confirmed; his worst fears were realized. He sprang forward and caught the young spy by the arms.

"You'll do nothing of the kind, Cassell," he panted in a half-whisper. "You'll keep your mouth shut—and breathe not a word of this affair, or I'll choke the life out of you, here and now. Look at me! I mean every word I say."

Cassell was a craven at heart; he cowered before Raymond's look and manner of fierce determination—and gave in.

"Promise me!" the detective commanded, with a light in his eyes the other could not face.

"I—I promise," the poor cowered faltered. Then, with a weak assumption of courage, "But don't you threaten me anymore, or I'll have you arrested—that's all."

"Listen," Raymond said, impressively. "I can have you arrested on two charges: for assaulting Miss Haskins, and for counterfeiting—of which you have been so glibly talking. If these men up here are counterfeiters, your father is guilty of harboring them on his property. Besides I find you in the immediate vicinity of the plant and giving me the information that it *is* a plant; and that would serve as proof that you have been aware of the illegal business for some time and haven't reported it to the authorities. Then, Bud Fogle comes to the farmhouse and carries away supplies of food. All these things together put you and your father in a tight place. But I don't want to take advantage of the compromising circumstances—I don't want to give you any trouble; yet I can and *will* do it, if you meddle in the matter—if you try to frustrate my plans. Keep a still tongue—in other words mind your own business and leave mine alone—and all will be well; but breathe a word of what you have seen or learned today, and I'll give you and your father a chance to prove your innocence."

"I—I won't say a word," the youngster stammered. "I'm innocent—you know I am, Mr. Raymond; and father—"

"Very well," the detective interrupted, hardly able to repress a smile at his companion's manifestations of alarm. "I bear you no lasting ill-will. Remember to keep your mouth closed. Good day."

Raymond strode away toward the river, leaving Cassell alone with his thoughts. The younger man ground his teeth and muttered: "Oh, no—you bear me no ill-will; but I do you! I'll get even with you, Mr. Claude Raymond, if I go to the penitentiary for it. You kicked me and slapped me; but I'll make you pay for it. You're a detective, eh? Well, that's no news to me; I suspected as much. And Fogle and the rest are counterfeiters; and the uppish Miss Haskins is a common criminal. I know what I'll do; I'll kill Raymond and let the gang swing for it—the haughty Miss Myra included."

Then, after a few moments thought and sundry shakes of the head, "No, that won't do; it's too dangerous. Perhaps they'd kill him themselves, if they knew all I know. I'll go up and tell them, this minute; Raymond'll never know."

He skirted the clump of trees and bushes, ascended to the house, and knocked upon the half-open door. The sound of his timid blows reverberated through the crazy structure, but no one responded to the summons. He knocked again with more force and a moment later heard steps approaching from the dusky interior. It was Crogan, and his appearance was not prepossessing nor reassuring. His suspenders hung at his side; his cotton shirt was open, revealing his hairy chest; his hands and face were grimy and his red eyes were scintillant with defiant anger.

"What's do you want?" he growled, suspiciously eyeing the intruder.

"Is—is Bud Fogle here?" Cassell inquired, retreating a step.

"S'pose he is—wh't den?"

"I want to see him a moment."

"W'at you want wid him?"

"I have some business with him."

"Is *dat* so? Well, out wid it."

"I'd rather see Fogle."

"Well, you *can't*—so dere!"

"Are you Crogan?"

"Sure—you bet! An' you?"

"I'm Frank Cassell, son of the man who owns this building."

"Well?"

"I want to tell you that the detective has been watching this place all morning."

The repulsive Irishman did not start nor appear surprised or concerned, as Cassell had expected. "W'at detective?" he demanded, coolly.

"Raymond, who boards at our house; Fogle knows him."

"Well,w'at's dat got to do wid us?"

"He thinks you're counterfeiters."

"Does, eh?"

"Yes."

"Dat don't *make* it so."

"No—o," answered Cassell, somewhat taken aback at the other's coolness.

"W'at 're you doin' over here—spyin', too?"

"No, I was over here looking after stock."

"W'at made de side of y'r face all red?"

And inspiration came to Frank Cassell. He would gain Crogan's gratitude and friendship. He answered:

"I caught the detective at his dirty work, and he struck me— tried to do me up."

"Dat's a lie!" Crogan cried, sharply. And, with the agility of a monkey, he sprang forward and caught the surprised and terrified young man by the throat. Then he dragged him into the house, shoved him into a chair, and demanded:

"Now, fer de truth; out wid it!"

Cassell was gasping for breath, but he managed to pant,

"Don't—touch—me; and I'll tell you."

"Oud wid it, I say!" Crogan insisted, fiercely.

"Raymond caught me making love to Miss Haskins; and he struck me. He's jealous of me."

"You was makin' love to Miss Haskins?"

"Y-e-s; I—"

"W'ere?"

"Down by the road."

"W'en?"

"Just now."

"W'at was you doin' over here?"

"I followed Miss Haskins."

"What fer?"

"To make love to her."

"Go slow!"

"That's the truth."

"Did she ask you to foller her?"

"N—o."

"W'at did you do it fer, den?"

"I—I don't know."

"Who is dis Miss Haskins?"

"Don't you know her?"

"You answer *my* question!" Crogan growled, savagely.

"She's the young school teacher boarding at our place."

"W'at was she doin' over here?"

"I—I don't know."

"Take care!"

"Hunting flowers and things, she said."

"W'at did you see 'er doin'?"

Cassell bit his lips and was silent. He wished in his inmost soul that he had not encountered the ogreish Crogan—that he had not come to the house at all. What should he say? Crogan did not give him much time to think. "Out wid it—'fore I choke you ag'in!"

"I—I saw—saw her take some silver coins—" the young man began; but Crogan brought him up with:

"No, you didn't!"

"Didn't I?"

"No! remember dat, now—'r it'll be de worse fer you. See?"

Cassell nodded sullenly.

"You saw de gal pickin' posies. See?"

"Y-e-s."

"Purty figure you cut, didn't you!" Crogan sneered.

Cassell bit his lips, and made no reply.

"W'at you goin' to do to him fer swattin' you?"

"I'd *like* to kill him!" Cassell cried, recklessly. "Curse him—I hate him!"

"Well, w'y *don't* you kill him, den?"

"I am—I'm afraid."

"Bah!"

"*You* kill him, Crogan," the weakling whined, wheedingly. "I won't tell; and he's trying to send you fellows to the pen."

"Tryin' to send *us* to de pen? W'at fer?" And Crogan assumed an expression of grieved innocence.

"Because you're counter—" Cassell began; but Crogan shut him off. "Naw! *I* ain't goin' to kill him; I ain't not'ing ag'in him—you keep dat in mind. But if *you* wants to stop his wind, *I* won't make no blow 'bout it. See?"

Cassell made no reply, and Crogan continued, "Dat's all; you may go. But keep y'r trap shut; you don't know not'ing 'bout dis place. If you cheep—well, look out fer *me!*"

Glad to escape, Frank Cassell retraced his steps to the farmhouse. And as he went he resolved, "I'll do it this very night. It will be laid at the door of the counterfeiters. He kicked me and slapped me! Oh, I'll get even with him!"

Crogan returned to his companions in the cellar.

"Who was it?" Fogle inquired.

"Dat young Cassell from de farmhouse."

"What did he want?"

"Said he was just passin', and t'ought he'd make a neighborly call."

"It took them quite a while to make it."

"Yes; we was talkin' over de lates' fashions, an' all dem society t'ings." And Crogan winked facetiously at Stoneman.

"Why didn't you ask him down to see the plant?" Fogle laughed.

"No, t'ank you; he knows too much a'ready."

"Does he suspect?" Stoneman inquired, with some concern.

Crogan shook his head and silently pointed at Fogle, who had his back toward the other two. Stoneman nodded knowingly, and nothing more was said on the subject—until the two were alone. Then Stoneman asked, "Are we going to have trouble with that smart young guy, Crogan?"

"Naw, he won't say not'ing; he hates de detective too bad to play into *his* hands. But dat cuss's got ev'ryt'ing ready to nab us; an' we must git away wid him tonight—'r skip out."

"Which shall we do?"

"I say kill him—an' take de chances. You see him an' de young smarty, Cassell, had a scrap today, 'bout de gal; an' de kid's b'ilin' mad 'cause de cop smashed him in de mug. Tol' me he'd like to kill him, an' all dat. If Raymond's found dead, Miss Haskins 'll swear she saw 'em scrappin'; an' nobody'd t'ink of layin' it on us. W'at's de young blood's first name?"

"Frank."

"Yes, dat's it. Well, I'm goin' to stamp his name on de gun dat I use to kill de detective wid, an' leave it close to de body. I'm goin' over tonight an' try fer a pop at him. Don't he go to de town 'most ev'ry night?"

"Yes. But, really, I don't know but it would be better for us to skip at once, Crogan."

"Look here, Stoneman! Dat don't go; you promised to stand by me."

"All right—have it your way; but we'll probably swing for it."

With an oath Crogan replied: "I'd kill dat Raymond, if I *knowed* I had to swing fer it."

At this point in the conversation Fogle rejoined them, and no more was said on the subject.

Chapter XIII

Raymond returned to the farmhouse and sought his room. Jap, the hired man, had brought the morning's mail from the village; but there was nothing for the detective, and he was in a fever of unrest. He felt that everything was ripe for a descent upon the gang of counterfeiters, and that further delay was risky. He reasoned that Fogle and his companions would not remain quiet and inactive much longer, knowing that he—Raymond—was aware of their business.

"They'll slip through my fingers if I'm not careful," he mused. "I wish Kennard would let me hear from him. What can be the matter? Can it be possible Travis never received my dispatch, and that things are at loose ends at Pittsburg, with no one to look after them? A woman in a case always complicates matters; and there is a woman in *this* case with a vengeance. I've delayed and bungled this job more than anyone I've ever worked. Yet who can blame me? Who would not have temporized under the circumstances?"

Miss Haskins did not come down to dinner, and at supper time she requested Ruth to bring tea and rolls to her room. So Raymond did not meet her again that day; for, much as he desired to see her, he felt it would be cruel to disturb her.

Supper over he took up his hat and walked to the village for the evening's mail. He was rewarded with a letter from Kennard. It ran:

"Raymond: Have carried out your instructions to a dot. 'Sarah H. Ormsby' is a blind—you understand. Have jumped into the stuff myself. Got Miss Haskins latest letters and the box. It contains some clam shells and one-fifty of the 'stuff.' I send you the letters. They are addressed to 'Mrs. Ormsby,' but are meant for Gimp, of course.

"Gimp is becoming nervous; he is still shoving, but slowly and cautiously. If you're ready at your end, I'm ready here. I think Gimp should be nabbed at once.

Kennard."

Raymond, standing by the little post office window, read Kennard's letter through. Then he hastily glanced over Miss Haskins' letters, which Kennard had inclosed. They contained nothing which the detective did not already know. In the daintily written missives the young woman went on to say that she had been grossly deceived by Gimp; that she had had no true idea of the business when he persuaded her to go into it; that she was heartily sick of the whole thing, and that she would have nothing more to do with it. And she asked—nay, begged and prayed—that Gimp would let her go in peace and not have her punished for what she had already done.

The detective thrust the letters into his coat pocket and walked away from the post office, muttering, "No further delay is possible or required. I'll wire Kennard to arrest Gimp at once, and tomorrow I'll put the nippers on Fogle and his pals. Myra shan't be known in the affair, if I can help it; and *I can*—Kennard's discreet. However, the others may peach[41] on her. If they do, I'll have to fight to clear her; but I think, with the evidence and the influence I have, I can do it. The stuff was shipped from the plant to Gimp, and Gimp shoved it through the bank. That's enough for the public to know." He went direct to the telegraph office and wired Kennard. Then he crossed the bridge and called upon the sheriff of the county, at his residence in the courthouse yard.

Sheriff Williams was a portly and rather pompous man of middle age and was fully aware of the dignity of his office. He met Raymond at the door, with the brusque inquiry, "What do you want, sir?"

"You are the sheriff of this county?"

"I am, Sir."

"I'd like a few minutes private conversation with you, on an important matter."

"Pertaining to my business and duties?"

Raymond smiled involuntarily as he replied. "Pertaining to *my* business and *your* duties."

"I'll be in my office at nine o'clock tomorrow morning. You can see me then."

"Stuff!" the detective snorted. "I must see you at once."

"Is your business so urgent?"

"Certainly, or I wouldn't be here at this hour."

"Very well, sir; come into my office."

The sheriff led the way to a room on the first floor of the court-

------

41 **peach** – inform on

house, near at hand. He turned on the gas and, pointing to a chair, said ungraciously: "Have a seat. Now, what's your business?"

Raymond tossed his card upon the table, with the words, "Please close the shutters and lock the door."

A marked change took place in the pompous Sheriff as he read the name upon the bit of pasteboard. The severe scowl left his features and an unctuous smile took its place, while his dignified demeanor softened to servile humility.

"Very glad to meet you, Mr. Raymond," he murmured, confused. "What can I do for you?"

"First, you may close the door and shutters, as I suggested."

Sheriff Williams hastened to comply with the detective's request. Then, seating himself in an expectant attitude, he silently awaited his visitor's pleasure. Raymond wasted no time, but went to the business in hand at once. He began with the question: "Have you two courageous and thoroughly reliable men, that you can bring with you to help me make a capture, tomorrow morning at daybreak?"

"I've the men—yes, sir—good men, too. But what—what's up?"

"I've run down a gang of counterfeiters—three in number," Raymond returned, briskly, "and I want your assistance in arresting them. I may as well tell you that they are desperate characters—two of them, at least; and you want to bring good men with you."

The sheriff bit his lip and was silent. He did not relish the idea of assisting in the capture of such a group as the detective described. Then a comforting thought struck him, and he said, "Of course you understand that I can't assist you if these counterfeiters are in another county."

"I understand that fact perfectly; but they are in *this* county."

"Near here?"

"Right under your nose—down here at Douda Run."

"At Douda Run!"

"Yes; in the Chalkley Grafton house. You know where that is, of course?"

"Y-e-s. But are you sure you're not mistaken, Mr. Raymond? I don't see how—"

"There's no mistake," the detective interrupted, briskly. "Will you lend me your help?"

"I will, certainly."

"Tomorrow morning at daybreak, then, be at the Cassell farm; I'm boarding there. If you don't find me, hurry on to the house on Douda Run. You'll find me waiting for you there. Remember— bring cool, level-headed men. Let them be well-armed, but caution them to keep their wits about them. I want to take these chaps alive, if possible. That's all. Good night."

He shook hands with the sheriff and took his departure. Fifteen minutes later he was hurrying down the river road toward his boarding place.

It was quite dark by this time. Heavy blanket-like clouds obscured the heavens and rendered the evening air oppressive. Great banks of black thunder-heads loomed up in the west, and pale flashes of lightning, followed by remote and rumbling thunder, gave indications of an approaching storm. Fireflies were flitting in and out of the foliage of the trees along the dusky road, and hoarse frogs were indulging in an unmusical serenade beneath the bank of the river.

But Raymond gave little heed to minor sights and sounds; he was too deeply engrossed with his thoughts. When he had arrived within a few hundred yards of the farmhouse, he became dimly conscious of footsteps behind him. Tall trees on both sides of the road interlocked their arms above it, completely obscuring the meager light of the cloudy sky. Again the detective's keen sense of hearing caught the sound of guarded footsteps in the rear, and a sense of imminent danger came over him. It was so dark he could not see his hand before his face, and he was groping with his feet to keep in the roadway.

Once more he caught the sound of footsteps—and this time very near at hand. He whirled in his tracks, whipping a revolver from his pocket, and demanded, "Hello! Who are you?"

A blinding flash of flame and the deafening report of a firearm was the answer he received. He felt the breath of a bullet as it whizzed past his head, and thought he caught a brief glimpse of a human figure outlined by the flash of the weapon. He took quick aim and twice fired into the dense blackness. Two answering shots came from his invisible assailant, and the last took effect.

Raymond felt a stinging, burning pain in his right temple, and a dizzy faintness overcame him. He staggered, caught himself, staggered again and fell upon the green sod at the roadside. He was fully conscious, but his brain was in a mad whirl and he could not rise. He heard someone rush past him, going in the direction of the farmhouse. He made a great effort to get up on his elbow and turn his weapon in the direction of the retreating footsteps. But his limbs were lead. He felt something warm trickling down the side of his face and knew that it was blood.

All this took place in the fraction of a minute. Raymond felt that he was not seriously wounded and did not give over trying to get upon his feet. Then, of a sudden, he became aware of someone standing near him and heard Frank Cassell's voice saying: "Did he wound you, Mr. Raymond? Are you bad hurt?"

The detective answered rather faintly: "I'm hit—yes; but I don't think it's serious—a mere scratch. It bled a good deal, though, and I feel faint and sick. Assist me to a sitting posture, please."

Cassell did as the wounded man requested. Then he suggested: "Hadn't I better go for help to get you to the house?"

"Wait a little while," Raymond answered. He was feeling better and thought he would be himself again in a few minutes. Presently he asked: "Have you a match, Cassell?"

"Yes."

"Strike it and take a look at this gash on my temple."

Cassell proceeded to make an examination. He found that the bullet had plowed a furrow two or three inches long across the temple. The laceration had bled freely, and Raymond's hair and clothing were soaked.

"Just a scalp wound, isn't it?" he inquired.

"That's all; but it still bleeds a little."

The match went out, and the two were left in pitchy darkness. The thunder storm was rapidly coming up from the west. Nearer and nearer rumbles of the thunder, and vivid flashes of lightning occasionally illuminated the roadway and danced over the foliage of the bordering trees, bringing into relief against the black wall of darkness the faces and figures of the two men—the two rivals.

"Help me to my feet; I believe I can walk," Raymond said.

Cassell obeyed, and the detective stood alone. "I'll be all right presently," he remarked. "I'm feeling ever so much better; but it was a close call. I don't want to go into the house with all this blood upon me. When we get there I'll go out to the cistern at the barn and have a wash."

At that moment a blinding glare of light for a brief second turned night into day. It was followed by a rattling crash that reverberated from hill to hill and echoed far up and down the valley. Raymond stooped and picked up an object lying at his feet. It was a revolver, and he silently shoved it into his pocket. Then together the two set out for the house. The detective found that he was able to walk alone, though his steps were a little weak and uncertain.

Young Cassell stopped in the kitchen for lantern, basin and towel; Raymond went on to the barn. When Cassell had rejoined him and had assisted him in removing the blood stains from his person, the detective took from his pocket the revolver he had picked up and carefully examined it. It was a murderous-looking weapon of the bulldog pattern; and stamped upon the breach was the name—"Frank Cassell."

Cassell stood holding the lantern. Raymond extracted the unexploded cartridges and, presenting the revolver to his companion, said coolly, "Here's your gun, Cassell."

"*My* gun!" cried the other, recoiling.

"Yes, it has your name on it. See?"

Cassell took the weapon in his hand, saw the name upon it, and asked: "Where—where did you get this?" His face was blanched and quivering. Visions of a crowded courtroom—the judge, jury, and himself a prisoner in the dock—thronged his brain and brought with them suggestions of the jail, the scaffold, the black cap and the hangman's noose. He heard the detective speaking, but the latter's voice sounded far off. Outside the lightning blazed, the thunder boomed, and the rain poured in torrents. Raymond said, "I picked it up in the road. You saw me. It was careless of you to drop it. Your aim was remarkably good, considering the darkness, but I had no idea you had it in for me—to the extent of wanting to kill me."

"It isn't—isn't my revolver," Cassell stammered.

"It's got your name upon it," Raymond returned, quietly, "and you will have some difficulty in making a jury believe it isn't yours.

Cassell's terror was growing upon him. He was shaking all over. He saw plainly the web of circumstantial evidence that entangled him—the weapon bearing his name, his encounter with the detective, his intemperate avowal to Crogan, his presence at the scene of the attempted murder; and the feeling of guilt in his soul made a cringing, abject coward of him. Leaning limply against the wall, he whined beseechingly, "I'm innocent, Mr. Raymond—before God I'm innocent! This gun isn't mine—I never saw it before. I *did* think of killing you; I thought your death would be laid on the counterfeiters. But I hadn't the courage; you know I hadn't. Crogan's the man who shot you—I'm telling you the truth! I was hiding in the bushes and saw him run down the road after he shot you. Oh, please believe me!"

Raymond pitied the wretch, but felt that he had not been sufficiently punished; so he asked harshly: "Why were you hid down there in the bushes?"

"I—I don't know; something seemed to *draw* me there—I couldn't stay away."

"That's too cheap a tale," the detective sneered. "The revolver bears your name."

"I *know* it does; and I can't understand it. Crogan must have put my name upon it. It isn't mine—I'm innocent!"

"You told Crogan you were going to kill me?"

"No—no! I—I—"

"You mentioned our troubles to him and what you saw Miss Haskins doing?"

"Yes—I did. And I tried to get him to say he would kill you; but—but I'm awful sorry for it now. Oh, please say you won't have me arrested!"

"I ought to send you to the penitentiary as an accomplice of Crogan's," Raymond answered, "but I shan't do it—provided you come to your senses, and heed what I say."

"I'll do anything—anything!" Cassell whined.

"You violated your promise today."

"But I won't again—indeed I won't."

"All right. Go to the house and keep your mouth shut. Do you understand? *Keep your mouth shut!*"

Cassell silently slunk away, and Raymond, taking the path across the hills, set out for the counterfeiters' den. The rain still fell in torrents, and the night was black as ink. The detective tied a handkerchief around his wounded head and, unmindful of the storm, plotted on, muttering, "I must keep an eye upon them tonight; they'll make a break for it before morning."

After his attempt on the detective's life, Crogan wasted no time in returning to the plant. He had seen Cassell crouching by the roadside, and he felt, as he figuratively expressed it, "dat de jig was up." Therefore he sped from the spot as fast as his legs would carry him; and a half hour afterward he dashed into the presence of Stoneman, who sat alone in the house.

"What's the matter?" Stoneman inquired quickly, alarm in his voice. "You are all covered with mud; you've been running; and you're *scared*—if ever I saw you scared. What's the matter?"

"Where's Fogle?" Crogan panted, as he dropped into a chair.

"Gone down to the river to run his trout line," Stoneman replied, keenly eyeing his companion.

"He better be here, gittin' ready to run from w'at's a-comin'."

"What's up?" Stoneman snarled. "I've asked you twice."

"Just dis: I've bungled de whole business; an' we got to git up an' dust—to de tune o' short meter. *Dat's* w'at!"

"So you've bungled the job, just as I told you you would," Stoneman cried, angrily.

"Naw! I ain't bungled not'ing; I killed Raymond all right enough. But dat young cuss of a Cassell saw me do it; I guess it was him—hid along de road."

"What did you kill him with?"

"Wid de gun I showed you."

"After the first shot?"

"Naw; I had to shoot two 'r t'ree times."

"What's that upon your sleeve—blood?"

"Yes, he winged me—but it's just a scratch."

"What? He shot at you?"

"Course he did, twice."

"Then how do you know he's dead?"

"Cause I seen him fall—an' he never groaned; dat's how."

"Where's your gun?"

"I t'rowed it down in de road—to make folks b'lieve young Cassell done de job."

"And *he* saw you do it! Crogan, you fool, you've bungled the job sure enough; you've messed it up a plenty. You ought to have used a knife, as I wanted you to do. Listen how the storm rages! Well, we must pack up a few things and get out of here. There's no time to lose—everything's off; the authorities may be hot after us by morning. I wish Fogle would come."

"I don't care if he don't come—I don't. I'm t'rough wid him. If he comes in time to go—all right; if he don't, I won't snivel none. He'd raise a devil of a row, if he'd happen to find out I'd killed de detective. W'en we git ready to go, we'll burn dis ol' shack to de ground an' hide all signs. Eh?"

"Yes, certainly. But now, to work. The sheriff and a posse will be after us just as soon as Frank Cassell can get to town and tell them of Raymond's death. We must be miles away from here by daylight. I say that we strike for the Ohio, cross, and hide in the hills of West Virginia. I wonder if they've arrested Gimp yet. There's one consolation: each of us has a neat little sum salted down. But you'll catch me in no more jobs with amateurs."

"N'r me!" Crogran cried, with an oath. "W'at'll we take wid us?"

"Very little; we don't want to be burdened."

The two went to work, packing a few valuables and costly tools that they could carry without interfering with swift and easy flight. Outside the summer thunderstorm was still raging; and Fogle had not come.

At last Crogan said, "Dere, I'm ready. Let's scoot."

Stoneman replied, "I'm ready, too; but we can't burn the building with Fogle's stuff in it—and it won't do to go off and leave things as they are. What'll we do—wait till he comes? It won't be very long, probably."

"As fer me, Fogle can look out fer hisself." Crogan answered, doggedly. "I ain't a-goin' to take no more chances. W'at was *dat!*"

The two stood and looked at each other in perplexity and alarm. Above the downpour of the rain and the sigh of the wind, each distinctly caught a peculiar grating sound. It appeared to come from the side of the house next to the hill and sounded like something scraping against the weatherboards. It lasted but a moment; then all was still again but the bluster of the elements.

"It sounded like something trying to climb up to one of the windows," Stoneman whispered.

"You stay here an' keep still; I'll just slip out an' see." And Crogan silently opened the back door and passed into the outer darkness.

It *was* someone trying to peep in at one of the windows on the upper side of the house; and that someone was the detective. Arriving upon the scene and finding everything about the place dark and quiet—for Crogan and Stillman were in the room next to the brook, with but a dim light burning—he thought it possible that the counterfeiters had already taken flight. So he resolved to raise a window and enter the house, or, at least, to peep in and ascertain the truth. In order to do this he must climb upon something. Procuring a piece of plank, he leaned it against the house, ascended his improvised ladder and attempted to raise the window to the sill where he found himself clinging. But the plank upon which he stood slipped from under him: and, scraping along the weatherboards, made the sound the two counterfeiters heard.

Raymond mentally cursed his ill luck and stood still and listened. Hearing no outcry nor other sound from within, he again placed the plank against the wall and was preparing to ascend for the second time, when a blow from a club in the hands of Crogan dropped him senseless and bleeding to the ground.

"Come out here, Bob!" The Irishman bawled lustily. "I've got de laddie-buck, good an' proper!"

A door opened and shut with a bang, and Stoneman joined his companion.

"What's the matter—who is it?" he inquired, peering and squinting.

"I've got de dirty sneak." Crogan answered: "an' I t'ink it's dat young Cassell—can't see his face, dough. I knocked him over wid dis club. Le's drag him in to de light."

Together they half dragged, half carried the inanimate form into the house and deposited it upon the floor of the room in which the lamp was dimly burning. Crogan bent and peered into the upturned face, staggered back—and said nothing. Stoneman turned up the light, took a look, and cried, "Why, it isn't Cassell, is it?"

"Naw!" Crogan gasped.

"Who the hell is it, then?"

"It's de cop—de detective."

"Crogan, you infernal idiot!" Stoneman roared. "You did do a *good* job of killing!"

"De cuss must be a cat wid nine lives," the Irishman grumbled. "He ain't dead yit; I see him a-breathin'."

"Give him another crack over the head or stick a knife into him," the other suggested. "Let's put an end to him and his future meddling."

"Not me!" Crogan growled, surly. "I've had two tries at him—an' I don't want no more. Dere's somet'ing bogy 'bout dat feller—he's a hoodoo!"

"Fool!" sneered Stoneman. "You haven't the sand—"

"Cut it short, pard." Crogan snarled, angrily. "'r me an' you'll come togeder!"

The other laughed uneasily, and replied: "There—don't be touchy. I didn't mean any harm. We've got to hide this fellow somewhere, before Bud comes back. Let's carry him to the cellar; he was so anxious to see the inside of the plant, we'll leave him there. If the house burns down by accident, we're not to blame. Come on! Bud will be back soon."

They bore the unconscious man to the cellar and laid him upon the stone flags in one corner. Then, taking with them a few light tools they thought Fogle might desire, they returned to the upper apartment. In their haste and confusion of mind, they left their lantern burning upon the lower step—and closed and locked the heavy oaken door behind them.

"Now," Stoneman said, "we'll wait ten minutes; if Fogle doesn't show up in that time, we'll touch a match to the old pile and skip. If he comes and wants his tools, we have them here: and he'll have no cause to go to the cellar—and find the detective."

"Dat's de stuff: dat suits—" Crogan began. But he stopped suddenly, raised a finger, and uttered a warning, "Hist!"

A moment later Fogle's dripping form appeared in the doorway; and Fogle's voice cried: "Hello! What's up—what have you been doing?"

"Packin' up, an' getting' ready to skip by de light o' de moon," the Irishman replied, smoothly. "You'd better get a move on; dere ain't no time to waste."

"What's the cause of your sudden resolution?" And there was a shade of suspicion in Fogle's tone and manner.

"Dat fly detective, along wid de sheriff o' de county, an' his posse, is makin' ready to put de bracelets on us in de mornin'."

"How do you know all this?" was the not unnatural question."

"Dis way: Bob was down by de road, an' two men rode along, goin' from town. Bob heard one o' dem say dat de sheriff an' his gang was goin' to raid dis coop at daylight."

Crogan uttered the lie as glibly as though it were an indisputable truth. But Fogle was not satisfied, apparently, for he answered: "I didn't see any man pass the mouth of the run, where I was fishing; and I notice Stoneman's clothes are dry, and it's been raining all evening. You'll have to fix up a slicker lie than that, Crogan."

The Irishman blazed up instantly and, brandishing his fists, shouted: "If you don't want to b'lieve w'at I say—you can do de odder t'ing!"

"What other thing?" Fogle asked quickly.

"Go to 'ell—dat's w'at!"

The younger man laughs scornfully, and cried, "What a vicious old viper it is! Well, we shan't quarrel over the matter, Crogan. I'm perfectly willing and glad to leave here. I wonder I haven't gone long ago. I'll be ready in a few minutes."

He made a step toward the cellar door, but stopped, petrified in his tracks. A deep, sepulchral groan sounded beneath his feet and sent the blood in an icy torrent to his heart. The last thing his companions expected had occurred. Raymond was reviving in the cellar!

"What was that?" Fogle asked, in a husky whisper.

"Not'ing but de wind," Crogan answered readily; "it makes funny noises in dis ol' trap."

"It wasn't the wind," the younger man muttered, with a positive shake of the head. "It sounded like someone in distress."

"Rats squealing, perhaps," Stoneman suggested, looking anxiously at Crogan.

"I tell you it was some human being groaning in distress." Fogle insisted.

By this time Raymond had regained consciousness. The blow from the club had but stunned him, its full force falling upon his shoulder, and not upon his head. Now he was sitting up, aimlessly passing his hand over his head and shoulder and groaning. At first he could not understand where he was nor what had happened to him; but soon a full realization of the situation dawned upon his numbed faculties.

The underground retreat in which he found himself was about thirty feet square. The floor was composed of smooth flagstones neatly fitted together and was comparatively dry. In one side of the room was an immense fireplace. Rough wooden steps led to the apartments above; and there was no other means of egress, except a small door leading out through the wall next to the valley. This door was nailed fast. About the cellar were scattered tools and appliances of the counterfeiters craft—a crude crucible, a stamp, a lathe, and a work-bench; and in one corner was piled a quantity of mettle—silver, tin, and copper, in bars.

Raymond's experienced eyes swept the room, dimly lighted by the lantern his would-be murderers had left upon the steps, and took in all these details before he was conscious of their import, even.

He managed to get upon his feet but could barely stand. He sank to the floor, crawled to the steps and drew himself upon them. His head ached excruciatingly, and his eyes burned like coals of fire.

"They've trapped me," he muttered, "and will make their escape while I'm secure. How my head aches! One of them must have slipped upon me while I was at the window. I must get out of here—but how?"

Then he caught voices in loud and animated conversation, in the room above; and he listened intently. Fogle was saying: "You've knifed him and thrown him into the cellar, and I'm going down there. I told you I wouldn't stand for any violence; and, if I find things as I think, you'll have to answer to me—that's all."

"Stop y'r clack!" Crogan growled. "You don't know w'at you're talkin' 'bout. Dere ain't nobody down dere—is dere Bob?"

"Of course not!" Stoneman answered emphasizing his words with an oath.

Again Fogle spoke. "How comes this blood's upon the floor, then?" he asked.

"From my arm," Crogan explained; "I hurt it on a nail. Come on, Bud; git y'r packin' done. We're losin' time."

"I don't believe a word you say;" Fogle cried, obstinately, "and I'm going down there."

Raymond heard someone rattling at the door over his head. Then came the sounds of a struggle and the sound of the heavy body upon the floor. The detective strained his ears. He caught the sound of whispered conversation and hurrying footsteps. Then, after a time, one of the outer doors opened and shut; and all was silent as the grave.

Chapter XV

Raymond sat for some minutes with his head in his hands. At last he tottered to his feet, muttering: "It won't do to sit here; Crogan and Stoneman will be putting miles between this place and themselves. I'm confident they've killed Fogle and that his body lies in the room above me. The infernal murderous devils! with all these tools lying about—surely I can get out in some way."

He laboriously climbed the steps and tried the door. It was securely locked. He descended to the floor, procured the lantern and a cold chisel[42] and returned to the top step. A dark-colored liquid oozing beneath the door attracted his attention.

"Blood!" he cried. "As I thought, they've stabbed Fogle to the heart while he was trying to come to my aid. Poor, misguided fellow! He wasn't all bad, at any rate."

The lock was a strong, old-fashioned one; and, although he hammered and battered at it with implements at hand, he could not get through the heavy door. Suddenly he ceased his efforts, sniffed the air and gazed wildly about him.

"I smell smoke! he whispered. "Can it be possible the villains have set fire to the house? If they've done that, I'm in a bad box. Whew! It grows stronger; I've got to hurry."

He renewed his efforts, with increased vigor and did not hesitate until the smoke in rapidly increasing quantities almost drove him from his position. Then he paused and listened and distinctly heard the crackle and hiss of burning wood. The discovery made him shudder, and the faintness stole over him. For a moment he leaned weakly against the door but quickly started away from it. It was growing hot with the breath of the blaze beyond.

"Great heavens!" he gasped. "Am I to die like a rat in the hull of a burning ship? It's plain that I can't escape in this direction; the fires in the room beyond. And there is but one other outlet—and that nailed fast, probably!"

His brain swimming, his limbs trembling, he again descended the stairs and groped his way through the volumes of stifling smoke, to the other door. It was nailed fast, as he had suspected. He set the lantern upon the floor and went to work—hewing and hacking at the barrier that stood between himself and safety. He realized that time was precious, and he made frantic efforts to get out. But on account of his weakness and confusion of thought his endeavors were blindly directed and he made little progress.

By a careless backward step, he overturned and extinguished

---

42 **cold chisel -** a chisel made of hardened tempered steel and used for cutting cold metal

the lantern, leaving the place in pitchy darkness. Then, indeed, did his courage falter. He felt that further effort was useless, and he dropped his hands and leaned against the wall for support, panting and gasping. He heard the fire overhead increase in volume and fury, until it was a roaring, seething furnace of flame, causing the walls of the crazy structure to groan and vibrate. Hissing, squirming serpents of flame darted their blazing tongues through the cracks in the floor and licked and lapped at his cowering form.

"Lost—lost!" he groaned feebly, sinking toward the floor. "No—no! I mustn't die tamely! I can't—I *won't!*"

He clenched his hands and sprang erect; but the next moment dropping upon the flags, clutching at his throat, panting and wheezing. Revived a little by the fresh air that stole in under the door he made one mighty effort to bring someone to his aid, by shouting, "Help! Help!"

To his distorted imagination, the dancing flames and gyrating smoke assumed the form of leering imps, and the crackling voice of burning wood was the crackling laugh of mocking fiends. His breathing became asthmatic, his parched tongue grew thick and stiff, and his eyes rolled in blood rimmed sockets. A thousand fiery fancies surged through his super-heated brain, till he went mad and laughed with the fiends that tormented him. Again a breath of fresh air drove the smoke and flames in retreat before; and again he revived and called: "Help! In God's name, help!"

Then he sank back, wrapped in the thrice blessed mantle of unconsciousness, as a woman's piercing scream outside sounded above the din of roaring flames and falling timbers—and a woman's brave voice called: "Claude—Mr. Raymond! Stay close to the door—where you can get a little air. I'll try to get you out. Do you hear me?"

But he was beyond answering.

It was Myra Haskins. The light from the burning pile lent an unearthly beauty to her pale face and turned her tangled tresses to ripples of molten gold. With an axe that she had caught up from the wood pile near at hand she rained blow after blow upon the stubborn door, and with her tender white hands she pulled and snatched at the loosened boards. Frenzy lent her strength. Soon her taper fingers were torn by the splintered wood, her face and neck were almost blistered by the intense heat; but she gave no heed. The last nail gave way, and the door fell inward with a crash. She threw down the axe and sprang through the opening—the entrance to a fiery furnace.

"Claude!" she screamed frantically, almost suffocated by the smoke and flame that met her.

But no answering voice greeted her ears. She called again and again, groping and gasping. Then—just when she felt that she could bear the torture no longer, and that she must retreat, leaving him to his fate—she stumbled against his unconscious form. How she got him out she never knew. Half crazed herself, but steeled by desperation, she partly dragged him, partly carried him through the opening in the stone wall and laid him upon the grass at a safe distance from the burning building. Then relaxation followed the terrible tension, and she fainted at his side.

When she revived the rain was falling gently but steadily, and she was soaked and chilled. The building had fallen in, and a few burning brands alone lighted the scene. She soon realized that Raymond was not dead, for his eyes were open and he moaned and babbled incessantly. He kept calling for water, water, in his delirium. She went to the spring nearby, found a battered tin-cup and carried him a draught of the cooling liquid. Then he was quiet for a time, and she seated herself upon the wet ground and pillowed his head upon her lap.

The hours dragged along. He kept babbling at intervals, in a low monotone. Once she caught her own name—"Myra." She gently passed her hand over his singed locks stroked and caressed his bruised forehead. Was he not all hers—all hers?

"Myra," he whispered again, "I—I love you—"

"Yes—yes," she replied in soothing tones. "I know, dear!"

She realized that this sweet declaration was but the figment of a disordered brain, yet—in spite of her own discomfort, in spite of her poignant fear that he would die ere morning dawned and she could bring him aid—she was happier than she had ever been in her life.

When the gray dawn came creeping into the little valley, she still sat holding him to her breast—soothing him as a mother soothes the fretful child.

It was just coming daylight, and Farmer Cassell was watering the work-horses at the barn pump.

"Hello!" called a gruff voice, from the lane.

"Hello, y'rself!" the old man answered. And three horsemen emerged from the gray mist.

"Is Mr. Raymond here? asked one of the men.

"Is that you, Sheriff?" Mr. Cassell inquired in turn.

"Yes. Where's your boarder, Raymond?"

"Left last night—him an' Miss Haskins both, the girls says; must 'ave eloped, I guess. Quite a storm we had last night. Must 'ave struck some barn out towards Pennsville; I saw a big light over that way, 'long 'bout midnight."

The old gentleman would have rattled on, but the sheriff and his men wheeled their horses and galloped away.

"Wonder what in the world he wants with Raymond," the farmer muttered, as he watched them out of sight. "An' where *is* that feller an' Miss Haskins? Williams 'peared to be in an awful hurry; couldn't even stop to be sociable. I'm afeared there's trouble in the wind; I don't like the look of things."

He little suspected how serious the trouble was.

Sheriff Williams lost no time in making his way to the appointed meeting place on Douda Run; and on his arrival, he showed himself worthy of the office he held by prompt and intelligent action. He dispatched one of the deputies for a physician and a carriage and turned his attention to Miss Haskins and her unconscious charge, doing all he could to make them comfortable. Nor did he leave them until they were again safely installed at the Cassell farmhouse. He performed his part with an ornate show of officiousness[43], to be sure—but he performed it well.

For the next twelve hours he busied himself in sending telegrams, in an effort to intercept the fleeing criminals and to apprise the authorities in Washington of what had occurred.

---

43 **officiousness** - marked by excessive eagerness in offering unwanted services or advice to others

Within twenty-four hours Kennard was on the scene, just in time to receive word from Marietta that Crogan and Stoneman were in jail there. He went down, identified the two as old offenders and arranged for their safe detention until they could be brought to trial. On his return, he joined Miss Haskins in her effort to nurse Raymond back to life and health.

Raymond's illness was a tedious one. For days he lay unconscious, tossing and moaning, whispering and babbling. Through it all Miss Haskins was his devoted attendant. When he was again conscious and on the road to recovery, he sent Kennard back to Pittsburg, to arrange for the trial of Gimp and his confederates. Crogan and Stoneman received life sentences for the murder of Fogle. Gimp would serve a long term, and come out a broken and ruined man.

Kennard gone, the whole care of Raymond was upon Miss Haskins; and she was thankful to have it so—and perfectly happy. They talked over the past and made plans for the future. She told him how Gimp had persuaded her to aid in "shoving" the spurious coin, how he had threatened her with disgrace and punishment to keep her at it, and how she had given up all hope of escape. Of course he knew all this, already; but it was sweet to have her tell him. On his part, he told her how he had gained his first clue and how he had followed it, step-by-step. Then he said, "You passed that coin in the bookstore at Zanesville, the day I arrived in the city; but you didn't come down on the train that night."

"No; I came down on the boat."

"You went up on the morning train?"

"Yes."

"How was it the conductor knew nothing of you, and the salesman at the bookstore described you as wearing glasses?"

"I'll answer your questions this once," she said, her voice vibrant with emotion, "then let's drop the subject forever; it hurts me to think about it. I concealed my dress, while on the train, under a linen ulster; and I put on glasses after reaching the city."

Both were silent for some moments. At last she asked falteringly, "Are you sure I won't be arrested—or won't have to appear as witness against the others?"

"Quite sure," he replied, smiling, "that's all been arranged."

Another silence. Then he whispered huskily, "Myra, tell me how you happened to come to my rescue."

"I don't know; I felt you were in danger—and I couldn't rest. I descended the stairs, met Frank Cassell and asked him about you. At first he claimed ignorance; but I pleaded so earnestly that at last he told me where he thought that you had gone. Then I followed you, without stopping to ask myself what I meant to do—what I *could* do. Oh, I can't bear to think of that awful night!"

A longer silence.

"A penny for your thoughts, Claude," she whispered.

"For once they're worth it," he laughed.

"Well, tell me. What are you thinking?"

"What—will—*Travis*—say?"

"That you've found a counterfeit coin," she replied, with a happy laugh.

The Undoing of Old John Chaney

John Cheney was a hard man. His neighbors so pronounced him, and old John did all that lay in his power, apparently, to give the color of truth to the pronouncement.

He lived in the principal street of the little town in a big ramshackle frame house that had once been the village tavern. In the flourishing days of stage-coaching and stock-driving he had been a loud-voiced and jolly landlord, so report declared, and had made much money by entertaining travelers—and much more by running a sly doggery[1] in the basement of his building. But all this was of the past. His wife and two children were dead long ago; his profitable business was no more, and he and an unmarried sister, as ill-favored and much disliked as himself, lived alone in the rat-infested old pile.

Yet it was known that Old John was quite well-to-do—was the rich man of the village, in fact. True, he never gave any evidence of being the possessor of wealth, either in the way of ostentation or charity: but the tax duplicate showed that he owned two good farms, several pieces of town property and a large block of stock in the village bank. As has been more than intimated, however, he was close-fisted. A dollar saved was a dollar earned, with Old John. He went clad in rags, he lived on the coarsest fare, and he drove hard bargains with everyone with whom he had dealings.

No one could point to a penny he had ever given to charity; no one could recall a kind word he had ever spoken. Stocky, square jawed, beetle-browed and sullen-looking, he inspired all timid persons with fear and all others with aversion. Men ignored him, women avoided him, children ran past him and dogs barked at him; and he didn't care, apparently, but rather gloried in his unpopularity and looked upon the aloofness of his fellows as a thing desirable. He was seventy-five years old, but erect and strong.

---

1 **doggery** - an illegal drinking establishment

One warm afternoon in the early part of May, the hard old man was working in his garden just back of his home. The latch of the sagging gate clicked, and he glanced up. A boy of seven and a girl of five were peeping through the paling[2]. Both little tots were bare-headed and bare-footed, and both little faces were flushed with heat and excitement.

"Here." Old John growled, surlily. "Don't you come in here."

He half straightened from his stooping posture, leaned heavily upon his hoe-handle and glared hard at the ventursome pair. The brown-haired laddie looked questioningly, wonderingly, at the yellow-headed lassie; and she returned his perplexed gaze. But they did not turn and scamper away, as the old man had expected. Instead the boy took his companion by the hand, lifted the latch of the gate and essayed[3] to push it open.

"Here—I say," Old John called crossly. "Don't you come in here: I don't want you. Clear out, now."

But the boy resolutely pushed open the creaking gate and entered the inclosure, pulling his companion with him. The merest shadow of a wintry smile lightened up the old man's somber features, and his voice sounded less harsh, as he demanded, "What do you want, bub?"

"Want you, mister—mister—" the boy made reply, sturdily advancing along the narrow path and literally dragging his more timid companion after him. Then he could say no more—and stopped, and stood embarrassed and silent.

"Well, what do you want of *me*?" the old man growled, his tone and manner hinting at lack of faith in his own senses.

"Want you to—to—" the lad began, but hesitated and quit.

Then the little fellow looked helplessly, appealingly, at his trembling companion; and she, after a comprehending glance and a few preliminary gulps, began volubly[4] and incoherently:

"We want you to—help the birdie, mister—the poor little birdie—up in the tree—and all fast and tied, and can't get loose; and it's all tied on a limb—with string, and its leg's hurt—and—and—"

---

2 **paling** - a fence made from pointed wooden or metal stakes

3 **essayed** - attempted or tried

4 **voluble** - characterized by ready or rapid speech

"Huh?" The old man muttered irritably. "What—what're you tryin' to tell, anyhow?"

The boy had partially recovered his composure; and now he made effort to explain, "It's a robin, in the elm down on the corner there, mister, and—"

"And it's all tied up," the girl broke in.

"It's tied with string"—the boy continued.

"And can't get unfast," the wee lassie interjected.

"And we want you to come and get it loose," the laddie concluded.

"And its leg's all hurt," the little miss added, as a postscript.

"Oh, *that's* all you want," Old John grumbled. "A bird fast, eh? Huh?"—contemptuously—"Well, I hain't got no time to be foolin' with birds—n'r with children, either. Now you two skeedaddle out o' here—and don't bother me no more."

But the tiny intruders failed to grasp the meaning of his unfeeling words—failed to catch the import of his merciless decision. They just stood and stared at him, opened-mouthed and plainly puzzled.

"Be off with you," he mumbled, crustily, pointing toward the open gate; "and don't you come in here no more."

"Won't you come and let the bird loose?" the boy inquired.

"The poor little bird!" the girl murmured, pityingly.

The old man stubbornly and impatiently shook his head.

"Won't you?" the laddie persisted. "I'd let it loose, myself, but it's way out on a limb where I can't climb to it."

"Won't you—*please*?" coaxed the lassie.

A grin warmed the old man's countenance.

"Well, I s'pose I'll *have* to," he said ungraciously. "I'll never get rid o' you little pests, if I don't. Wait till I get a ladder."

When the three of them were under the tree at the corner of the street Old John looked down at his small companions and asked, "Whose kids are you two, anyhow?"

"We're Mr. Carter's children," the boy explained; "we just moved here last week."

"Yes," the girl volunteered, "and my name's Lucy; and brother's name's Harry."

"Well," the old man chuckled, rearing the ladder against the tree and sliding the top of it out along a large drooping limb, "I thought you hadn't been in town very long, 'r you wouldn't 'ave come into *my* garden after *me*."

The children did not understand him; indeed, it is doubtful that they heard him, so intent were they upon the rescue of the unfortunate bird frantically fluttering among the branches over their heads.

The old fellow continued reflectively, his gaze directed upward, punctuating his words with dry and asthmatic giggles, "Purty how-d'ye-do—now, *this* is; me down here with a couple o' barefooted kids, trying to save the life of a measly robin. Ort to be 'shamed o' myself; must be gittin' childish—by cracky! An' if I save the robin's life, it'll pay me by comin' an' stealin' my cherries, I reckon. Humph! That's gratitude in this world, I've found out. An' if anybody sees me,"—glancing apprehensively around.—"I'll stand a right smart chance o' losin' the repytation I've earned; an' that 'ld be my final an' everlastin' undoin' in *this* town. That bird's got fast tryin' to steal somebody's twine to make a nest of; don't know but it serves it right."

Then, suddenly, to the boy: "There, bub, I got the ladder in place, but I can't climb it; the limb won't bear my weight. Think you could go up an' git the bird?"

"Yes, sir," the lad answered promptly, eagerly.

"'Yes, sir,' eh?" Old John grinned. "You got your manners with you, I see. It's been a good while sence I've been sir-ed an' mister-ed by little folks; sounds kin' o' good. Well, up you go. There, take my knife, you have to cut off the branch that the cord's 'round. An' be careful—don't cut yourself, an' don't fall. Sis,"—to the little girl,— "you stand out o' the road; he might let the knife drop—'r the ladder might slip." Again to the boy—"That's it; pull the branch down an' whack it off. Be careful! Don't lose y'r balance, bub. That's it—whack it off; an' bring the branch an' bird an' all down. Never mind the bird fluttering; you won't hurt it—guess its leg's broke, anyhow."

"Oo—h!" murmured the wee maiden. "Poor little birdie; I'm so sorry for it."

Old John looked at her in scowling silence. Then, at sound of approaching footsteps, he turned his head and swept swift glances up the street and down.

"Hurry up, bub," he called to the boy; "here comes a lot o' fool meddlers. That's it; shut the knife up an' throw it down. Don't be afraid; I won't let the ladder fall—if it does shake. Don't miss that rung with y'r foot. All rightee! Now, hand the bird to me." Then in a fierce aside: "Confound the meddlers, anyhow! Pity they can't tend to th'r *own* business; alluz pokin' th'r noses into other people's." All the while he was cutting and disentangling the cord that bound the hapless robin's leg to the severed bench.

Moved by idle curiosity and wonder, quite a crowd of men, women and children had gathered on the opposite corner; but, knowing the disposition of Old John Cheney, no one ventured to approach closer. In the crowd were the village doctor, the corner grocer, the jeweler and others of the town's professional and business pillars.

Presently John had the bird released. Then, to the infinite surprise of one and all of the villagers, he called out curtly, but not unpleasantly:

"Doc, come over here."

"You want *me*?" Dr. Herdman called in reply.

"Of course," snapped the old man.

The doctor leisurely sauntered across the street. Several of the crowd slowly straggled after him; and soon the whole number were assembled around the tree, open-mouthed, wide-eyed and wondering.

"Who asked all you folks to poke y'rselves in?" Old John demanded, grumpily. But, getting no answer, he turned to the doctor and said, his manner evidencing the embarrassment and irritation he felt, "This robin,"—smoothing its rumpled feathers,—"tied itself to a limb up in the tree there, with a piece o' twine; an' nothin' would do these silly little kids, but I must take the ladder an' let it loose. It's got its leg broke, as you see. Can you fix it up any way?"

Very soberly the doctor bent and carefully examined the limb of his tiny patient. Then he said, "The leg's almost entirely severed just above the foot, John—just hanging by shred of skin. I can't do anything but cut it off."

"Oh, don't do *that*!" The little boy pleaded, his voice thick with pity.

"No, please – *please* don't do it!" the wee girl cried, her lips trembling, her breast heaving.

"Can't do nothin' else, can't you, Doc?" Old John grunted, hoarsely.

"Wrap it up—wrap it up!" coaxed the little girl.

The doctor slowly and sadly shook his head.

"It would drop off," he explained to Cheney, whose keen gray eyes were fixed upon his face.

The old man stooped and laid his horny hand upon the child's yellow curls.

"No use to wrap it up, sis," he mumbled huskily, his rugged old features twitching;—and the people crowded closer to view the miracle!—"the doctor says it 'ld drop off."

"But the birdie can't fly any more!" the little miss wailed.

"Oh, yes, it can—yes, it can!" the old man answered her, half testily.

"And can it sit on a limb?" the boy inquired, sturdily trying to hide his emotion.

"Of course—of course!" the old man jerked out.

The children offered no further objections to the necessary procedure. The doctor deftly amputated the bird's dangling foot; old John muttered:

"Now we'll let it go, kids; it'll be all right—you needn't worry. Run along home to y'r mother, now—run along."

Then turning savagely upon his assembled neighbors: "You folks clear out; an' the next time 'tend to y'r own business."

And he shouldered his ladder and climbed up the path into the garden.

The villagers dispersed, winking, grinning and giggling; and by nightfall the report of the miracle was all over town.

A few days afterward Mrs. Ruskin, the wife of the druggist, met Old John upon the street and thus accosted him—coolly, confidently:

"Mr. Cheney, the window Hammond has lost her cow and we're trying to raise money to buy her another. How much will you give?"

"Not a cent," the old fellow vowed decidedly.

"Oh, yes you will!" Mrs. Ruskin urged sweetly. "Mrs. Hammond has three children and can't get along without a cow, you know, Mr. Cheney. You'll give something."

"Well, I won't."

And he tried to get past the determined little woman; but she kept in front of him, and persisted, smiling patiently:

"Yes, you'll give something, Mr. Cheney. You don't mean what you say; you can't fool me anymore—I've heard all about your rescuing that robin for those children."

Old John's jaw dropped; and he just stood and stared at his audacious tormentor. Then he puckered his features, squinted an eye and slowly and reluctantly thrust a hand into his trousers' pocket—and more slowly and reluctantly withdrew it.

"Here is a dollar," he snarled; "but don't never come to me no more."

She thanked him and bid him good morning. He stood and watched her around the corner; then he clumped on his way, shaking his head and chuckling, "Jest as I expected—jest as I pr'dicted! I said that fool bird business 'ld be my everlastin' undoin'. Now I won't never have a minute's peace; I'll be at their mercy. Mercy? Huh! They hain't got none."—He set his jaws and frowned, "Well, I've brung it on myself; an' now I'll have to take my medicine, I reckon."

A week later, one dewy, sunshiny morning, the old fellow knocked at the door of the Carter home and in answer to Mrs. Carter's mute look of surprise and inquiry—not unmixed with mild alarm, for she did not know her visitor, and his disreputable appearance was against him—he stammered:

"Good—good morning, ma'am. Where's—them little fellers o' yours?"

"My children?" She asked.

"Yes."

"Playing in the backyard."

"Just thought I'd come down an' tell 'em," he went on, rubbing his callused palms together, "that that stump-legged robin's buildin' a nest in the black-heart cherry tree in the corner o' my garden; gittin' ready to hatch a brood to eat up all my cherries, I s'pose. Thought the children'd be kind o' glad to know the bird was all right, and—and maybe they'd want—want—"

He hesitated, and stopped.

"Oh!" Mrs. Carter murmured, smiling. "You're the man who rescued the bird for the children; you're Mr. Cheney."

"Y-e-s," he said slowly, "that's my name. 'Old John'—I'm mostly called, though."

"And you'd like to have the children go with you, to see the lame robin and the nest it's building?"

"W-e-ll, yes—if you don't care."

"I'll call them," she consented, with alacrity[5].

The tiny tots accompanied the grizzled old man to his garden and saw the lame robin at work and marveled over the nest it was constructing in the crotch of the cherry tree. And they held his hands and prattled to him; and he answered with nods and grunts and surly monosyllables; and when the two little ones had gazed their fill and had fully expressed their wonder and admiration over the handicraft of the handicapped bird, their aged companion took them to the corner grocery and bought each of them a sack of candy.

"Now, run along home," he grinned. Then, as a swift afterthought, he called to them: "Come up an' see the ol' stump-leg bird ag'in; don't wait fer me to come fer you."

Ah, John Chaney—John Cheney! That illy-considered and impulsive utterance was your final undoing, indeed. Almost every day the two children went to see the lame robin—and the old man. With keen and quick intuition, they learned to understand and love him; and, with a heart-hunger that was never fully satisfied, he learned to look for them, long for them—and fairly adore them. He trundled the yellow-haired lassie in his wheel-barrow; he let the brown-haired laddie ride the old gray mare to water. The children came and went at their pleasure; they played in the shade of the black-heart cherry tree in the garden, they romped over the hay in the mow of the stable. And the old man smiled—

---

5 **alacrity** - brisk and cheerful readiness

smiled frequently, smiled smiles that were good to see!—And offered no word of objection or correction. The three became inseparable companions; wherever the old man went the children tagged him. Not only did he smile upon his wee comrades, but his manner toward mankind in general—with dogs, even!—underwent a perceptive change. Other children played in front of his house, unrebuked, and festive curs frolicked in his stable yard, unmolested. His nighbors noted the marvelous change in him and commented upon it—and took advantage of it. They spoke to him whenever they met him; and he returned each greeting—grumpily or graciously, as the notion took him. They appealed to him to contribute to this charitable fund and that; and not always did he refuse. A few times, even, he gave money unsolicited. Old John Chaney was undone!

But while he might tolerate his neighbors and their offspring—and their dogs!—and show them more consideration than he ever had been his wont, he made no move that would lead to a closer and warmer intimacy. Was he waiting for them to make advances indicating a real friendship? Had he been waiting, all the sad years, unwisely holding himself aloof, for them to understand him and know him? Who can say? I doubt if Old John could have said himself.

But, as has been shown, the Carter children, knowing nothing of his reputation as a miserly and crusty old curmudgeon, had forced their way into the stout citadel of his lonely soul; and now it was led captive by them, helplessly enmeshed in the cords of love they had thrown around it. His vinegary sister called him a fool and then enticed the children into the house and surfeited[6] them on cookies and peach preserves.

In the Fall Old John fell ill, afflicted with that terrible form of heart disease that will not permit the patient to move about or lie down, but compels him to sit erect in a chair day and night. He suffered greatly and not uncomplainingly; he was no angelic invalid. But he was markedly pleased when his old acquaintances called upon him; and he took those sincere, if somewhat perfunctory, expressions of sympathy kindly.

---

6 **surfeit -** to feed or supply to excess

Every day Mrs. Carter brought the children to see their ailing comrade; and every time he was delighted. Even while fighting for breath, he would put his loving arms around them and fix his sunken eyes upon them—hungrily, rapturously.

One day, the boy said:

Mr. Cheney, the stump-legged robin's gone."

"Eh?" The old man queried, panting.

"The stump-legged robin's gone," the lad repeated.

"And we s'pect it's gone to a summer place," his sister broke in, "where there's flow'ers and other birds—and—and everything."

Old John put out a shrunken, wrinkled hand and tenderly toyed with the wee maiden's yellow curls. Then he wearily closed his eyes and panted:

"The stump-legged robin's gone; one of us—is gone. An' it'll be my turn next—to go to a sunnier place."

That evening when he was alone with the doctor, and was a little easier, he asked abruptly:

"Doc, how long will I live—this way?"

The doctor started.

"You really want me to tell you, John?" he said.

"Of course—'r I wouldn't have asked you."—with a show of his usual petulance.

"You will live but a few days," was the doctor's answer.

"Then."—slowly and firmly,—"I'll make my will tomorrow."

And he did; and all the village heard of it, of course, and speculated as to who were his beneficiaries. Some thought he had given his property to his sister; others thought he had not, as she had property of her own. Many held that he had willed everything to the Carter children; many others held that he had not. But nothing definite could be learned as to what disposition the old man had made of his considerable wealth; and speculation rioted, and all sorts of idle reports became current and gained credence.

The morning of the day Old John died, the minister came to see him, with the hope of offering him spiritual consolation.

Don 't you want me to pray with you, Mr. Cheney?" asked the young divine.

Old John pettishly shook his head.

"Nor to pray for you?"

"No!"—testily.

"Then, shan't I read you something from the Bible?"

"Guess not."—wheezingly, painfully.

There was a momentary and embarrassing pause; then the old man breathed stridently:

"Say!"

"Well, Mr. Cheney?"

"Ain't ther' somethin' in the Book 'bout the sparrow's fall?"

"Yes." replied the minister. "Shall I read that to you?"

Old John nodded, his eyes closed.

The minister turned to Matthew 10, 29-31, and read:

"Are not two sparrows sold for a farthing? and one of them shall not fall on the ground without your Father. But the very hairs of your head are all numbered. Fear ye not, therefore, ye are of more value than many sparrows."

"Means robins, too—I reckon," the old man commented.

"Certainly," the minister replied wonderingly.

"An' ain't there," Old John pursued," somethin' in the Book— 'bout the wolf an' the lamb—an' a little child leadin' 'em?"

"Yes," said the young divine; and quickly quoted: 'The wolf also shall dwell with the lamb, and the leopard shall lie down with the young goat, and the calf and the lion and the fattened calf together; and a little child shall lead them.'"

Old John nodded and smiled.

"Thought it was in there some'er's," he whispered, hoarsely.

"Shall I explain what it means?" The minister suggested.

"No!"—snappishly—"It don't need no explainin'. *I* know what—it means,—a good 'eal—better'n *you* do."

"And there's nothing more I can do for you, Mr. Cheney?"

"No;"—with infinite weariness, "I'm all right. I *thought* I— was; now I *know* I am."

Just before he died he asked that the Carter children be brought into his presence. He could not embrace them; but he caressed them with his eyes. The little ones looked upon him wonderingly, pitingly, and fondled his wasted hands. Then, as the weeping mother led them from the room, the dying man hungrily stared after them and murmured gaspingly:

"Suffer—little children—to come—unto me? Suffer—little children—" The sentence broke; and the cord of life snapped with it.

Old John's will was a surprise—and a revelation. To the Carter children "that understood me from the very first—and in spite of myself," he left a sum of money sufficient for their maintenance and education; to his native village, to build a town hall and found a library, "for the people that never understood me, and never tried to understand me—and that I wouldn't let understand me." he left the rest of his wealth.

And then the villagers simply couldn't understand Old John Chaney at all!

Locales Based on Actual Locations

Naylor's descriptions of locales in his stories were often so vivid that they were easily recognized as actual locations. The names he created were often similar to the real name.

Castleton, also East Smalleyville. Both these monikers were used in "Did It Pay?" for McConnelsville.

Cranston Plow Factory. The Manley Plow Factory was a major employer in Malta for many years.

Crooksburg. A locale mentioned in "Two Consultations at Mam Starlings" would be Crooksville, 22 miles northwest of McConnelsville.

Dartmore. Because Captain Stanwood, a "moving and directing spirit" of the village in "The Coming of Sawlus" had a large controlling interest in half a dozen other industries," this locale fits the description of Malta rather than Stockport. Captain Gibson, Naylor's first father-in-law, appears to be the model on whom Stanwood's character was based.

Douda Run. Doudna Run, used in "A Counterfeit Coin" and "Wild Tom" was a favorite haunt of Naylor's.

Foxtown. This is the community of Pennsville where Naylor started a practice after he married Lena Ervilla Naylor, his second wife.

Grangerville. The locale for "The Blackmer Affair" fits the description of McConnelsville where Matthew Blackmer's magnificent mansion "occupied a slight elevation and was surrounded by beautiful and extensive grounds, containing gravel walks, fountains, statuary, and groves of stately trees."

Hookton. This locale in "Wild Tom" probably referred to Hooksburg.

Kikertown. From the description of the locale in "A Spike from the Underground Railroad" this was Pennsville – "a few miles from the picturesque Muskingum river" that "occupies the crest of a high ridge, with Bald Eagle creek on the one hand and Wolf creek on the other and is hedged in by a fruit and grazing country." It was the "center of a large Quaker settlement" where their descendents… still cling tenaciously to the religion, dress and manners of their forefathers." A stopping place on the old stage road from Zanesville to Marietta, it was one of the main stations on the great Underground Railroad.

Malconta. This is the name that Naylor coined for the two villages of Malta/McConnelsville in "Wild Tom." He later used it in *Ralph Marlowe.*

Marlow. Mentioned in "A Spike from the Underground Railroad," Bassett had sent to Kikertown for a search warrant, but believing the abolitionists were stone-walling him, he sent his comrade to Marlow, in all likelihood Stockport, the locale for his best seller, *Ralph Marlowe.*

Onionville. This locale in "Two Consultations at Mam Starlings" is thought to be Uniontown or perhaps Neelysville.

Quakertown Road. The road to Chesterhill.

Smalleyville. The locale for "Did It Pay?" describes Malta/McConnelsville so well. "…it occupied both sides of the ribbon-like river that zig-zagged its way through the beautiful valley in which the village was situated. The two parts of the town seemed a pair of ragged Siamese twins, connected by an old, covered wooden bridge, a vital link—as it were—that creaked and groaned in every gale and appeared in danger of breaking in two…."

Stoverton. This locale in "Stuff of Which Doctors are Made" matches the description in *Ralph Marlowe* of Stockport, with a population of about 600 inhabitants.

Unionville. A locale identified in "Jud Trainor's Ghost" that is likely Uniontown.

In a number of instances, Naylor did not disguise the names and referred to locales by their actual name, as in the following examples:

Bald Eagle creek. Referred to in "A Spike from the Underground Railroad," this was a stream that Naylor grew up exploring

Columbus. The capital of Ohio was referred to in "How Tom Evans Won His Wife."

Eagleport. This was the town referred to in "One of Morgan's Men" where General Morgan's raiders crossed the Muskingum River.

Graysville. A town along the road that the boys in "Beggars Awheel" pass through is about 35 miles due east of McConnelsville in Monroe County.

Meigs Creek. "Jud Trainor's Ghost" refers to this location.

Missionary Ridge. Mentioned in "Did It Pay?", where Naylor and the character Dr. Jeffrys lost their fathers during the Civil War.

Neill House. "How Tom Evans Won His Wife" refers to the Neill House in Columbus where Naylor stayed when he visited the city.

Pennsville. One of the episodes in "Two Men and a Boy" takes place in Pennsville, a small community not far from where Naylor grew up and where he established a medical practice after his marriage to Villa.

Red Brush. "Stuff of Which Doctors are Made" refers to a place now rarely mentioned. It was also referred to ***Ralph Marlowe***.

Wolf creek. "A Spike from the Underground Railroad" mentions this creek that runs just a bit south of Pennsville

Zanesville. The main character in "Ol' Cap Mingo," a river boat captain, used to make a daily run to Zanesville, twenty-six miles north of McConneslville.

Although no locations were given actual names in "Two Men and a Boy," " the village is said to be two miles from the boy's home, which was the distance from Naylor's home to ***Pennsville***, and the second part of the story no doubt describes ***Stockport.*** No actual names were used in "Ben's Adventure" either, but the farm and the forested area surrounding it fit descriptions of Naylor's boyhood home on ***Newton Ridge***, between those two villages.

In a short article in an area newspaper under local news from Newton Ridge after Naylor's death it was noted that "The community was sadly shocked to learn of the passing of a former resident,

Dr. James Ball Naylor. Regardless of the heights of fame to which he soared, meeting of old friends or mention of the old ridge always brought a sparkle of pleasure to his eye."

Writings of James Ball Naylor

Collected Verse

1893 *Current Coins Picked Up at a Country Railway Station*, S. Q. Lapius, Columbus, Ohio, Hann & Adair, Printers and Bookmakers.

1896 *Golden Rod and Thistle Down*, S. Q. Lapius, Columbus, Ohio., Hann & Adair, Printers and Bookmakers.

1906 *Old Home Week*, C. M. Clark Publishing Co., Boston, Mass.

1906-1907 *Old Home Week*, C. M. Clark Publishing Co., Boston, Mass. Governor Rollins Version, (double copyright).

1906-1907 *Old Home Week*, C. M. Clark Publishing Co., Boston, Mass. Mayor Fitzgerald Version, (double copyright).

1907 *Songs From the Heart of Things*, New Franklin Printing Company, Columbus, Ohio.

1927 *A Book of Buckeye Verse*, Tucker-Kenworthy Co. Press, Chicago, Ill.

1935 *Vagrant Verse, Morgan County Herald*, McConnelsville, Ohio.

1968 A *Second Book of Vagrant Verse*, Preface by Lucile Naylor, D. W. Garber. (One copy only).

2011 *Vintage Verse*, Edited and Annotated by Theresa Marie Flaherty, Turas Publishing, Corpus Christi, Texas.

Serialized Writings

1896-1897 "Beggars Awheel," *Ohio Farmer*, December 3, 1896 to January 21, 1897.

1897-1898 "In the Days of St. Clair," *Ohio State Journal*, December 5, 1897, to February 27, 1898.

1898-1899 "Under Mad Anthony's Banner," *Ohio State Journal*, November 27, 1898, to March 5, 1899.

1900-1901 "The Sign of the Prophet," *Ohio State Journal*, October 28, 1900, to February 10, 1901.

1904 "The Witch Crow and Barney Bylow," *National Magazine*, V. 21, No. 3, December, 1904 through V. 22, No. 1, April, 1905.

1905 "The Little Green Goblin of Goblinville," *National Magazine,* V. 22 and 23, September and October, 1905.

1906 "From Jim to Jack; Letters to an Old Time Schoolmate," *Ohio Magazine*, V. l, 1906.

1907-1908 "A Counterfeit Coin," *Ohio Magazine*, Columbus, Ohio, Vol. 3 and 4.

1926   "Physicians of Morgan County," *The Weekly Herald*, January 21,
            1926 through March 4, 1926.
1927   "Rambling Reminiscences," *Morgan County Herald*, McConnelsville,
            Ohio, March 29, 1927.
1939   "Straight Sticks from the Brush of Old Morgan County," *Morgan
            County Herald*, McConnelsville, Ohio, June 15, 1939 through
            September 7, 1939.

Novels

1899   *Under Mad Anthony's Banner, Ohio State Journal,* Chauplin Press,
            Columbus, Ohio, 1899.
1901   *Ralph Marlowe*, Saalfield Publishing Co., Akron, Ohio.
1901   *The Sign of the Prophet*, Saalfield Publishing Co., Akron, Ohio.
1902   *In the Days of St. Clair*, Saalfield Publishing Co., Akron, Ohio.
1903   *Under Mad Anthony's Banner*, Saalfield Publishing Co., Akron,
Ohio.
1904   *The Cabin in the Big Woods*, Saalfield Publishing Co., Akron, Ohio.
1905   The *Kentuckian*, C. M. Clark Publishing Co., Boston, Mass.
1907   *The Scalawags*, B. W. Dodge and Co., New York.
1908   The *Misadventures of Marjory*, C. M. Clark Publishing Co., Boston,
            Mass.
2011   *Ralph Marlowe*, reprinted with additional material, edited and
            annotated by Theresa Marie Flaherty, Turas Publishing, Corpus
            Christi, Texas.

Children's Books

1906   *Witch Crow and Barney Bylow*, Saalfield Publishing Co., Akron, Ohio.
1907   *The Little Green Goblin*, Saalfield Publishing Co., Akron, Ohio.
1909   *Dicky Delightful in Rainbow Land*, Saalfield Publishing Co.,
            Akron, Ohio.

Pamphlets

1907   *From Jim to Jack*, Herald Printing Co., McConnelsville, Ohio.
1911   *Across the Miles*, Rustcraft, Kansas City, Mo.
1911   *UCT Booklet*, United Commercial Travelers, Zanesville, Ohio.
1911   *Angelina's Ardent Lovers*, Advertising Poem.
1912   *For You*, Rustcraft, Kansas City, Mo.
1912   *If You Were Here*, Rustcraft Co., Kansas City, Mo.
1912   *The Old Time Friend*, Rustcraft Co., Kansas City, Mo.

1921   *Old Morgan County*, Poem, Herald Printing Co., McConnelsville, Ohio.

1921   *The Muskingum Valley*, Malta, Ohio, June, 1919.

1927   *Rambling Reminiscences*, Herald Printing Co., McConnelsville, Ohio.

--   *Flinch*, Advertising Poem.

Short Stories

1897   "Ben's Adventure," S. Q. Lapius, Copyright 1897.

1903   "Ol' Cap Mingo," *National Magazine*, V. 17, No. 4, January, 1903.

1903   "How Tom Evans Won his Wife," *National Magazine*, V. 17, No. 5, February, 1903.

1903   "The Mishaps of Ol' Andy Perdue," *National Magazine*, V. 17, No. 6, March 1903.

1903   "A Lucky Opal," *National Magazine*, V. 18, No. 4, July, 1903.

1903   "Sim Spike's Misadventures," *National Magazine*, V. 19, October, 1903 (reference to)

1903   "The Youthful Indescretions of Jim Whiss," *National Magazine*, V. 19, October, 1903 Reference to *Ohio Star*, August, 1909.

1906   "The Undoing of Old John Chaney," *Ohio Magazine*, V. 4., 1906

--   "Coming of Sawlus," S. Q. Lapius.

--   "Did It Pay?," S. Q. Lapius.

--   "Jud Trainor's Ghost," *Ohio State Journal*.

--   "Mamie's Prisoner," *Ohio State Journal*.

--   "The Diversions of Dicky Dare."

--   "The Blackmer Affair," S. Q. Lapius.

--   "The Mills of the Gods," S. Q. Lapius.

--   "One of Morgan's Men," S. Q. Lapius

--   "Spike from the Underground Railway," S. Q. Lapius.

--   "Story of a Skeleton," S. Q. Lapius.

--   "Stuff of Which Doctors are Made," S. Q. Lapius.

--   "Two Consultations at Mam Sterlings," S. Q. Lapius.

--   "Wild Tom," S. Q. Lapius

Newspaper Columns

1913   *The Ohio Star*, Marion, Ohio.

1913   "Sunshine Corner," *The Marion Star*, Marion, Ohio.

1915-1923 "Life's Vaudeville," *The Marion Star*, Marion, Ohio.

1920-1923 *The Chicago Journal of Commerce*, Chicago, Illinois.

1925-1928 *The Week.*

Political Sketches (Who's You in Ohio)

--	Allen Oh! Meyers
--	An'-drew Lightning Harris
1907	Charles Hungry Grosvenor
1907	Elmer C. Dover
1907	George Boss Cox
1907	Jon'ah McLean
1907	Joseph Beensome Foraker
1907	Kernel William Alexander Taylor
1907	May-Jar Charles Dick
--	Nickle-Us Longworth
1907	Theodore Energy Burton
1907	Tom Lofty Johnson
1907	William How-Hard Taft

Campaign Songs

1920	Republican Campaign Songs, Ohio Republican State Executive Committee, Columbus, Ohio.

Presented in Programs

1904	A Voice from the Past
1904	Down Upon the Rappahannock
1904	Flinch
1904	Follerin' the Fife and Drum
1904	My Skies are Seldom Gray
1904	The Fifer of the Buck Run Band
1904	The Girl Who Sings Popular Songs
1904	The Ol' Country Dance
1904	The Physical Culture Fad
1904	The Song in My Heart
1908	Foolin' Ma
1908	Song of the Motor Car
1908	The Cumberland Stage
1917	Old Glory, April 19, 1917
1917	Some Singers, June 4, 1917
1923	Minor American Singers, August 20, 1923
--	Boyhood Days
--	One Country, One People, One Flag
--	Pop Goes the Weasel
--	Snip, A Study of a Boy and his Dog
--	The Diversions of Dicky Dare
--	The Jester

The Millionaire Dude
When You and I Were Boys
Whistling Jimmy

Christmas Cards

Christmas in the Heart
From a Friend in Old Morgan County
Good Luck to You
Holiday Greetings
The Home Light
The Old Home Place

Broadsides

Bully Yankee
Call Him, Can Him and Cuss Him
Dr. John Goodfellow--Office Upstairs
Foolin' Ma
Gallery of the Immortals
Hands Across the Sea
My Laddie's Life Lesson
The One Flag
To Her Who Keeps My Dwelling Place
Ye Doctor's Life
Yours and Mine
What America Means

Unpublished Material

1908 — Castle of Doors and Shutters, Children's story.
The Fate of the Valley Belle, (A Barefoot Avenger), Story.
Two Men and a Boy, Story.
The Adventures of the Elephant, the Monkey and the Clown, Poem.
The Cowboy and the Doctor, Comedy Sketch.
Two of a Kind, Comedy Sketch.
1916 — The Little Town of Toddville, Play.
The Jackies, Play.
One Country, Entertainment Program.
When You and I Were Boys, Entertainment Program.

The Final Test
A Biography of James Ball Naylor

by
Theresa Marie Flaherty

Vintage Verse
by James Ball Naylor

Edited and Annotated by
Theresa Marie Flaherty

ISBN: 978-0-9832342-8-9 Softcover $18.95
www.JamesBallNaylor.com
www.TurasPublishing.com
Also Available from Ingram - Amazon.com

Ralph Marlowe
by
James Ball Naylor

Edited and Annotated by
Theresa Marie Flaherty

A reprinted/reformatted edition of his 1901 best-seller
with additional material: a foreword, afterword,
contemporary reviews and period photographs

ISBN: 978-0-9832342-7-2 Paperback $23.95

www.JamesBallNaylor.com
www.TurasPublishing.com

Also Available from Ingram - Amazon.com